E-Day
Book 1:
Shattered

STACEY LIVINGSTON

ACKNOWLEDGEMENTS

Writing this book has been quite an adventure. There have been ups and downs, with many fits and starts. As with any major accomplishment, there will always be things that hinder you. There will also be people who help you achieve your goal. I would like to take this opportunity to recognize those friends of mine who helped make this happen. First and foremost, I'd like to thank my best friend and business partner, Jil Daniel. When I would slack off or feel lazy, she would remind and encourage me. My good friend Anne Marie Gentry Rowe. I thank you for your endless hours of editing and unwavering pep talks. To my long lost friend, Debbie Grose Darnell. Thank you so much for taking the time to edit the book. You're still great at English and I took your edits to heart. Last but certainly not least. To the Cache Oklahoma class of 1986, this one's for you!

1

He could feel it deep in his bones. Today was going to be another beautiful spring day. Jack Denton was sitting astride his horse on a bluff overlooking the ranch. Five hundred acres of some of the most breathtaking land just outside of Cody, Wyoming.

Striker shifted underneath him and Jack, distractedly, pulled on the reins to bring him back around.

He could see Grady, the grizzled foreman, and his sons, working down near the barn. It was time to brand the cattle, and Jack was riding up into the north part of the box canyon to check for mavericks.

Turning his horse away from the majestic view, he rode back down through the gullies and into the trees. As he did, his thoughts returned once again to what he came across eleven years ago as an intelligence and investigative officer in the military. Not a day went by that he didn't think about it.

He and his team had been stationed in Afghanistan and Jack had been part of a team that would go in after a bunker had been "cleaned and cleared." Their job was to sift through the Intel and try to glean anything useful about what the enemy was planning or where certain key target personnel may be hiding. On the latest search, Jack had come across credible, detailed documents stating that the enemy had the technology to build and, with help from unnamed accomplices, to unleash a large EMP or electromagnetic pulse bomb against the "Western infidels." He took this information very seriously. Jack's superiors and on up the food chain, however, had not. They had brought in many civilian and military scientists who chuckled as they told him that the equipment to produce an EMP blast large enough, and long enough, to do significant damage would have to be the size of a football field. Jack argued with them, saying that in some of the documents he had found nano technology had been mentioned. Nano technology is the science of making working parts smaller, almost microscopic, and was being perfected in the Far East. They condescendingly told him it couldn't be done.

A sudden movement and sound to his right brought him out of his reverie. Two squirrels were fighting over something. Probably one of their caches. Smiling to himself, he looked around and realized he was almost into the foothills where the mavericks liked to hide. Striker skittered down the last gully before the foothills and Jack had already spotted two white-faces staring dumbly at him from fifty feet away.

Circling them and whistling loudly, he steered them back the way he'd come. They seemed content enough to be heading home, kind of like Jack.

Once again on autopilot, he went back to musing on what had happened to him in the military long ago.

Even though the scientists, nor his supervising officers, would not take the EMP threat seriously, Jack could not shake the thought that this was a real threat. It began to affect the way he did his job and the way he thought of the military. In the end, he spoke to his immediate supervising officer, and agreed on an honorable discharge. He had done his job and done it well.

While he had been in the service, Jack was devastated when his mother and father had been killed in a car accident. As the only child, he had been left a sizeable inheritance and life insurance policy. Jack invested well and had a substantial amount when he was discharged.

Because of his prior knowledge of a possible impending catastrophe, and his gut instinct, ten years ago Jack had researched the best place to be in case of an EMP bomb. He had learned that being isolated from large cities would be key. A large ranch in Cody, Wyoming, had come up for sale and being single, with no children, he set out to buy the ranch.

He chuckled to himself thinking of Grady Hudson, the foreman's, face when the man found out that Jack had no prior experience with a ranch. Especially one this size. Grady's face had turned red but to his credit he just blew his walrus-style mustache out, looked Jack dead in the eye, and said, "I guess we better get started."

Grady was sixty years old, in good health, and had a classic western cowboy mustache and beard. He had plenty of common sense and when that let him down, Maria, his spunky wife of thirty-eight years, would bring him back around. There was also a quiet understanding between Jack and Grady of the father figure he'd become to Jack. Grady and Maria had three children: a daughter, Emma, thirty-seven, and two sons, Scott, thirty-five, and Danny, thirty-four.

Emma. He couldn't bring himself to think about that

right now, there was too much pain.

One of the mavericks suddenly bolted and he reined Striker to intercept it. Jack had come to love the ranch and all it entailed. The early mornings and quiet evenings. It was hard work but extremely satisfying.

Shortly after he had purchased the ranch, Jack had learned that Maria was an expert at canning vegetables, and had a small vegetable garden in the northeast corner of the backyard. She canned anything that couldn't be eaten right away, but had limited area to store the food. Jack wanted to build a root cellar. He also wanted to start smoking meat and storing it in a smokehouse. He dug three more wells for water and had bought an arsenal of weaponry that would make the ATF extremely interested if they knew. In his extensive research, Jack had learned that wood might be extremely important in this type of crisis. To that end, he had been cutting down trees and replanting new saplings for future use.

He may be wrong about things, but he may be right too. Better to be wrong and not need all that he built than be right and not have what was needed. He had learned a lot in thirty-eight years. Number one was to be prepared. Regardless of how people perceive you, if you did the right thing, you win in the end.

He had driven the two mavericks into the corral and was dismounting when Grady ambled up on slightly bowed legs.

"Have any trouble up there?" he asked.

"No, these fellas were in almost as big a hurry as I was to get back. Does Maria have some of those famous biscuits and coffee ready?" Jack asked.

"She sure does. Go get you some. The boys and I ate earlier. She asked where you were. Grumbling something about you and skin and bones."

Grinning, Jack said, "She's going to make me fat. Good thing I'm not trying to impress a woman."

"She said something about that too!" Grady laughed.

"I'll just bet she did." Jack said somberly.

Maria was devastated eight years ago when Jack and Emma had broken things off. Maria had been planning a huge wedding. Actually, Jack had been pretty devastated himself. He still wasn't sure why Emma had suddenly decided after a year and a half of constantly being together, she would break it off and move to Atlanta. At first Jack thought he had done something wrong, but after years of replaying it in his mind, he still could make no sense of it. She insisted she got cold feet and wanted to further her nursing career.

Jack sighed. He loved Emma with all his heart, and for that reason he knew he had to let her go. For now. He was sure she loved him as much as he loved her. Jack just hoped she'd see the light and come back home soon.

He'd arrived at the back door and pulled open the screen, "Mama Mia!" he laughingly called when he saw Maria. It was an endearment he'd called her for years. Knowing she secretly enjoyed it, he grinned when Maria shot him a glare.

"You sit down there and I'll bring you some biscuits. You run off first thing every morning before I can get any food down you. You're going to dry up and blow away," she grumbled.

"Maria! I'm six-feet tall and two-hundred pounds. I don't think I'm in danger of starving to death," Jack snorted.

"Still, I'm starting to think you don't like my cooking," she sniffed, acting put upon.

Jack smiled to himself as he bit into a biscuit that melted in his mouth. Everyone around knew Maria had the best cooking in four states. The people at church were always asking her to make cakes for bake sales and Maria never turned them down.

Finishing two biscuits and a cup of excellent coffee, Jack looked up and asked, "I'm going into town for supplies in a bit. Do you need anything?"

"We could use some more Mason jars and seeds for the garden. I'm going to put some squash in this year and make some of that squash relish you like so much," she said.

"About time you made something my stomach could handle!" he said, standing up and turning to the door.

"Oh! Get out of here!" she said, throwing the dish towel at him and smiling.

Jack smiled to himself as he walked down to the corral. It still amazed him how well all of them got along. Even Scott and Danny. Danny had recently married his high school sweetheart, Denise Franks. She had broken up with Danny after graduating high school and gone off to college. While there, she'd met a Hispanic man named Ricky Valendez and married him. Danny, heartbroken, had gone into the Army for four years. When he told

Maria he was thinking of reenlisting, she sat him down and told him she'd heard some talk about Ricky hitting Denise. Danny promptly drove to their home, knocked on the door, and asked Denise if it was true. When she started crying and nodded, he beat Ricky to within an inch of his life. Last fall after buying a corner of Jack's ranch to have a horse farm of his own, Danny had popped the question. It turns out Danny had just signed an agreement with the forest service in Yellowstone to sell them a set number of horses every year. Denise was a perfect complement to Danny's tall, dark, and quiet personality. She was short, fair, and quite a spitfire. She had gone back and finished college and now worked part time as a substitute English teacher. Jack got along with her just fine. He just stayed out of her way, he thought with a grin.

Arriving at the corral, Jack hooked an elbow over the top and watched as Danny held the last calf and Scott branded him.

"That bar D brand's a little crooked isn't it?" It was always easy to get Scott worked up.

"You just step up here and take over, big shot, if you think you can do better!" Scott said mock threateningly.

"That's easy to say now, you just branded the last one!" Jack shot back.

Sighing loudly, Scott tossed the iron back in the water bucket and took his gloves off.

At five foot eight, a hundred fifty pounds Scott was whip thin, lean with all muscle. He had a shock of black hair that he kept pretty short and blue eyes. Scott was charismatic which was evident in the thickness of his "little black book".

In contrast, Danny was only an inch shorter than Jack and built like a bull. Quiet and unassuming, Danny had always been in Scott's shadow, but he didn't seem to mind. Danny had the same coloring as Scott only his hair was cut in a buzz cut.

"Either of you want to ride into town with me?" Jack asked. "I've got to get some feed and Maria wants some squash seeds. I thought we'd stop by the post office too." he said, sliding a side long look at Scott.

Scott's latest woman was Janine who worked at the post office counter.

Scott rolled his eyes and Danny was smirking when Scott said, "Yeah, I guess since you're twisting my arm, I'll go with you."

Danny said, in a deep bass "I'll stick around here and clean up. You think you'll be back by lunch? You know mama will ask."

Sliding in to the passenger seat of the beat-up F-150, Scott said, "Tell her we wouldn't miss it for the world."

Getting behind the wheel, Jack glanced out to the West. Some clouds were gathering on the horizon, looked like possible rain this afternoon sometime.

Scott was looking out the window as he casually said, "I talked to Emma yesterday."

Everyone knew how Jack felt about her, and went out of their way not to talk about her or bring her up.

Just as casually, Jack said, "Yeah? How's she doing?"

Scott turned and looked at him then, "She said she

wants to come home. She misses the ranch and mom and dad too. She'll be finishing up her Master's in a couple weeks. As soon as that's done, she'll be heading this way."

Jack felt conflicting emotions. On one hand he was stunned; he'd hoped she would come back, but really hadn't counted on it. On the other hand Jack felt a little hurt because Scott said she missed the family but didn't mention him specifically. Underlying it all was the outpouring of love he felt just hearing Emma's name.

Jack was quiet for a time. Before he could say anything, Scott went on, "I don't know exactly what happened with you two, and I don't want to know because it's personal, but you two made a great couple and I have this feeling, you know, just a gut feeling, that she still loves you."

Scott was fiddling with the seat belt in his embarrassment. He and Emma were always close and if he said that, then there must be something to it.

Clearing his throat, Jack decided to change the subject, "Do you want to help me dig the root cellar after lunch? I'll let you run the backhoe."

Thankful for something else to talk about, Scott looked up and grinned. "You sure? Did you forget what happened the last time?"

"I didn't forget. Mama Mia is who you have to watch out for. She still hasn't forgiven you for tearing through her garden!" said Jack.

They both smiled for a minute, remembering Maria's rampage.

Then Scott said, "What's all this for, Jack? I mean, I

know you're not crazy. I've never asked because, well, you're the boss, but three wells? All Mama's canning, now you want to dig a root cellar and an old-timey smokehouse? Don't get me wrong, I love mama's canning, and venison's good too, but well, you know what I mean. Sometimes I can tell you're worrying something to death in your head but I've never got the nerve up to ask before. I think we know each other well enough now I can ask. What's going on?"

Jack thought about putting Scott off, beating around the bush, but they were as close as brothers and Scott deserved answers. Hell, he worked hard and was loyal, well beyond what he was paid for.

Jack took a deep breath and pinched the bridge of his nose. It was a big step from people thinking you were eccentric to opening your mouth and letting them think you were plain crazy, but this was Scott. He had never told anyone after he left the military for just this reason. Jack was afraid people wouldn't believe him. Well, if he wanted to start somewhere, Scott would be the best person to start with. If he believed Jack then maybe it only sounded crazy in Jack's head.

So Jack told Scott everything—abbreviated version, of course.

For his part, Scott just let Jack talk and by the time they reached town, Jack had finished. When they pulled up in front of the store, Jack cut the engine.

He could hear the ticking in the engine as it cooled. Jack hadn't even looked at Scott yet, afraid of what he might see.

"Did you tell Emma any of this?" Scott asked. Jack could see that Scott wondered if this was the reason Emma had left.

"No, I didn't tell anyone anything about this until I just told you."

Minutes passed as they both sat looking out the windshield in silence, mulling over the secret Jack had just revealed. Scott ran his fingers through his hair. "Well...now I know why folks around here think you're crazy, but I for one believe you, man. Don't ask me why I do, but I do. Why hasn't it already happened?"

Jack shrugged his shoulders. "I don't know. Could be it's never going to happen, but my gut instinct tells me, for some reason, to be prepared."

"It all makes sense now, what you're doing at the ranch," Scott said, nodding his head and looking off to the mountains.

"So if and when this bomb goes off, what exactly will happen?" Scott asked.

Jack looked out his side window while he contemplated his answer. All he knew for sure was that anything that used electricity would no longer work. Cars would no longer run, airplanes would fall from the sky, and there would definitely be no computers or cell phones. Basically, wherever the bomb went off, civilization would be set back to the frontier days. Guns and ammo could be used, but no refrigerators or lights. Pacemakers would also cease functioning and those people would drop dead in their tracks. As a matter of fact, there would be many, many deaths in the beginning and more would come later with the riots, and other results of the catastrophe. Complete chaos for a society like the United States.

Jack related all this to Scott.

Scott sat stunned, absorbing it, trying to get his mind around it. If what Jack said was true, if this event happened, their very lives were at stake.

"Jack, I sure hope you're wrong. That's all I can say."

Jack nodded, "I've been wrong so far. I hope it stays that way."

Jack opened the truck door and got out, "Meanwhile, we've got supplies to get."

Scott came around the front of the truck and they walked into the store.

When his eyes had adjusted, Jack looked around and noticed Jim Carson manning the register. He raised his hand and said, "Hey Jim, couldn't get any help today?"

Jim owned the Feed and Seed and was always grumbling about the help he hired, but deep down everyone knew he was a softie. Jack couldn't help teasing him just to get him going.

Scott elbowed Jack and whispered, "Don't get him started, Jack, we'll never get out of here."

Sure enough, true to form, Jim said, "Good help is so hard to find. Shawn called in and *said* he was sick. Do you know how many times I went to work with a hundred and one fever? Plenty! I told him I'd let him off this once, just once, mind you."

Jim continued mumbling under his breath. Smiling to himself, Jack strode on down the aisle picking out supplies he knew they needed. He came across the squash seeds Maria wanted and grabbed those as well.

Jack looked back for Scott and saw him arranging for the feed bags to be loaded in the truck.

By the time he got back to the register, Jack saw Scott was facing him with his hand out and with a roll of his eyes said, "Please give me the keys, I don't know if I can take any more."

Jack glanced over at Jim, who was still grumbling, and with a laugh, gave Scott the keys.

Jack placed the items he'd gathered next to the register. "Looks like we might get some rain this afternoon," he said.

Jim stopped grumbling when he heard Jack talking about his second-favorite subject.

"Yeah, this morning the weatherman said possible thunderstorms late this afternoon. Could get nasty."

"I hope it doesn't get too bad, I wanted to dig that root cellar today." Jack replied.

"You still planning on doing that?" Jim questioned, "I thought you had gotten out of that notion."

"Nope, still going ahead with it. Kind of like they had in the old days," said Jack.

Jim shook his head, "It's your money and your time. Nobody else will, but I'll tell you Jack, you have some peculiar ideas."

Smiling big, Jack said, "Why, thank you, Jim! It does my heart good to know you're so honest."

Jim just snorted and handed Jack back his credit card.

"See you later!" Jack said.

Jim waved back and Jack stepped out the door. Scott had the truck loaded and was in the driver's seat waiting for him in front of the store. Jack placed the supply bags on the floorboard at his feet and climbed in the passenger side.

As Scott turned the truck around, Jack asked, "Do you think I'm crazy Scott?"

Scott looked over at Jack and soberly replied, "I've known you for ten years and I've never known anyone else whose instincts were always right on target. That's what worries me. Not that you're wrong, but that you're probably right. That's why I was thinking about that root cellar you wanted to dig while you were still in the store. Now I want to get that done as bad as you do. At least all the things you've done can't hurt even if they don't drop a bomb."

"OK, when we get home we'll start on the cellar and be able to get a jump on it before Maria has lunch ready." Jack replied. "Maybe we'll get a lot dug before the rain comes."

They arrived back at the ranch and unloaded the truck. Jack took Maria the squash seeds and Mason jars. He asked her what was for lunch. She told him baked ham from their own hogs, mashed potatoes, green beans, and fresh rolls. All came from the ranch except the wheat for the flour in the rolls. Jack told Maria they'd be up in an hour for lunch. She just shooed him out and turned back to the boiling potatoes.

Before leaving, he turned back and politely asked where Denise was, he hadn't seen her. Maria confirmed what he'd guessed by saying Denise had been called to fill in for one of the high school teachers who was ill. He nodded and walked out. Maybe it was his military training, but he always liked to know where his people were.

Danny was checking the backhoe over and Scott was looking at the plot of land Jack had chosen to hollow out as Jack walked up.

Jack stepped up next to Scott. "What do you think?"

"I think it'll work great. We dig far enough back and deep enough, it'll stay plenty cool in the summer."

They turned around as they heard Danny climbing the slope. He had a quiet strength about him and nothing ever seemed to ruffle his feathers.

Jack asked him where Grady was.

"He saddled Midnight and rode out to check the west fence. He said if Mr. Jamison's bull has knocked a hole in it again, he was going to bulldog him. I was afraid to ask if he meant the bull or Mr. Jamison."

They all got a good laugh at that.

"Fire up that backhoe, Scott."

Hours later, the root cellar was almost complete. All they had to do was shore it up on the inside and add a door. They had only stopped once, briefly, for lunch. The clouds had continued to build and darken and a steady West wind had kicked up. Fat raindrops were starting to pelt them as they dashed the last few yards to the house.

"Wow! It's really coming down out there now," Scott said as he shook water out of his hair. "We barely got it done in time."

"We'll finish it up tomorrow," Jack replied.

Grady walked in sipping a cup of coffee. "You've got company, Jack."

Jack turned to look behind Grady and just stared.

"Hey Jack. You're a hard man to find." Jason Evans had been Jack's immediate superior in the military and now he was standing in Jack's living room. At six foot, Jason and Jack were the same height, but that's where all similarity ended. Where Jack was blonde with green eyes, Jason had dark hair with a bit of gray at the temples and light brown eyes. Jack didn't remember the gray, but then again, it had been ten years.

"To what do I owe the pleasure of this visit?" Jack asked sarcastically.

"Now Jack, I'm hurt. Is that any way to treat an old friend?"

Jack snorted, "Old friend my ass! How many times did you send me into the most hostile environment imaginable? Not to mention denying R and R leave when it suited you."

Jason lifted his hands in an innocent gesture and lifted his eyebrows, "But Jack, that's my job!"

Jack stepped up and slapped Jason on the shoulder, "It's good to see you, Jason. You got here just in time for supper. Let me wash up and we'll eat. Then you can tell me what you're doing here."

Jason smiled, "Fair enough."

Twenty minutes later, they were all settled at the table with Jack at one end and Grady at the other. They had passed around the country-fried steak and leftover mashed potatoes and green beans.

"So how is Washington?" Jack asked between bites.

Jason hesitated, he wanted to talk to Jack alone, and so he said, "Same old same old. You know how the machine works."

Denise and Marie had finished in the kitchen and came to the table to take their places.

Jack looked over at Denise and asked playfully, "How was school today, dear?"

Denise looked squarely back at him and knowing this was for their guest's benefit said, "It was fine. I'm glad we have finals in a few weeks and are graduating the end of May."

Pleased that she had played along, Jack surreptitiously watched Jason's reaction out of the corner of his eye and wasn't disappointed. Jason was trying not to stare at Denise. Jack could tell he was trying to guess how old she was. Finally, Jack let him off the hook by saying, "Denise substitute teaches over at the high school."

Jason glanced back and forth between Jack and Denise and mumbled, "Ah."

Jason turned to Marie, "Supper is delicious, ma'am. Thank you."

Marie just turned to him and nodded. She was very protective of Jack and she had a feeling this wasn't just a cordial visit. "You're welcome."

When they'd finished, Jack stood up and told Maria, "I promise to do the dishes tomorrow night if you'll let me off dish duty tonight."

"I suppose I could give you tonight off, seeing how you have a guest," she sniffed. "Just don't let it happen too often."

Everyone but Jason was looking anywhere but at Jack and trying not to smile. Jason just lifted an eyebrow as if to ask, 'I thought you owned this ranch?' Smiling to himself, Jack thought, don't ask.

Jack pointed his chin to the back porch, "Let's go out there, Jason, and we can talk. Coffee?"

"No thanks, I won't be able to sleep tonight if I do."

"You used to drink coffee day and night and it never seemed to bother you," Jack said as they settled on the porch. Jack could see it was still sprinkling, but it seemed to be almost over.

"I've gotten older and hopefully wiser. Things tend to change."

There was something in the way Jason said that last part that had Jack swinging sharply around to face him.

"You have something to tell me, Jason?"

Jason let out a big breath and glanced around, "They're building it, Jack."

"What do you mean, Jason? Spill it!" Jack's tone was just a little bit sharper than he intended.

Jason had his palm up in a placating gesture, "Just relax, Jack. We don't even know how far along they are into this. Let me start at the beginning.

"Several days ago, we received intelligence from our person in China. Apparently, they've been working on what they call an FCG or flex coil—"

"—Generator," Jack finished for him, "also known as an EMP device. Go on."

"Anyway," Jason continued with an irritated scowl, "as I was saying, they've been working on their FCG for a while. We have very limited information, unfortunately, but we think they are at least halfway done building it." He paused to see Jack's reaction. Up to this point he had been pacing with his hands on his hips and scanning the floor with his eyes. Jack looked up and motioned to Jason with a gesture to go on.

Jason hesitated, then said, "They've also made noises to the effect that they've finished an EMP shield. I guess I don't have to tell you what that means."

No, he didn't. Jack knew that, in theory, if you've built a shield, effective against EMP waves when an EMP bomb goes off, supposedly whatever is shielded will be protected. Hence, whatever is protected will still work while the rest of the unshielded area will cease to function electrically, theoretically. Of course this was all conjecture, a lot like the a-bomb back in the 1940s. Until you actually test an EMP bomb, you just really don't know what's going to happen. That's why it was so terrifying. There were so many unknowns.

Jack looked up at Jason, "No, you don't. Physically, how big is their EMP bomb? I know that's been the problem in the past, theorists said it couldn't be reduced to a manageable size in proportion to effectiveness."

Again Jason hesitated, "Jack, it was just as you said before you left. They've refined nanotechnology and have reduced the bomb to the size of a briefcase."

The words hung in the silence between them.

Jack was stunned, and had to sit down. He lowered himself onto the rocking chair.

"A briefcase...a briefcase?"

The ramifications of what Jason had just revealed to him were just sinking in. If this were true, it would mean that the bomb would be extremely mobile. If a bomb were that size it could be maneuvered almost anywhere with little to no detection before being deployed. Depending on the strength of the bomb...the strength would determine how widespread the affected area from ground-zero deployment.

"What is the strength?" he asked not looking at Jason. He was afraid Jason would see he was holding his breath.

"Strength...?"

"Strength, Jason. The power of the bomb, whatever the hell you want to call it! How powerful is this briefcase sized bomb!" Jack yelled.

Jason sat down too. Seeing Jack's reaction, and knowing the research Jack had put into the subject over the last ten years, he was beginning to understand how devastating this could be to the United States.

"We're not sure. I told you our Intel was incomplete. One of the things we don't know is the bomb's effective radius. We know the Chinese are very excited but that's about it on the power level."

All of a sudden Jack remembered something else

Jason had said. With growing horror Jack looked at Jason and said, "You said something about a shield. Tell me about their shield."

"Um, yes, we were able to learn that they've come up with a shield to block the EM pulse supposedly to protect their country from losing power. Of course, you and I know that without actually testing it, they won't know how well it will work against an EMP bomb of the magnitude they're planning."

"How do you know they haven't tested it yet?" Jack asked quietly.

"We would have learned about it."

Jack sat still, silently staring a hole through Jason, then just as quietly again said, "It took your team almost ten years to the day to learn about this. How do you know, Jason, that this isn't information the Chinese are feeding you. This could be information they want you to know because maybe, just maybe, they couldn't keep it from you any longer."

Jason laughed a little unsteadily, "Now you're just being paranoid, Jack."

"Am I? I seem to recall you stating that same thing back when you cut me loose, and yet, here you are. What are you doing here, Jason? What do you want from me?" Jack sat back and studied Jason with a hooded gaze.

Jason sat back also and Jack could see his shoulders slump a little. "Well, Jack, to be perfectly honest with you, my superiors don't know I'm here." He paused, gauging Jack's reaction and seeing none, he went on, "The United States government, based on what happened with you ten years ago and the information you discovered, delegated a team of scientists to further study an EMP event. With unlimited funding, they were told to research all aspects of EMP bombardment, its effects and possible ways to shield against said event."

Jack's face had been getting redder the more Jason talked. Finally, he jumped to his feet again and said, "You mean to tell me, while the government made me look like a paranoid fool, behind everyone's back they were listening to me, and not only listening, apparently taking notes and making detailed plans!"

Jack was back to pacing. Then he went still and with sudden insight he understood. Slowly he turned toward Jason.

"You built one too, didn't you?" he asked.

Jason held up his hands. "No, Jack, we haven't. We're getting there but we're nowhere near the Chinese. What we have built is the shield against an EMP device, or at least we think we have. We really won't know its capability or range, unfortunately, until we have to use it."

Jack sat back down. "So," Jack said, running his hand through his hair, "let me get this straight. You're way behind the Chinese in technology to make an EMP device. You have information that they have built, or are building one of these bombs now. If they have already built one, you have no idea whether they have more than one or even where it is or how they are deploying it. They may have a shield to protect their country but you don't know if it works. Jesus! That is a hell of a lot of uncertainties, Jason!"

Jason was looking straight at Jack, "I know it sounds like a lot of what ifs, but I remember a certain intelligence officer coming to me with a lot less. Please, Jack, I need you to come to the facility and look at our schematics. When you were in the field, you saw those plans before they burned and I know you have a photographic memory. At least take a look at our stuff and see if it resembles anything you saw back then!"

Jason sat back, clearly distraught. He wished he didn't have to be so blunt with Jack, but now was not the time to let ego interfere with survival.

Jack was torn. He knew if he didn't go and the Chinese deployed the bomb, he would always feel he might have done something to prevent it. If he did go and he couldn't give Jason what he needed, he'd feel like a failure.

Ultimately it came down to this. In his gut, what was the right thing to do? Not ego, not whether the government did him an injustice ten years ago. It came down to whether innocent people deserved to die because a crazy regime was trying to take over the world, or whatever they were trying to do.

Jack was a simple man, always had been. It had always been black and white to Jack, never gray. That's why he'd never got along with bureaucratic bullshit.

He had to think.

"Look, Jason, I'm going to have to think about everything. You've thrown a lot of shit my way. Why don't you grab your things and I'll show you to one of the guest rooms. I'm sorry things have been a little tense, but you have to admit, after ten years I just wasn't expecting to see you. Let me think about everything tonight and I'll let you know in the morning what I'm willing to do."

Jason looked at Jack and tilted his head, "That's all I'm asking."

Before they went upstairs, Jack had one more question, "Where do you have your base of operations?"

Jason hesitated only for a second, "Knoxville, Tennessee. We had to go somewhere inconspicuous. The powers that be want us to fly under the radar. We've set up a dummy corporation for funding purposes. We've named it Atlas Research and Development Inc."

Jack nodded, "Well, let's go get your things and I'll show you where you're sleeping. By the way, how are Sarah and Jay Jr.? "

Jason looked away and quietly said, "Sarah and I have separated and Jay's almost eighteen now. Sarah was sick and tired of not seeing me, and Jay's just bitter over the whole thing."

Jack faced him and not knowing what else to say, mumbled, "I am so sorry, Jason."

Clearly not wanting to talk about it, Jason broke the spell by standing and changing the subject. "I'm really sorry, Jack. You were the only other option left. I'm out of ideas."

Jack nodded and said, "That's what I was afraid of."

2

Emma Hudson was exhausted. This was her third day in a row working a twelve-hour shift. Two more weeks left and she'd have her master's in nursing. She smiled quietly to herself. Finally, after eight long years of working a while then school a while, she'd finally done it.

She went around the next corner and almost ran into Bryan. He grabbed her arm and steadied her. "Whoa, easy Emma, you almost plowed me under!" he said with an easy grin.

She smiled back tiredly, "Sorry, Bryan I guess I'm just a little tired."

"Three twelve-hour shifts will do that to you. I wish I was on my last twelve of the week, I'm just getting started. Oh, I wanted to tell you, you were great in that Code. You had x-ray down there before the doc thought to call us. It ran smooth as clockwork."

Emma tiredly thanked him and made to move on down the hall.

"Would you like to have a drink later, when I get off?" he queried, raising one smooth eyebrow.

He was a handsome devil with his surfer blonde hair and blue eyes, but Emma had never really gotten over Jack. She came back with her ready reply she'd used again and again, "I'm really beat tonight, Bryan, maybe next week."

Bryan made a mock serious face and said, "That one's really getting old, Emma. You need to think up some different ones. Don't you know we bachelors in the hospital have compared notes?"

She laughed, but shook her head and jauntily replied, "You bachelors have too much time on your hands."

With that she turned and with a quick smile over her shoulder she walked on down the hall to the time clock. Swiping her badge, she pushed open the employee exit door and strode outside. Atlanta in the springtime always rejuvenated her. The mixture of smells from fresh-cut grass, magnolia trees blooming along with gas fumes even, always had her picking up her step. It didn't hurt that she had three days off to relax. Well, sort of relax. She had to study for her finals. That thought brought her back to earth a little. She had called her brother Scott, knowing he'd say something to Jack, and told him she was coming home.

Emma had reached her car. She unlocked the door to her 2000 Ford Taurus and slid behind the wheel. She sat there a moment musing about her intentions. She was interrupted by her cell phone. She looked down and saw it was Lori, her best friend. As she answered, she was already thinking of excuses not to go out and have drinks. Lori always wanted to go out.

"Hey girl!" Lori said, before Emma could say hello, "You busy?"

"No, I just got in the car and was heading home."

"OMG! Really! It's only seven o'clock! I thought we'd go to Cow Tippers. They make the best martinis. What do you think?"

"Lori, do you realize I have just come off a three-day twelve? I am absolutely exhausted! I couldn't raise a martini to my mouth, much less enjoy it."

Laughing heartily, Lori said, "Calm down, calm down, you're going to hurt yourself. I know your hours, remember? I work with you. I was just yanking your chain. So how did it go? Par for the course?"

Emma was pinching the bridge of her nose but smiling at the same time. Lori Bubar was the most infuriating person you could meet, but she was true blue. What you see is what you get with Lori. That's why Lori was her best friend. She could tell her anything and Lori would be right there.

"Same old thing. You know how it is. Nothing exciting. Oh, except Bryan asked me out again." She grinned knowing Lori would melt. Lori had the biggest crush on Bryan Peterson.

Lori thought she had a few screws loose because she wouldn't go out with Bryan. True to form, Lori inhaled noisily, "No! Are you serious? How many times does that make? I've lost count. Are you insane? Are you sure you're not a lesbian? Just kidding, I know you aren't, anyway, what did you say? Please tell me you said yes!"

Emma waited for the Energizer Bunny to finally run down before devastating her by replying, "I told him I was tired," and waited for the explosion. She didn't have long to wait.

Emma stifled a giggle as Lori's rant took on unheard of proportions. As Emma waited for the flood to die down, she looked at herself in the rear-view mirror and did a critique. Medium-length black curls that framed a heart shaped face and light hazel eyes. She had to admit she had a great smile and dimples on each side.

Finally, something Lori had said caught her attention.

"I'm sorry, Lori, what did you just say?"

"Sheesh! I said, is this about that cowboy you've mentioned a couple of times? I wish you would tell me THAT story." Lori hesitated, waiting for Emma to elaborate. When she didn't, Lori rushed on, "Anyway, I guess you're not going out with me and I know you're not going out with Bryan, so, what are you doing tonight besides sleeping? And if you say eating I'm going to scream."

Emma didn't miss a beat, "Eating."

"AARRGGH!" screamed Lori.

Emma threw her head back and laughed. Good Lord but she needed that, "I'm sorry, Lori, you stepped right into that."

She'd started her car and headed down the street to her apartment ten blocks away. Emma knew Lori well enough to know she'd better head home now or spend the night in the parking lot. She chewed on the inside of her lip for a moment, then made a split second decision.

"I tell you what. Let me get some sleep tonight and tomorrow you can come over when you get off work and I'll tell you about the cowboy."

There was dead silence for a good three heartbeats, long enough for Emma to think she got cut off.

Then there was a huge intake of breath and Lori gushed, "Are you serious? You'll tell me? OK, OK, you get lots of rest and call me when you wake up. Ooh, this is gonna be SO good!"

Emma rolled her eyes but smiled, "Yes, I will call you tomorrow, probably around eleven, OK?"

"All right! Sounds good. I'll talk to you in the morning."

Emma could hear her squealing as she disconnected. She shook her head and hung up her own phone just as she pulled into her parking spot. Lori was so A.D.D., sometimes Emma wondered if Ritalin would work on her. It seemed not to affect her job, checking patients in to the Emergency Room, and all her co-workers liked her. How could you NOT like Lori? They had hit it off from the first day Emma had gone to work at Piedmont Hospital. Lori could see Emma was so confused by the large hospital that she took her under her wing. Lori introduced her to everyone and made sure she could get around without getting lost. Emma smiled thinking about her friend. Lori had made it easy for Emma.

Despite her talkative nature, Lori was a great listener. She'd been meaning to talk about Jack to Lori for the last couple of weeks, but had been too busy.

She went into her apartment and closed the door. She needed to think about supper, not Jack Denton. Emma shook her head, as if to clear it of thoughts, but by the time she entered the kitchen, she was right back at it.

Emma had met Jack about ten years ago when he had bought the ranch from the movie star who owned it. She had never thought much of the movie star and had assumed Jack would run the ranch the same way. The movie star had been absent ninety percent of the time and only came to the ranch to bring his friends and impress them. Emma and her family had made sure the ranch ran smoothly. It was difficult for Emma, growing up, to remember that her parents didn't own the ranch.

Then they had received word that the ranch had changed hands and a sense of foreboding had made the Hudson family worry that they would have to move. Emma hadn't realized until that moment, just how much she loved that ranch.

She realized she was standing in the middle of the kitchen. Emma stepped to the refrigerator and removed some raw vegetables. She let out a large sigh. Thinking of the ranch made her want a big juicy steak and baked potato. Like women around the world, however, Emma knew steaks and potatoes were not conducive to a 'girlish figure.' While she peeled the carrots, Emma went back to her musing.

The first time Emma had seen Jack, it was not love at first sight. She laughed out loud thinking about it. They were more like oil and water. Well, she was the oil on the water. Jack was always calm and thought things through, then acted fast as lightning. He had a sharp mind and wanted things done the way he wanted it. Usually his way was the right way, and that irritated Emma the most. He was the only person she knew who was usually 99.9% right.

It took six months of wrangling back and forth over little things before Emma suddenly found herself in love with this six-foot hunk of blond-haired, green-eyed manhood, who had a brain. That's what Emma couldn't believe. She'd gone out with handsome guys before, only to find out there was nothing between their ears. Very frustrating. When she figured out Jack Denton was the total package, she was already totally, hopelessly in love with him. The thing she liked most about him was that when she was mad, he would let her keep going on and not say a thing. Then he would look at her and quietly ask, "Well, Em, what do you want to do about it?"

Jack always valued her opinion, treated her as an equal. Nobody else Emma had ever known, outside her family, had ever shown her that respect. She thought that was the point that made her fall in love with Jack Denton, dammit.

Emma viciously snapped a carrot in half and ate it. Why was she thinking about this now? She grabbed the bowl of veggies and moved to the sofa in the living room. Eight years. Maybe she had grown up enough to face what had happened.

Jack didn't even know why she left. Why hadn't she told him? The simple truth? She had been young and scared. Emma had run away.

Emma resigned herself to finally think this thing through.

Jack had wanted children. Emma knew this, she wanted them too. After she and Jack had been together for a year, they started planning a wedding, talking about having kids, their own family. Jack was so excited when they would talk about names and whether they wanted boys or girls.

As is Emma's nature to cover all the bases, and because of her nurse's training, she decided to get a checkup with her OB/GYN doctor. The moment the doctor walked back into the room, Emma knew something was wrong. She found out that she had a condition that would never allow her to have children. She had done all this without Jack's knowledge, and knowing how much he wanted children, she vowed then and there not to tell him.

Thinking back on it now, Emma thought that maybe she should have told Jack. She realized now that she had been feeling sorry for herself and very insecure. Jack wanted children and she couldn't give them to him.

She never gave him the choice of her without children or another woman who *could* give him a family. Emma had been afraid to find out what his choice would have been. Instead, she made the choice for him. Emma had cut all ties and recited some nonsense about wanting to further her career in nursing. It was true, she did want to get her master's, but she didn't have to do it the way she did. It just made it easier on herself.

The first year after she had moved to Atlanta, she talked to Scott a lot. He never asked her what had happened between her and Jack, and for that Emma was grateful. She didn't think she could have lied to Scott, or told him the truth for that matter. Scott, tentatively, kept her abreast of the ranch and along with it, what Jack was doing. Emma had been torn, back then, about her feelings for Jack. On one hand, she loved him fiercely. On the other hand, she had moved so far away hoping he would find someone else to love and make a family with.

Apparently, it hadn't worked. Scott said Jack had

thrown himself into learning the ranch and making a lot of odd additions. Occasionally, at dances, Scott said Jack had danced with women, but for the most part he was totally devoted to the ranch. Emma was both relieved and frustrated. If only Jack would have married someone and gone on with his life, then Emma could have tried to pick up the pieces of her own life and somehow moved on as well. As it was, Jack was still single and Emma couldn't get over him. She knew this now.

With a huge sigh, Emma pushed herself off the sofa and started to go out on the balcony where her exercise bike was located. She might as well keep exercising, she'd need it when she got back to the ranch. She planned to live at the ranch and work there when she wasn't doing nursing in Cody.

Out of the corner of her eye she saw movement and turned that way. Sauntering towards her was Bella. Bella was her calico cat that had claimed Emma as her human about five years ago.

Emma had taken the trash out back one day and returning to her apartment she heard a high-pitched squeak coming from the bushes next to the steps. When she squatted and pushed part of the bush aside, out strode the tiniest kitten she had ever seen. She had walked right up to Emma and clawed her way up Emma's leg to her knee. From that day forward, Bella had owned a piece of Emma's heart. She had promptly taken Bella into her apartment and here they were five years later. So many lonely nights when Emma came home, Bella had always been there.

Now she walked toward Bella and asked, "I guess you expect me to feed you. I know, I know. You don't have any thumbs. That excuse is getting lame, Missy!"

Emma gave her a mock stern look and Bella went into her act of rubbing on Emma's leg, purring and peering into her eyes routine, as if to say, 'I absolutely adore you!'

Emma couldn't keep a straight face, she grinned ear to ear and reached down to scratch the cat's chin. Then she turned to the pantry and got a bag of Meow Mix out and filled the bowl. Immediately Emma was forgotten, and she laughed, thinking of how fickle Bella was. She really loved this damn cat.

Continuing on to the cycle, her thoughts picked up where they had left off.

The ranch. God how she'd missed it! Then she sobered. It was going to be hard saying goodbye to all the friends she'd made here in Atlanta. Some would understand, some wouldn't. Most of her co-workers would understand. Lori would be hurt but after Emma told her about Jack tomorrow, she would definitely understand. Bryan would definitely NOT understand. He'd been trying so hard to date her, it was almost like she was his by default. Emma rolled her eyes as she pedaled. It was not going to be fun telling Bryan. Oh well, somehow, she'd make him understand.

Emma stopped pedaling and got off the bike. She was back in her zone now and was going to take a shower and go to bed. Like they said in *Gone with the Wind*, "Tomorrow was another day."

Emma opened her eyes to morning sunshine streaming in between the curtains in her bedroom. She barely remembered going to sleep the night before. The last thing she remembered, she'd slipped in a movie and had watched about fifteen minutes of it before her eyes slid closed. Emma loved having that satisfied feeling of a hard day's work, but then there were the side effects of exhaustion. Well, that was over with, for a few days anyway.

She threw the covers off and stretched. Looking at the clock, she saw it was eight fifteen. She'd had eleven hours sleep. Feeling renewed, she went to put on the coffee and do her exercises. Push-ups and sit-ups in the morning. It was a love/hate relationship with these. She loved them because they kept her fit, but she hated exercise in general. It's a good thing she was self-disciplined. As she walked into the kitchen, Bella eased her way into Emma's path.

"Bella, I know it's been a few hours since you ate, but do you mind?"

Emma navigated around her to the coffee pot. First things first. She got the coffee going, then got the cat some food.

"There...satisfied?"

Bella answered with a swish of her tail then stuck her head in the bowl.

With a shake of her head, Emma detoured around the cat and headed for the study. She used this area for her exercises. When she finished she was ready for her shower and already thinking of her studies.

Looking forward to a shower, she called out to the cat, "You stay and eat your breakfast. I don't need you staring at me this morning...'Kay?"

Bella loved to sit on the bathroom counter and wait for her to get out. Very annoying.

Emma remembered that she needed to call Lori. After she was dressed and ready to face the day, that's exactly what she did.

"Hey girl, what's going on at the big house?"

"Did you get some rest? You were so damn tired last night," Lori said.

"It was heaven," Emma replied, "I came home, fed my baby, did my exercises, and died."

"You are the only successful, gorgeous thirty-seven-year-old woman I know that would brag about the evening you just told me about! Anyway, because you're my BFF, I'll let it slide."

Teasingly, Emma said, "We're BFF's?"

"Oh please! All right, I'm just going to ignore that. Anyway, so what time can I come over? I'm dying here!"

"Ok...Ok...I'm just kidding, you are my BFF. I tell you what, I'll be done studying by five thirty. Does that sound good?"

"You know it! I'll stop, get some beer, and be over around six. This is going to be juicy, I can tell!"

Emma smiled as she replied, "Just make sure they're

Coors Light. Anything else gives me a hangover."

She said goodbye to Lori and hung up her phone. For the next few hours, with just a couple of breaks, she studied. Bella lay in her lap and purred. Emma got up at one point and made herself a turkey sandwich with some unsweetened tea.

She'd accomplished a lot by late afternoon, and rewarded herself with a brief time of mindless television.

At six o'clock, Emma was lounging on the couch and rubbing Bella's ears.

The doorbell rang and Emma jumped up to answer. She looked out to make sure it was Lori and slid the bolt back.

Lori breezed into the room with a "Hey girl!"

Emma grabbed the twelve pack of Coors Light out of Lori's hand and said, "Hey yourself!"

She took the beer to the fridge with Lori following. Bella trailed the little procession and all convened in the kitchen.

"I didn't think I'd make it on time, the traffic is awful! I was behind a little old man, who shouldn't have been driving, doing twenty five in downtown Atlanta! Then nobody would let me over."

Lori pulled out a bar stool and plopped down. Bella promptly jumped up on the next bar stool and gazed adoringly at her. She was such a ham.

Lori reached down and absentmindedly started scratching under her chin and continued, "I know you love this place, but honestly, Em, it's a bitch to get here."

Emma handed Lori a beer then cracked her own and

leaned against the counter. "I love it just for that reason." She took a swallow and pulled her own stool out. "It suits me fine. All the humanity, even Bella loves the traffic sounds."

Lori glanced down at the cat and stroked her head with her other hand, "Oh, she was born here, she's used to it."

"You shouldn't pet her when she wants you to, you spoil her."

"You're one to talk. Who had a pet door installed in the back door?" Lori teased.

Emma wrinkled her nose. "You know I don't do litter boxes. Besides, Bella can take care of herself. She even tries to take care of me. She keeps bringing me animals to eat, a squirrel here, a bird there. She's a very good hunter."

Lori wrinkled her own nose. "Ew! That's just gross. Why does she do that?"

"She thinks I'm her family and has an ingrained sense to protect and feed. I think it's sweet."

Lori took another swig of beer then leveled her gaze at Emma, "So, you knew I'd get around to it." Quietly, and that was saying a lot for Lori, she asked, "Tell me about Jack?"

Emma took a breath and said, "This may take a while, let's go into the living room."

They grabbed their beers and, with Bella in tow, moved to the couch.

Emma got herself situated and turned to Lori. "I've been in love with Jack Denton for a long time." From there Emma poured out her heart to her friend. The fact that it was her longtime friend made it easier to tell the tale. She told Lori everything. From the first time she saw Jack, to the medical diagnosis she went through, to moving to Atlanta. Through it all, Lori nodded at times and touched her hand at others when Emma was near tears. Emma hadn't realized how much she had been holding in, until she said it out loud. She hadn't known the torment she had gone through to try to let Jack have the kind of life she felt he wanted and deserved.

Emma came to a stopping point and Lori held up her hand, "You need another beer and so do I. Hold that thought. I'll be right back."

As Lori went into the kitchen, Emma wiped her eyes and looked down at Bella, "I'm such a fool."

Bella turned her head upside down in Emma's lap and stretched her paw up to touch her hand as if the cat actually understood.

Emma laughed and rubbed Bella's head. When Lori came back, she had two beers. She gave Emma one and opened her own.

"So..." Lori said. "What are you going to do next?"

"What do you mean?" Emma asked, confused.

Lori sighed and rolled her eyes, "You said you're in love with this guy?"

Emma sat a moment, then got up from the couch and went to the balcony to gaze at the sunset.

Lori joined Emma on the balcony. "You haven't dated any one since him, and I've watched you as you were telling me all this. I may seem like a schitzo most of the time, but I can see how much you love him. You're head over heels for this guy Jack." She turned to Emma, "Like I said, what now?"

Emma continued to stare out at the darkening night. "I've already decided. I'm going back to Wyoming."

Emma held her breath, waiting for Lori's reaction.

She didn't have to wait long, "Woo hoo! I was so hoping that would be your answer!" Lori yelped.

Emma looked at her strangely, "So you want me to leave?" she asked, teasingly.

"Well, hell no, but when it comes to a love story as sweet as that? I can't see any ending better than you going home." Lori was quiet for a moment, as she looked out across the city. She turned to Emma and said softly, "I'm going to miss having you around, girlfriend, but Wyoming's not that far away." she winked and then put her arm across Emma's shoulders and squeezed.

After Lori left, Emma sat awhile and thought about what she'd told Lori. She did love the city, but once she was back in the mountains for a while she'd have no regrets.

Emma yawned and got up to go to bed. She realized that she'd already made her decision to move home before she'd mentioned it to Scott on the phone the other night. She was going home! Emma had a little smile on her face as she turned out the lights.

3

Dai Ji Kuan was worried. Actually, that was putting it mildly. He was terrified. He was the leading projects scientist for The People's Republic of China, so he had a lot to be worried about anyway. He was also sabotaging the secret project currently being carried out against the world, and America specifically. Add to that staging his own death and defection, well, it's a wonder he didn't have bleeding ulcers. Kuan shook his head and pulled the blanket up higher on his shoulders.

It had all started fifteen years ago. Dai Ji Kuan had been a promising student at the University of Hong Kong. Kuan's uncle was the supervisor of a new branch of combined science and military project. He had tapped Kuan for the lead scientist because he knew that he could trust him. He had also chosen his nephew because Kuan was brilliant at what he did. Kuan's genius was in nanotechnology and electromagnetism.

He bowed his head as he thought of his naiveté back then. He had been so proud to be chosen above all the others. He had not thought to question what the Chinese leaders had in mind for his combination of talents. Dai Ji had a new wife, Tang Sheng Hui, and a whole bright future ahead of him. Little did he know that life rarely follows the course that we intend for it to go.

Bitterly, Kuan clenched his fists around the railing of the ship. As had happened so often before, his past memories assaulted him once again.

The first few years with his new wife were happy. He

was working on the project and she was doting on him. They didn't try to have a child because they weren't ready yet. They wanted to put that off until he could advance in the political system. Things proceeded as they wanted and after four years they began planning for a family.

Kuan squeezed his eyes shut as the next series of images played across his memory. He had been coming home to celebrate with Tang that he had broken the nano barrier. That was his name for the final obstacle that had been plaguing him. He had to break the nano barrier before the EMP bombs could be built small enough to fit into the communications satellites. Now he had done it! Finally they could create an FCG or EMP bomb, as lay people called it, to target the Chinese's most dangerous enemy. He was reliving the entire problem as he pulled in the drive and stepped out of his car. They'd had to make something small enough to fit the size of a briefcase and he'd figured it out! As he opened the door and called out to Tang, he heard the television in the living room playing a live news report of an uprising and subsequent shooting of insurrectionists. Kuan continued to call out for Tang Sheng and got no answer. Puzzled, he had stopped in the middle of the living room and looked around. This was Tang's day to go to market. She usually got back by four o'clock in the afternoon. He looked at his watch, it was now five. Suddenly he looked up from his watch at the television and everything came horribly into focus. The news story came to Kuan's attention and his hand shook as he reached to turn it up.

"In an ongoing struggle with our great political

leaders, these wretched antagonists have killed several innocent bystanders at the central market."

When he forced himself back to the present, Kuan realized he was still gritting his teeth and gripping the rail. He found out soon after, that his wife, the love of his life, had been one of the innocents who had been murdered. Kuan had an epiphany that day and his life and feelings had changed. Over the next few weeks and months, he had begun to question all his beliefs, all he'd been taught. Tang had been everything to him and maybe everything you saw wasn't always the truth. Back then, as his eyes opened and he began to see the way things really were, he began to notice people weren't who they seemed to be. He began to make contact with people who knew people, because he began to hate. He began to hate the idea of what the project stood for and what it would do.

He began to really examine what it was the project was supposed to do. He didn't like it, he knew Tang wouldn't like it and he was ashamed that he was a part of it. He endeavored to change his life and who he was. He began gradually over time to meet some of the people that weren't what they seemed. Wouldn't you know it? It turns out they were spies. CIA. American agents. At first, Dai Ji was extremely nervous, he knew what could happen. But as time went by and he fed information to the Americans and tried to sabotage the project, a plan began to form in the back of his mind. He began, gradually, not to care, because of Tang. He felt her approval, her love. She would want him to do this. So, in the end, he cooperated with the CIA and they made a plan to get him out.

Kuan looks up, now, at the stars off the ship's bow and grins. He was so lucky that it had all came together. Or was he? Dai Ji's grin faded as he thought of Tang. She was better than him. She was better than he deserved, he always knew that. She'd always been with him and always will.

The CIA had finally met up with him and hatched a plan. After he finished sabotaging the project, they would help arrange his disappearance. An auto accident would occur with Kuan. They would then switch his body with another corpse and torch the entire scene so his "remains" would be unrecognizable.

A very simple plan, and yet it had worked. Afterward they had whisked him away to this cargo ship and here he was on his way to some small, obscure port in Oregon. When he reached Oregon, Kuan and the three agents who had met him on the ship, would board a private plane and fly to Langley, Virginia. There he was to be debriefed and try to help the Americans work on their EMP shielding.

On the surface it sounded easy, but the underlying intricacies had been tricky. Up to this point, amazingly, all had gone as planned. Kuan just wished he had done all that he was supposed to do. This was what had him frightened. His American benefactors did not know that he'd failed to disable all of the EMP devices. The reason for that failure was a good one. He could ease his mind knowing that he'd disabled all of the nuclear bombs. Those bombs were meant to be deployed after the EMP devices had disabled the American defenses. Still, there were the EMP devices that were left, and they would cause major death and destruction themselves. Kuan sighed deeply and lowered his forehead to the rail. He had done all he could to stop what his home country was trying to do and had simply run out of time.

He straightened and gazed off to starboard. Six weeks. They had six weeks to try to finish the shield. The plan was for China to release the EMP bombs from orbiting satellites on June 1st and tomorrow was April 16th. Kuan had a lot of work to do. Explaining to the Americans why time was critical was not something he was looking forward to.

4

Jack stood on the back porch with his hands on his hips. He stared at the night sky and thought about all that had happened. His brow was furrowed. He was worried about what exactly to do. His first instinct was to call Emma. What would he say? He definitely needed to tell his extended family what was happening. But there again...was something happening, or was it his paranoia?

Jack closed his eyes then turned and sat in the rocker. He had always trusted his instincts. When others had died, he had made it through. No matter what.

So, nodding to himself, Jack picked up his cell-phone and, by memory, dialed Emma's number. After four rings it went to voice mail and Jack was frantically searching his brain what to say. He had expected Emma to answer.

Deciding on a plan, he responded

"Hey Emma, things are a little out of the usual here. Nothing bad. Everyone's OK, but, well this may sound strange to you but...if anything out of the ordinary happens, I want to meet up. No, make that, I will meet you where we began our life. You know where I'm talking about, our special place."

Jack brought the phone close to his head and closed his eyes as he uttered the next words, "I hope I'm wrong, but if I'm not, I will be there." with a quirk of his lips he uttered, "and you better be too, or I'll kick your ass into next week! Anyway, I'll explain next time I see you. Just take care of yourself and keep safe. I love you Emma, I think you know that."

Jack hung up the cell phone and stood back up in agitation. He paced along the porch and thought about how there wasn't anything more he could do for Emma. He had responsibilities here he had to take care of. He knew in his heart now that he had been right all along. As he paced, he began organizing, in his mind, what he had to do. It would be a long while before he'd get to sleep, if at all.

———————————————————————

Jack woke up early the next morning, as usual. He'd had four hours sleep and felt every bit of it. He sat up on the edge of the bed and rubbed his eyes. They felt like they had sand in them. He decided last night to wait and tell everyone at breakfast what was going on. That way everybody would get at least one more good night's sleep before worrying. At least everyone but him.

Jack took a shower and dressed and was going downstairs for breakfast when he saw Jason coming out of his room with a frown on his face.

"What's wrong?"

Jason turned to Jack and looked him in the eye, "I just got a call on my secure satellite phone." he said quietly.

Jack immediately understood and gestured back to his room. They went in and closed the door.

"What's up?" Jack asked warily.

"Seems like the Chinese have cut out the Middle East connection and are going it alone. According to my contacts, the EMP device has been built and it's not just one." Jason hesitated then looked straight at Jack. "There are twenty five devices and they are already placed in small, satellites orbiting around the globe. The Chinese placed all of them in that large satellite that was launched last week. Remember? That communications satellite they made a big to-do about? Apparently it held a lot more than just communications equipment. Since launch, this satellite has been periodically releasing these small EMP devices at strategic locations all around the world. Unknown to anyone but us, once these devices are in place they will be detonated and all electronics worldwide will be shut down."

The words hung in the silence. Jack was stunned and sat down in the chair by his bed.

Quickly, Jason held up his hand "Wait a minute though, I haven't told you all of it. There is good news." He ticked off points on his fingers, "We turned one of their scientists, that's where we're getting our information. He's been working with us for a while. As a matter of fact, he's the lead scientist on this project and before you ask, he's doing this because he had a humanitarian change of heart. The Chinese also had nuclear devices deployed in camouflaged satellites ready to strike at us after the EMP's did their jobs but Kuan managed to disarm those before they launched. I'm also told that he thinks he has disarmed all the EMP devices, we'll know more when he arrives here."

Jack had been mulling over what Jason said and jerked his head up sharply at this last bit.

"HERE? What do you mean here?"

"Dai Ji Kuan is the scientist's name and after sabotaging the project we helped him defect. We had to help him disappear. He has information regarding the devices and the EMP shield that we absolutely have to have. Specifically, me. I have to have. I was made the senior coordinating member of this counter operation. I'm made aware of all details and information regarding this situation and on a need-to-know-only basis I delegate information and tasks to those people on the team who take care of them. I don't have time to go back to Virginia and wait for them to make their way there from the West coast. It's much easier to meet them here and go on from that point. I guess I should have told you, Jack. I'm sorry."

Jack glared. "You don't seem to be all that upset that you're trying to turn my home into another Langley." he said between clenched teeth. "I don't work for you anymore! You damn sure should have asked me. As it is, the only reason I'm going to ALLOW it is that you're gonna give me what information you get from this Kuan." Jack continued speaking over Jason's protests, "Oh yes, you will give me the information because you owe me that!"

Silence rang in the room for about five heartbeats, both men staring dangerously into the eyes of the other. Jason dropped his gaze first and let out a huge sigh. After a moment he lifted his eyebrows and said, "Price of being wrong, eh?"

Very quietly Jack nodded and said, "Payback's a bitch

isn't it?" and he actually grinned.

Jason grinned back and shook his head, "Now I remember why you use to piss me off. Fine, I'll interrogate Kuan and let you know what I can."

Jack narrowed his eyes and said, "NO! I'll be with you when you question him! After all, it was you who made me keep my top secret clearance." He beamed at Jason with a self-satisfied little smile.

Jason tilted his head to the side and seemed to consider. After nodding to himself he said, "All right Jack, I guess you're back on the team." And with that he turned on his heel and strode to the door, but not before Jack saw a quirk of his lips and a gleam in his eye.

"Oh no you don't!" Jack said, "What do you mean 'back on the team'? I'm retired, remember? I don't want to be on the Team! Jason! JASON!"

Jason just kept walking. Finally, at the top of the stairs, Jack caught up to him and grabbed his shoulder and stopped him. When Jason turned to him he had an innocent look on his face.

"You did this on purpose, didn't you?" Jack asked.

Jason spread his hands and asked, "Whatever do you mean?"

"Cut the crap, Jason! You came here, not only to pick my brain, but to get me to help you. To get involved again! I told you when I left, that I'm through with this, and with you, and I am! Nobody would believe me and I swallowed my pride and begged all the powers to be to listen to me and none of you would! It hurt, Jason. A man can only take so much humiliation and I hit my limit!

Now, you and the Machine find out I've been right all along and you want to suck me right back into this thing like nothing ever happened. No 'Hey, Jack, you were right, I'm sorry' or how about 'Hey, Jack we were assholes and we should have listened to you'! Jesus, the least you could have done is stood up for me when it all went down! I thought we were friends, dammit!" Jack was breathing hard when he finished and was surprised at how strong his feelings still were on the subject.

Jason was standing very still and his fists were clenched in, Jack was surprised to see, barely controlled fury. Jack couldn't ever remember seeing Jason furious but he was now.

With visible effort, Jason closed his eyes and took a deep breath. When he opened them he was much more under control. "Jack, you didn't see what went on behind closed doors and I never told you. I went to bat for you so viciously that my superiors thought I had lost my mind. I had to undergo psych evaluation for two weeks because of it! So don't tell me I didn't stand up for you. Now that's the last time we're going to talk about this! Yes, I want you on the team. I have and Washington has since we learned everything you said was true. I guess I came here hoping you'd just want to be part of the solution but I should have remembered how hard-headed you were and apparently still are. The point is, Jack, this thing's going to kill a lot of people unless WE, you, me, Kuan, whoever it takes, tries to put a stop to it and pride be damned! If you want to help, fine. If you don't then get the hell out of my way and let me do my job!"

Without blinking, Jason turned and started down the stairs.

Jack closed his eyes and thought to himself 'Damn, he's right. The whole point of my discharge was that they didn't believe me and people were going to die. Don't let your pride get in the way now.'

Jason was halfway down the stairs when Jack raised his hands and said, "OK, OK, you're right. I'll be part of the team but in a limited capacity. I'll be a consultant. That way you don't have control over me, agreed?"

Jason smirked as he looked back with a shake of his head. "Fine, you suspicious bastard," and went on down the stairs. Jack followed him down and they both entered the kitchen. Maria was pouring coffee for Grady. Danny and Scott had their own at the table.

Jack looked around and asked, "Where's Denise?"

"She went out to gather eggs and should be here any minute," Danny said.

"Good. We all need to talk about something and I want everyone here," Jack said.

He grabbed his own coffee and motioned Jason to do the same, ignoring the pointed looks everybody was giving each other. They'd find out soon enough. He and Jason sat at the table while Maria finished shoveling eggs and bacon onto a platter. She brought them to the table as Denise walked through the back door carrying a basket. Everyone mumbled good morning to her as she breezed to the sink and washed the eggs off. Maria gave her a heads-up by casually mentioning that Jack had an announcement. Denise cut her narrowed eyes at Jack and briefly nodded. Couldn't put anything past this family, Jack thought with pride. No, he amended with a smile to himself, his family.

Denise grabbed some coffee and sat. Maria did the same at the kitchen bar and all attention turned to Jack. Jack introduced Jason again to everyone and added that he used to work for Jason in the military. That was Jack's subtle way of informing all that Jason was government, since everyone knew Jack's history. Jack caught Scott's eye and barely nodded, and Scott sat up straighter. He just realized what this would be about.

Since all of their family meetings were informal, this one would be too. Jack grabbed some eggs and bacon and passed the platter to Grady, who did the same and passed them on. Jack waited until everyone was served and starting to eat, then he began. He started by recapping his history in the military and what he'd found. He told of the government's disbelief and humiliation and subsequent discharge. More than one pair of eyes were leveled at Jason and he studiously kept his eyes on his plate. Jack drew them back to him and it took more than an hour to relay the information Jason had just given him concerning Dai Ji Kuan with minimal input from Jason. Jack could feel the natural reticence of Jason from long years in his line of work. Jack had no such tendencies. This was his family and, by God, they would know the truth.

As he finished, Jack realized you could hear a pin drop, and all eyes were turned to him in stunned amazement.

"Well," Grady drawled finally, "now we know why you did the things on the ranch that you did." He stroked his mustache and grinned. "You weren't crazy after all!"

Everybody let out a little laugh including Jack, which relieved some of the tension.

"No, Grady, I probably am crazy but at least I had reasons for my craziness and this was it," Jack said with a grim smile.

At that point everyone started talking at once and Jack held up a hand. "One other thing. Jason is going to be bringing someone here who can answer some of the questions that you all are probably thinking. Until he gets here in a few days, it will be business as usual. After Jason and I talk to him I'll be able to tell you more. Until then I'd like you to not tell anyone outside the ranch about this. This person may have neutralized the entire thing. We won't know for sure until he tells us. Until then, this is Family Business." Jack said this last with grave finality. Everyone knew, when it was Family Business, it was hush-hush. No one mentioned it outside the ranch.

Everyone nodded and finished up breakfast. Dishes were taken to the kitchen and the men were headed to the door when Grady stopped and asked, "Before we go, I have one important question to ask."

Everyone stopped and looked at him. He turned to Jack and said, "When was this shindig supposed to happen?"

Jack turned to Jason and raised an eyebrow.

Jason cleared his throat and said, "June 1st."

Grady nodded and said, "This is April 17th so if this

fella you're talking about tells you it's still on, we have six weeks, right?"

Uncomfortable, Jason silently nodded.

"We've got work to do, boys," Grady said solemnly. "Let's get to it."

They all continued out into the morning.

Sometime later that morning, Jack was helping Scott finish up the root cellar when Jason walked up and said, "I've had contact with my agents. They've docked on the coast of Oregon safe and sound." He didn't need to tell Jack it would be an obscure port and they would have debarked under cover of darkness.

"I've brought them up to speed and given them the ranch's address. They have to drive in, so best possible speed puts them here sometime tomorrow if all goes well." He waggled his hand back and forth in a so-so gesture.

Jack pulled his gloves off and signaled Scott to take a break. He glanced over and saw Maria and Denise going out to the barn to get their gardening tools. Maria was talking animatedly and Denise was nodding. Jack was glad that everyone got along well.

"What are the powers that be saying about you bringing him here?" Jack asked.

Jason looked him in the eye and quietly said, "I have complete autonomy."

"I'm impressed," Jack said with raised brows.

Nobody ever has that level of confidence from Washington and they both knew it.

Jason looked away for a second, than swung his gaze back to Jack. "This is serious, and they seem to have finally figured that out. I need complete control over this situation to do my job and, to be honest, I think they're scared."

Jack looked away for a second then said, "I've spent more than ten years studying the effects of what an event like this could cause and trust me when I say Washington damn well better be scared."

After lunch, Jack found Grady and handed him a sheet of paper. "I need you to take the truck and fill this list of supplies."

Grady looked down at it and harrumphed. "I don't know where I'm gonna get that much kerosene and so many matches and lighters." He cocked an eyebrow at Jack.

"Just do your best. Also, you might stop by that antique store and see if they have any lanterns. We've got a few but I'd like to have more. Thanks Grady." Grady shook his head and walked off towards the truck.

Jack frowned thoughtfully as Grady walked away. He just hoped he remembered everything.

5

Emma hung her phone up and just looked at it. That had been a voicemail from Jack, the first one in eight years. He sounded strange and she couldn't put her finger on it. What was it?

She tapped her fingers on the arm of the couch and frowned. Then, like a light bulb it dawned on her. She had never heard that emotion in Jack Denton's voice before and it surprised her. Fear. That had been fear in his voice. What was it he said? Emma listened to her voicemail again. Special place? Then she remembered. They had gone to Pigeon Forge, Tennessee, a few months before everything fell apart. Back when everything had been perfect, before she decided to get a checkup. It had been the most wonderful week of her life. How could she have forgotten? Selective amnesia no doubt. She hadn't wanted to remember and now it all came rushing back. The evenings on the balcony of their mountain cottage watching the stars come out and making plans for a wedding and a family. The nights spent trying to start one. These memories still made Emma blush almost nine years later. Jack was a gentle and compassionate lover but had a bit of a wild side. All of these things had combined to make her fall even deeper in love with him. All the more reason, she'd thought back then, to cut it off cleanly.

She shook her head, back to reality. Pigeon Forge? What was Jack talking about? What the hell was going on? She'd have to remember to call Scott later, she didn't have time right now. She had errands to run. Bills to pay, groceries and on and on. Anyway, Scott would tell her later.

Emma grabbed her purse and dropped her phone in it. Snatching her keys from the kitchen, she scratched Bella under the chin and said, "I guess you want me to get you a squeaky toy?" She laughed at the feline's version of rolling the eyes and then Emma swooped out the door.

As she climbed into her car, Emma's cell phone rang and she fished in her purse for it. When she looked at the number, she saw it was her supervisor at work and let it go to voicemail. She knew they'd want her to come in for someone who had called out. That's the only reason they ever called. She was not going to give up her day off. Not today. She had too much to do. It rang again as she pulled out into traffic and Emma muttered, "Persistent little buggers," and looked down at the number. It wasn't the hospital this time, it was Lori. She answered with one hand and Lori said, "Hey girl, whatcha doing?"

Emma smiled and said, "Just going to pay some bills, you want to go for me?" She could almost see Lori wrinkling her nose.

"And pay with what, an IOU?" You could always count on Lori for a snappy come back.

"But seriously Emma, Bryan and I are going to lunch and we want you to come with us." Quickly she added, "Only as a friend. He called me last night to ask why you wouldn't go out with him or anybody else." She giggled and added, "He wanted to know if you were a lesbian." Then Lori really started laughing.

Emma was already shaking her head and grinning. She saw that coming halfway through Lori's monologue. "Are you serious, Lori, he asked you that?"

Lori quit laughing just long enough to stammer, "Yes, oh God, yes, he sure did!" Then she went back to laughing. This was getting annoying now. "And you said...?" Emma queried, and squeezed her eyes shut.

"Hunh? Oh I told him no way, and then explained about Jack," she said after getting herself under control.

"No, Lori, please tell me you didn't!" she groaned.

"Of course I didn't! I was just kidding! But I had you going for a minute, hunh? Anyway, I did tell him you weren't a lesbian and that you and I were having lunch today. I also asked if he would like to come along. This is the perfect opportunity for YOU to tell him about Jack."

"Of course," Emma said sarcastically. She sighed and rubbed the sides of her temples. This would be the perfect time to break everything to Bryan about leaving after school and moving back to Wyoming. Get it all over with. A thought struck her and she slowly said into the phone, "This would also pave the way for YOU and Bryan! Hmm, two birds with one stone?" Laughing inside, Emma waited for Lori's answer. She wasn't mad at Lori but she loved to get one over on her and make her think she was. She didn't get to see Lori squirm often, so she tried to enjoy the opportunities when they arose.

"Well," Lori said sheepishly, "if the truth would set him free?" She left it hanging.

Emma burst out laughing, "You are one sly woman. You know that?" More soberly she said, "God, what am I going to do without you?"

Lori was quiet a moment then said, "Visit as often as you can!" Emma could tell Lori was struggling to change the subject and heard her say, "So, are we having lunch?" She was trying to keep the conversation light and Emma let her.

"Oh, all right! Let me get a couple of errands done and I'll meet you at the Busy Bee Cafe."

"Oh man! I haven't eaten there in a while!" She hesitated, "Um, is Bryan welcome?"

Emma rolled her eyes, "Yes, bring your puppy along."

Lori squeaked, yes, actually squeaked, "OK, what time?"

Emma thought about it a minute and said, "How about one thirty?" That would give her time enough to pay two bills and she could get groceries when she was done.

"One thirty sounds great!"

Emma hung up about the same time she pulled into the electric company parking lot. She turned off the car and just sat there a minute thinking. How exactly to tell Bryan. She would just tell him like she had told Lori, from one friend to another. Hopefully, now, he'd see Lori in a new light. Shaking her head and smiling, Emma got out and went in.

Far above the earth, multiple satellites were switching on and starting a countdown. For many, it was the beginning of the end, they just didn't know it yet. Three hours. The Chinese discovered what Dai Ji Kuan had done and came to the conclusion that he'd defected. They decided to start things a little early. Unfortunately, Kuan had not disrupted the plans of the Chinese as much as he thought. Nuclear devices and EMP bombs were still in play. Nobody, not even the Chinese, knew what would happen. It was anybody's guess now...

6

Kuan and his "handlers" had debarked in a small port on the mid-Oregon coast. He was now safely tucked away in an inland safe house. The agents escorting him, a woman and two men, weren't very talkative. Kuan determined that Ray Burch was the one in charge since he gave orders and carried the satellite phone. Catherine Simmons, or Cat as the others called her, was the least talkative and Kuan had yet to hear her say more than a few words strung together. By contrast, Greg Morrison talked more than the other two put together. That seemed to be because he was more nervous. They were all built like athletes but each in a different way. Burch was muscular across the chest and shoulders and reminded Kuan of one of those American bulldogs. Simmons had more of a feline grace and Morrison made Kuan think of a greyhound. All of them made Kuan feel they were supremely competent in their jobs. He supposed they were, since escorting and guarding him from his now-avowed enemies was an extremely dangerous undertaking. His new American benefactors were well aware of this.

Kuan sighed tiredly and glanced around. He had just entered the living room. He set the small duffel bag filled with his worldly possessions on the floor next to an overstuffed chair. The house was starkly furnished, as one would expect a government safe house to be. It had minimal and utilitarian furniture, but as tired as he was, Kuan thought it looked like Shangri-La. He slumped in the chair and leaned his head back on the headrest. Burch came back into the living room after checking out the rest of the house and said softly to the other two, "It's clear." Simmons put her gun in its shoulder holster and headed into the kitchen to check out the food situation. Morrison was next to the windows facing the front street and edged the front window curtain aside to check for anything suspicious. Burch got out the sat phone and typed in a number. He walked away toward one of the bedrooms. Kuan relaxed his breathing and lowered his heart rate. He'd learned to do that when he was young, as he'd learned to do a lot of things. Self-defense. Sanshou, Tai Chi, hand-to-hand combat, you name it, he knew it. Call it an occupational hazard of growing up in his family. He wasn't a violent man, far from it, but if he had to protect himself and his family, he could. His handlers probably didn't know this and they didn't need to know. Kuan was just glad he had these talents. It could come in handy.

Cat returned to say she was going to make sandwiches. She pierced Kuan with a dark look and asked if he wanted a sandwich.

Following Cat into the kitchen, Kuan said, "I'm famished, what do we have to eat?"

She jerked open the fridge and laid out the contents, roast beef, ham, turkey, and bologna and snapped, "Take your pick."

Kuan stopped and looked at her. Softly he asked, "You don't like me. Why?"

Cat slammed the refrigerator closed and turned to him.

"No, I don't like you. You and your kind have

plotted against MY nation, the country that I love. I have family and friends out there that you have been trying to kill! What the hell do you expect?"

She turned sharply to leave and he gently grabbed her shoulder.

She turned to face him with menace in her eyes and slowly, deliberately looked down at his hand on her shoulder. As she raised her eyes to his, he slowly let go of her.

"I was once a soldier of evil, and did not know it," he said. "But I've learned from many experiences that I would not wish to learn again. I know better now. Not that your country has a better perspective of Right and Wrong or, better put, that not one religion or country is Right or Wrong. I have learned that all humanity has a right to live the way they want to. Not governed by religion, politics, or any other way except simply put, 'I am happy.' You've heard the saying 'Live and let Live'? I believe in that, completely. That's why I have done what I have done and find myself where I am."

As she listened to his soft spoken words, Cat sensed the strength of spirit Kuan embodied and knew the truth as he spoke it. The severity in her eyes relented a little but she couldn't let it go completely and Kuan saw this. It would do for now. If he was going to be with these people for any length of time he would like there to be no underlying issues. It was his way and it made life easier.

He turned away from her and made himself a bologna sandwich. He'd always wanted to try the stuff.

Cat made sandwiches for herself and the other two

agents. As she did, she studied Kuan out of the corner of her eye. He was taller than most Chinese and stood about the same height as she did. There was something about him that troubled her. Cat had had several relationships with some guys and none had radiated the strength of conviction that Kuan had. It's almost like he knows he's right. That should be a good thing, but it felt off somehow. As she made the sandwiches, she mulled over what it was about him that bothered her. She finally shook her head. She would have to think on it later.

She picked up the plate of sandwiches. As she went to the living room to deliver supper to Ray and Greg, she heard the sat phone ring. Curious, she put the plate on the coffee table and turned to Ray.

Ray answered and Cat knew he was talking to Jason, their immediate superior and the only one who knew this leg of the operation.

Ray listened for a bit and said, "un hunh" and "yeah" a couple times. Then Ray listened a while longer. Time seemed to draw out and Greg glanced at Cat. When there was a long, drawn-out silence on this end, they knew from past experience it was not good. Possibly a change in plans. Nobody liked a change in plans.

Cat turned to the kitchen, and realized Kuan was eating his bologna sandwich and listening in. There wasn't much to hear, but Kuan was smart enough to realize something was wrong. He slowed down chewing and looked between Greg and Cat with his eyebrows raised but they ignored him. He continued to chew but looked more sharply at Ray, who paced to the window and listened.

Ray turned and saw that everyone was paying attention to him. He finished up the call and as Ray hung up the phone, he cleared his throat.

"Jason says that we have to meet him in Cody, Wyoming. So, we have to figure out where it is and how to get there. When we get there, Jason is going to talk to Dai Ji and figure this all out."

Cat walked over to the desk that had an encrypted computer and switched it on. Meanwhile, Greg walked over to Ray and asked in a low voice, "Cody? What's in Cody?"

"I don't know and he didn't explain. I guess we'll find out when we get there. It has to be important to keep him away from Washington right now. Why don't you go see how Kuan's doing and you might as well fill him in. We'll all be traveling a long way together and he seems like a pretty bright guy. There's no reason he should be in the dark at this point. I'm going to go get some chips to go with my sandwich and see if there's a soda."

Ray walked through to the kitchen and Greg filled Kuan in.

Cat had finished printing the directions. She brought the papers over to Ray when he returned from the kitchen. They all sat at the table and Cat said, "Eleven hundred miles. It says it'll take us seventeen hours by car."

Ray looked around at Greg and back at Cat, then sighed. "We'll just have to take turns driving. I saw an ice chest in the garage. We'll pack some of the food and drinks into it. Let's get a good night's sleep, wake up early, and be on the road. Set your alarms for six am. Sharp. I don't know about you all but I'm exhausted. I'll go to bed last and set the alarms."

Everybody grabbed their gear and headed off. Ray muttered to himself, "I don't know what you're up to, Jason, but I hope you have a good reason. Jeez, seventeen hours."

7

Emma walked into the Busy Bee and looked around. The place smelled exquisite. This was one of the best restaurants around. She was standing on tiptoe, looking for her friends when a woman at her shoulder asked if she could help her. She looked over and saw a hostess.

"Yes, I'm with Lori Bubar?" she asked smiling.

The hostess smiled back and looked down at her tablet. After consulting her seating chart, she looked up and said, "Follow me, please."

Turning on her heel, she wound her way through the tables and Emma followed. At the back of the cafe, she made out Lori and Bryan at a booth. She waved, smiled, and then slid into the booth next to Lori.

"How are you guys?" Emma asked.

"Good, girl!" Lori said, smiling. She seemed a little tense and Emma glanced at Bryan, "Hey Bryan! I've got a bit more energy today."

Bryan gave an easy smile and replied, "Glad you let me into the girls club."

He took a sip of his beer and looked across it at Emma.

Emma smiled back at him and noticed Lori out of the corner of her eye. She looked concerned.

Trying to break the tension, Emma asked, "Have you guys ordered? I'm starved."

Lori, relieved, answered, "No, we just got here and were checking the menu."

She handed one to Emma. "I was just telling Bryan

that you would be done with your master's in a couple of weeks."

Emma forgot about the appetizers she was perusing and looked up at Bryan. He was looking up expectantly from his own menu. She glanced at Lori impatiently, then smoothed her face before looking at Bryan. "Yes, I'll be finished by the end of the month."

She didn't know what else to say right then, so she went back to checking out the menu.

Bryan cleared his throat and said, "That's great, Em! What are you going to do next?"

Emma was afraid of this and took a deep breath before setting down the menu and looking over at him. "I'm thinking of going back home to Wyoming. They have a great hospital there and I miss my family."

She held her breath, waiting for Bryan's reaction. She didn't care romantically for Bryan, but she liked him as a friend and colleague. She had always hated to hurt anyone's feelings if she could help it.

Bryan looked steadily at her for another minute and then with another slow smile he said, "Good for you Em," and seemed like he meant it.

Releasing her breath, Emma smiled and felt Lori was smiling beside her too.

"Thanks, Bryan. It means a lot to me to have the support of my friends."

She subtly emphasized the friend portion of that last statement. She knew Bryan was intelligent enough to pick up on it and she was not disappointed. Emma could tell by the look in his eyes that he did.

The server came around and they ordered, giving them all time to readjust.

After ordering appetizers and beers, Bryan sat back and proceeded to take on a teasing tone.

"So you can take the girl out of the country but not the country out of the girl, is that it?"

Lori and Emma both laughed and Emma said, "Something like that." They all chatted easily after that and laughed about work until the food came.

The server had just set the sample platter down when there was a blinding flash of blue-white light. A sound like slow, rumbling thunder accompanied the lights going out. Immediately following this were two heartbeats of dead silence and then pandemonium.

Outside the café there were tires screeching and loud sounds of cars crashing together. Inside the restaurant people were screaming and yelling back and forth. There was a mad rush for the front door. In the gloom, the three friends glanced at each other with puzzled expressions, but not very alarmed yet. Working in the medical field, they all had learned to keep their head in a crisis. Bryan pulled his cell phone out and tried the touch screen, wanting to get information on what was going on.

"It's dead!" he announced. "What the hell is going on?"

The two women had their phones out and had just noticed that theirs were dead too.

There was a huge explosion across the street and they could all feel the heat as a massive fireball, carrying debris, blew in the front door of the café. It instantly killed all the people that had rushed the front door. The three friends, as one, ducked under the table in their booth but not before a flying glass shard grazed Lori's cheek, just under her eye. It then sliced through the tip of her ear.

As the friends huddled under the table, the first thing Emma thought of were the twin towers. But then, that didn't make sense because they now had Homeland Security. They were always on high alert since THAT tragedy. She was confused and terrified. She looked over at Lori and saw her bleeding cheek. "Oh my God! Lori, are you okay?"

Quickly, she peeked up over the table edge and grabbed the cloth napkins lying there. She scooted next to her friend. Lori looked dazed and confused. Emma knew she was going into shock. She eased Lori back against the base of the booth seat and examined her wound.

Unbelievably, people were still shoving to get to the front and out the door. Trampling one another in their frenzy to escape.

She saw Bryan move out of the corner of her eye and glanced over to see what he was doing. He was peering out towards the front of the building, apparently trying to make sense of the chaos. Smoke and dust lay over everything. It was swirling around the inside and outside of the building. More explosions continued outside along with screams all around them. Moans from the injured and dying threaded through the other sounds adding to the unrealistic feeling of it all. Emma tuned all this out and returned her attention to Lori's wound. It was a deep gash that had laid open her cheek to the bone under her left eye. It was about two inches long and skipped a distance before continuing at an upward angle to slice through her left ear. Emma saw right away that it would need stitches but that would have to wait. She folded the napkins and pressed them to Lori's cheek and ear telling her to put pressure on it. Lori complied without saying a word. Which REALLY concerned Emma. She took a deep breath to calm herself and tried to focus. When she felt under control, she eased over to Bryan and said loudly to be heard over the tumult, "What's going on?"

"I don't know," he said just as loudly, "but I can tell you, the electricity's out, no cell phones, cars are crashing out there still and that was a plane crash across the street. I can see the nose of the damn thing out in the street still burning!"

Emma sat stunned. A total nightmare. She couldn't even begin to comprehend what was happening. Then immediately she thought of her family. Were they going through the same thing, was Jack okay? That thought immediately made her remember Jack's phone call from the day before. It had been puzzling at the time and damn weird, but she had promptly forgot it with all the errands she had to run. Now, however, she remembered his words with clarity: 'If anything out of the ordinary happens, get to our special place.' Which of course was Pigeon Forge. Jesus! Jack somehow had known something was going to happen! She didn't have time to think it through right now about HOW Jack had known, but he had and he'd told her where he would come for her. The fact that Jack had tried to warn her told her that this wasn't just a local event. She closed her eyes and a tear streaked down her sooty cheek. She hurriedly wiped it away and returned her attention to the present. They had to get out of the city somehow. Her thoughts were in overdrive now…in survivalist mode. She'd grown up on a ranch and even though that training had been slumbering for the past eight years, it all came snapping back to the forefront now. They had to get to her apartment somehow. She had a bunch of supplies there that they would need: First-aid kit, handgun, knives, canteens and food. She also had a compass, maps and matches. She raised a prayer of thanks that she was an avid outdoors person on the weekends and kept her supplies at the house.

Emma grabbed Bryan's sleeve and pulled him back where there was less noise. They were hearing gunshots now as well as the other noises. She looked over at Lori to check on her before leaning over to Bryan's ear.

"Whatever is going on is huge. I have supplies at my townhouse that we need to get to! Whatever has to be dealt with can be better handled with the things in my apartment." She gave him a level look, and he hesitated.

"Lori has a deep laceration and we can stitch that up at my place too. It's only a couple of blocks away, plus we need to stick together, right?"

"Yeah," he finally relented, "you're right. But how are we going to make it through that mess out there to go fifty feet, much less two blocks?"

Emma thought furiously. She knew there was a back

alley on the other side of the wall they were leaning against. She closed her eyes and mentally followed it to the fenced vacant lot at the end. It was surrounded by a low chain link fence which they could go over and through the lot to the edge of the apartments farthest from hers. She opened her eyes and looked at him as she grabbed his arm, "I know how to go a back way if it's clear. Come on," she said turning to Lori. Lori's gaze looked clearer, she just looked scared now.

Emma leaned over to Lori and said with a forced smile, "Hey girl. I've got a plan, you with us?"

Lori gave a little smile and said, "Sure, nothing better to do right now." Then winced as the motion caused her cheek to throb with pain.

Emma knew with that sentence that Lori was going to be all right. She put her hand up to let Lori know to wait there. Emma then caught Bryan's eye and motioned to the table above them. He seemed to understand and they both edged their heads above the tabletop. As her eyes cleared the top of the table, she furtively looked around the cafe and saw that most of the patrons were either dead, injured or hiding. Nobody else was poking their heads out. 'Probably smarter than we are,' she snorted to herself.

She scanned the tabletop looking for the steak knife she remembered being there and spotted it. At the same time, Bryan spotted another one. Their glances met knowingly and they both reached out at the same time and claimed their prizes. They both ducked back under the table breathing hard as if they'd run a mile. Looking up sheepishly at each other they both kind of chuckled before the seriousness of the situation descended on them once again and they sobered. Lori looked quizzically back and forth between them. Emma shook her head and said, "Never mind. Look, we're going out to the back alley. Hopefully it will be clear. Then we'll go down to that vacant lot that backs up against the other side of my apartment. You know, the one those kids played in last summer? From there it's just a little ways to my apartment where we'll regroup and make further plans."

Lori took in Emma's confident voice and look and said, "Lead the way, El Capitan."

Emma nodded and turned to Bryan, "You ready?"

He gave a brief, nervous nod and followed Emma. He was holding the knife with one hand and guiding Lori's elbow with the other.

They squatted low and eased toward the door separating the kitchen from the dining area. Every time they heard an explosion or a scream they flinched, but less and less as they became use to it.

Emma had just reached the door and was pushing through it when someone from the other side came barreling through shooting off a handgun. The door flattened the three of them against the wall and shielded them from the gunman's sight. He continued straight through the cafe and out the gaping hole that use to be the front door. Emma rested her sweating forehead to the metal door she was holding and could hear Lori sobbing against Bryan's shoulder. She gathered her strength and looked back at Bryan over Lori's head. He gave a nod of conviction and the same thought passed between them. They had to get to Emma's place, it was the closest place of probable safety. Taking a deep breath, Emma eased her head around the door and looked into the kitchen. Nothing moved. It was darker even than in the dining area and Emma took a moment to assure herself that nobody was moving in there. When she felt sure, she slowly stood up in a crouch with her knife in front of her. Going through the door, she slid up against the inside wall. That way she wouldn't present as much of a target. Jack had taught her that.

She looked around to get her bearings and spotted the back door. It was partially open and she stared at it a minute to make sure it wasn't moving. When she was certain, she glanced back to wave her friends through, but they were already coming up beside her. Emma pointed at the back door and Bryan nodded. Creeping through the smell of burning food, Emma peered out the door and looked around at the alley. There was a lot of debris clogging it, but she felt that with some effort they could make it to the lot. The firecracker sounds of gunshots and screaming were louder here. She pulled her head back to ready herself and encourage her friends. Bryan had removed his sports jacket at some point and rolled up his sleeves. Lori snapped off the heels of her shoes so she could maneuver better and Emma felt a moment of relief that her friends were thinking sensibly. Emma looked down at her own outfit and realized that she was actually dressed well for the situation. Jeans and a t-shirt with Timberland boots. It's what she usually wore to lunch with friends. She shook these thoughts off and pushed on the door but it would only go so far. She pushed harder and felt it give a little more. Bryan must have seen her dilemma and tapped her shoulder. Emma looked back to see him gesture first to himself then to the door. She got it. She was kind of petite and Bryan had some muscles. This was no time to play the feminist, so she stepped back by Lori.

As Bryan began trying to dislodge whatever was blocking it, Lori leaned over and asked, "Do you have any clue what the hell is going on!"

She sounded just a bit hysterical, but then Lori had every right to be. Emma herself *felt* a bit hysterical and was using every ounce of self-control to focus on the problem at hand.

She looked her best friend in the eye and said, "I can make a hundred guesses but it won't change what we have to do. I only know that cell phones aren't working, electricity has gone down, and there are a lot of scared, hysterical people out here trying to save their own asses. There's no way to call the police even if they could get to us and help. We're just going to have to help ourselves and that means we start by getting to my place."

Here Emma took a deep breath and turned to apologize to Lori for talking more sternly to her than she intended. Lori had her hand up and the right side of her mouth quirked in a little smile. She still held the napkin to the cut on the left side of her face but said, "You would have made a great drill sergeant!" She then hissed in pain. Bryan had the door opened and motioned them on.

They stepped into the alley and glanced around. The sky was leaden with smoke, ash, and dust, but Emma noticed a green glow between the clouds. It seemed slightly familiar to her but she couldn't put her finger on it.

She forgot about it as Bryan called over to them from across the alley. Emma looked over and saw he was sheltered behind a dumpster strewn with wooden and metal debris, some of it still smoldering. She grabbed Lori's hand and scuttled over next to Bryan. He was rubbing his eyes and coughing from the smoke.

"We've got to get some air, which way?" He asked Emma.

She pointed left down the alley and he squinted that way, trying to see what was ahead. Leaning towards them he asked, "You said there's a vacant lot down there on the left?"

A little out of breath, Emma again nodded then said, "About fifty yards down you'll start seeing chain link. When you see that, we need to find a way over, under or through it." Glancing at Lori she said, "Preferably through it." She then squeezed Lori's hand who squeezed hers back.

Bryan nodded then moved off in the gloom with the two women at his heels. They all flattened on the ground when they heard a loud noise like a dumpster lid dropping directly ahead and then footsteps running away up the alley in the direction they were going. After a minute they all carefully raised up to a squat and, glancing around, started toward the lot.

More explosions and angry shouts were heard in the distance. Nearer at hand they could hear gunfire and glass shattering. Emma's heart was in her throat, and she could feel Lori's hand shaking badly in her own. Finally after passing the offending dumpster and about fifteen more minutes of slinking through the alley, they came to the edge of the building on the left. Sitting squarely in the middle of the lot was an entire wing of an airplane which had been sheared away at the fuselage. It was burning and they could all smell the sharp odor of jet fuel.

"We can get over the fence, but what about THAT?" He gestured to the wing and lifted his eyebrows in a question.

Emma felt her spirits drop for a second, then her thoughts focused on one thing. They HAD to get to her apartment. Her resolve returned and she looked up to take in the burning wing with new eyes. When she first looked at it, the wing seemed to take up the entire lot. On second look, she saw that the part of the wing that had sheared off the fuselage was resting on the building they'd just walked past. There was a small space between the wing and the building. It also wasn't burning as much as the other end. She saw that they could make it under that section. They would have to hurry before the fire claimed it but she was willing to take that chance. Quickly she turned to her friends and with fire in her eyes she said, "We've got to get to my apartment. If we hurry, we can shimmy under that end of the wing before the fire gets bad. Are you with me?"

They were all breathing hard and covered head to

foot with dirt. Lori and Bryan looked over to where she was pointing and squinted, judging the distance and the fire.

Frustrated, Emma said, "I'm going."

She put one hand on top of the fence and swung her legs over it like she used to do on the ranch. She turned to look at her friends and saw surprise on their faces.

"We don't have a lot of time to dick around here, guys!" she stated. "I'm not leaving you here so come on. We've got to move it before we draw attention from whoever is shooting those guns!" She practically screamed the last and that finally mobilized them.

They glanced at each other and then Bryan glanced down and ripped his right sleeve off. This, he tied around the bandage on Lori's face so her hands could be free. Emma stifled a laugh and they both glanced up again in surprise. Emma beat down the laughter and looked at them apologetically. "I'm sorry, Lori, it's just that you look like you're wearing a turban. Oh, never mind. Just temporary insanity."

She reached up her hands to help Lori over while Bryan helped from his side. After Lori was over, Bryan vaulted the fence and they all ran to the last remaining section of wing and scooted under on hands and knees.

After they squeezed through, they checked each other out and patted out fires on each other's clothes. They had only suffered minor burns on skin and clothes, but Lori's bandage was smoking. Emma and Bryan worked together to get it out. They had all turned to look at the wing when a new noise began to emanate from it.

At first they all looked puzzled. But when Emma realized what she was hearing, her eyes flew open wide and she turned, grabbing her friends, and ran. "Oh shit!" she screamed as she dragged them away as fast as she could. She heard Bryan screaming "What!" as he struggled to keep up with her. Emma had no time to answer as they sped toward her apartment. They all sprawled behind a cement wall and she yelled, "Cover your head!" Instantly her friends complied.

There was a sound gearing up to a high-pitched whine and Emma tensed as she heard a loud WHUMP!

Emma continued to stay curled in a ball as debris rained down all around them. When she heard less debris falling, she peeked out between her arms and saw her friends doing the same. She breathed a sigh of relief and relaxed back against the wall.

Breathing heavily she felt Bryan look at her and ask, "What in the hell was that!"

She looked over at him and Lori, and said, "On the ranch, we burned a lot of trash. When I heard that sound, I remembered that aerosol cans in the trash would make that sound just before they exploded. I just put two and two together."

They both blinked at her with what she thought was renewed respect, and she felt uncomfortable.

Emma tried to change the subject and looking around she said, "Look, we're not far from my place. Let's get up there and get my supplies."

Lori snorted and said, "Jeez, MacGyver, what kind of supplies do you have up there?"

Bryan guffawed too and Emma rolled her eyes.

"Come on you guys, really, we gotta go!"
Emma's two friends stifled their laughter and looking around, sobered up.

They all trudged through the weeds at the back of her townhouse property and finally reached Emma's back door. Surprisingly, her place seemed to be intact.

She was reaching for the backdoor handle when there was a rustling in the weeds and a blurry, multicolored shape shot out at Emma at light speed. Emma tried to jump back, but the shape was on her. Before she could react, she recognized the noise coming from the furry blob and embraced the object to her chest.

Emma hiccupped out a cry and brushed her cheek next to the calico fur and breathed, "Oh, Bella! Oh my God! I didn't even think about you! I'm so sorry."

Bryan and Lori had jumped back at the furry motion too. They eased back next to Emma and Lori actually chuckled. Bryan, who didn't know Emma's cat, still stood back a ways. Lori stepped up next to Emma and rubbed Bella between the ears. She glanced over to Bryan and said, "Emma loves cats. She's a cat magnet and Bella is her cat. She's pretty much her baby. If you want to be friends with Emma, you better pass Bella's approval."

She stepped back to let Bryan have access to Bella and he eased up to look at the cat.

Bella narrowed her eyes at Bryan and waited to see what he would do.

Bryan smiled crookedly at the cat and reached up to scratch her under the chin. Bella started purring, and

Emma laughed, "What a cheap date. Okay, let's get into the apartment."

She put Bella down and grabbed a small rock next to the steps. Flipping it over, she slid the bottom off. She dumped the key out in her hand and replaced the rock.

She went up the steps and entered the back door. There were no lights on. Well, she hadn't expected any. Emma took a deep breath and felt herself start to tremble. 'We made it!' she thought. The overpowering sense of relief in that one thought was enough to bring her to her knees, but she couldn't let it. She had to focus on one thing at a time. She turned to Lori and said, "Come into the kitchen, we've got to wash out that cut and get a better bandage. Bryan, can you go to the bathroom, and on the top shelf of the linen closet is a black bag. Meet us in the kitchen with it." She pointed down the hall and he walked away.

Lori had slumped down on the couch and had her head in her hands. Emma gently helped her up by her shoulders and walked her into the kitchen. Sitting Lori on a bar-stool, she quickly went to the sink and tried the tap. Fresh water gushed out and Emma smiled with relief. At least one thing still worked. She quickly grabbed a recently washed milk container from the cupboard and started filling it with water. Bryan walked in and set the bag on the counter.

"How can I help?" he asked.

"Since you take x-rays and I sew people up, why don't I take care of Lori and you fill the jugs. There are three or four more in the pantry. Fill as many as you can and then start filling other containers. I've got a feeling we might not have running water for long."

Both Bryan and Lori stopped what they were doing and just stared at her.

Before Emma could say anything, a light dawned in Bryan's eyes and he said, "It makes sense. If the power's out then the water treatment plants can't keep running. The beauty of it is that even if you're wrong, it's better to be prepared."

Emma saw that Lori got it too, now, and so she just nodded.

Before getting started, Emma wanted better light. It was still daylight outside, technically, but the green haze caused it to be darker than it should be. She pulled out three candles, put them on saucers, and lit them. Much better, she thought.

She walked over to her clean rag drawer, pulled out several, and laid them on the bar.

They could still hear ongoing chaos outside, rife with yelling, screaming, and explosions, but it was muffled in the apartment. In any event, Emma had a job to do and her training kicked in to tune everything out but her patient. She reached into a different cabinet and brought out a bowl. Nudging Bryan out of the way she filled it half full of water and took it to the bar next to Lori. She also put the rags and first-aid kit next to the bowl. She looked Lori in the eye and said, "This is going to hurt some but it's got to be done. I'm going to give you a painkiller and wait fifteen minutes. Then we'll do it."

Lori grabbed Emma's hand with both of hers and

tried to smile, "I trust you, Em, and I know you're doing what you do best, so let's get it over with."

They hugged and then Emma gave Lori the pills and turned to ready her instruments.

After what they thought was fifteen minutes, Lori was groggy and said she couldn't feel the pain so much. Emma glanced at Bryan, who'd finished filling every available container. He gave her an encouraging smile then moved away to find food for Bella. For just a moment, Emma hesitated, wondering if this situation would be temporary. Surely somebody out there is mobilizing the Guard and bringing troops in to control this mess. She shook her head to refocus on the task at hand. Lori needed her now, so she went to work.

8

Since yesterday after lunch, everyone had been working at a higher level. With a deadline bearing down on them, they had all felt the need to get things done. Jack had been overseeing projects all morning that he'd let go until now. Lunch was ready and everyone else was up at the house. Jack stood for a minute and looked around. He was proud of their accomplishments. Now there were just a few little things left to do. He looked over at the garden and saw it was planted. The root cellar was finished. After lunch he'd help Maria and Denise carry out the new batch of canning to be stored there. Scott and Danny were going hunting this afternoon and checking the traps. If they caught anything, he'd help them get the meat ready for the smokehouse.

He thought again about Emma and wondered what she was doing. Nobody had heard from her since Scott had a couple of days ago. He just hoped she had gotten his message.

Jack had just climbed the steps and was reaching for the front doorknob, when suddenly there was a loud crack that sounded like a bullwhip. A blinding blue-white wave of crackling light seemed to come from the southern sky and consume everything. Jack instinctively flattened to the porch as a loud rumble of thunder passed over the ranch. As the noise receded and the light became less intense, Jack slowly opened his eyes and looked around. The sky had turned a sickening shade of green. His heart was pounding as he pushed himself to his feet, jerked open the door, and almost ran flat out into Scott.

"Was that what I think it was?" Scott asked.

"I think so," Jack said, striding past him.

"I thought this wasn't supposed to happen until June?"

"Obviously, somebody's information was wrong," Jack said, his thoughts going into overdrive.

The rest of the family had filed into the living room as Jack had said this last part, but he didn't see Jason.

"Where's Jason?" he asked.

Maria spoke up, "The last I saw he was going up to his room."

Jack noticed that all the power had gone out as he grabbed the railing and raced up the stairs.

"Get the lanterns out and somebody go check on the animals!" he called over his shoulder.

Reaching the top of the stairs, he stepped over to Jason's door and saw him sitting on the bed with his head in his hands.

"Don't say it, Jack. Dammit! This wasn't supposed to happen!"

He dropped his hands and stood up facing Jack.

"I've already checked the sat phone. It's dead, as I knew it would be. We're on our own."

Jack took a deep breath and suppressed his anger and fear. Venting at Jason would not help. What was done was done. They had to make plans.

Nodding his head at Jason, Jack said, "Let's go see the others."

They went downstairs to find Grady just coming

back in from checking the livestock.

"They're pretty spooked, but everything seems fine," he said.

"Good," Jack said. "Let's all sit down. We've got to talk about what we're going to do."

Someone had put some lanterns on the table and lit them and now everyone gathered around the table and stared expectantly at Jack. He knew they were counting on him and he just prayed he wouldn't let them down. He realized in that instant that he loved these people like his own family.

"All right, Scott, I need you to saddle up a horse and head into town. Find out what's going on and report back. Don't get too close, but close enough to see what's going on there."

Scott nodded and started off.

"Maria, you and Denise please inventory all the canning and see what we have. Also, inventory all the things we have planted already and when they should be ready for harvest."

Maria and Denise nodded and headed off.

Jack turned to Grady, "I need you to ride the fence and check it. Make sure there aren't any problems. Come back and let me know."

Danny looked at Jack and raised his eyebrows.

Jack looked back at him and said, "I need you to get a better check on the livestock. Get an accurate headcount of the horses, cows...you know. Make sure the Ranch is stable, A-OK."

Jack turned to Jason, "I need to know where your

people were and what was going on before this happened."

Jason had his hands on his hips and was staring at the table.

"My team is already on the way here. They were supposed to have left Oregon before dawn yesterday and they have Kuan. We'll know more about this when he gets here. I just don't know when or if they'll get here, now."

Jack didn't know what else he could do. He did know that they were away from airline flights and any major interstates. They just needed to make sure that everything stayed secure.

Jack looked outside and could see the green glow. This puzzled him and he walked out on the porch. Jason watched and followed him out.

"What do you think it is?" Jason asked, staring up at the unpleasant jade sky.

Jack shook his head and said, "I'm not sure...but it feels familiar."

Jason looked around and said, "I'm worried, Jack. What am I going to do about my family?"

Jack turned to him and said, "The same as we are. Wait."

"I hate waiting." Jason snarled.

"Join the club." Jack said with a curl to his lip he couldn't control. He remembered many assignments that Jason wouldn't change and he felt vindicated.

Jason noticed and said, "You don't have to like it, damn it!"

"You're on MY territory now. You'll have to do what I say!" Jack didn't like being heavy handed, but he knew he had to let Jason know where things stood.

Jason looked at Jack and conceded he had a point.

There had been a time when Jason could tell Jack what to do. No more. He acknowledged that Jack knew what he was doing.

Jack knew his stuff. He always thought about everything and Jason knew Jack was thinking about Jason's wife and son as well as every other factor in the problem. He would let Jack mull everything over and ask him later. It was killing him, but it was the best, the quickest way. He had to keep his mind on the immediate problem.

The problem was getting his people and the agent to Jack's house. If they make it, Jason and Jack can quiz the agent and possibly get more information. He's not going to think about if they don't make it.

Jason had put the best three agents he had on the assignment. They had to get Kuan here. The agent had the answer to a lot of questions, including hopefully how to neutralize this situation.

Jack and Jason now watched as Scott rode out to check on the situation in town. Each man hoped everything would be good. That's all they could hope for.

Jack turned and walked off toward the barn. Jason looked after him then followed. Jason caught up and asked, "Where are you heading now?"

Jack looked straight ahead and answered, "I've got to check on the guns and ammunition. If you want to help, we can start taking them up to the house and cleaning them. We can also do inventory on everything as we bring them up. It'll give us something to do until Scott gets back. It will also give me time to think."

"Sure, it'll keep my mind off everything and focused on something different." Jason replied.

They reached the barn and Jack slid the door back. Reaching to the side without thinking, he flipped up the light switch. When nothing happened, Jack instantly realized his error and rolling his eyes pulled out his flashlight.

"I've got a feeling I'm going to be doing that a lot today."

Walking to the back of the barn he brushed hay away from the trap door in the floor and pulled the ring up.

"One of the first things I did after buying the ranch," Jack explained, "is to create an arsenal." Glancing at Jason, he continued "I know human emotions and read a few things about what might happen. People are going to become desperate and I want my family safe."

Jack went down the stairs and Jason followed him. As Jack shined his light around, Jason whistled, "Wow! I thought I had a stash!"

Jack ignored him. He started grabbing weapons and ammo.

"Come on. I've got home defense and military grade weapons. We need protection. Just in case. We'll have to make several trips." His hands full, Jack went back up the stairs and to the house. When they got there he directed Jason to the den.

"Let's clean everything and organize it by size. I want to get everyone a weapon and some ammo. The women will need size appropriate weapons and I know they can shoot. I'll pick something out for them."

Jason followed directions and got things laid out. Two hours later they were done. They had lit the lamps and stood looking down at their handiwork.

"Denise likes the Glock, and I want to give Maria that sawed off shotgun. The guys will get whatever they want. They probably already have theirs. If they don't, they can choose. Everyone will be armed." Jack motioned to the table and then asked, "What's your poison?"

Jason looked over the arsenal, then chose a Sig Saur 1911.

"I like it short and sweet."

Jack grinned lopsidedly and chose a 357 standard revolver.

"I like simple."

Jason nodded and put a shoulder holster on. Jack did the same.

Feeling better, the men stepped into the hall and looked around. Denise was going to the kitchen and Jack asked, "Have you seen Scott?"

She nodded and pointed to the front door. "He just rode up. He'll be up in a minute."

"Thanks." Jack said, "How is the inventory going?"

"Good. Maria is so meticulous anyway, she had half of it all done before you even asked."

Jack watched her pass by, then headed for the front door. He was anxious to hear from Scott.

"What do you think happened in town?" Jason asked.

"Same as all around the country. Bad shit. Pure pandemonium. I just hope it was better than I expected."

Jason matched strides with Jack. "So what can we expect here?"

"If we're lucky? We'll have about a week of relative peace. When our neighbor's water starts running out we'll probably start getting visits. When the food starts running out we'll get visits with weapons. People you thought were your friends or neighbors? They'll shoot you first and ask questions later. When people get hungry they will kill for food. Especially since America's not use to starving...in general."

Quietly Jason said. "I never thought of it that way."

Jack glanced at him and said, "That's America's problem, they never have."

Jack looked up and saw Scott walking towards him with his rifle. He stopped and waited for him.

"Well?" Jack asked.

Scott sighed and looked at Jack. "I eased up into a stand of trees on a hill, that one right before Carson's store, you know? Anyway, half the town was burning, from the looks of it, probably still is. I could see bodies everywhere, injured in their cars, lying on the sidewalks. I heard gunshots across town and also saw smoke from the direction of the airport." He shook his head and looked right in Jack's eyes with a tortured expression, "I felt so helpless, I couldn't help anyone. I knew in my gut that if I rode down there, whoever was shooting might have tried to kill me."

Jack knew what Scott was feeling. Many times, in the field, Jack was put in that same voyeuristic position. Painfully helpless, that's how he'd felt. Like watching two cars coming to an intersection with no stop sign, knowing they couldn't see each other and yet too far away to warn them.

Jack had years of preparing himself for this eventuality. Scott and, basically, the rest of humanity had let themselves be blindsided.

Bringing himself out of his reverie, Jack said gently, "You did the right thing, Scott, as hard as it was. If you would have ridden down there, you probably would have been shot. If not for your horse, than for no other reason than that people are afraid. We can't afford to lose anybody. All of us depend on each other. We're on our own, now, until this situation is corrected." Jack didn't say out loud what he was thinking, which was, 'If it ever is.'

The sky still held that weird green glow which, subconsciously, Jack had been thinking about. Some areas of the green seemed to be darker than others and if Jack's suspicions were correct they could all be in a lot more trouble than they already were. He kept all this to himself for now, he had to wait to see if he was right.

While they were standing there, Danny and Grady walked up to join them.

After Danny had checked on the livestock, he'd ridden off to help his dad check all the fence lines. It was a lot of area to cover for just one person.

"Everything looks pretty good." Grady now said,

"Danny came up from the East and then North. I rode the South, West, and part of the North before meeting Danny about where you found that maverick the other day. It all looks sound. At the time, I thought you were crazy, but now I'm glad you had us put up those ten-foot fences with razor wire. I see why you did it now." Amazingly, Jack saw behind Grady's beard that he was blushing, and he knew it had taken a lot for Grady to say what he had. It was an admission and apology all in one breath and Jack could see, as he looked around at Scott and Danny, that they felt the same way and Jack was touched.

He let them off the hook by saying, "I kind of thought I was crazy too, had kind of hoped I was. Unfortunately I wasn't. Now we just need to get organized and make plans. We've already inventoried everything, so let's go up to the house and talk about what to do next."

Grady and his sons looked relieved and they all walked up to the house.

Entering the front hall, they sat the rifles down but kept their sidearms on.

It felt funny to Jack but he realized this would be the way of things from now on. Passing through to the dining room, Jack noticed that Maria and Denise had reheated the food and set it on the table. They must have used the wood stove, he thought. Immediately on the heels of that thought was how hungry he was and, smelling the food, mentally praised the women's thoughtfulness.

As the women entered from the kitchen Jack said,

"Thank you, Maria, Denise," and he nodded to them, "for remembering what us men tend to forget until it's placed under our noses." He grinned to get everyone to relax a little, and it helped. All the men chuckled and the women smiled graciously.

Everyone found a chair, and after being seated, Jack nodded to Grady, who said a prayer. Food began to be passed around and Jack decided to wait until all had eaten before discussions began.

Nobody said a thing until lunch was finished and everybody pitched in with the dishes. Tap water was still running, but Jack knew it wouldn't be long until it stopped, two, maybe three days at the most. He planned to stop using it after tonight anyway because it might be contaminated from the water treatment centers having been down too long. He was not taking any chances. He had chemical purification pills and there were cases of Clorox in the underground warehouses he had built. Pure water was not an issue. They had water from the creeks on the property and the wells they had dug. Might as well start getting used to hauling it.

They all gathered back in the dining room and Scott lit a lantern. Everyone got quiet and waited for Jack to begin.

He pulled out the notebooks he'd gone up to his room to retrieve and cleared his throat.

"Okay, earlier, Scott rode down as close to town as he could get. From a grove of trees he saw all hell breaking loose. Dead and injured in the streets. I told him, when he left, not to get too close. We can't afford to lose anybody." This last was said again for Scott's benefit and for anyone else around the table who might have questioned this.

Maria had closed her eyes and was slowly shaking her head. All the others were in various degrees of the same shock, but all in all they seemed to be accepting it.

Jack went on. "The town is burning and Scott said he saw smoke billowing on the other side of town, about where the airport is. It's probably burning also. He heard gunshots, from who or for what purpose, we just don't know. First and foremost I shouldn't have to say this, but keep your weapon near you at all times. It's going to get worse before it gets better. I just hope it will eventually get better. If so, we need to make sure we get through it in one piece. Any questions so far?"

No one moved a muscle.

"All right." He looked down at his notebooks, then glanced around. "I've done a lot of thinking on what to do in case this happened." Jack raised the notes. "This is my best guesses as to what to do in an orderly manner. Really, we've already executed the first major step which was inventory. I'm going to set each of you on top of a certain duty but it will probably be common sense for you. Just like every day, each of us will have to help each other. If you come across a problem or something doesn't seem right, don't hesitate. Let someone know." He looked steadily at each one of them. "Our lives may very well depend on it. We're going to have to learn new skills to help us get through this, like how to be a blacksmith, weaving, and more extensive leather working.

If these conditions continue for an extended period of time, we'll need to know how to do these things. I've stocked a library of these books in the underground warehouse, where the guns are kept. I want everyone to learn a new trade in your spare time. I know there won't be much of that at first, but hopefully we'll settle down into a routine."

Jack looked around then down at his notes. "Danny, you're good with the animals so I'd like you to be in charge of them. It's going to get demanding, because as food gets short, they'll become more valuable. Carry both rifle and sidearm. I'd also like you to read up on how to blacksmith, you've got the build for it."

Looking over at the old man, Jack continued, "Grady, I want you to be the sentry, keep up with the fences. Check the grounds and buildings on a regular schedule. Keep an eye out for anything out of place. You are the law when I'm unavailable. Fill in where we're shorthanded, since you know this ranch like the back of your hand and I'd like you to read up on—"

Grady cut Jack off before he could finish. "Jack, if you tell me to take up knitting, I'm going to hit you right between the eyes!"

This got a loud round of laughter, even Jason, and especially from Scott, who was envisioning his dad with a pair of knitting needles.

Jack immediately saw Grady's ploy for what it was. An attempt to defuse the awful tension of the situation, even for a short time. With a smile and a slight nod in Grady's direction, Jack silently thanked the man for reminding him that they all needed a good laugh.

As the chuckles receded, Jack continued with a small smile, "I was thinking more along the lines of leather working and fur making, but if you want to try your hand at knitting, I've got a pair of socks with a hole in one of …"

Before he could finish, his last words were drowned out by another loud round of laughter and Jack glimpsed the older man across the room nod his approval. Jack filed that away for later. He couldn't be all gloom and doom. As bad as everything was, he was a leader and he had to know when to be serious and when to lighten things up just a bit. Once again Grady had taught him a valuable lesson.

As the laughter died away and people were wiping tears from their eyes, Jack started again.

"Maria and Denise. When you two get some time, we're going to need more soap and candles. I've got books on that too." Jack saw everyone staring at him and suddenly knew what they were thinking. Emma. He knew this was as good a time as any to address it. He knew this would not be an easy conversation.

He scooted back in his chair and said, "I see all of you, except Jason, are thinking the same thing I am." After he said this, you could have heard a pin drop. Jack ignored the puzzled look from Jason. He'd figure it out in a minute. Jack continued, "I am as worried as you are about Emma," he stated quietly. "I will tell you this. I am going to get her." Out of the corner of his eye, he saw Jason's jaw drop.

"I didn't tell anyone, but the night before this happened, I called and left her a message." He continued, "I let her know that if anything," he paused, searching for the right words, "strange happened, she was to get to Pigeon Forge and I'd meet her there."

There was stunned silence as this sunk in. They had all gotten somewhat used to Jack's uncanny sense of intuition, but this was surreal. Jack became uncomfortable and added as an explanation, "It didn't take a rocket scientist to put two and two together. Jason shows up making this announcement. I'm an amateur expert on what would happen if this event went down. I then took into account the Government's record on being too conservative in estimating past events, and last but certainly not least, I think everyone here knows how much I love Emma. Even if she is two thousand miles away." This last was said quietly into the growing darkness.

He let this last part sink in before going on. "I haven't had a chance to tell you what Jason told me yesterday. His team from Oregon was supposed to be here sometime today. Obviously now, this estimate is out the window. However, when they do get here, Jason and I will still interrogate this Chinese guy and get all the information we can from him." Here he looked at Jason and went on, "After which, we will ready our horses and head to Pigeon Forge." He knew this last statement would cause an uproar, and it did.

Everyone, except Jason, began talking at once and Jack had to hold his hand up for quiet. He glimpsed Jason out of the corner of his eye, and saw he had a thoughtful expression on his face.

Scooting forward in his seat, he said, "Let me explain. When Jason's people get here, this person Kuan possibly has information we need to resolve this EMP effect. He was a scientist high up in the Chinese government and instrumental in developing the bombs. He also, supposedly, knows how to build a shield, or in our case, turn one on. If he has this knowledge, Jason and I need it, and him, before we go to Pigeon Forge." Here he held up his finger for effect. "After we get Emma we're going to Knoxville to try and get the shield started that the government has built there. Before you ask, they didn't get the shield started before this happened simply because they ran out of time. We don't know how far they got, but I'm hoping this guy can help. It's a long shot, I know, but it's the only shot we have right now and I'm going to get Emma anyway. Knoxville is only 30 miles from Pigeon Forge, which makes it too close not to try to do something about this."

He looked around and could tell everyone was trying to digest it all. He continued, "Also, I've been thinking about this green glow and going over it in my mind. From the material I've seen, nobody really knows what would happen during an event like this. They made guesses and hints but, reading between the lines, I gathered, nobody knew for sure. An EMP blast from a high altitude was supposed to be a non-lingering, one-time occurrence that did not have ongoing effects. It happened once, fried all electronics, but then, once they were repaired, things could go back to normal. With this green glow, I have a suspicion that, if we repaired things, it still wouldn't work. From what I've read, it has to do with a phenomenon called 'pumping of the Van Allen belts.'"

At this statement, Jack could see Jason was startled. Before Jason could question him, he went on, "I've spent some time in Alaska and Northern Canada and this glow has the same distinct coloring as the aurora borealis. I believe that the explosion and corresponding electromagnetic burst has affected our atmosphere in the same way as a solar flare does, only on a much greater scale. The Northern Lights, as most people call them, are a phenomenon caused by the interaction of solar winds with the Earth's magnetic field. It's my thinking that this blast has caused the same disruption in our ionosphere. The reason I think it will continue is evidenced by the fact that the artificial green light is still there and I think it will be until something shocks it back into normalcy."

Jack could tell that with all that had happened, nobody had had time to wonder what the lights might mean. Now, something like dawning horror began to cross their faces at the realization that this might be how things would be forever. Before this thought could take hold, however, Jack reiterated what he'd voiced earlier.

"I said earlier that Jason and I are going to try to change all that. I don't know if we can, but we're going to try. While we're gone I need you all to keep the home fires burning, so to speak." He looked each person steadily in the eye then went on gently, "It won't be easy but you've got to keep things safe here so we all have a home to come back to, whether things are back to normal or not." With more confidence in his voice than he felt, he continued, "I'll bring Emma back, either way, and she needs to know her family is safe and waiting on her."

Scott spoke up then, and with quiet conviction said, "You can count on us Jack, you just bring Emma back. I know nobody's ever said this but, we love you. You've been one of the family for several years now, and I love you like a brother."

There were nods all around and murmurs of agreement. Jack felt his throat tighten with tears and fought it back so he could finish. Hoarsely he said, "Thanks, Scott and everyone. I hope you all know the feeling is mutual." They all took this last in stride, as if they'd known it all along so he continued. "One last thing for tonight. We need to set shifts for the watch. Everybody gets a turn."

With that, they all gathered around the table to plan the watch, even Jason.

Later, as Jack sat on his bed writing in his notebook by lamplight, there was a knock on the door. "Yeah?" he called.

Jason eased the door open with raised eyebrows, "So, when were you going to tell me about the girl?" he asked. "Or were you?"

Jack dropped his pencil and ran his hand through his hair. He knew Jason would come asking. Jason didn't like surprises, Jack remembered. He gestured to the chair beside the bed and leaned back against the headboard.

Jason brought his hand from behind his back in a peace offering. He held a bottle of Jack's good whiskey and two highball glasses. He partially raised them with a quirk of his brow.

Jack grinned crookedly and said, "Yep, just about what I need right now."

Only Jason was aware of how close Jack had come to almost drowning himself in alcohol after his service ended. Between his parents both passing away at the same time, the honorable discharge, and above all, his integrity being challenged, he'd nearly lost the struggle with that one vice. He had battled back though, and after six months of self-pity, he'd gone dry for good. Only occasionally now did he allow himself to drink and only because he was able to say 'when.' Self-discipline, Jack reflected, that's definitely what makes the man.

He reached out for the glass Jason poured and let him stew a minute more. Jason had poured two fingers and Jack swigged it down. Setting the glass on the side table, he said mock seriously, "You know if I tell you, I'm going to have to kill you."

For a split second they both sat staring at each other. First Jason burst out laughing, and Jack soon joined him. It was an old joke between them on that cliché. They let the laughter die down and shared another drink, this time Jack just sipped his slowly, something else he'd learned.

"Ah, Jason," Jack said, leaning his head back against the wall, "I hadn't planned any of it to happen, but then again, we never do." He started at the beginning and told his old, estranged friend the not-so-funny tale of Jack and Emma.

9

Ray Burch was in a foul mood. More so even than usual. They had awoken early yesterday and driven all day, making good time. Twelve hours on the road had put them in Butte, Montana, by the time they had stopped. Now, however, it seems their good luck had run out. They were sitting in a diner eating breakfast while the rental agency took its time swapping the vehicles. Apparently, the Chevy Tahoe they had driven from Oregon hadn't taken too kindly to the twelve-hour trip and had decided it wasn't going to start. No matter what he tried, Ray had been unable to get the damn thing going, so here they sat, waiting. Ray hated to wait. He was an action guy. Cat was the one with patience.

Ray looked across the table at the other two agents. Greg had been finished eating for a while and was playing with the salt shaker. Cat was taking her time eating eggs and sausage. Ray was too pissed and wound up to eat. He glanced next to him at Kuan and saw him calmly sipping the tea he'd ordered. Ray shook his head in disgust and said "Jeez, what is taking so long?"

Cat didn't even look up, like she had expected this. "It hasn't even been an hour, Ray, give them some slack."

Ray sighed heavily and slid out of the booth, "I'm going for a walk."

"You want some company?" Greg piped up.

"No." Ray said a little too harshly. He tried to soften it somewhat, "You stay here and listen for the phone in case the boss calls."

That seemed to do it. Greg subconsciously sat up straighter and quit playing with the salt.

Ray walked out the front door and looked at his watch. Damn! Almost nine o'clock. He stretched his arms up and the muscles in his shirt bulged against the seams. He felt better with the fresh air and walked to the corner of the building. Reaching into his inside jacket pocket, he dug out a pack of menthol cigarettes. He'd quit five years ago but with this assignment, he'd been craving the damn things again. His wife was probably rolling over in her grave. She had hated his smoking. He smiled a little thinking of her, then turned serious again as he lit up. He reflexively scanned the parking lot and surrounding area, noting every little detail. It was why Jason had given him this assignment. Simply put, he was the best. He never lost the target. Luck just seemed to follow him. As for Cat, they had worked many assignments together and they just seemed to know what each other was thinking. Greg, on the other hand…Ray wasn't sure why Jason had brought the kid in. He didn't know much about Greg and neither had anybody else he'd asked. Greg was an enigma. It wasn't that he was a bad agent, he seemed to know his stuff well enough. Ray just didn't like someone so young on his team. You usually equate youth with inexperience and in this line of work, inexperience could mean death for one or all team members.

Ray had stamped out the cigarette and turned toward the door when the others came out. Cat was in the front with that graceful feline walk she had. Kuan was next and had a quiet, steady air about him. Greg was last with a slight grin on his face. Ray was quick to notice, however, that Greg was covertly scanning everything Ray had. All of a sudden a thought occurred to Ray, 'He reminds me of myself fifteen years ago!' Ray vowed to watch the kid more and see if it was true. Maybe that was why Jason had put him on the team: he saw something in Greg that other people hadn't. He'd think on it later.

"The rental agency called and said they'd meet us at the Tahoe in fifteen minutes. Perfect timing." Cat was grinning at him.

"Perfect timing, my ass! We could have been on up the road an hour ago if they hadn't drug their feet," Ray snorted.

He thought he heard Greg snicker and whipped his head around to glare at him, but Greg was studiously looking at nothing and Ray let it go. The kid just might turn out all right.

They walked down to the motel and the new rental vehicle was just pulling in when they got there. This time it looked like they got a Ford Expedition. They all grabbed their stuff out of the Tahoe and exchanged vehicles. Ray grumbled something at the poor guy and tossed him the keys to the Tahoe as they peeled out of the parking lot.

Cat, who was riding shotgun, noticed Ray was looking all over the dashboard for something.

"What's wrong?" she asked.

"This thing doesn't have a GPS thingy."

"What, like a Tom-Tom?"

"Yeah, one of those things."

Cat pulled out a map of Montana and said sarcastically, "I guess we're going to have to do it the old-fashioned way."

Ray just rolled his eyes, and again heard something from the back seat but decided to ignore it. He did look at Kuan in the rear view mirror, however, and noticed the guy watching the by-play with interest and not a little humor. 'This guy is a lot smarter than I thought he was,' Ray thought. He had been so quiet from the first, it had been easy to misjudge him. Ray looked at him now with a bit more respect, not just as a target.

He returned his eyes to the road after Cat called out the next turnoff which was I-90 East.

As they merged with traffic, Ray turned to Cat and asked, "How far?"

"According to this thing, 209 miles to our next turnoff, then about ninety miles south on a two-lane," she stated.

"I'll drive 'til we get to the two-lane, then I'll switch with you." Ray adjusted his shoulder holster and got comfortable for the three-and-a-half-hour drive. Glancing at his watch, he saw it was now almost 10 o'clock. With any luck, they'd make it to Cody by about 3 or 4 o'clock. Then maybe he could relax for a bit.

They had just seen a sign that said Livingston was two miles away, when all of a sudden a brilliant blue-white light seared the back of Ray's retinas. Along with the light came a loud snapping-crackling roll of thunder. Ray was startled so badly that he swerved off the road. Cat had been dozing and let out a confused, startled yelp as she reflexively grabbed for the dash. Ray continued to fight the wheel as the SUV tipped up on two wheels and slid into the ditch. He heard gasps and grunts from the back seat, then nothing as he focused back on the task at hand. He was still blinking his eyes, trying to clear his vision, when he felt a thump and the car went airborne. He cringed as he waited for the SUV to land and tried to relax his arms as he'd been taught. The Expedition came crashing down and slewed to one side and he twisted the wheel to compensate. At the same time he tried to slam the brake and felt their forward momentum slowing. As they came to rest, he was breathing hard and anxiously glanced next to him at Cat. She had her hands out on the dash and seemed to be praying. He took a quick look over his shoulder to see about Greg and Kuan but both seemed to be okay. They all sat still for a second and then Greg said, "What the hell was that?"

Ray didn't answer, but said, "Is everyone okay?"

Everyone seemed to mumble something, so he took that as a yes. Taking a deep breath he said, "Okay, I'm going out to take a look, now that I can see."

He stepped out and looked around. He noticed a green glow in the sky, but filed it away for later. Looking back in, he said, "Looks like we got lucky. We didn't hit a tree, but we need to see if we can get out of the ditch."

Greg was getting out and looking around. He seemed to be limping, and Cat was shaking her left wrist.

"Any broken bones?" Ray asked, nodding to Cat and Greg.

They both flexed the offending parts and shook their heads. Ray guessed they were still shook up and he needed to focus their attention.

He realized he'd heard other crashes when he first got out, but now there was silence up on the road and that puzzled him. Shaking it off, he went back around to the driver's side and tried starting the SUV. Nothing. He couldn't even get it to turn over. 'Well, shit.' He thought, 'That's just great.' He whipped out his cell phone to call the rental agency for another car. Dead. The sat phone was dead, too. He knew he had charged it last night. At about the same time, Cat had been trying her cell phone out and it dawned on both of them at the same time. They jerked their heads up, looking into each other's face for a split second, then scrambled for the door handles.

Greg noticed their quick motions and, following suit, yelled "What! What the hell is it?"

Without replying, Ray and Cat scrambled up the ditch and reached the interstate just as what looked like a 747, whose pilot must have been trying to glide in on the road, crashed nose-first into a pile of already wrecked cars, causing a tremendous fireball.

The shock wave knocked them both back down into the ditch and they came to rest in a heap mere inches from the Ford's rear bumper.

Greg had been hobbling around the passenger side to the front when it hit and he and Kuan, who'd been helping him by the arm, went flying back into a holly bush. The concussion caused the glass in the SUV to explode, but luckily Greg and Kuan had been blown into the bushes. Cursing noises were coming from the holly bush along with some frantic rustling. There was some liberal Chinese coming from the area also. Ray lifted his head and saw Cat was okay and shooting his thumb over his shoulder said, "I guess that answers if they're still alive."

Cat was leaning on her good hand and wiping grass off a scrape on her cheek. "I'm getting a bad feeling, Ray. You know I don't believe in coincidences and if you think about it, either this is one damn, big coincidence, or somebody's dropped one of those EMP bombs. Early." she said, glaring at Kuan where he was crawling out of the holly bush.

Ray blinked in surprise, "Shit! I knew it! The cell phones, the Ford, and then the airplane!"

Greg had stumbled out of the holly bush and overheard their conversation. "How the hell are we supposed to get the rest of the way to Wyoming? You read the briefing that Jason sent us. If it's true and a device went off, nothing electric works now!"

They all froze for a minute as they heard another, smaller crash and explosion. Probably an automotive gas tank.

Ray forced himself to calm down and focus. Now was not the time to panic.

"Greg, get off that leg and put your back against that tire. I'll get the atlas. Cat, you go around to the glove box for the first-aid kit. We gotta get organized."

Ray's chest muscles bulged as he gripped the handle on the back door and raised it. He was thinking furiously as his eyes darted from bag to bag and he realized his adrenaline was racing now. 'Calm down,' he told himself. He took a deep breath and felt better. He looked at the bags again and reached in one for the main atlas. It was where he remembered it was and he reached around and gave it to Greg. "Figure out where we are, exactly, and try to plot a course."

"Um, I think I remember a sign saying Livingston ahead."

Good, now he's getting focused. "Find it on the map."

Meanwhile, Ray was setting packs out side by side and unzipping them. He had to figure out what they had to have and what they didn't.

Cat came around the bumper with the first-aid kit and headed toward Greg. Ray grabbed her good elbow and said, "You first."

He sat her on the bumper and took the kit. He first grabbed a bottle of water and poured some on her cheek, washing off the scrape. She didn't say a word. Then he took the Neosporin spray and put some on.

"Any little cut could be lethal now," he said. Their eyes met and a silent understanding went between them.

She nodded and said, "I just sprained my left wrist, not broken."

He said, "Good, I can't afford to lose you."

Trying to lighten the mood, Cat said, "I bet you say that to all the girls."

Realizing what she was doing, Ray chuckled and said, "Nope, just you."

More relaxed, they quickly got Cat fixed up and she attended to Greg. While she did that, Kuan came around and quietly asked, "Can I help you, Mr. Burch?"

Ray couldn't understand how a man as quiet as Kuan could exude such strength and competence but he took what he could get.

"Start going through these bags and find any food, ammo, weapons, and maybe lighters or matches you can find." Glancing up he said, "In other words, anything that we may need to survive in the wild. Any questionable things, ask me." After a pause he added, "Thanks." Kuan politely nodded and went about his business. Ray took the ice chest out and flipped the lid off.

They had brought along sandwich meat, bread, condiments, a few canned things, and—miracle of miracles—a can opener. He took an emptied backpack and started repacking things.

The sandwich meat would go bad first, so they had to go ahead and eat it. They could save the canned goods for last and the bread would last a few days.

Out of the corner of his eye, Ray thought he saw movement, and with lightning-fast reflexes, he pulled his gun and went down on one knee. Nothing. He panned side to side and still didn't see anything. Easing up on the hammer, he slipped the gun back in its holster.

Must have been smoke from the plane or an animal. Shaking it off, he finished filling the backpack. Looking over at Kuan, he said, "Let's see what you found."

Bending at the waist, Ray surveyed Kuan's take. Rubbing his jaw he said, "All right! Looks like we've got a box of matches, a lighter, ammo, um…what's that?" He pointed to a kit-like contraption and Kuan said, "A sewing kit." Ray looked at him for a beat and considered. "Okay, good job, we'll probably need it."

Ray then turned to Cat and Greg. "How's he doing?"

Cat finished packing the first-aid kit and said, "Bruise on his shin, right leg. Multiple cuts and scratches from his argument with a holly bush."

"Damn, man. Those things sting!" Greg said.

"Make sure you got them all with Neosporin," Ray said.

"She did. I guarantee she did!" Greg bitched.

Ray smiled a little and turned away.

Yep, Ray thought, Greg was going to fit right in.

"What the hell are we doing, Ray! Do you have a plan? I have the route."

Ray looked around at everyone. This was his team. He could have done worse.

"Okay. This is what's going on. We've got an EMP bomb down. We have to get to Jason who is maybe 200 miles south, southeast. We have a map, we have some supplies. I doubt my compass will work. We'll just have to make it as a team."

At this, Ray looked up at the only member of his team he wasn't absolutely sure of. Kuan.

Kuan was looking back steadily at Ray and said, "I assure you, Agent Burch, you can count on me."

Ray wasn't assured, but still nodded because he had

no choice. Kuan would have to prove himself along the way. They were all in this together.

"Are you okay to walk, Greg?" Ray asked as he rested on the bumper and reached for the atlas.

Greg handed the map to him and stood up gingerly. "I won't be running any marathons for a while, but I'll manage."

Ray concentrated on the map and said, "Looks like we have two choices. We either cut through Yellowstone, which is shorter, or follow the roads and the route we're on now."

He pointed out, on the map, what he was talking about and they all gathered around.

After a minute of studying the map, Cat spoke up, "If we go on foot through Yellowstone, it's a lot more rugged, but shorter. If we keep going through Livingston, we'll probably run into a lot of folks."

Ray was nodding before she finished. He'd hoped they'd see for themselves what he'd noticed right off. They had to start thinking like frontiersman because, in a nutshell, that's what they were now. Only, years ago, the frontiersmen didn't have a lot of refugees running around, scared out of their minds and probably a lot of burning wreckage between them and Cody to contend with.

Ray could see the light dawning on Greg, too, the moment Cat said it.

Kuan spoke up then, surprising Ray.

"Horses," Kuan said softly.

"What?" Ray asked. They were all looking at Kuan

now.

"This is America, and Montana at that. Surely there are some horses around here somewhere?"

Greg blew out a short laugh. "Yeah, right. Let's just go out in the next pasture and wrangle some up!" he said sarcastically.

"No, no, wait, Greg. That's a good idea," Ray said, thinking, "It definitely would cut down on time, which we don't have, and possible injury to ourselves. Okay, here's what I think. We split up the supplies and each carry a share. We cut across to Highway 89, here," he said, pointing to the map. "We'll miss most of the town and enter Yellowstone the back way. We want to avoid people as much as possible. As we travel, one of us is scouting out a ways farther from the road to look for ranches or farms or whatever. If anybody spots a ranch, hightail it back to the group and we'll go from there."

He looked around at his ragtag group and asked, "Questions? Okay, how about suggestions?"

After a moment, Cat said, "I think we should grab our stuff and move away from the road and into the woods. For some reason, I'd feel safer, less exposed that way."

Evidently, everyone else liked the idea. They all started gathering their things and after two tries again, by Greg, futilely, to start the SUV, they trudged through some bushes to a group of pine trees. Here they dropped their bags and started pulling everything out and sorting by groups. Food went in one pile, while ammo and weapons went in another. When they were finished, they had a better amount of supplies than Ray had thought they would. They had a pack of shaved ham, a loaf of bread, some uncut fruit, and several canned sandwich spreads. They had four knives and four handguns. Ray glanced up at Greg and, knowing what Ray was thinking, he said, "I got an ankle holder for the .32."

Ray nodded and said, "Okay, let's get this stuff separated into four piles of equal weight; no, on second thought, make mine heavier. I can take more weight than any of you." Everybody nodded because they knew he was right. This was no time to be modest or petty. They all got to work, and within ten minutes had three duffel bags pretty equal and one about half that much more.

Ray looked at the weapons and while Greg and Cat retrieved their handguns and knives, Ray reached down and grabbed his old KA-BAR. Then he took up his second knife and looking at it decided something. He looked up at Kuan and held out his trusty Buck knife to him. Shaking his head, Kuan said with a little smile, "I will pick out a weapon along the way."

Ray scrunched his eyebrows together in puzzlement for a moment, then shrugged and slipped the Buck in his belt. "Suit yourself."

Once the bags were packed up, they all sat down to share out the food. They would have to ration, but for now they could eat the ham. It would spoil soon, anyway, so everybody got a hardy share. They only divvied up one slice of bread apiece however. They shared a bottle of water and Ray made a mental note to keep an eye out for water along the way. They only had three bottles left.

Silently, everyone picked up their bags and cinched their shoulder straps. By unanimous decision, Ray was chosen to go first and Greg would bring up the rear. His leg was barely hurting now, but he'd have a bruise tonight.

They were on the south side of I-95 and were going to head south/southeast, skirting between Livingston and butting up against the mountains just southwest of them. With luck, they'd encounter little to no people and reach Highway 89 and enter Yellowstone Park. Their plan was to cut through Yellowstone to Cody. It would minimize confrontations with people, but also, the terrain would be harder. They'd just have to be careful.

"Cat, when we start off, I want you to scout first," Ray said. "Stay a few hundred feet to the group's right and keep your eyes open for horses. We're also going to need blankets or sleeping bags, so if you come across a residence, come let us know."

She nodded and smiled at Ray to reassure him.

Ray looked around. This was his team. They all looked back at him and he said, "I'll just be damn glad when the sky's not green anymore!"

Everyone shared a shaky laugh and started off.

10

Emma had finished stitching Lori's cheek with much hissing between teeth and tears from the patient. To Lori's credit, however, she hadn't cried out once. Surprisingly, Bryan found other things to do in the house after gathering water in containers, and Emma suspected he had a weak stomach when it came to blood. Maybe that's why he took x-rays—they usually didn't see a lot of blood. Silently she forgave him. He'd been productive by going through the apartment, at her urging, gathering up supplies they would need.

Emma finished drying her hands and checked in on Lori. She was laying back on the loveseat with Bella rubbing her head against Lori's lap. She opened her eyes as Emma walked in and gave her a weak smile.

"How you doin'?" Emma asked.

Lori nodded her head and said, "Better than I thought, now that you sprayed that numbing stuff on it." She continued to pet the cat and said, with a somber expression, "What do you think has happened, Emma?"

Emma sat down beside her and shook her head, "I don't know, but it's bad, real bad. I didn't tell you that Jack called the yesterday and left a mysterious message. When I told you about him before, I neglected to tell you something about him, mainly because I'd almost forgot it myself. Jack has a very sharp talent for sensing things ahead of time, almost like ESP. When we were together before, I saw firsthand several times when Jack would almost know something was about to happen and would do something or not do something and it invariably would turn out all right. I told you a minute ago that he called, and he did, but I wasn't there and he left a voice mail. He said that if anything out of the ordinary happened that he would meet me in Tennessee, in particular, Pigeon Forge."

Emma looked at Lori to gauge her reaction. Startled, Emma saw that Bryan had walked in as she'd been telling Lori this last part. They both had puzzled looks on their faces and Bryan's expression was also clearly disbelieving.

"Who is this person, Jack?" he asked, "Some of your family?"

Glancing at Lori, Emma knew she'd have to tell Bryan everything now, as well.

She patted the chair next to the loveseat and Bryan sat. She started at the beginning and retold Bryan everything she'd told Lori. She knew it would probably hurt him, but if they were in this nightmare together, they might as well get it all out on the table.

When she finished, she looked up at him with a pleading for understanding.

He stood up and went to the window to look out, stalling for time, she assumed.

She looked over at Lori and Lori silently shrugged.

After a few minutes, Bryan turned around and with a sad smile said, "Well, it all makes sense now. It wasn't that you thought you were better than me, you had an old flame. In a way that's better. I'm just going to have to give up on you going out with me, Em." Jokingly, he said, "Will this guy be okay with us just being friends?" He said this last part with a quirked eyebrow.

Relieved, Emma and Lori both laughed and Emma said with her old jauntiness, "I don't think he has a say in the matter!"

This last part made them think of their current situation, which sobered them all.

Bryan broke the silence by asking, "Do you think your boyfriend knew what was going to happen?"

"His name is Jack and no, I don't think he knew what would happen, just that something serious might. Kind of an impending doom feeling about ten times more powerful to him than to us average folks. At least, that's how he described it to me once." She had a thoughtful look on her face as she went on, "He must have got that feeling the day he left the voicemail or else he would never have called. I didn't tell you guys that we haven't spoken to each other directly for eight years. My brother Scott, who lives on the ranch, is an unbiased go-between for us. He talks to Jack and tells him how I'm doing, I feel sure. He and Jack have become great friends, as have all my family. Scott also makes sure when he talks to me that he lets slip a few things here and there about Jack." She smiled wistfully, thinking of the past phone calls with her brother. She knew there would probably not be another one in the near future. "Anyway," she said, going on, "he lets a few things slip, thinking he's being clever, and I cherish every bit of news I can."

Realizing she might be hurting Bryan, she quickly looked up at him, but he didn't seem to notice, he seemed to be deep in thought about something else.

Curious, Emma asked Bryan, "What are you thinking?"

Distracted, he said, "Hmm? Oh, I was thinking ahead about our predicament and what we need to do now. We need to talk about worse case scenarios, don't we?"

They both looked at Lori and realized the painkillers must be still working, because she had fallen asleep with Bella in her lap, purring peacefully. They looked back at each other and Bryan grinned. Emma smiled back and motioned to the kitchen.

After tiptoeing to the kitchen bar, they sat and started discussing their next move.

Bryan indicated the living room where Lori snoozed. "Back there, I said something about worse case scenarios. I think we'd better consider it. This guy, Jack?" He asked with a lift of his brows and Emma nodded. He went on, "Jack. If he's as intuitive as you say he is, we have got to consider the worst and plan accordingly."

He looked at Emma with pain in his eyes. "My mother and little sister live in California and there's no way to reach them or, even to find out about them until this is all over. I talked to them just this morning, thank God, and they were going to go shopping this afternoon. I just hope they found safety, if this nightmare even reached that far. I'm just going to hope that it hasn't."

Emma understood the distress Bryan was going through. Thinking of her own family brought a sinking feeling in her stomach, so she gently laid a hand on his shoulder and said brightly, "It may just be Atlanta this has

happened to. We won't know until we get out of town."
She took a deep breath and voiced her decision to Bryan,
"I want to go to Pigeon Forge. If this isn't widespread,
Jack will be there waiting for me. If it is widespread,
again, Jack will make it there eventually. I know at least
one of my brothers will be there with him. I have two and
one of them will have to stay and help dad run the ranch.
Either way, getting out of here is the best thing we can
do. We have to get away from populated areas. People are
too unpredictable. I want you and Lori to go with me."

She dropped her hand as Bryan rose to pace. Bella
must have heard them talking. She jumped up on the
table and for once, Emma let her stay there. Why make
her get down? They were leaving anyway.

Bryan quit pacing and turned to Emma, "Okay, it's
not a hard decision for me, none of my family lives here.
We need to ask Lori though. Does she have any family
here? Do you know?"

Emma thought back to last year when Lori's mother
had died from ovarian cancer and how she'd broken
down on Emma's shoulder. That was really when the two
of them had become like sisters. She knew Lori was an
only child and her father had run off with another woman
when Lori was young. She hadn't really known him
before he'd run off because he was never home. So it had
always been her and her mother against the world. When
her mother got sick and they found out about the cancer,
Lori had moved back in with her mother and taken care
of her through the terrible illness.

"I think she has a long-lost Aunt, her mother's sister,

whom she hasn't spoken with in years, but she lives in Florida somewhere. I don't think there's anything holding Lori here. She had her mother's house, but that's a little irrelevant now, don't you think? Especially if this isn't just Atlanta where it's happening." After the words left her mouth, Emma knew she'd misspoken. Bryan winced, but to his credit, recovered quickly.

"What's irrelevant?" Lori said from the doorway.

Emma looked around and saw Lori gently rubbing the bandage on her cheek.

"Bryan and I were just discussing options. Sit down and we'll all talk about it. Decisions need to be made and right now we're all each other has. I think we should stick together and Bryan agrees. We were just about to wake you up anyway. We need to know if you're going with us to Pigeon Forge."

Clearly, to Lori's groggy mind, she hadn't thought that far ahead. She pulled out the stool and collapsed on it.

"Pigeon Forge?" she said now. "Why are we leaving? This could just clear up as soon as the National Guard gets here."

She looked at her two friends as Bryan and Emma glanced at each other. Lori clearly wasn't thinking straight or, more likely, she was still in a bit of shock.

Emma turned to her and took her hands across the table to soften the blow. "Lori, Bryan and I think there is a good chance this is nationwide, maybe even worldwide. When the electricity is out," she said slowly, "and the cell phones don't work and several airplanes fall from the sky, it's definitely a possibility that this is much more widespread then we at first thought."

Emma looked to Bryan and saw he was nodding his agreement.

She looked back at Lori to see her reaction and was relieved to see acceptance and resolve in her friend's eyes.

Lori sighed heavily and closing her eyes, pulled her hands slowly from Emma's to rub her temples, "Okay, dammit. What's the plan? I hate having my whole world, literally, blow up in my face but I'm a realist. Let's get down to business." She looked up at them both then, with conviction in her eyes. Emma smiled inside at the strength she saw in her little friend as she bounced back with a vengeance.

"I guess Emma told you my situation, I only have one sister to my name, and she's sitting across the bar from me, so count me in." She grinned at Emma's happy surprise at the compliment and Emma grinned back.

"What's your status, Bryan?" she asked and again Bryan flinched. He recovered a little quicker each time, Emma noted, and listened while Bryan brought Lori up to speed about his family in California. Emma could tell Lori really hurt for Bryan as he retold his story and with a shock, Emma realized how deeply Lori really cared for Bryan. She'd have to remember that. She needed to remember it wasn't puppy love like she thought, and needed to not step on her feelings by joking with her as she'd done in the past.

Bryan had finished and both of them were looking at her.

Bryan broke the silence by asking a question with serious eyes, "Do you really think Jack will meet you in Tennessee?"

"Yes, I do," she said with no hesitation. "When you meet Jack, both of you will understand. Oh, one thing I don't think I told either one of you, Jack used to be in the military before getting an honorable discharge. He has a deeply inherent sense of valor and honor. Trust me, unless he dies, he'll be there."

They were staring at her, with Lori openly gawking.

"What?" she asked.

Her friends turned to each other and laughed. "She doesn't get it, does she?" Lori asked Bryan. Bryan, still chuckling, said, "No. I bet this Jack guy was pulling his hair out when she left, wondering 'Why's she leaving? I know she loves me.'"

Emma was glancing back and forth between her friends in consternation and not a little puzzlement. "You want to let me in on the joke?"

"Um, you'll figure it out sooner or later." This latest from Bryan brought on a new snicker from Lori and made Emma throw up her hands in an I-give-up gesture. She walked past her two friends to the fridge and jerked the door open. She'd realized during all this that they hadn't eaten lunch and now she was starving. Trying to ignore her giggling friends and trying to change the subject, she said, "We need to eat something and let's start in here. If the power doesn't come back on, this will spoil."

She started laying lunch meat out on the counter

along with the bread. She sent up a silent prayer of thanks that she'd gone to the store only yesterday and she had a bad habit of buying more than she needed.

She felt Lori and Bryan gathering around her and said, "I've got mustard and mayo. I'm sure it's still okay, the fridge hasn't been off long. We'd better take advantage of the tomatoes and other vegetables, because if things stay like this they may become a luxury."

Emma continued to lay things out and she felt Bella winding around her legs. Absently, she murmured, "I'm not forgetting you, big-head."

While the others were opening packages, Emma opened a container of five-day-old smoked salmon she'd had for supper last week. Grabbing a dish, she set the salmon on it and placed it in front of the cat.

Bella started purring and eating at the same time, making an ungodly noise. She glanced up once at Emma and she could have sworn the cat winked at her. Smiling to herself she turned to make her sandwich and Bryan said, "I KNOW you're not leaving that cat here, she's like your kid or something."

She turned to him in genuine surprise and replied, "Of course I'm not. Bella goes with us. She catches her own food all the time, when I don't spoil her. Believe it or not, she likes to ride in a backpack."

Shaking his head with a crooked grin he said, "I should have known. A backpack, wow!"

Lori eye-rolled and bit into her leftover chicken sandwich. Bryan had made a ham and cheese and before anybody had thought about it he opened the microwave and shoved the dish in, then froze.

The light hadn't come on and that jarred his memory. Looking around sheepishly, he smiled crookedly and pulled out the sandwich.

"I guess that's gonna happen a while before I catch on," he said.

The girls both nodded good-naturedly and kept on eating. Emma had already flipped the switch twice for the kitchen, before thinking, and Lori had flipped the bathroom switch.

Emma was thinking while eating. "Hey, Bryan, what all supplies did you find?"

"Oh yeah, um let's see, of course, I found a shitload of medical supplies and prescription meds. Where did you get the meds, by the way?" he asked.

"I worked extra a few months ago for a home health care place and they were sort of left over. The family was going to throw them out and asked if I wanted them, I said sure." She looked up and they had both stopped chewing and were looking at her.

She was still chewing and glanced back and forth between them. "What?" she asked and spread her hands, "I'm an opportunist, they were going to throw them away, and so I took them off their hands. They were going to waste, and believe me, I'm glad, now that I did."

They had continued eating and with a head bob back and forth, Bryan said, "Yeah, you're right. Things have changed and our thinking has to change too. If you hadn't taken those meds, we wouldn't have had them for Lori."

"Okay," Emma said, "so what else did you find?"

"All right," Bryan said, wiping his mouth, "I found two hand guns, a 357 and a 9 mm Glock." He glanced at Emma with a cocked eyebrow, then went on. "Hollow point ammo that matches." He cocked another brow her way and she eye rolled this time to Lori, who shrugged.

"I also see you have plenty of canned goods and dry foods along with a shitload of camping gear. I think we're good." Before they could say anything he added, "Oh, and I also found two *Playgirl* magazines under your mattress."

Dead silence, then Emma, "You did not!" and Lori blew breadcrumbs across the bar laughing.

Emma hit Bryan on the shoulder as he danced away, grinning, and Lori finished choking on her sandwich.

"Seriously, though," Bryan resumed, "I think we have everything we need. Emma even has a .30-.30 in her closet."

Lori looked questioningly at Emma and she explained, "It's a large rifle for big game."

Lori's eyes widened and Emma quickly said, "I don't use it here. I used to go hunting in Wyoming with my brothers. I was pretty darn good, too, if I say so myself. I just couldn't bring myself to leave it there."

Lori finished up and threw her napkin in the trash. Emma thought she looked less groggy and said, "I guess we need to decide if we should leave tonight or early tomorrow."

Bryan said, "I didn't find any maps, do you have an atlas?"

Emma chewed her lip in thought. "I think there's one in the hall closet, top shelf. You're right, we need to plot a course."

As Bryan went to find the map, Emma looked at Lori and asked, "How are you?"

Lori was still rubbing her cheek, and her left hand kept going to the notch in her ear, "I don't think this little nick in my ear is fashionable, but, thanks to you, I'll live." She said this with a smile and Emma smiled back. Just then Bryan returned, brandishing the atlas and two flashlights, "I struck gold!" he said, flicking the flashlights on.

Lori clapped and Emma smiled.

Laying the atlas on the bar, Bryan flicked off the flashlights. "To save the batteries," he explained, and started flipping through the pages.

"Do you have a highlighter?" he asked Emma. "I don't think they require electricity," he stated sarcastically, and Emma chuckled.

She reached in a drawer and got one out.

"Okay...let's see," he said as he perused the Georgia map.

They all gathered around and Emma moved one of the candles closer to the map. It seemed to be getting dark fast and she glanced down at her watch, 4:45 and it was still running. Miracle of miracles, but it *was* a Timex.

"Looks like we need to go 75 north through Knoxville and then cut back on Highway 411 to Pigeon Forge." He leaned back. "That's if we walk and follow the roads."

He looked over at Emma.

"We're going to have to get out of the city on foot, but I want to try to find a four-wheel vehicle when we're out of the populated areas. If we can't find a jeep or something like it, it's going to take forever to get there. Unfortunately, other people will have thought the same thing, so we'll have to keep a sharp eye out. By the time we get out of Atlanta, we'll know if this is a major event. Either way, we need to get out of this nightmare first. Do you all agree?"

Bryan looked briefly at Lori and her at him and then they both nodded.

"Okay, let's bring all the supplies to the living room and sort through it. We need to start thinking like we're in the wild." Her brain was in high gear now, helped along by the explosions and gunshots that seemed to be getting closer. "We need to find out what we have and what we need. What we don't have, we'll try to get along the way. I hate to say it but, we need to have a list in our head of what we need. When we see it, we need to bargain for it or grab it. When you're packing things, try to think of extra things we have that we might be able to trade, extra candles, knives, food, you know." Bryan and Lori both nodded.

"There are some duffel bags and backpacks in the same closet you found the atlas, Bryan. Take everything into the living room and I'll be with you in a sec."

As Bryan moved off, Emma went to her bedroom and closed the door. She turned to the closet and, once inside, she turned on the flashlight. Moving to the back, she opened the lid on a basket. To anyone else it would look like a dirty clothes hamper. It was actually filled with old clothes for disguise. Reaching under the clothes, she pulled out several hard plastic rolls of Liberty head silver dollars. For the last two years she had been dabbling in the metals market as a hobby and had made money when gold had sky-rocketed. She had put some of the money back in silver this time and had just been sitting on these rolls hoping the market would turn.

She transferred the rolls into the bottom of her backpack and hefted it to check the weight. Not bad. She then packed some clothes she'd need and returned to the living room.

Bryan and Lori were just lugging the last stuff into the room when there was a knock on the front door. The noise was so out of place that everyone started and looked at each other. After a second, Emma shrugged and, grabbing the Glock, went to answer it. She looked through the peephole and saw Mrs. Roskam, her next-door neighbor, standing there. Emma undid the deadbolt and tucking the handgun under her shirt, swung the door open.

Carl and Sophia Roskam, along with their white poodle, Toto, lived next door to Emma. He had retired from Delta last year and they were planning on moving back to where their kids lived, somewhere in the Midwest. Sophia and Emma had traded numerous cups of sugar and had chats over coffee. They were a sweet couple.

Now, Sophia was wringing her hands and had a worried look on her wizened face.

"Sophie?" Emma asked, "Where's Carl?"

"Well, that's why I came over. I know you're a nurse and all, and I was hoping you could come over and check on my Carl?" She ended this last bit in a question. Continuing, she said, "He was sitting in his chair a while ago and I was in the kitchen peeling some potatoes when that flash of lightning put out the lights. We had been talking and then he didn't respond and I thought he was sleeping and didn't bother him but then, a few minutes ago I went to wake him because I got worried, and now he won't wake up!"

Emma realized Sophia was in a state of shock and rambling, so she put her arm around her to try to comfort her and gently led her back to the couple's apartment, afraid of what she might find. Outside the door, she could hear Toto yapping away. After stepping through the doorway, Emma left Sophia in the foyer and walked into the living room. Carl was sitting in his favorite recliner, seemingly, by all appearances, to be asleep. Emma steeled herself and knelt down next to him.

She placed two fingers on his carotid artery and found no pulse. Carl Roskam was dead. Briefly, she closed her eyes. Not now, not this sweet couple. What was she going to say to Mrs. Roskam? What would Sophia do now? Where would she go? These thoughts chased each other through Emma's mind in about two seconds, then she inhaled deeply and focused. Something Sophia had said flashed to the front of her mind and got her attention, something about a flash of lightning. Then it clicked. There had been a flash of light before all this nightmare began. At the cafe. It came to her, a show she had only half-listened to on the Discovery Channel about electromagnetic pulse, what had it said? She tried to remember but could only remember bits and pieces because she had been studying at the time and the show had seemed so far-fetched. She even remembered chuckling at the screen. Science fiction, that's what she remembered thinking. Oh God! Could it be? Something else came to her that the show had said and scared her badly.

Emma looked down into Carl's pale face and then to the collar of his button-up shirt. Sophia had stepped a little closer and in a background drone, Emma realized she was still rambling about something but Toto, thank God, at least had stopped barking. Blocking all that out, Emma reached out and with trembling hands, undid the top two buttons of Carl's shirt. She pulled down the left collar, baring the area over the left side of his chest. Her eyes widened as she saw the scar there, caused from the surgery to place a pacemaker. Good God! It was true! Emma remembered that when she saw that show, they had said that people who had pacemakers would drop dead from the pulse disrupting the devices. She remembered that part vividly because of her medical training. She had to think. This put a new twist on EVERYTHING. She rubbed her forehead and tried to regroup. This was seriously turning out to be a bad day. She had to take care of Mrs. Roskam first.

Getting to her feet, she strode over to the tiny lady and putting her arm around her again, she led her to the kitchen. Emma sat her down at the dining table and took her hands. Sophia had quit rambling the minute Emma had stood, as though sensing something. Looking into the woman's eyes, Emma saw Sophie's mouth begin to tremble, and tears start in her eyes; her heart ached for her neighbor.

"Sophie," Emma started gently, "Carl isn't sleeping." She let that last hang for a moment, hoping Sophia would come to understand what she was trying to tell her. Apparently, she didn't, so Emma pushed on, "Honey, I'm so sorry, but it looks like Carl has had a heart attack." Still, Emma got no reaction other than the tears. Trying to get through to the woman as gently as possible, she went on, "I see he had a pacemaker, right?" Sophia barely nodded.

"Something must have happened to it, Sophie, it must have failed. I hate to be the one to tell you, but Carl has passed away."

All of a sudden, something in Sophia's eyes changed. She narrowed them and her jaw firmed. She glared at Emma with such malice, it felt to Emma like a physical blow.

"You don't know what you're talking about!" The woman almost shouted, "You are not a damn doctor!" She stood up and pointed, "I want you out that door, Missy! My husband is just sleeping. Why, if you were a doctor, I'd sue you for malpractice!"

During this tirade, she had bodily herded Emma to the door and Emma was so shocked at this change in personality she was over the door sill with the door slammed in her face before she could even think to protest. When she recovered herself, she blinked twice at the door and realized that knocking would be a waste of time. Something in the woman had snapped. She felt bad for the lady, but with the realization of what was really going on, Emma knew she had to get back to her friends and tell them about it. She turned abruptly and walked back to her own apartment. Glancing over her shoulder once more, she closed the door and went to the living room. There, she found her two friends sorting the supplies into piles. Lori had changed into more relaxed clothes. They both looked up then froze at the expression on her face.

"What is it?" Lori asked, as Bryan pulled her to the couch. They all sat and Emma proceeded to tell them what had happened next door and the dawning realization of the probable events that had caused their current situation. In finishing she said, "I wish I had paid closer attention to that damn show, but I only remember a few things. Luckily, it'll help us plan better for our trip. Let's see," she said furrowing her brows in thought, "I remember the pacemaker thing, oh, and the fact that cars won't work." She snapped her fingers in dawning horror. "The airplanes! That's why they were crashing, shit! It's all making sense now!" She realized, all of a sudden, that Bryan and Lori hadn't said anything through this whole rant and she looked back and forth at them on either side of her.

Bryan had a stricken look on his face and was staring wide-eyed at the floor. Lori had a look of absolute horror

on her face and was looking past Emma at Bryan. With
dawning realization, Emma knew what Bryan was
thinking. With this news, all hope of an isolated event
went out the window. Bryan was thinking of his mother
and sister in California.

She laid a hand on his shoulder and said, "Oh, Bryan,
I am so sorry. I'm sure they got to a safe place."

He nodded his head slowly and then turned to
Emma. "You really think so?" he asked hoarsely.

Emma forced herself to sound more confident than
she was. "Absolutely," she said with a big smile. "If
they're half as resourceful as you are, they are holed up as
we speak, with the doors barred in a house full of food."
She knew it sounded over the top but Bryan seemed to
grab on to what she said with both hands and calmed
down a lot.

Out of the corner of her eye, she saw Lori relax at
the same time Bryan had. She was glad she was able to
comfort them. They all needed to concentrate on getting
ready to leave. They could not stay in Atlanta.

Patting Bryan on the leg, she changed the subject.
"Looks like you guys found a lot of stuff. I didn't know I
had all that."

Bryan nodded and she could see him refocusing on
the task at hand. "We divided it into piles: foodstuff,
weapons, medical, clothes, and whatever was left."

"Have either of you fired a gun?" Emma asked them.

Lori shook her head but Bryan replied, "I used to go
hunting up in the Sierra Mountains with my uncle until I
left for college."

"Fantastic! You can carry the rifle. I'll carry the handguns, and Lori," she said with a wink, "I'll give you one of my knives and my mace. I've got a gut feeling we're all going to have to have some kind of weapon before it's all over. Let's get the stuff evened out into three piles. Would you mind carrying the food, Bryan? It's going to be the heaviest and you're stronger than either one of us." She hated using flattery but it seemed to work as Bryan stood up straighter and said, "Of course, that's the way it should be."

They started going through things and sorting. Emma told Bryan, "Lori and I wear about the same size, so we can share my clothes. We'll have to get some for you along the way."

She grabbed three canteens and some water purifying tablets from the camping gear, as well as a pup tent. She put both handguns in holsters on her hips after checking the ammo in them, and handed Lori one of the knives and pepper spray. She thought Lori would balk, but again her friend proved her resilience by accepting and then stashing the items about her person.

As they went back through the apartment a final time, Emma realized she was really hurrying now. She forced herself to calm down, lest she make any mistakes. Attaching the Buck knife to her belt, she arrived once more in the living room, then called for Bella. The cat came strolling leisurely down the hall and Emma swept her up into the backpack with the silver. She wanted to make sure Bella knew they were going on a trip. She didn't know exactly what they were up against, but she didn't want the little cat to get scared right away and run off. Bella hunkered down contentedly and began to purr. She looked up then to see her friends ready and watching this spectacle, bemused.

"What? I told you she liked the backpack. We take walks all the time, she even goes camping with me."

Grinning, they looked at each other and shook their heads. "I've seen it all now!" Lori stated.

Emma ignored that and asked, "Did you get the candles, matches, and flashlights?"

"Roger," Bryan said with a little salute.

Emma knew he was trying to be upbeat and silently commended him for it. After a beat she cocked an eyebrow around the room and blew out the last candle. "All righty then, let's go."

At the back door, Emma eased it open and stuck her head out. The green glow was still lighting the early evening sky and she was glad they didn't have to use their flashlights yet. She looked back at her friends and nodded, then slipped out to the backyard and waited for them to follow. They could still hear some gunshots and the roar of fires but not as many and not as close as before. They eased back to the vacant lot where the airplane wing had been burning and saw the fire had mostly burned out. The air was filled with greasy smoke and dust which brought back memories of the cafe. Emma dismissed the memories and peered ahead, under the wing section, back the way they'd come. She didn't see anything moving, which was good. According to the map, they were going to have to return to the corner of the cafe, then cut over to MLK Blvd and then Northside Drive. They would then take Ivan Allen to Williams Street, eventually getting them to I-75 North onto Tennessee. If they made it to I-75 without incident she'd count themselves lucky.

She glanced back at Lori, whose eyes were huge and then Bryan bringing up the rear. He had a hand on the rifle case which was slung over his shoulder and trying to look in every direction at once.

She could feel her own heart pounding in her chest and knew she looked as wild-eyed as they did. She cocked her head at the wing of the plane they'd gone under earlier and Bryan made a shooing gesture with his hand. Easing forward, she made sure the Glock was loose in the holster and easy to get to. She shimmied under the wing and her friends followed. Making it to the fence, Emma swung her legs over as she did before, then crouched with the Glock pulled, watching out for her friends. They made it over and Emma returned the gun but kept a hand on it. They were all breathing hard with their backs up against the building. 'So far so good,' Emma thought and about that time she heard a rock skitter down the alley, like it had been accidentally kicked by someone. As one, they all three froze. Downtown Atlanta was not the safest place to take a stroll in the best of times and these were definitely NOT the best of times. Squinting down the alley, Emma strained to see any sign of movement.

Suddenly, down the alley by the cafe's back door, several figures appeared from around a dumpster. Emma saw they were walking towards her and her friends. Her heart skipped a beat and she put her hand back where her friends could see it. Making a fist, she hoped they understood to hold up.

The distant figures were still coming their way, and Emma's eyes darted everywhere looking for an escape. A loud sound came from the group down the alley, jerking Emma's eyes back that way. Another loud sound and the back door of the store next to the cafe crashed inward. Looters! Emma figured out it was probably a gang going store to store. Dangerous, but they may be able to slip past them while the gang was preoccupied. Glancing back to Lori and Bryan, she saw they had figured it out as well. Emma cocked her eyebrows skyward in a question. Lori looked to Bryan and he nodded back to Emma. Slipping the gun out of its holster she crept quickly up and past the doorway. Emma heard sounds of breaking glass and slurred yelling coming from within. Beads of cold sweat slipped down the back of her shirt as she ran in a crouch to the other side of the dumpster the gang had come from. Sliding to a stop, she quickly glanced back and saw her friends kneel down next to her. She listened for a second to see if they'd been heard. Not hearing anything but their hushed panting, she slowly raised her head to eye level over the dumpster and saw they were safe. She slipped back down and went to one knee.

"You okay?" she whispered to Lori.

"Oh yeah, never been better," she whispered back sarcastically, and Emma could imagine her friend's eye-rolling.

Bryan was watching up the alley the way they needed

to go. After a few minutes of catching their breath, Emma took the lead and headed on up the alley. A gunshot sounded back down the alley and had come from inside the store where the gang was. It startled Emma and her friends badly and caused them to drop down again. This time Bryan whispered, "Let's get the hell out of this damn city!"

Emma agreed and nodded and they got up and moved. Emma was determined to get to the interstate and with a lot of slinking from shadow to shadow, they finally made it to Williams Street. Emma knew they weren't far from the on ramp to I-75, but she wasn't sure they should actually get on the Interstate. They all needed to talk about this and she looked around for somewhere less in the open.

She took a deep breath and closed her eyes for a second. If they went to the on ramp, there was a place UNDER the interstate where they could hide. It was almost dark now, and they needed somewhere to hole up for the night anyway. Hopefully, nobody had the same idea at this particular street.

She turned to her friends, who looked as exhausted as she felt from the heightened alert their bodies were in, and whispered, "We need a place to hole up. I say we get up underneath the Interstate."

Bryan nodded tiredly and Lori shrugged.

Emma kept her hand on her pistol and led the way across the street. Once on the other side, they all slipped to the corner. Between the alley behind the cafe and now, there were more bodies then Emma wanted to remember.

If they hadn't died in a car accident or plane, which they'd all seen more of, they'd been shot by someone. As a nurse, Emma was appalled. As someone who used to live on a ranch, it was reality. The last part was what kept her going. Survival, and that was why she had her hand on her gun. They were at the corner of Ivan Allen and Williams and she could see the shadow of I-75 stretching away from them north and south into the darkness.

She turned to her friends and said, "Not too far now."

She knew they were all at the end of their rope but she kept pushing. They had to get somewhere safe. They had developed a hand signal language to get from place to place and she used it now. Fist for 'Hold 'til I get to the other side.' Scampering across the street, Emma pulled the Glock and motioned them across. They slipped over to Emma's side and she looked up the street to their destination.

Bending down, she whispered, "Follow me." With confidence she didn't know she had, Emma looked up and down the street and raced up underneath the Interstate.

Glancing back to make sure they followed, she scooted back up against the concrete. Surprisingly, there was plenty of room and nobody was there to share their shelter. Hunched over a bit from the cement ceiling, Emma stowed her gun and helped Lori the last few feet. They all collapsed, breathing hard, and Emma could hear Lori saying a prayer under her breath.

They all just sat there a while, recovering. Some time

had passed, and their breathing had slowed, when Emma's backpack rustled and out popped Bella with her fur all in disarray. She threw a glare at Emma, as if it were her fault, then promptly sat down and began cleaning herself. Emma had jumped when the bag moved because, in the thick of everything, she'd completely forgotten about Bella. After Bella appeared, Emma relaxed and let out a shaky laugh, glancing over at her friends. They were grinning too.

Bella finished cleaning herself and sauntered off.

"Hey!" Bryan said, "Where's she going?"

Emma shrugged, watching the cat leave. "Out on the town, I guess."

"Is she gonna be okay?" he asked.

"Sure. She comes and goes."

Emma had pulled the backpack with the food close to her and had switched a flashlight on, down in the bag so they wouldn't draw attention.

Emma knew they had to eat something and set up a camp of sorts.

Lori was rubbing her cheek and Emma said, "Here, let me put some more Neosporin on it."

Meanwhile, Bryan was starting to sort through the food and said, "What do you two feel like—we've got chicken spread, ham salad, spam, tuna, oh wow! Here's a big can of stew, I love stew!"

Emma looked to see if he was being a smart-ass, but no, his eyes were gleaming.

"Okay," she said, "executive decision, open the stew and one slice of bread apiece. Sound good?"

Lori just nodded, getting ready for Emma to tend to her; Bryan was actively trying to ignore Emma's actions. He rummaged in a bag and came up with a can opener, candle, and lighter.

"What do you think caused the green glow?" Bryan asked.

"I've been thinking about that," Emma said. "I think it has something to do with charged particles in the atmosphere. I don't remember them saying anything about it during that show I watched, but then again, I think we're on new ground here. I remember the guy saying no one knew for sure what would happen, since an EMP bomb had never been fired, or even tested."

Bryan had opened the can of stew and got three plastic forks out.

Emma had finished with Lori's wound and was replacing the bandage.

The small candle gave off just enough glow to see by, just what they wanted, as they didn't want to attract notice.

"It reminds me of pictures of the Northern Lights," Lori stated. "Only, not as pretty."

Emma nodded, and took the can of stew from Bryan. "As long as the sky is green, I bet our nightmare continues." She passed the can to Lori after getting a bite.

"Are you serious?" Bryan asked startled.

With her mouth full, Emma nodded, then swallowed. "Think about it, charged particles in the atmosphere equals no electricity down here. It keeps disrupting the flow."

Then Lori spoke up and asked the question that had just occurred to them all, "I wonder when it'll go away."

But nobody replied, since they didn't know the answer.

Hearing Bryan open the can, Bella wandered back into the candlelight.

Emma saw her and dug out one of her own cat food cans. She opened it and spread the contents on the cement a few feet away. Bella eased up to the food and began to eat.

Returning, Emma could feel the exhaustion starting to creep in. She dug out two blankets, all they could carry, and brushed away leaves as far up under the overpass as she could get.

"We're going to have to take turns at watch," Emma said and opened her mouth to volunteer but Bryan beat her to it.

"I'll go first, you two get some sleep."

Lori and Emma nodded gratefully and Bryan took the Glock Emma was handing him. He grabbed one of the blankets and walked into the shadows of the farthest pillar and sat back against it.

The two women got their blanket and scooted up as far as they could in the crevice.

As they settled in, it dawned on Emma that this was the safest she had felt since the cafe. They were well hidden and Bryan was out there watching out for them.

She was just drifting off, when she noticed Bryan blow out the candle. She had been so tired she forgot. Then darkness claimed her and she slept.

11

Jack awoke early, as was his custom. He'd had the midnight watch and after his two hours, fell into bed and right back to sleep. Ever since being in the service, he'd never had trouble sleeping whenever he could. He lit the lamp next to his bed and rubbed his eyes. He wasn't looking forward to a cold shower, but then again, he'd be glad if they still had running water. It was just a matter of time before they lost that. Then they'd have to rig something up to haul water.

He got up and went into the bathroom, taking the lamp with him. Setting it on the counter, he grabbed a towel and jumped in the shower, gritting his teeth. After roughly 5 minutes of brisk scrubbing, he was out and quickly drying himself with the thick towel. Even in cold water, taking a shower felt great. He hadn't had time to have one since the night before the bomb went off. He dressed quickly and, taking the lamp, headed down the stairs.

He entered the kitchen to find Maria and Denise already cooking on the wood stove. He felt a moment of pride and vindication as he silently watched his years of precaution in use. Then he chided himself for these emotions and reached for a mug and the old tin coffee pot on the corner of the wood stove.

"Morning," he said to them. They replied back to him about the time Scott and Jason entered from the stairs.

"Where's Danny?" Scott asked Denise after looking

around.

"He had the last watch, so he and Grady went to make the rounds."

"He brought me some fresh eggs for breakfast and some smoked ham," Maria said. "You all sit down and we'll have it ready in a minute. We made biscuits last night, so they're not warm, sorry."

"I'm just glad to have something to eat, ma'am," Jason said.

They sat and after sipping his coffee, Jack spoke up, "I was thinking this morning about going to Carson's place. I want to see what's happened to him and I've been thinking about his old Dodge pickup."

Scott shrugged, looking back and forth between Jason and Jack. "Why do you want to look at that clunker? You said vehicles won't run and we've proven that here with our trucks and the backhoe."

Jack glanced at Jason as the women put the food on the table and joined the men.

"We said that vehicles with microchips won't work. They started putting microchips in automobiles in the seventies, I believe," Jack replied. "An old car, made before microchips were installed, theoretically, may work."

There was stunned silence as the possible implications sunk in.

Scott stated what everyone else was thinking, "You could drive to get Emma! It wouldn't take weeks, it would take days!"

Slowly, Jack nodded but then held up his hand. "We

don't want to get ahead of ourselves though, I said, theoretically. That's why I want to go to Carson's place. I'll saddle Striker and leave after breakfast."

About that time, Grady and Danny walked in and headed to the kitchen.

"All seems pretty quiet out there," Grady said. "I sure am glad the flashlights work."

"Jack is going to Jim Carson's place after breakfast," Scott said after swallowing.

Grady came back to the kitchen doorway and leaned against the jamb, waiting.

Looking at Jack, Scott gestured with a biscuit.

Jack told Grady what he'd said earlier about cars made before the seventies.

Danny had returned by then with a plate and said, "That's if old man Carson will let you borrow it. He loves that truck."

With his mouth full, Scott bobbed his head in agreement.

"I know Jim can be cranky, but maybe if I go with you, we can tell him about Emma, and he'll realize how much we need it. That is, if it starts," Grady added. "He always thought the world of Emma. Maybe he'd lend it to us for her." He stepped back into the kitchen to fix his own plate.

Jack had finished his own breakfast and, as he stood up to take his plate to the kitchen, he said, "We need to rig something up for a bathing and shower place so that when the running water stops, we'll have some way to bathe and shower. We'll be hauling water from the well, so, closest place would be the back porch. Everybody think about it and have suggestions ready when Grady and I get back."

He quickly washed his plate and silverware and refilled his mug with coffee.

As he was stirring cream into his coffee, Jason said, "I'm going to go with you, if that's all right. There's not a lot for me to do around here except get in the way."

He looked steadily at Jack and Jack said, "Sure Jason, come on along." He placed the spoon in the sink and grabbing a flashlight, carried it and the coffee to the front door. "I'll be saddling the horses when you two are ready."

When he got to the front hall coat tree, he set the flashlight and coffee down and buckled on his revolver. Retrieving the mug and light, he switched it on and went down to the barn. He'd been trying not to think about Emma, but now, by himself, he couldn't help it. He kept imagining her broken body thrown from a car, or men with guns taking advantage of her. He forcefully shook his head, dispelling those thoughts from his head. He knew Emma better that that, he would continue to think she got his voice mail and, knowing Emma, armed to the teeth, she was even now making her way to Tennessee. He grinned as his imagination had Emma outfitted in bandoliers crisscrossing her chest, rifle in hand and sombrero on her head. His smile faded as reality came back to him and he sighed to himself.

He entered the barn and without thinking, flipped the light switch. Of course nothing happened and Jack rolled his eyes at his stupidity. 'Come on, Jack,' he chided himself, 'you gotta get over that.'

Keeping the flashlight on, he whistled through his teeth and hoof beats sounded as the horses trotted up to the barn. He chose Striker and two others and shooed the rest away. "Don't act like you haven't been fed. I know Grady fed you when he and Danny were down here." The rest of the horses turned and wandered away. Closing the gate, he turned and set down the now-empty mug. He started saddling the horse Jason would ride. She was an easygoing mare named Molly and he chose her for Jason because he didn't know how well the man could ride. After saddling her, he had turned next to Bear, Grady's horse, when Grady and Jason entered the barn.

"Hey, boy," Grady said with mock sternness, "you think I'm too old to saddle my own ride?"

Jack smiled at the horse's belly where he was tightening the cinch and said in the same tone Grady had used, "I wasn't sure an old man like you would remember all those darn straps and buckles!"

He stood up and turned around about the time Grady threw a fake punch at his belly.

Laughing, Jack moved back out of the way and Grady chuckled lightly.

Jason watched this interplay with curiosity and amusement. Jack noticed him and said, "I've got your horse ready, Jason," gesturing toward the mare.

Jason looked at the horse with trepidation and the mare looked back at him with the exact same expression.

"He doesn't bite does he?" Jason asked in a small

voice

The corners of Jack's mouth quirked as he tried not to smile but Grady had no such inhibitions and guffawed out loud making the horses jump. Jason's face turned red and Jack tried to relieve his discomfort as he said, "No, SHE doesn't bite. Well, unless you bite her first, of course." Which made Grady laugh even harder.

Jason frowned and said, "Let's just get going!"

Jack shrugged, and smiled. He and Grady finished saddling Striker and Bear, then mounted. He could see Jason out of the corner of his eye, watching Grady's technique and he took two tries to follow suit. In the end, he made it aboard and Molly swung her head around to eye Jason warily. He asked her, "What? Did I do something wrong?" and she nickered and turned back to face the barn door.

Jack made sure that his .30-.30 was in the boot behind his right leg and nodded to Grady, "Let's go."

About 2 hours later, the trio arrived at the gate that stood at the entrance to Jim Carson's driveway. It wound around and down into a small, cozy little tract of land. In the distance they could see Jim's house. Looking at Grady, Jack said, "I'd hate for anything bad to have happened to that old codger."

Grady spit a stream of tobacco off to the side and said, "I'd be surprised if anything *did* happen to the old codger."

Jack looked back at the house and didn't see any movement, which made him worry. Kicking his horse's flank, he started down the dirt drive. The sun had come up, but the sky still held that green tint that Jack was finally getting used to.

Jason brought up the rear, and Jack could still hear him trying to cajole Molly into following the other horses.

"Did you pick out this horse on purpose, Jack? I swear to God she hates me. Why couldn't you have given me a male horse, maybe we could have bonded?"

Jack let the quirk of a smile bend his lips and said, "I remember you telling me once, 'Give me any female and I'll wrap her around my little finger.'"

Dead silence for a moment, then Jason stated, "Aw, Jack, I was young and stupid and I damn sure wasn't talking about a horse!"

A rifle shot shattered the day and all three men dove for cover. Behind a bush, they all had their guns out. Jason said, "I thought you said this guy was your friend?"

Jack replied, "He is. With all that's happened, think about it. It's either someone else, or he's shooting now and asking questions later."

Grady piped up, "If it was me, I'd shoot first and ask questions later."

"Thanks, Grady, you're a big help!" Jason said.
They were all squinting through the bushes, trying to figure out what was going on.

Jack finally said, "I'm going to shout out and see if it's Jim."

"HEY JIM, IT'S JACK! JACK DENTON."

Nothing for a few seconds and then, "JACK? IS THAT YOU? WHO'S WITH YOU? I SAW SOME OTHER PEOPLE."

"I GOT GRADY WITH ME, AND ANOTHER FELLA." He squinted at Jason, to tease him and yelled, "A GOOD FRIEND OF MINE. CAN WE COME UP?"

"WELL THANK GOD! YEAH, BRING YOUR HORSES AND COME ON UP," Jim shouted back.

Jack grabbed Striker's reins and eased through the bushes. Jason had to go find Molly and, grumbling, he chased after her and finally walked up behind Grady and Bear. Molly was reluctantly in tow.

Jim had come out on the front porch and was looking anxiously past the men at the road. "See anyone else on your way?" he asked.

"We've been the only ones between my place and yours," Jack assured him.

Giving a decisive nod, Jim lowered his rifle and said, "Come on in. I've rigged up a wood stove and got some coffee on."

The men went in, with Jim following. He gave another look at the road and closed and locked the door.

Turning around to Jack he demanded, "What in the HELL is going on?"

Jack looked at him and said, "Let's get some coffee and I'll tell you."

Jim decided that was a reasonable request and led the way to the kitchen. He set out mugs and sugar and powdered cream, apologizing for not having real cream.

"My fridge went out with the power. Had to make do since yesterday. I figured the power company would get it all back on, but," and he shrugged, "don't look to be happening anytime soon."

Jim poured and everyone chose their poison. After getting the coffee and settling at the kitchen table, Jim looked expectantly at Jack. Jack took a moment to organize his thoughts. Taking a deep breath, he turned to Jim and decided to introduce Jason. "Jim, this is Jason Evans. You probably know I was in the military. Well, he used to be my boss." He let this sink in a minute, and when he saw Jim look at Jason and narrow his eyes, he quickly went on, "He's a good friend of mine and helped get me an honorable discharge when I wanted out. We've kind of stayed in contact over the years," he glanced meaningfully at Jason and went on, "and when the government came up with a certain problem, one we're dealing with now, he came to find me. Unfortunately, it was too little, too late, and here we are."

Jack saw Jim relaxing back as he took in the explanation and proceeded to explain everything to Jim. When he finished, Jim had a few questions. Jack answered them the best he could and sat back.

"So, what are you all doing here?" he asked.

Grady spoke up before Jack could and told Jim, "You know my little girl, Emma?"

Jim looked at Grady with a surprised look on his face. "Yep, cute little young 'un. She always came in my store sweet-talking me into giving her candy." He chuckled and said, "She could talk a leopard into changing his spots!" Dawning horror crossed his face and he asked in a hoarse voice, "Oh my God, Grady, where is she now? Is she still in Atlanta?"

Grady had Jim's attention now and nodded. "You're getting it now. She's in Atlanta, trying to make her way back home, we hope. Luckily, Jack left her a voice mail on her phone the day before this happened, and hopefully she's making her way to a place in Tennessee as we speak. Jack has to go get her. She can't make it safely all the way back here." He crossed his arms in front of him on the table and said, "Jack's got an idea, Jim. Listen to him and I'm in your debt."

Jim was looking bewildered, back and forth between Jack and Grady. "What the hell do I have that can help you? You know I'd help that little girl out! Tell me what I can do."

Jack told Jim about his theory and Jim got excited. "Yeah, I just got a tune-up six months ago. I didn't even think to check the ole' Dodge. My new Ford didn't work, and none of the other cars worked! I just thought everything was dead!"

Jack asked, "What other cars?"

"I was at the store, yesterday, when it all happened," Jim said with a pained look on his face. "That bright light and the thunder. Shawn had come in to work—miracle of miracles—and was helping load feed in the back. When that bright light went off and that loud clap of thunder, it scared me so bad, I fell to the floor. I thought we were getting nuked. I lay there for a minute, waiting for something to happen and when it didn't, I yelled to

Shawn. He yelled back and I asked if he was okay. He said he was. I heard him get up then and walk back toward the front where I was. I started to get off the floor, when a big crash from the back of the store threw me flat again. Turns out, some older lady drove her car through the back of the store where Shawn was coming from. He never had a chance. I jumped up and ran back there, but the lady was dead at the wheel, probably from the impact. Shawn was under the car and when I saw him, I knew right away he was a goner." There were tears in Jim's eyes when he finished and Jack knew better than to say anything.

After a minute of staring at the table, Jim shook his head and pulled out his handkerchief and gruffly scrubbed at his eyes and blew his nose. Replacing it, he cleared his throat and went on, "I couldn't help them, so I went to the phone to call 911 and it was dead. I noticed then that the lights were out, but I figured the crash did that. Then I realized I was hearing crashes outside the store and walked out on the front stoop. The cars were all wrecked or stopped, some right in the middle of the street. People were getting out and walking away, kind of in a daze. Some were helping each other. A couple of buildings were on fire. I watched one of those puddle jumpers they got out at the airport, you know, Jack, like the one Steve Nance flies all the time? Anyway, I saw this one coming down over by the airport and I thought it was going to land, only it was coming in too steep. Then it went out of sight and there was a crashing sound and I saw a big fireball go up. That's when I made up my mind to get out of town 'til this was over. There wasn't nothing I could do to help and I was too scared to go looking for anybody." Jim looked around sheepishly, and Jack knew he thought they would say something about him leaving town. Jack spoke up to comfort him. Gently he said, "Jim, there wasn't a thing you could do. If you had stayed, you could have been killed too."

Jim looked relieved and went on. "I locked up the store as best I could, with that car in the back. Then I went out to my truck, but it wouldn't start. By that time, I was pretty spooked. I just started walking home. It's a pretty good ways and I had to stop to rest a couple times. When I got here, I got my rifle out and loaded it, but haven't seen a soul until y'all showed up. I even saw a couple of cars abandoned along the way, but none of them started either."

"Were the cars you saw older or newer models?" Jack asked. Jim tilted his gray head in thought, "Nope, they were all newer, like my Ford."

Jack let out his breath in relief; maybe he was right. He hoped so.

"Let's go see if that Dodge will start," Jack said and stood up. The rest followed suit and Jim led the way through the kitchen to the back door, grabbing a set of keys on the way out.

"When I was walking home, I noticed that green cast to the sky. Any ideas about that?" Jim asked.

Jack told Jim his theory about the charged atmosphere and the similarities to the Northern Lights. As he finished, they arrived at the barn where Jim kept the Dodge. Jim opened the barn door.

They all stood stock still, staring at the truck.

Jim broke the silence first. "There she is boys! My pride and joy, a 1965 Dodge d100. I had a fresh paint job put on her about 4 or 5 years ago. Black Beauty, that's what I call her."

The truck was nice but that wasn't why the other men were staring. They were all thinking the same thing, 'Would it start?'

Jim tossed the keys up and caught them, then handed them to Jack, "Go see if she'll start."

Jack was afraid to move. It reminded him of when he was young, back in Tennessee. He'd be out in the woods holding real still, like his daddy showed him, and along came a rabbit. He didn't want to move because he'd frighten off the rabbit. He knew it was irrational, but he felt the same way now.

He mentally shook off the fear and gripped the keys hard. Stepping forward, he grabbed the handle, opened the door, and swung into the seat. All in one smooth move. He froze again, for a second, and a bead of sweat trickled down his temple. He glanced up at the other men and they all suddenly had grins and were nodding at him in encouragement. He tried to grin back and did a stupid thumbs up. Before he could stall again, he jammed the keys in the ignition. Scrunching his eyes closed, he turned the ignition. The big engine tried to turn over once, then twice. Jack could feel his heart skip a beat. Opening his eyes, he could see the goofy grins sliding from their faces like hot wax. He had just started to get a sinking feeling in his stomach when, with a cough, the big engine turned over and began to purr.

Jack really did grin then, from ear to ear. The three other men were jumping up and down and slapping one another on the back. You would have thought they had just won a Little League game. Jack slumped in relief and after a moment he turned the truck off.

Jason stopped jumping up and down and yelled, "Hey, what happened!"

"I turned it off to save gas," Jack replied.

"Oh, you turned it off. You scared the shit out of me, Jack. I thought it died." Everybody but Jason started to chuckle, and then even he was outright laughing. Jack knew stress relief when he heard it, and smiling, he let it run its course.

He slid out of the cab and closed the door. Walking around the back of the truck, he saw all the tires were aired up and surprisingly, they were new. By the time he returned to the front of the Dodge, they had regained their composure and Grady asked Jim what Jack had been thinking. "Do you have extra gas?"

Jim turned around and grabbed a two-gallon plastic canister and proudly shook it to show it was full. "I once ran out and had to walk a ways. Now I always keep a little extra. It's got an extra gas tank on it though and both of them are full. Each hold sixteen gallons."

Jack looked at Jim and said, "I'll do my best to bring her back to you in one piece."

"You just bring little Emma home in one piece and we'll call it even," Grady replied.

"I'm sure gonna try," Jack said and patted Jim's shoulder. "Let's go in and finish our coffee, we've got plans to make."

As they walked back to the house, Jack was thinking about Jim and his generous loan of the truck. He was trying to think of a way to repay the man. He remembered Grady telling him, after he first moved here, that Jim was a widower. He'd been happily married to his wife Francis, until about twenty years ago when she developed cancer. He thought they had said stomach cancer. They had never been able to have children but Grady had said Jim and Francis had seemed content. Then she had passed away. Grady said it nearly broke old Jim. Jim had told Grady once, after that, he would never love anyone else and that had been that. The man only had his friends. His mind made up, they had just walked in and refilled their mugs when Jack told Jim, "We've got plenty of room out at the ranch. You're welcome to come and stay if things get bad around here."

Jim glanced over at Grady, who was nodding, and with a sad smile replied, "I sure appreciate the offer, Jack, but this is my home." He emphasized this by spreading his hands. "I wouldn't know how to act under someone else's roof. I've lived here for forty-one years and I'm comfortable."

Jack nodded and let it go. "Just saying, you're welcome."

Changing the subject, he turned to Grady and Jason who, like him, were just about finished with their coffee. "I guess we'd better get going. Jason and I are going to ride back in the truck. Do you mind leading our horses back, Grady?"

Cracking a smile, he looked at Jason and said, "What? You don't want the horse whisperer here to bring 'em home?"

Jason rolled his eyes and said, "It's the first time I've ever been on a horse, for God's sake, and you won't let me live it down."

Grady chuckled, then looked back at Jack, "You two go on. I'll be there shortly. Me and this old man are gonna jaw a while. I'll bring the horses back."

Jack and Jason left the house to a chorus of good-natured ribbing of what constituted an 'old man.' Jack understood by Grady's parting glance that his visit with Jim was Grady's way of thanking the man without embarrassing him. Jack still had a lot to learn about life in Wyoming, but he felt he was getting there.

Getting in the truck, Jason looked over at Jack and said sarcastically, "That Grady is a really funny guy."

Jack smirked and said, "He must like you. If he didn't, he would ignore you."

Jason looked straight ahead and said, "Hunh."

Jack laughed and turning the key, once again started the truck.

"Hey, we almost forgot the gas can," Jason said and jumping out, put it in the bed. He got back in and they eased out of the barn and made their way slowly up the drive.

Jack was thinking about what they needed to take on the trip to Tennessee, when Jason interrupted his thoughts. "We can't leave right away, Jack."

Jack had been waiting for this and he stayed silent to give Jason his say.

He didn't have long to wait. "We've got to wait on my people to bring Kuan in. We need him, Jack. He has things in his head that we might need!" he insisted.

Jack looked over at Jason and said, "Do you think your team made it through? If so, how long do we have to wait?"

He waited Jason out and he said, "I'm not sure, Jack. I mean, I know they made it through, they're the best I've got, and I'm just not sure how long to wait." Jason looked back at Jack and Jack could see the sincerity.

Jack quickly went over things in his head. Emma was strong. If she had made it through the blast, he just knew she'd make her way to Tennessee. On the other hand, how long would she wait for him in Pigeon Forge before becoming impatient and trying to make it to Wyoming? She was smart enough to know it would take him awhile to get there, but, and here Jack smiled inwardly, Emma was not a patient person. His smile faded as he thought of Emma trying to make her way, by herself, to Wyoming. An impossibly long way. Checks and balances, it came down to checks and balances. Sighing, Jack knew his friend was right. Waiting on Kuan was worth the anxiety he would suffer thinking of Emma on the road alone. A lot hung in the balance of what this Chinese scientist knew about EMP effects and shields against them. If he knew as much as they hoped, he could, possibly, help them use the shield in the Knoxville facility to shock the ionosphere back to normal.

Jack heaved a big sigh and said, "Okay, Jason, where were they when you last spoke to them?"

Jason looked off in the distance, thinking. "They called me on the sat phone in Butte. That was a couple of hours before the bomb, so...let me see, I would guess somewhere around Bozeman or maybe Livingston? I'd have to look at a map."

He looked over at Jack for help. Jack was thinking.

He said, "Walking? We're talking, maybe a week? That is, if they didn't have problems. Best case, they get horses and maybe three to four days. God, if we're really shooting for the moon, and they found an old car or truck like we did, hell, they could be here tomorrow. So...I guess we'll just—"

Jack slammed on the brakes and Jason reflexively threw his hands up to the dash.

"What the!—" Jason yelled, and as they came to a sliding stop, he jerked his head around and stared at Jack, "What IN THE HELL was that all about? Are you out of your mind?"

Jack was grinning like a crazy man, staring out over the steering wheel. He slowly turned to Jason and asked, "How well do you know your people? Do you know what route they would have taken if this bomb went off? Please tell me you briefed them on what to expect."

Recovering from the shock, Jason looked back at Jack and began to understand what he was thinking.

"Of course I briefed them!" he said. "I've got to get my hands on a map of the area." He paused, thinking of the possibilities. "I'd have to figure out what Ray would do. He's the lead agent on this and he's pretty smart. Let's get back to the Ranch and a map, then I'll be able to figure out his moves."

"You know what I'm thinking, Jason. We have the vehicle, we've just got to go get them. It would take, maybe four hours, tops. IF we know which way they're going. There are only two routes to Cody from Butte. I'm hoping they take the route through Yellowstone. It's harder terrain, but shorter distance," Jack stated, pulling back on the road, now, with a purpose in mind.

A short time later, they pulled up to the ranch. Jack killed the engine and got out. Denise came running out the back door with a grin on her face. "Oh my God! I can't believe it runs!" She stopped short and lovingly caressed the hood. "I never thought I'd be so glad to hear a car pull up!" She exclaimed, still with that goofy grin on her face. Jack knew how she felt and he knew he had an answering grin on his own face.

Jack looked back toward the house and saw Scott and Danny walking toward them with smiles of their own and Maria was even smiling, standing on the back porch.

"How's that old man, Jack?" Scott asked when he got closer.

Jack said, "Still kicking."

Then Danny said, "I guess you talked him into letting you take it."

"Well, actually, your dad talked him into it. He used Jim's fond memories of Emma as a child to kind of bribe him."

Danny snorted and said, "Jim never got to know her when she got older." He glanced at Scott and rolled his eyes. "'Fondly' probably wouldn't have been how most folks remember our big sister in her teenage years, 'hellion' would be more like it."

Maria had walked up by now and she whacked Danny on the back of the head and demanded, "You take that back! Emma could be struggling for her life right now and here you are bad-mouthing her."

Jason had come around the front bumper and only caught part of this last exchange and looked to Jack with puzzlement. Jack just shrugged as Danny rubbed the back of his head and replied, "Ma! You know Emma's fine! If anything, she's giving bad guys a run for their money. I was just joking."

Maria sniffed and said, "You better be!"

Denise had watched this exchange while trying to cover a laugh by coughing into her hand.

Jack spoke up then and told them where Grady was.

Maria nodded and said, "I feel bad now, we should have visited him more. He sure loved Francis and it had to have been hard after she died." She shook her head thinking about it.

"Well," Jack said after a moment, "on the drive back, Jason and I decided we're going to go get his agents. We figure they're on the other side of Yellowstone making their way here. We can drive the truck there and intercept them along the way. It should only take about a day, so we need to pack some food and we'll take some extra gas from the barn. Let's go look at those maps and get some food ready, Jason. Danny, I'd appreciate it if you'd put the gas in the back of the truck."

"Denise and I will pack the food, you two go look at your maps."

Scott said, "I'll check out those maps with you, Jack, you know I go camping up there a lot."

"Yeah, Scott, I'd appreciate that too."

They all split up to go to their separate tasks. After getting the maps from his bedroom, Jack rejoined the other two men in the kitchen and spread them on the table. Studying the map for Cody and the surrounding area, the three men stood with their hands on their hips.

Jack said, pointing to a squiggly line, "This is 14 and leads west then north through the park up to Livingston." He then pointed to another yellow winding line and said, "This is 296 and it leads northwest to Cooke city and then onto Livingston. What we need to figure out is this: Which way will they go?"

He continued to study the map as Scott spoke up. "The terrain up 14 is a lot rougher but definitely shorter. Highway 296 is longer but easier." He looked over at Jason and asked, "Are any of your agents from this area, or familiar with the park?"

Jason, still looking at the map, shook his head and said, "No. I get what you're thinking; if they don't know how rough it is, they'll take the shorter route."

"One more thing," Scott said, holding up his finger

to Jason. He looked over to Jack and asked, "What are your feelings, your intuition, Jack?" He gazed at Jack as Jack closed his eyes and appeared to be semi-meditating.

After about ten seconds, Jack opened his eyes and reached down and placed his finger on the Yellowstone river right outside of Livingston and on the way to 14 through Yellowstone. "I got a feeling they're here and taking 14 through the park."

Jason coughed out a laugh and stared incredulously at Jack. "You're going to base which direction we go on some random feeling!"

Scott looked over darkly at Jason and said, "Since I've known Jack, I found out something. I've never seen Jack be wrong about anything when it comes to gut feelings. I'd trust Jack's intuition over anyone's 'facts' any day of the week." He finished with conviction. Jason looked surprised at Scott's vehemence and turned a cocked eyebrow at Jack.

With a shrug, Jack quietly confirmed, "I've been honing this little talent since getting out of the military. I seem to be right when I have a gut feeling."

Jason saw they were serious and his face fell. "You're serious?" he asked quietly.

"Yep," Jack said sincerely.

Jason turned back to the map and heaved a sigh. "It's the best we've got, so let's roll with it. Logically, that's probably the route Burch would go anyway, just looking at a map."

"At least we won't have to go through town," Scott stated.

Jack nodded and said, "We're going to have to bring a log chain for moving cars out of the way. Let's roll the map up and see if Maria has some food ready. I want to leave as soon as possible. Allowing for obstacles, it'll take us a good four hours, I bet, to get to Canyon Village. We'll need some jackets too. It's going to get cold up in the mountains at night."

Scott nodded and asked Jason if he'd brought a jacket.

"No," he said, "I didn't think I'd be here this long."

"You and I are about the same size," Jack said distractedly, "you can borrow one of mine."

Jack was going over, in his mind, a list of the things they would need.

Maria came in the room, then, with a worn leather satchel and handed it to Jack. "I put smoked ham, biscuits, a jar of my canned pickles, some leftover cold chicken with two hunks of cheese and three canteens of water. I wasn't sure how long you planned on being gone, so I packed extra."

"Thanks, Mia," Jack said with affection and gave her a peck on the cheek.

Flustered, she slapped him on the shoulder and said semi-gruffly, "Just don't you go wasting any of that food, you hear? And bring yourself back home safely. I don't want to have to send anybody out after your rear-end!"

Jack gave her an easy smile and said smartly, "Yes ma'am!"

Then she huffed, turned on her heel, and marched back toward the kitchen.

Grinning, Jack watched her go and said, "I think the world of that woman."

The other two men were grinning too, and Scott said, quietly, "We know. She loves you too, Jack."

His smile fading, Jack turned and clapped Scott on the shoulder. "I know you wanted to go with us but I need to ask you to stay and watch over everyone. Can you do that for me?"

Jack could see the disappointment in his eyes before Scott quickly recovered and said, "Of course, Jack." Then he lifted his chin and said, "You know you can count on me."

"Good," Jack said and inwardly breathed a sigh of relief. He wanted everyone he loved back here on the ranch, safe, if he could help it. He was also thinking that if things got desperate, folks in town may remember that Jack had been building up foodstuffs and come causing some trouble. They'd need every hand in that case. He prayed it wouldn't come to that. Scott had seen the thoughts pass over Jack's face, and seemed to understand. He nodded silently to Jack and Jack smiled again.

"All right, Jason," Jack stated, a bit too loudly, "let's go grab our gear and get this show on the road."

Twenty minutes later, after loading up the truck and checking everything twice, Jack and Jason were trundling down Highway 14 toward the first town they'd be coming to, Wapiti. Jack had no idea what to expect and said so to

Jason.

"It's a little town and there's usually not a whole lot of traffic on this road anyway, and we might get lucky."

Jason didn't respond so Jack glanced over at him in the passenger seat. He looked distracted and Jack asked, "Penny for your thoughts?"

He took a minute to answer, looking out the front windshield deep in thought. Jack thought he was going to have to ask again but then Jason answered, "I was just thinking of Sarah and Jay."

Guilt suffused Jack as he suddenly remembered Jason's estranged wife and little boy, well, not so little. Jason had said he was 17 now.

Not sure what to say, Jack decided to ask Jason some questions and let him talk about it. He asked, "Where are they?"

Jason flicked a glance to Jack and said, "The day before I flew out here, they were going up to visit her parents for a long weekend. Up in D.C., that's where we met. Sarah had taken Jay out of school a couple extra days, which didn't hurt anything. He's got a 4.0 grade point average, you know?"

Jack could tell by Jason's voice he was proud of him. He smiled over at his friend and said, "That's great! Chip off the old block, eh?"

Jason chuckled, then sobered as they sat silent again. Jack waited him out and listened to the deep growl of the old engine and scanned the road ahead. They were now skirting Buffalo Bill reservoir and not a vehicle in sight. Yet.

Jason spoke up then, "Sarah and I had an argument before they left. ANOTHER one," he amended, bitterly.

"We said a lot of hurtful things and then Jay walked in and put in his two cents. So, all in all, it was pretty bad. I stormed out of the room and they left." He put his head back against the glass. Softly, he muttered, "I wish I could take it all back, you know?"

They were quiet again for a minute and Jack was trying to figure out what to say when Jason said, "I was thinking about the nukes. Remember? There were some nukes mixed up in all this. I can't help but think, if some of the EMP's got through, what if the nukes did too? I know there's nothing I can do about it, but it's driving me crazy worrying about them, and the way we parted."

Jack had opened his mouth to say something to comfort his friend when they came around a turn and almost ran into a stalled Toyota pickup. Jack's lightning fast reflexes saved them as the Dodge swerved around the back of the Toyota just barely clipping its back bumper. Jack had slammed on the brakes at the same time, and even though he was only going about 45, they slid sideways a few more feet. The Dodge came to rest in a cloud of dust from the roadside. The men were frozen for a second in stunned relief, then Jason who was propped against the dash said, "I'm only going to let you throw me into that dash one more time, buddy, then I'm kicking your ass!"

Jack, breathing hard, blinked at him and then wheezed out a laugh. Jason looked over and then joined him with a shaky laugh himself. Finally, Jack took a deep breath and opened his door. "I hate to, no telling what we'll find, but I'm going to have a look."

Jason opened his own door and together they eased over to the Toyota. Jason stealthily drew his sidearm and stood back to cover Jack. Jack looked at him and nodded. He eased his own gun out and opened the driver's door. Nobody home. Swiftly his eyes took in the details. Baby blanket, some cheese cracker crumbs on the passenger side seat. There was a photo showing a young man in a cowboy hat with his arm around a woman of the same age as she held a baby. The photo was wedged in a corner of the rear view mirror. Jack relaxed and stowed his gun. Jason saw him and did the same. Walking up to the cab and peering in, Jason asked, "Where do you think they went?"

Jack was looking around now and saw some boot prints heading off toward Wapiti. He pointed them out to Jason and then headed back to the truck. He was glad to see everything seemed to be okay with the family, but this was only their first encounter.

He needed to be more careful in his driving and watch the corners. He mentally slapped his forehead as he reminded himself that there was no calling 911 anymore. Hell, there was no calling for help, period. If they had crashed, it could have been the death of them or, if the family had still been by the Toyota, one of the family members. Jack couldn't let this get him down, he just resolved to be more careful.

Jason noticed he hadn't said anything since getting out of the Dodge and intuiting the reason, he said, "You can't save everybody, Jack."

This hit a nerve in Jack and before figuring out why that was, he'd rounded on his friend and yelled, "Why not, dammit! I've done the best I could, so far, in preparation! I let people call me crazy in this town AND in Washington so I could try to save as many as I could! If nothing else I could at least save my family! It did NO GOOD in D.C. to try to tell those arrogant, egotistical and narcissistic windbags what was coming! If they hadn't been so damned intent on keeping everything quiet, we could have prevented this! Or, at the least, been prepared, but no! Your buddies in Washington know what's best for everyone and won't tell anybody a damn thing!"

Jack's rant had taken on unheard of proportions and Jason, understanding that it was his frustration talking, or rather, yelling, he let him go on. He just stood off a ways, watching, with his arms crossed, as Jack paced and, intermittently, pointed at Jason to pound some point home. Finally, Jack ran out of steam and breathing hard, with his fists on his hips, he stood staring out at the reservoir.

"Feel better?" Jason asked, sympathetically.

Immediately from Jack, "Hell, yes." After a moment he went on, "I haven't done that since, well, since I was back in the military and you were my supervisor." He shot Jason a look with his eyebrows raised. "Maybe you just bring out the best in me," and quirked a smile. Actually, he was a little embarrassed but he did feel better.

"I'm sorry, Jason. I know you said you stood up for me back then, and I believe you, but, dammit! You could have told me. I held a lot of resentment toward you, not to mention, I felt pretty let down. Being an only child, after my parents died I felt I didn't have any family. Then, you got transferred over, and I got to know you. You had the same values I did and saw things, most of the time, anyway, as I did. I came to think of you as an older brother. That all ceased when I got drummed out."

Jason knew this was a lot for Jack to come out with and he sought for the best answer to give him, because he deserved it. He decided on the truth. "I'm sorry, Jack. I hated the way it all played out. All I can do is apologize and ask you for your friendship once again."

Jack could see in Jason's eyes, complete truthfulness. He'd felt betrayed years ago. As he got older, however, he had thought about how Washington worked and knew Jason had done what he had to.

Heaving a sigh, Jack said, evenly, "All right, you sorry bastard, let's get in the truck."

He looked up at Jason and smiled, letting Jason know everything was okay. Jason smiled back and they slid into the cab.

As Jack started the Dodge, Jason said, "Now that you got that shit off your chest, I really would appreciate it if you'd quit slamming on the damn brakes."

Jason laughed when he saw Jack narrow his eyes at him.

They drove a little slower on towards the little town.

They'd been driving for two and a half hours when they came over a rise and Jason saw a lake spread out before them. The land had steadily become more rugged and more beautiful. Despite the green-colored sky, he could tell, now, why Jack loved this country. "What lake is that?" he asked Jack.

"That would be Yellowstone Lake," Jack replied.

They had made pretty good time, even though Jack had been overly cautious. Most of the stalled vehicles they had come to could be driven around. Only a handful had to be towed or pushed out of the way. The only time they had seen any people was back at that first town, Wapiti.

They had driven slowly through the middle of town and, hearing the engine, several people had come out on their porch. They had all been older people and when he and Jason had discussed it, later, they theorized the older people didn't want to leave. Kind of like in a natural disaster, the police always had trouble making the old folks leave.

As they were leaving town, they had had to navigate around a bunch of motorcycles outside a bar and as they were passing in front of the bar, a group of rough looking men and women came rushing out the door, chasing them drunkenly. They were yelling and throwing bottles. Jack had hit the accelerator, quickly leaving them behind.

Now, Jack was hungry. This was as good a place as any. They could see in all directions, in case someone tried to jump them. He said, "Hand out some of that food, Jason. I'll pull over here and we'll sit on the tailgate." Jason grabbed the satchel as Jack turned off the truck and they both got out and sat on the tailgate.

Passing out the food, Jason said, "You know, I haven't told you much about my team."

He looked up as a hawk caught his attention. Jack took his ham biscuit and said, "You always had a knack for picking good team members."

Jason finished chewing and, pointing at Jack with his biscuit, he said, "My lead guy is a lot like you, Jack."

He knew Jason wanted him to ask so he did. "How so?"

"Well," he said, "he's smart, thinks before he acts, and has that logical thinking thing foremost and upfront."

Nodding, Jack swallowed and said, "Yep, those are good qualities there, Jason."

Jason heard something condescending in Jack's voice and looked at him with narrowed eyes. "I'm serious, Jack. Ray is a good man and Cat has been in the business for years. I have more faith in her than I do my male agents. You know that means a lot. I handpicked this team, Jack."

Jack knew Jason was right. If he handpicked them, they got the job done, period.

"If this Ray thinks like me, he'll follow the road and we'll meet up with them," Jack stated. Wiping his hands he stood up and stretched.

"That's what I'm hoping," Jason replied as he finished his biscuit. He grabbed the canteen and after taking a long swig, he handed it to Jack. They jumped in the cab and headed off down the road.

12

Ray awoke with a start. For a moment, he had no idea where he was. He smelled hay and the skin on his neck was itching. He was lying on his back and breathing fast. In a rush, it all came back. The assignment, Kuan, and an apparently little-used barn in Montana. He couldn't see anything; it was pitch black and he was bone cold. Now that his brain was working again, albeit sluggishly, he thought about yesterday's trek and where they'd ended up. What a fiasco! If he didn't know better, he would have thought yesterday was Friday the 13th.

After a great beginning and good organization, his team had moved fluidly and flawlessly through the countryside. Even Kuan had operated as a player and they'd made pretty good time. Cat had been scouting for a while when she had come back to report houses seen, but occupied, so they had avoided those. Ray had opted for going around occupied homesteads because people were more likely to shoot now and ask questions later. He just wanted to get the target to Cody.

He took a deep breath, now, and listened for team members. He heard Cat off to his left. Someone, probably Kuan, off to his right. It was Greg's watch so he was glad not to hear him. He was starting to trust Greg a bit more. He pushed himself to a sitting position and rubbed his neck. He had a crick, but at least they'd found a place to stay.

Cat had seen one house after they'd all walked about four hours. It had been pretty quiet. Ray had made a decision, after surveying the place, to approach it. He silently let Greg know to sit on Kuan. He and Cat had made their way quietly toward the house. When they were within 50 yards of the place, someone yelled out, "HEY, I SEE YOU MOVIN' OUT THERE. PLACE IS OCCUPIED. MOVE ON SOMEWHERE ELSE!"

Seeing they were spotted and Ray didn't want bloodshed, he had looked across at Cat and nodded back to where Greg and Kuan were. Arriving back at the place they had left them, Ray told them what had happened, and said the group was moving on.

Ray had looked up at the sky, yeah, still green. They were cold, it felt like about 50 degrees. They were also tired and hungry. A dangerous combination for moving a group of people any distance. They were going to have to find shelter soon, as the sun was going down.

They had then gathered up their bags and started off. After slogging through two tributaries to the Yellowstone River, which they were shadowing, they had dodged a grizzly bear and her cub. The sun had almost set when Cat had come back saying she found a barn. It seemed to be falling down but not used, and was only 500 feet away, up against the foothills.

Ray had taken a deep breath and, glancing meaningfully at Greg, gestured Cat to lead on.

They had arrived at a shrub and peered through at the decrepit building. Visually inspecting the barn and surroundings, Ray could tell it had been a while since the structure had been used. He took a chance, mainly because he knew they had run out of time. He nodded to

Cat and standing up, he walked in full view toward the barn. With his senses honed from adrenaline, he could hear the bird calls and squirrels fussing with each other in the trees. He kept walking right up to the barn doors. Having nobody yell out or challenge him in any way, Ray reached up and simply slid the door back. He immediately smelled mildew and dust and knew nobody had been here in a while. No animals, and so he moved on inside. It was marginally warmer and Ray could see there was potential, ahead of him, to build a fire. They would need it for food and warmth. He was thinking of his socks—hell, his feet—getting warm.

He walked back outside and asked Cat to go get Greg and Kuan. Meanwhile, he swung his pack off and grabbed a flashlight. Switching it on, he reentered the barn, went up a ladder to the loft, and saw the roof was intact in this small corner. Inspecting the corner, he realized the mildew wasn't as widespread as he had first thought. Ray went back down the ladder and saw the rest of the group coming in the barn door. Ray went to his bag and retrieved the matches. The hay should help start the fire.

He went back outside and got some wood after asking the others to get some food out. While they passed around the food, he had built up the fire. He removed his shoes and peeled his socks off. He then placed the socks on a rock next to the fire. Watch duties were figured out by flipping a quarter and thank God, he had the last watch. Slipping on some clean socks, he watched long enough to see everyone to their assigned places. He then climbed to the loft, rolled up in his jacket, and promptly went to sleep.

Ray had been remembering all this as he tried to shake off the tiredness. As he stood up, his knees popped. Grimacing, Ray stretched. Turning on his flashlight, he made his way down the ladder. Jesus! It was cold! He had to get a fire going, so slipping outside, he went to find some wood. God, what he wouldn't give for a cup of hot coffee! There were things he was going to miss, but he really hadn't known just how much he would miss them.

He heard a noise off to his right and he spun and crouched, reaching for his gun. He realized he had left it behind about the same time he figured out it was Greg.

"Hey," Greg said, as he walked up, "what are you doing up?"

Ray relaxed a bit, chastising himself mentally for his laxness, and said, "It's my shift." He finished picking up some wood.

Greg yawned and Ray asked, "How did it go?"

"Some wolves, some raccoons, Jesus, I've seen animals I've only read about before!"

Ray took this opportunity to ask Greg, "So, where are you from?"

Greg turned away and swept his flashlight back and said, "Chicago. Bad district."

Ray started walking towards the barn and Greg followed. The way Greg had said that last part, Ray could tell it was a sore subject, so he let it go for a bit.

Meanwhile, Greg had his own questions. "How far

did we walk yesterday?"

Ray dropped the wood in the makeshift fire pit before answering, "I'd guess about eighteen, maybe twenty miles, give or take."

He went to one knee and shoved some hay under the wood and struck a match.

"Is that all?" Greg whined. "It's going to take us forever!"

Ray smiled to himself. Like most young people, Greg was impatient and used to fast, easy living. Cars that go fast, fast food, fast internet. That was gone for now, maybe forever, who knew. Everyone was going to be forced to have patience.

Ray watched the wood catch and saw movement out of the corner of his eye. Glancing that way, he saw Cat coming down the ladder. He should have known she'd wake up. She was an early riser too, and that habit was hard to break.

He returned his attention to the fire, seeing that it was catching nicely now, and moved in closer.

Rubbing his hands together for warmth, he replied to Greg, "We don't have much choice. Until we find some horses, best speed is about three to four miles per hour by walking, depending on the terrain. I'm not happy about it either but look at it this way, at least we're making progress."

He saw Kuan was coming down from the loft as well and thought 'The gang's all here,' and then perked up at the thought of getting an early start.

Cat reached the fire and standing as close as she

could, grumbled, "I sure could use some coffee."

Ray next to her nodded and opened his mouth to agree when Kuan spoke up and reached in his bag for something. "I have some tea and sugar packets, if we can rig something over the fire to heat it, and something to put it in."

Stunned silence all around. Caffeine! You could see by the dawning realization on all their faces that the same thought had occurred to all three. Not only that, but something hot to go in their bodies, pure heaven. Ray gave a low chuckle and happily said, "You're on, Mr. Kuan!" and began casting around in the barn with his flashlight for something to hold the tea in and to place it over the fire. He saw Greg and Cat searching too and the thought of some hot tea lifted his spirits. It was the little things.

Greg yelped in triumph and held up a small, battered coffee can. "I'm going to go wash it out in that stream I found out behind the barn."

As he started walking toward the doors, Ray yelled out, "Bring back a couple of good-sized rocks." Which stopped Greg in his tracks for a minute, but then he shrugged and went out.

Ray was looking down at a square of chain link, obviously left over from some repairs, and three concrete blocks. He grabbed two of the blocks and the chain link and made his way back to the fire. Cat was already there and had a smug grin on her face as she held up two chipped white porcelain dippers. "Miracle of miracles, look what I found."

Ray cocked an eyebrow in question and she said, "They were hanging on that pole over there, above a wooden barrel."

Ray positioned the blocks on end on opposite sides of the fire and laid the chain link across them. He stood back and admired his handy work, then adjusted the blocks closer together. About that time, Greg came back in and said, "It still has a couple of rust spots I couldn't scrub out, but I guess it won't kill us." He handed the can to Kuan who was reaching out for it and gave the two rocks he'd brought back to Ray. Ray placed them on top of the blocks covering the chain link for support against the weight of the can full of tea which would be in the middle. The trio stood around admiring their creation with satisfied smiles as Kuan knelt and filled the can with water from a water bottle. He then placed it on the chain link and proceeded to withdraw a box of Earl Grey teabags and sugar packs. These he placed on a tree stump he had positioned close to the fire.

Ray motioned to Greg and said, "I saw some more tree stumps out back. Let's go get a few to sit on." They started heading to the door as Cat said, "I'll go up and get my bag and see what we've got left for breakfast."

Returning from their second trip, the men set down the stumps and everyone had a seat around the fire. Cat had piled on more wood and the water was just beginning to bubble. They were starting to see outlines of shapes in the barn as dawn approached and birds were beginning to sing outside. While they waited for the water to boil, Cat passed around packs of crackers and beef jerky and everyone, even Kuan, dug in. If it wasn't for the circumstances, the scene would have seemed almost a peaceful one. Ray took this time to thank Greg for letting him sleep, but told him not to let it happen again. Greg gave him a mock salute. Then winked at him! Damn that boy! Ray shook his head with a smile.

Everyone sat thinking their separate thoughts and chewing as the day got lighter and the water began to boil. Kuan had set up the dippers after breaking off the long handles and had produced, incongruously, his own small, delicate teacup from his bag. With teabags already snugged in the cups, he produced a towel and using it as a potholder, poured the water in the cups. When he was finished, there was just enough water left in the coffee can so he plopped a bag in there for the fourth person.

Ray raised his hand and said, "I'll take the can. I'm so excited about the tea, I don't care what it's in."

Cat and Greg muttered agreement and then added the sugar, using their knives to stir.

As Ray let the can cool next to him, he watched Kuan surreptitiously. What a strange bird. Ray couldn't figure him out; he was too quiet, but then again, he gave off calming vibes. Even after a couple of weeks being around the man, Ray still didn't know that much about him, just what had been in his dossier. The little China man had a way of growing on you though, and coming up with the tea definitely hadn't hurt. There was still something about Kuan that Ray didn't like.

His tea can cool enough now, Ray still blew on the lip and sipped cautiously. It was bitter but the warmth was beautiful.

When they'd all finished their tea, Ray looked over at Kuan and said, "Thank you, Dai Ji. That hit the spot."

Cat and Greg thanked him as well and Kuan nodded to them all in a gesture of 'You're welcome.'

Cat began packing up and Greg said he would go up in the loft and retrieve his and Ray's bags.

Ray took the cups and coffee can out to the stream and rinsed them out while Kuan readied his own things. When he got back, he saw Cat and Greg studying the map spread across two stumps and Kuan was rummaging around in the back of the barn. Ray stepped over to the map and studied it for a minute. He placed a beefy finger on a place not too far from a town called Emigrant. Still in Montana.

"We're about here, see the little stream and the mountains to the west and east? The Yellowstone River and Highway 89 run right down this corridor and straight into the park. We'll keep shadowing 89 like we did yesterday and eventually we've got to find some horses."

He heard a sigh from Greg and looked at him. "It just looks like such a far distance. I know, I know," he said raising both hands at Ray's stare. "I'm just saying, okay? Can't a guy vent a little?"

Deadpan and not moving a muscle, Ray said, "No."

Rolling his eyes, Greg muttered, "Great." Cat let out a snicker.

Kuan walked up quietly then and he had what looked like a long broom handle standing upright in his right hand and his bag over his left shoulder.

Ray asked, "Walking stick?"

Kuan quietly replied, "Quarterstaff."

Ray narrowed his eyes slightly and replied, "Okay."

Turning back to the rest of the group, Ray visually checked everything and made sure they hadn't forgotten anything. Reaching into his bag, he brought out his holstered weapon and knife and clipped those on. By this time it had gotten light enough to see without flashlights. The woods outside had enough screeching going on that it rivaled the San Diego Zoo.

Giving his party the once over, he shouldered his own bag and asked, "Greg, how's the leg?"

Greg lifted a shoulder and said, "Just sore, but one hell of a pretty bruise!"

Ray nodded to him and asked, "You want to be point man today and scout us out some horses?"

Greg brightened up at this relief from Kuan's caretaker and said, "Sure thing, Ray!"

Cat had been kicking dirt on the fire, and now she grabbed her things and, hearing Ray's question to Greg, took up position beside Kuan.

In an attempt to lighten the mood, and just because it's who he was, Ray said, "Okay troops, your mission today, if you choose to accept it, is to find viable transportation that surpasses 3 miles per hour."

"Hell, yeah!" Greg uttered, and Cat quirked a smile. Kuan just had a puzzled look on his face and opened his mouth to say something but Ray started off without giving him the chance.

It was now full daylight outside and Ray looked to the sky for confirmation. The sky still had that green cast and Ray thought it was incredible what the human mind could get used to. He thought about blue skies with Jessica, his former wife. Just ordinary days of coming out of buildings from paying bills and that blue sky, that blue sky...it just seemed right. Still walking, Ray forcefully shook off the old memories and focused on the here and now. They had a long way to go and he had a mission to complete.

He became aware of Cat walking beside him and his mind wandered to her. He'd heard the talk around the office about Cat, but he had never really thought about it. He had heard she had changed careers in midstream, so to speak, and had decided, after a bad marriage, to divorce her husband. Before he could think about what he was doing, he turned to Cat and asked, "What did you do before doing this?"

She jerked her head around and stared at Ray.

Realizing his misstep, he verbally back-pedaled. "I mean, what made you decide to go into the spy business?" he tried with a self-deprecating grin.

Cat finally looked away but didn't say anything. They continued walking in silence.

Ray had just about decided Cat wasn't going to say anything, when, finally, looking straight ahead, she quietly said, "I had help in my decision to change careers." She had her chin tilted up and her eyes narrowed.

Ray knew that look. Miss Determination, he secretly called it. Many a time Ray saw that look when they'd shared missions. When Cat sported that look, shit got done. Ray voiced his next question very carefully. "You know people talk in this business. I hope you also know I consider us friends. Having said that, I just wanted you to know, it was an innocent question. I honestly was curious about what happened, but if you don't want to talk about it, I understand." He ended this last with a shrug.

They walked on for a while and Ray shook out a cigarette and fired it up. He looked up as a meadowlark sang out. There were gray squirrels chattering at each other and Ray was also aware of Kuan softly walking a few steps behind them. He thought of Greg off scouting and mentally wished him luck. They had been walking about an hour and Ray had been automatically glancing left from the tree line they were walking in toward Highway 89 and the Yellowstone River. They had to keep far enough away to try to keep from being seen, but close enough to shadow it. So far they were doing a good job.

Cat broke his musings by muttering, "You probably heard I had a bad marriage." She said this as a statement of fact.

Ray followed her lead and looked straight ahead, but knew she'd see him so he nodded.

She was quiet for a while, gathering her thoughts. At last, she seemed to come to a decision and in a small voice said, "I'm a totally different person now than I used to be. I got married too young. I was stubborn and naive. I grew up on a farm in Oklahoma. My mother died in a car accident when I was six years old and my dad got remarried when I was twelve. I've got a full brother two years older than me, a stepsister a year younger than me, and a stepbrother three years younger than me. Then there's my half-brother who's twelve years my junior. I love them all, but I haven't seen them in years. We're not very close because of the decision I made to get married when I was 18. They all tried to tell me about the asshole, but I wouldn't listen."

Ray had been listening quietly, but now he heard something and, stopping, he grabbed Cat's arm. Pulling her down next to him, he knelt behind a bush. Voices were coming from the road and he quickly swiveled his head to find Kuan and motion him down, but Ray saw that Kuan had already taken cover. They were only about fifty yards from the road and voices carried in this canyon they were in. Ray sent up a prayer that no one had heard their voices and his prayers seemed to be answered when he heard a burst of laughter at something that had been said on the road. He peered over the bush, trying to take in the circumstances.

After a couple of minutes, he deduced that they were close to the town he'd pointed out this morning, Emigrant. It looked like the citizens had a road blockade up. He looked down for a moment, thinking. This part of the country was, relatively, law-abiding citizens. Before E-day, as Greg had coined the event yesterday, you could leave your car unlocked around here and expect it to still be there in the morning. On the other hand, these people had, most likely, come to realize they were on their own.

So, factoring all this together, Ray decided that human nature would be at the forefront and the barricade was just the town protecting its own. He thought a moment, then turned to Cat and said, "I'm going to go down there and talk to them. I want you to stay here with Kuan in case Greg comes back. I'm going down to feel them out and maybe see about some horses."

Cat looked at him with her customary trepidation for a moment, then nodded quickly. He glanced over to tell Kuan, but found Kuan had been close enough to hear.

Taking a deep breath, Ray scooted over about twenty feet, in case anyone was watching. He then stood up and, bending over, hurried next to a tree. He looked back, saw Cat behind the bush, and winked at her. She nodded back and Ray eased around the tree and walked toward the barricade.

Ray had gotten within twenty yards before they realized he was there and one man called out, "Hey! Who are you?"

Ray stopped as he heard shells racking into rifles and hammers being pulled back on handguns. He raised his hands in a supplicating gesture and said loudly, "My name's Ray Burch. I was wanting to talk to someone in charge."

They all looked nervous and glanced at a man amongst them who was older and wearing a cowboy hat. This man called out, "You by yourself?"

Ray nodded and said, "Yeah, I guess something's happened. My car broke down and now I see you all have barricaded the town?"

Cowboy hat slowly nodded and replied, "You could say that," and he glanced at the sky.

Cowboy hat motioned Ray closer and Ray complied. He was ten feet away from the barricade, made of dead cars and useless appliances. The man in charge alertly looked Ray over and motioned with his .30-.30 for Ray to flare his jacket. Ray complied and everyone saw his gun and knife.

Cowboy hat looked into Ray's eyes and saw something, then said, "My name's Thomas Bradford, Tom to most. I guess you got a reason for carrying, besides the obvious."

Ray was looking back into Tom's eyes meaningfully and nodded, saying, "Yeah, I got my reasons."

Tom nodded back and said, "I understand, Ray, but I hope you don't mind leaving them with me. We've had a little trouble and I just want to be sure there's not any more." He had his left hand out while his right hand had the rifle pointing at Ray's belly.

Ray felt he could trust this man and slowly removed the handgun and knife. Reversing them, he held them out to Tom. Tom looked over at the youngest fellow and said, "Gavin, grab the man's iron." Turning back to Ray he spoke. "After you talk to the mayor, you'll get 'em back."

Gavin nervously walked out and took Ray's weapons.

Ray felt naked but pushed the feeling aside by thinking of his team.

Tom motioned with his rifle and Ray climbed through the barricade to stand beside him. Ray could see

Tom looked to be in his mid-forties. He had intelligent eyes and a military bearing about him. Ray had a knack for sizing up people and he was rarely wrong. This guy had probably gone into the armed forces right out of high school, spent some time, then come back to run the farm or ranch. Whichever the case may be.

They walked away from the barricade toward the middle of town with Tom in a slight lead.

Ray saw that Tom seemed to be a quiet man and he decided to wait to say something to the mayor.

They neared the town square and Ray saw it was a pretty town. He felt a pang of regret that this may be history in the making. Squashing the feelings, he followed Tom up the steps and stopped at the front door.

Tom turned to Ray and said, "You're Government something, that's why I haven't frisked you. You've got a reason for being here and I hope to God it has something to do with righting what's going on. I wanted to give you a little information. The mayor is a mite bit strange, but he's all right. If he doesn't answer all your questions, come back and see me and I'll do the best I can to fill in the gaps."

With this, he pulled open the door and ushered Ray in, closing it behind him.

Ray saw he was in an office and a man was behind the desk with maps and papers all around and a candle lit to the side. This man was dressed in a grimy white suit and had silver hair with a trim goatee. He stood about six inches shorter than Ray. He could also tell the man had a feisty air about him. He looked up at Ray and said, "Who the hell are you and what do you want?"

Ray took a step towards him and he pulled out what looked like a .45 revolver and pointed it at Ray. Ray raised his hands in a surrender motion and the man gestured with the gun to a chair.

"Come on over and sit down. Tell me who you are. Tom wouldn't have let you in without a reason."

Ray slowly eased into the chair and said, "My name's Ray Burch. I work for the Government and I am on a mission to, um," he quickly tried to think of what was best to say, "help the Government in this situation." He nodded to give credibility to his statement.

The man looked at Ray for a moment and then said, "I'm sorry, I didn't tell you my name. I'm Griffin Harris, Mayor of Emigrant." He walked around the desk with his right hand out. His left hand still held the pistol. He followed Ray's gaze and, seeing the gun, shook his head before setting it down on the desk. He then turned and stuck his hand out and Ray shook it.

"Sorry about the gun. Unfortunately, desperate times call for desperate measures," he said.

Ray nodded and replied, "Believe me, I know what you mean."

Griffin gestured Ray to a chair as he went back behind the desk and sat in his own. "So, tell me about this 'mission.'"

Ray took his time getting comfortable as he thought about how much to say. If he told Harris about his colleagues, he would have to bring them in. That might not be a bad thing, IF he could get some horses from this man. Studying the mayor, Ray decided to chance it.

"I have some people with me," he said, gauging the man's reaction. When he saw Harris nod, he went on, "I'm supposed to take them to a place in Cody, Wyoming." He saw recognition in the man's eyes and continued, "My superior is there, waiting for us and it's important I get there as soon as possible." Ray lifted his brows in what he hoped was acknowledgment of how important this was.

Griffin sat back and looked at Ray. He tapped a pencil on his desk while he thought. Abruptly he sat up and asked, "Does this figure in to what the hell is going on around here?"

Ray stared right back in the man's face and softly said, "Very much so."

Harris rubbed his hand across his goatee and seemed to be thinking. Ray stayed silent and mentally held his breath.

After a few minutes, Harris quietly asked, "You can't tell me what's going on, can you?"

Ray stayed quiet for a moment then shook his head and scooting forward on the chair said, "I can tell you this, if my team and I don't get to Cody at all possible speed, the sky might stay green forever, I just don't know."

He sat back and looked at Harris. Ray had a thought while he waited on the mayor to answer. This was like negotiating a deal. Almost like poker. Ray had his hand, the mayor had his. Who would bluff whom?

Harris sat looking at Ray a moment then slouched a

bit and said, "Look, why not bring your folks in. At least we can get them a bath and food then we'll work something out." Ray thought a moment about the alternatives and about the mayor's personality and nodded his head. "Fair enough," he said. "Is there a way to bring them in so not too many people know?"

Harris sat back and tapped his front teeth with the pencil. Ray took the time to study the mayor. He was a stout man in his mid-forties, Ray guessed, seemed to be in good shape, probably exercised but judging from the broken vessels in his cheeks, had a few drinks every night.

Harris, putting the pencil down, interrupted his observations.

"I think we can bring them in on the south side. Wait, how many are there?" he asked Ray, his eyes squinted.

Ray told him three and Harris nodded.

"Yep, we can sneak 'em in on the south side of town. It's still early and I've declared martial law. Most people are scared to death and like Chicken Little, they think the sky is falling." He snorted and shifted in his seat. "Not hard to understand why, with the sky being green and all. Hell, my wife's at home right now getting ready to go plant vegetables in the garden! I told her it was just a matter of time and the National Guard would show up and put things to right. Which brings me to my next question for you." He gazed steadily at Ray and asked, "Are you the front man for the guard?"

Ray could see restrained hope behind the man's gaze and wished he could give him the answer he was looking for, but Ray knew he'd have to disappoint him.

Ray took a breath and shook his head, "No, I'm sorry to say, Mr. Harris, that I'm not part of the guard. There's no easy way to tell you this, but you're probably on your own for a while."

"I guess you wouldn't tell me if I asked you point blank: what the hell is going on?" Harris asked.

Ray had a somber expression when he told the mayor, "I wish I knew." He paused, thinking, "I will tell you this, my team and I are escorting a scientist to my superior in Cody, Wyoming. This scientist COULD be the key to fixing this problem. I'm sorry I can't tell you more." Ray sat casually on the outside, but on the inside he was holding his breath.

The mayor sat gazing steadily at Ray. After a few moments, he seemed to nod to himself and stood up.

"Well, we better get that team of yours on in here. We can, at least, offer some hospitality. Let's see," he said, looking down at the map, "where are they located?"

Ray stood up and stepped over to the desk. He traced a line down from where they'd walked and tapped his finger on an area just outside the town. "Here. They should be waiting for me here."

The mayor seemed to think of something and turned to Ray. "Before we go through with all this, I was just wondering. Why all the secrecy?"

Ray looked back at the mayor and said, "I don't have a lot of time. To be honest with you, if my team and I march straight in here, there are going to be a bunch of questions. You see, the scientist I told you about is

Chinese and you all don't seem to have many of those in this part of the country. I seriously don't have time to try to answer questions about things I'm not sure about in the first place. To be blunt, we're just escorting him to my higher ups."

This seemed to satisfy the man and he turned back to the map. The mayor then pointed to an area on the south side of the town, "There's an empty building here, on the edge of town that has been boarded up. It used to be Joe's Pizza Shack but Joe didn't make very good pizzas so it went under. That was a few years ago and with the recession and the building being on the edge of town, nobody else has been willing to lease it. If you can go to your folks and get 'em around to the back here," he said pointing the way on the map, "I'll have the back door unlocked and y'all can scoot inside. There's a bathroom and shower in the back and I'll bring around some towels and other things after unlocking the door."

He stopped and Ray looked down at himself and realized just how dirty he was. He was covered in spots with a combination of smoke, dirt, leaves and hay and wondered that the guys out at the barricade hadn't just shot him.

He remembered something the mayor had just said and asked, "You still have running water?"

Harris nodded, sitting back down behind the desk, "Yep, for now anyway, but no hot water so it'll be a brisk shower."

Ray didn't care about the hot water, he was thinking about getting clean and perked up a little at the thought.

He and Cat had been on assignments before where cold showers were called for, so he knew Cat would be okay, but Greg was so new he wasn't sure how the kid would take it. Ray sighed to himself, he guessed they would find out.

He looked up and met the mayor's eyes. "I want to thank you, Griffin, for your hospitality."

Harris narrowed his eyes and said, "If what you say is true, and this scientist can help get America back on its feet, then anything I can do to help, well, the pleasure's all mine, Ray."

With this, he smiled and folded the map and handed it to Ray. "Give me about thirty minutes—no make it forty-five. I'll go get the sundries first and have the building open. There's no heat, as you know, so it's gonna be chilly. I wish I could do something about that, but..." and he spread his hands.

Ray shrugged and smiled saying, "You've done plenty, thanks."

Walking back outside, Ray saw that Tom had stuck around. Tom smiled and walked over. "Well?" he asked.

"Well what?" Ray queried back.

"What did you think of Harris?" he asked as they started walking back to the barricade.

Ray shrugged, puzzled, "He was all right, why?"

Tom said, "Yeah, I guess you being a stranger and all, he would have acted how he needed to and been the mayor. This all hit him a little harder than the rest of us." Tom gestured around them with his hand. Ray waited for him to go on.

Tom sighed, "Griffin was heavy into gambling over the internet before this all happened and now he's desperate for everything to come back up." He looked over at Ray with a sad look on his face and stopped, forcing Ray to stop with him. Quietly, he asked Ray, "It's not going to come back up, is it?"

He looked at Ray with such open honesty that Ray didn't have the heart to lie to the man and he had a feeling Tom just wanted to know for himself.

He rested his hands on his hips and said, "No, Tom, just between you and me, I don't think it's ever going to be the same. I have reason to believe that instead of waiting for the power to come back on, we better start learning how to make do with what we've got. I'm going to tell you something and I want you to keep it to yourself. I'm taking a man to my superiors and he just might be able to help things, but even if he does, it could be years before we get the electricity going again. If ever."

Tom's eyes had gone wide but then, as Ray guessed he would, he seemed to get a hold on himself and relaxing his shoulders again started walking. "I guess that sums up, in a nutshell, the answer to most of my questions. Once the mayor figures that out, I don't know what will happen. I'm glad you told me, though, I'm kind of his second-in-command and it's better if we're prepared."

They were nearing the barricade and Ray could see there were different faces now, they must have changed shifts.

Before they got too close, Tom asked him in a low

voice, "Anything I can help you with before you leave?"

Ray realized then that Tom hadn't listened in on the mayor and Ray's conversation so he stopped, forcing Tom to this time, and said, also in a low voice, "I'm going to bring my people around to that empty building on the south side of town—"

"Joe's Pizza Shack?" Tom interrupted.

Ray nodded, "That's the one, and we're going to get cleaned up, courtesy of the mayor, and then make a plan." He quickly assessed Tom and said, "If you wanted to come to the back door, say, about one o'clock, I could use your help on some things."

Tom eyed him speculatively for a moment then agreed. "That sounds good, and maybe I could pump you for some more information."

Ray doubted it but said, "Maybe so."

They had begun to walk again and had now reached the barricade. The other men had fallen quiet, probably having heard about the stranger from the night shift. Ray turned to Tom and shook his hand, seeming for all the world to be the last time. "Thank you, Tom, for the information. I'll just be heading back to my RV." Tom reached to his belt and withdrew Ray's gun and knife, handing them to him. Ray turned on his heel and went on down the road. He could feel the other men's eyes on him, but he wasn't worried. He had an ally in Tom, and the other men thought the crises would be over shortly. They had no idea.

Ray reached the spot where he'd left the others and filled them in on the plan. Cat was thinking things through and Kuan, as usual, was sitting with his back against a tree saying nothing.

True to form, Greg spoke up. "Cold water?" he asked. "I've never taken anything but a hot shower!"

Cat rolled her eyes and said, "Geez, Greg! Stop whining all the time. Do you know how many times Ray and I had nothing but cold showers? I'm just glad Ray got us a place to go and any water at all!"

Ray smiled to himself as Greg walked over to his bag, grumbling under his breath. Ray grabbed his own things as Kuan stood up and Cat shook her head. When they were all ready, Ray unfolded the map and showed them the route. "We've got to circle around south of town and come up back here," he said, placing his finger on the back of the pizza building. "I'll go first and Greg, you take the rear guard." Ray put away the map and, hitching up his bag, led off. Cat followed with Kuan, gripping his quarterstaff, right behind her. Greg brought up the rear and as Ray turned to look at him over his shoulder, he noticed how intense Greg's vigilance was. True, the kid may be a complainer, but he took his job very seriously. Ray was beginning to think that all the whining was a ruse, a way to tease and annoy his co-workers. If that was true, it certainly worked on Cat. Ray chuckled under his breath, thinking of Cat and Greg's byplay again. He looked at his watch and saw it was close to ten. If they hurried, they could be there by about 10:20, plenty of time to take showers and be ready for Tom by one o'clock.

Ray heard a loud crash to his right in the underbrush, startling him, and dropping to his knee, he whipped out his gun. Before he could shoot, however, a deer came running full out, about fifty feet in front of them, cutting across their path. It was gone in the next instant.

Greg had run up from behind and now he asked, "How many damn animals does this place have?"

Ray put away his sidearm and said, "A lot more than Chicago."

Greg put his own gun away and muttered, "Hunh."

Ray took a quick drink of water from a bottle out of his bag as he tried to slow down his heartbeat. He saw Cat do the same, but when he looked at Kuan, the man seemed as calm as if he was attending an afternoon tea.

Ray finished his water and shook his head. The man seemed imperturbable. Did nothing shake the man up? Putting the empty water bottle back in the bag, Ray became aware of some of the wildlife around him. A squirrel was chasing another one high up in the tree next to him, chattering away at each other. Somewhere off to the right, from the direction the deer came, a meadowlark was singing for all it was worth. As he started off again, he could hear rustling off to the left and as he glanced that way he saw, between some bushes, a brown rabbit eyeballing them suspiciously. Ray thought to himself that maybe humans should take a page out of nature's book because this big 'crisis' humans were having wasn't upsetting the animal population one bit. If anything, they seemed downright cheerful about it. Of course, animals weren't stupid enough to rely on electricity either.

Ray's musing came to a halt as they emerged from the trees at the highway and, reflexively looking both ways, Ray and his team crossed without a problem. A little way ahead, they all had to slog through the Yellowstone River, and cutting through some more bushes, arrived at their destination. They all pressed their backs up to the building and Ray tried the door. True to his word, the mayor had unlocked it. Ray looked over at his team and nodded, and one by one they entered.

Closing the door after Greg, Ray set his bag down inside the entrance. Looking around in the gloom, he made out they were in a storage area. Cat must have pulled a flashlight out, because she flicked it on now, and flashed it around. Ray got his own out and started looking around the place. In the back corner to the left of where they came in, he found the bathroom and shower and pointed it out to the others. Cat had already gone forward to the next area and she softly called out that she was in the pizza kitchen. Ray followed her through the entrance way and saw she was heading to the dining area. Everything was dusty and there was junk everywhere. He saw on a counter where the mayor had left some supplies and what looked like a note. He went over and, setting the flashlight down, took a look. There were towels, soap, razors, candles, matches, what looked like fresh biscuits, and a small jar of honey. Gambling debts or not, God bless that little man, Ray thought. Cat came back from her investigation and checked out the stash.

"Nice! We haven't had fresh food since..." She thought a moment, "Since the day this all happened." She looked Ray in the eye then and with a sober expression asked, "Are we going to make it through this, Ray?"

There was a vulnerable look in Cat's brown eyes that put Ray on protective mode. He had always thought Cat was pretty; hell, half the bureau wanted to date her and nobody ever had been able to get close. Ray quickly reined in his feelings and said, "We're going to make it in spades." Changing the subject, he picked up the soap and handed it to her. "Why don't you go take that G.I. Jane shower?" He also gave her one of the towels and turned away.

Cat stopped him with her hand on his forearm. He looked back, guardedly, at her and she seemed to think better of what she was going to say and instead took the towel and soap and smiled. "Just like old times, right?"

Ray smiled back and said, "Right."

Cat left to take a shower and Ray walked back into the storage room where Greg and Kuan sat on some chairs.

"What'd you find?" Greg asked.

Ray had carried the supplies back with him and now he laid them out between Greg and Kuan.

Greg checked it all out, but Kuan didn't seem interested. Greg picked out a biscuit and grabbed the jar of honey. "Oh wow! Fresh food!" He bit into the biscuit after smearing it with honey and moaned, "Oh God, this is so good! It's only been, what, twenty-four hours. If I'd only known when we were at that last restaurant...I would have ordered takeout biscuits!"

Ray grinned, seeing Greg's joy, and grabbed a biscuit for himself. "Kuan? You want a biscuit?" he asked the man, but Kuan smiled, slightly, and said, "No thank you, Ray. I am content."

Ray and Greg saved enough for Cat, and when she emerged, Ray asked Greg, "You next?"

Greg made a face and Ray shrugged. "Okay, guess I'm next, don't you eat Cat's biscuits." He said to Greg as he grabbed his stuff. He was still laughing at Greg's scowl as he passed Cat on the way to the bathroom. She smiled at him as she passed and, not thinking, he winked at her. She gave him a funny look and then he was in the bathroom. He closed the door and turned on his flashlight. Setting it on end, he put his things out and threw the towel over the shower curtain. He turned on the water and prepared himself. It would be good to be clean. That's all he thought as he got the job done. When he finished, Ray realized he was gritting his teeth and tried to relax his jaw, but until he had finished drying, he couldn't. Ray hadn't realized how cold he was until he had finished. He thought about Cat coming out of the bathroom and marveled at how composed she was. Well, if she could handle it, so could he.

After getting dressed, he was a lot warmer and, grabbing his clothes, he walked out to find everyone bedded down and taking a nap. He looked at his watch, and saw they had about an hour and a half until Tom came. Maybe it was a good idea to take a quick snooze. He rolled his bed out and saw an extra couple of towels from the mayor. Grabbing those for a pillow, he rolled up in his jacket, again, and after a few moments, went to sleep.

Ray came awake with a start. He heard knocking on the back door. Cat was already moving and had her gun out pointed to the back door. Greg had his left hand planted squarely on Kuan's chest, pinning him to the floor, and with his right hand pointing his weapon at the back door. Ray looked down to see his own weapon pointing at the back door. Everything was frozen for a moment, as everybody realized where they were. Ray exhaled, then stood up and waved everyone to relax.

Greg got off of Kuan, Cat relaxed enough to holster her gun, and keeping his weapon in his hand, Ray eased up to the back door and said, "Tom?"

"Yeah, it's me," Tom said.

Ray unlatched the door and eased it open. Glancing at his watch, Ray saw they'd slept through the rendezvous time. It was ten after one. Green-tinted sunlight shone in the back door as Tom entered. Closing the door behind Tom, Ray made introductions. Out of the corner of his eye, Ray saw the accusing glares Cat and Greg were giving him, and turning to them, he said, "I'm sorry I didn't tell you Tom was coming by. You two were asleep when I got out of the shower and I thought there would be time when we woke up."

This seemed to pacify them and he went on, "Tom is kind of the mayor's second in command, and I asked him to come by to discuss some things."

During all this, Tom stood watching back and forth between the team members but looking at Kuan with open curiosity.

"Kuan is the scientist I told you about, Tom."

Tom dragged his gaze away from Kuan and told Ray, "I can see now why you wanted things private. He doesn't exactly blend in. No offense intended, Mr. Kuan."

Kuan tilted his head to Tom and said, "None taken, Mr. Tom."

"No, I mean that's okay," Tom said. "Just Tom, no Mister."

Kuan looked to Ray with a puzzled expression and sighing, Ray said, "Never mind. Anyway, Tom, we've got to ask you some things. Let's go in the front room to one of those tables."

Grabbing some things, Ray, Cat, Tom, and Greg headed to the dining portion of the building. Cleaning off a table, they pulled up four chairs, laid out the map, and lit a candle to save the batteries for the flashlight.

They all sat and Ray told Tom, "Remember when I told you I was taking Kuan to my superiors?"

Tom nodded.

"Well, I found out just before this happened that my superior was in Cody, Wyoming, consulting with someone." When Tom nodded, Ray went on, "That's where we're going, to Cody. We have to get there as soon as possible." Glancing at Greg and Cat, Ray continued, "Walking is kind of slow. Cars don't work, so we've been looking for an alternative, and I hope you can help us."

Tom looked at Ray for a brief second, processing this, then understanding came into his eyes and, another emotion. Sadness.

"Horses. You want horses?" Tom asked.

Ray nodded, "Yes. If we had horses, we could get to Cody a lot faster."

Tom had a sad look on his face as he told Ray, "That's why the barricade was put up, and martial law was enacted." Seeing Ray's incomprehension, Tom went on, "Right after this happened, we had some folks come from out of town, Motorcycle people. After a few hours of the power not coming on and their rides not working, they got rowdy. They wanted to leave and were drunk. There was a confrontation at the Town Hall and Mayor Harris tried to calm them down, but they weren't having it. Being unprepared, we weren't able to stop them and they rounded up the horses we had. Took off north, down the highway, and we haven't heard nothing since. Pissed the mayor off pretty bad. Since then, everyone's been armed and the barricade went up. I wish I could help you, but we don't have any horses left."

Ray felt the blow as if it was physical. He hadn't realized how much he was counting on this speedier mode of transportation. He took a moment to compose himself. Quickly accepting this predicament, Ray moved on to the team's next needs.

"Okay, Tom, I understand. My next question deals with supplies. We're going to have to get more food, water, and other supplies. Especially if we're on foot," he added bitterly.

Tom looked at Ray sympathetically. "Sure, Ray, I can get you whatever you need."

Ray knew it wasn't Tom's fault, but it was a setback that they didn't need. He looked up at Tom and realized Tom was feeling guilty for not having the horses. Feeling bad about putting Tom in this position, Ray put on a smile and said as cheerfully as he could, "We're going to get there, Tom. You get us our supplies and you'll be doing the U.S. Government a huge service."

Tom seemed to know what Ray was doing, but being polite, he smiled back and nodded.

"I need to know exactly what you need and when you need it. I'll do the best I can but, since I'm working in secret, it'll take me a bit."

Ray laid out what they needed with input from Cat and Greg while Kuan watched them with interest from the shadows.

Tom finished taking notes with the pen and notebook he had in his back pocket. He flipped it closed and after looking at his watch said, "I'll have it to you by say...five?"

Ray looked back at him and smiled, "That's perfect. We'll take another nap and be ready to go by then."

Tom reached out his hand with a somber expression. "I hope you all succeed in your mission."

Ray nodded and shook Tom's hand.

After Tom left, Ray looked around at everyone and said, "Let's get some sleep. I don't know about you all, but I need some more." Everyone settled in and Ray wondered what would happen to all of them. Without horses, it was going to take forever. Ray yawned once. They would just have to keep going. He shook off the despair just as sleep took him.

Ray was awake this time when Tom came around. Tom was able to knock once and Ray let him inside the door. Tom's hands were full of stuff and he set it down inside the back door.

Ray and his people had woken up early enough to go through the building and clean out things they might need. They'd found two metal forks, four coffee cups, some match books, and one of those multi-use tools that went on your belt. If Tom was able to get what they'd asked for, it should see them through to Cody.

Ray asked Tom, "Were you able to get everything?"

Tom nodded, and still looking miserable said, "Yeah, all but the horses."

Ray consoled him, "Don't worry about that, we're tough hombres. We'll make it through and hey, we might even find some along the way!"

This seemed to perk him up a bit and snapping his fingers he said, "Oh, I got you all a little present."

Beaming, he reached into the bag he had brought, and lifted out a jar of instant coffee. "Ta-dah!" he said.

Ray found himself grinning back at the man while there was a collective gasp behind him, from Greg and Cat. You would have thought the man had pulled out a handful of gold coins.

Ray said, "You are the man, Tom!" and pounded him on the back.

He was still smiling as he returned the coffee to the bag and handed it over to Ray, "It's the least I can do for the folks trying to put things back on the right track. Good luck everyone." He turned to go but then stopped, "After you get everything fixed, and I know you will, come back and see me and I'll buy you all a drink."

"You bet!" Ray answered. Then Tom was gone.

Ray wanted to go through the items Tom brought and get organized, so he told everyone to bring their bags. Walking into the dining area, he had his flashlight on and placed everything on one of the tables that was still standing. Everybody else followed suit. They gathered around the table as Ray brought out the items one by one. There were several packs of batteries to fit the flashlights. And a bag of sugar and powdered creamer, which brought another round of oohs and aahs. Some metal spoons, four tin cups, which Ray replaced the ceramic ones with. There was also a roll of nylon climbing rope and four thermal blankets. He pulled out four jackets that were all larges, except one, an xx large, probably his. The rest of the items in the bag were canned food, biscuits and rolls, as well as more water bottles. At the bottom of the bag was a container of warm fried chicken that they were amazed at and decided to go ahead and eat before they started off. Everyone took a piece, including Kuan, and pulled up chairs to the table.

Ray pulled out a bottle of water and filled cups and

then everyone set to. None had realized how hungry they were and all had finished off the chicken before they knew it, even Kuan had a second piece.

Greg broke the silence by asking, "I've been looking at the map, Ray, and I've been wondering. When that split comes, which way are we going?"

Ray knew what split Greg was talking about and had his answer ready. "We're gonna take the east road. I've looked at it and think it's marginally shorter."

Greg nodded and replied, "I agree. What do you think, Cat?" He pointed his chin at Cat, since his hands were full of chicken and his water cup.

Cat was picking at her chicken and shrugged. "I really haven't had a chance to look at that stretch on the map. I'm sure Ray knows what he's doing." She glanced quickly over at Ray, who saw, but Greg didn't. Ray knew Cat well enough to know she'd perused the map as much as he and Greg had. She was just letting everyone know she backed Ray. Ray felt a swell of pride and appreciation and quirked a one-sided grin at Cat to let her know.

As they finished up, Ray spoke up in a cheerful voice and said, "Okay everyone, we're leaving in about ten minutes. Anyone needing to use the facilities should." This got chuckles as everyone slid their chairs back and turned to get their stuff ready.

Ray thought about waiting until morning, but he was anxious. He felt time slipping away, and he was, subconsciously, fighting time. He had to get Kuan to his superior, Jason. Every time he saw the green sky, he was reminded of this.

After everyone seemed ready, Ray hitched his bag up on his shoulder and led the way out the back door. They waited as Greg, bringing up the rear, softly closed the door. They turned and, walking single file, slipped out of town like a thief in the night.

13

Emma came awake slowly. For a split second, she was confused. It was dark and she could feel a lump under her hip. She could hear the familiar sound of Bella cleaning herself, which is what woke her up. As she woke up more fully, she caught her breath and suddenly sat up. It had all come back to her, and she looked around. She could see Lori still under the blanket beside her, her chest rising and falling evenly in sleep. Bryan, she saw, was still sitting with his back against the pillar. The gloomy condition was provided by multiple fires out on the street, none close enough to endanger them yet. She felt her heart starting to slow back to normal and looked around for her flashlight. Finding it next to her leg, she hooded the lens. She flashed it over her watch, then turned it off. It was four o'clock. Bryan should have awoken her hours ago for her shift. She grinned to herself, ruefully. He was going to make someone a great husband one day, so chivalrous and good looking. She just hoped it'd be her friend Lori. Emma struggled out from under the blanket and tried not to wake Lori. Bella had paused in her cleaning to glance at Emma, hopefully.

"Not yet, girlfriend." Emma whispered to her, and she promptly went back to her grooming.

Emma made her way over to Bryan, making sure to make some noise so she wouldn't startle him. He heard her and turned his head her way.

"Hey," Bryan said, standing up.

"You were supposed to wake me for my shift," she

said, mock angrily.

He looked away and mumbled something.

"What?" she asked.

"I thought I'd let you two sleep," he said.

Emma stretched to get the kinks out and said, "Well, I sure appreciate it, but now you need to catch a few winks. I'll keep watch for a couple of hours and then I'll wake you two at six. How were things?"

She could see him shrug in the gloom. "It was pretty quiet over here. I could hear muffled explosions and gunshots in the distance, but nobody really got close here."

Emma nodded and said, "Get some sleep. I'll wake you."

Bryan handed her the gun and moved off to where she had been sleeping. Emma watched him a moment, then turned to where he'd been keeping watch. She settled down to lean her back against the same pillar and heard Bella purring as she walked up to snug against Emma's leg.

Emma had a sudden urge to curl up and cry. It was all so overwhelming, she didn't know what to do. After a few moments of self-pity, she shook her head and brought her eyebrows down in a frown of focus. She thought about what needed to be done. She'd always been like that. When something needed to be done, she was a bulldog about pushing through and getting to the other side. It's what made her who she was.

As the sky began to brighten to light green, she thought about what needed to be done first. She needed to feed Bella while the others were asleep. Then, they all needed to eat and get ready to move. She needed to look at the map and figure the best way out of town to the Tennessee state line. She wasn't even sure of the distance, but she knew it was quite a way. She hoped they could find some horses, that's what they needed.

Emma started as an explosion sounded, loudly, one street over. Gas main, had to be.

Bella had jumped too, and this is what got Emma started in the right direction. Once again checking the street, Emma stood and went to her bag. She brought it back and, covering the flashlight, she shone it around and found another can of cat food. Tuna this time, and it had some juice in it, which she put in a hollow for Bella to drink after finishing breakfast. Bella was purring heavily, now, and Emma smiled knowing someone was content. She also rummaged in her bag for the map. Finding it, she went back and sat against the pillar. She covered the flashlight again and let the glow show her the route they would need to take. As she peered at the map, it occurred to her how different looking at the map was now, as opposed to looking at it when you had a car. The distances were so much bigger when you were on foot. Almost overwhelming. She turned the flashlight off and set the map aside. Resting her head back on the concrete, Emma decided not to think of the daunting trip ahead of them. She vowed to think simply, one step at a time. They had to get out of Atlanta as soon as possible.

Emma hadn't realized how tired she was, until she suddenly woke up with someone's grimy hand across her mouth and a gravelly male voice behind her saying, "Well look at what we have here!"

Emma's eyes flew wide and she tried to shake off the person who had her pinned to the pillar but they just chuckled and held her harder.

Emma thought furiously as the shadowed man pressed his body hard against her.

"Thought you'd take my house, hunh?" he said, wrestling her to the ground.

She tried to feel where the gun was, but realized she didn't have it anymore. The man must have grabbed it out of her hand before he woke her. She stopped struggling in order to let him think she was giving up, but all the while she was planning her next move. Emma thought about the knife she had secured on her belt, and tried to slowly get to it with her right hand.

Since she had stopped struggling, her captor had eased up, marginally, on pinning her to the ground.

Emma used this to her advantage and eased her hand around to the knife handle.

The man put his face next to Emma's and she could smell his rank, fetid breath. She could feel him grin against her face and instinctively rebelled against it, but making herself be still, she gripped the knife handle and slowly, quietly drew it out.

It was light enough outside, they could each other's features. Emma was on the bottom and the stranger was on top. He was bigger than Emma and, unshaven, was grinning triumphantly at her from six inches away now. Expecting to see someone scared or in shock, his smile began to fade as he saw the raw determination and anger in Emma's eyes as she deftly eased the knife point to a place just shy of 'Do you want children?'

The scruffy stranger felt the knife point against his privates and went slack-jawed with surprise.

"If you don't want to be singing soprano in the church choir, you better slowly place my gun next to my left hand." Emma growled between his fingers.

The man lay motionless for two heartbeats as he searched her face. Seeing that Emma was entirely serious, he eased his right hand up and placed the gun next to her hand.

Emma could see he was seething at the abrupt change in the situation and pressing the blade more forcefully in his crotch, she eased him up away from her.

She snatched the gun up, and with a steady hand, aimed it point blank between his eyes.

"I believe there's been a misunderstanding about your living arrangements. I didn't see your belongings here, so I think you might have moved?" She ended on a question.

He glanced at the gun barrel and Emma's trigger finger, both steady as a rock, and nodded quickly, "Yeah, I think you may be right." He anxiously licked his lips and stepped back another foot.

Emma quickly realized she didn't need to shame the man and make a mortal enemy right now, so she said, "Good. I'm glad we didn't take your spot." She was still pointing the gun at the bridge of his nose, and even with her slightly more pleasant demeanor, he was smart enough to realize she was giving him an out.

The man took a breath and shakily blew it out, just now realizing how close he had come to dying, and wiping sweaty palms on greasy pants he flashed her a smile full of yellowed and missing teeth and backed away. "Sorry for the misunderstanding then, lady." He eased on out of the overpass and Emma held the gun on him the entire time. When he disappeared around the corner of a building, she slumped back against the pillar and released her breath. She was saddened by the thought that this was reality now. The world had lost that innocent feeling of safety and security, maybe forever. This was what they had to look forward to. She took a shuddering breath and emotionally drew herself up. She was stronger than this. She had grown up with two brothers on a ranch and could do anything she put her mind to, including shoot someone in self-defense. It was how she was raised, she was a Hudson, after all.

Glancing back to where the stranger had disappeared, Emma holstered her weapon and felt Bella ease up against her leg. She looked down at the cat and said, "Gee, thanks. Where the hell were you when I needed a big German Shepherd to take this guy down?"

Bella looked up at her placidly and Emma could just imagine her saying, 'You had everything under control. Why are you worried?'

Emma couldn't help but smile at Bella and scratch her between the ears, then asked ruefully, "I guess you're hungry after all your hard work?"

Bella just walked over to Emma's bag and sat down, waiting for Emma to pull out the goods.

Emma shook her head and told Bella, "You just ate, so I'm only going to give you a piece of jerky. You're so chunky!"

Emma sighed to herself and paced to the edge of their hideout and watched as the day began to lighten. As she watched, she wrapped her arms around her shoulders and thought about the day ahead.

There was a noise behind her and she spun, relaxing as she saw Lori stretch from under her covers. Smiling, Emma strode toward her friend and said with concern, "How's your cheek?"

Lori grimaced, touching the wound. "Better. Just a little sore and stiff."

"We need to clean it and keep Neosporin on it," Emma said.

"Yeah, yeah," Lori said, waving her hand dismissively, "let me get something to eat first."

She rose up stiffly and Emma handed her some beef jerky.

Looking at it, one side of Lori's mouth quirked and she said, "Not exactly a bagel with cream cheese, but I guess beggars can't be choosers."

Emma took a bite of her own jerky as Bryan stepped up stretching his back muscles. Without looking, Emma handed him his own ration of jerky and casually said, "I had a visitor just a while ago."

This got everyone's attention and after glancing at each other, Bryan and Lori started talking at the same time. Emma held up her hand and said, "Guys! Guys!"

They stopped and listened to her. "A man jumped me," she said with a shrug. "I pulled a gun on him and he moved on." Emma looked both her friends in the eye. She wanted them to know this was status quo, this was the way things were now. She saw the bafflement at first in both, then slowly she saw understanding in both. First Bryan and then Lori. Something else flickered there, briefly, behind both sets of eyes. With Lori, it was equal parts of sadness and longing. Longing for a way of life now past.

For Bryan, Emma could see him run through the gamut of emotions: innocent surprise, denial, frustration, and then, slowly, Emma saw realization dawn on both their faces. Emma nodded to herself and, turning away, she began to pack up. She hated to do that to her friends, but if she hadn't, they may have gotten lax and another man, like the one she met, may have surprised one of them.

Emma heard movement behind her and knew her friends were helping her pack.

In the distance, Emma realized gunshots were starting back up and more fires were becoming apparent. She was anxious to get started and get out of town.

Emma turned her attention back to putting things away.

"How long do you think it'll take us to get out of town?" Bryan asked.

Emma finished packing the supplies, putting Bella's water bowl in the top and cinched the opening. "If we don't meet up with trouble, probably three hours, lunchtime at the latest."

Lori nodded and said, "That sounds about right."

They all hitched their gear up and Emma glanced around for Bella.

She was standing, perfectly still, at the edge of the cement and looking off into the sky. Emma could tell something was wrong as she saw Bella tense. Emma lowered her hand to the pistol and followed Bella's gaze. At the same time, a strange noise reached her ears.

There was a distant, building sound, a lot like you hear when coming into a packed stadium.

Emma saw her friends tensing, out of the corner of her eye, and knew they heard it too.

Not knowing what was happening now, Emma whipped out the pistol and motioned her friends back with her against the concrete wall. She looked to where she last saw Bella and found the cat had, prudently, disappeared. As the noise continued to increase, Emma could now make out an odd warbling sound and in the early morning light she could just see a huge cloud coming over the nearest building to the west.

"What the hell is that?" Bryan shouted over the noise.

Emma knew he couldn't hear her and besides, she had no idea, so she just shook her head and continued to watch the cloud grow as it approached their position. She listened closely to the noise and cocking her head, thought she recognized it for a moment. The cloud was now almost upon them and Emma realized it covered at least one city block and was blotting out everything behind it. The noise was deafening now and Lori had covered her ears and hunched down under the overpass.

All of a sudden, Emma felt a powerful, sharp sting in her upper chest and the sound of something thudding to the ground. Another and another object struck her body and the friends crowded up in the small space provided by the overpass. As the black cloud shrieked under and around the concrete, Emma had a split second to look down at the first object that had struck her and, in a moment of confusion, wasn't sure she believed what she was seeing. Then, in a rush it all came to her. Birds, it was a gigantic flock of birds. Swallows, to be exact.

She glanced back down at the flopping, dying animal and realized the entire flock was out of control. Reaching quickly in her bag, she jerked out the blanket and hurriedly pantomimed to Bryan to cover themselves with it. She saw that her friends had come to the same conclusion she had just a few moments ago and they all huddled under the blanket just as the main body of the flock swept up under the bridge. They tried to make themselves as small as possible as the screeching continued and they were incessantly pounded by tiny bird bodies.

They cringed that way for a good five minutes until slowly, Emma realized she was getting hit less often and the noise seemed slightly less. After another minute, the torrent had died completely away along with the noise, and the trio eased the edge of the blanket off their heads to look around.

Lori gasped as they all stared around them, awestruck. Hundreds of dead and dying birds littered the ground around them, literally carpeting the ground under the bridge. Some birds were still flapping their wings and others lay completely still. There was a ringing in Emma's ears after the unbelievable cacophony and she shook her head to try to make sense of it all.

"Holy shit!" Bryan proclaimed, "Unflipping real!"

Emma heard Lori crying softly and stood to comfort her friend. Just as she did, she hissed with pain and found that her whole body was sore. Lifting the edge of her sleeve and examining her arm she checked out other parts of her body and saw that hundreds of tiny bruises covered the parts of her body hit by birds. Looking up, she saw Bryan and Lori doing the same. They were all three covered in bruises.

Emma squeaked out a little laugh, in a forced moment of levity and said, "Almost death by flocking."

Lori had stopped crying and blinked at Emma's words. She let out a small giggle with a smile and nodded at Emma that she was okay.

Bryan looked back and forth at the two and shaking his head muttered, "Women!"

Emma winked at Lori and gathering up the blanket, she stuffed it back in her bag. She nudged some of the bodies away so she wouldn't step on them, then picked her gun up from where she'd dropped it to get the blanket. She took a shaky breath to calm herself and looked around for Bella.

She saw the cat at the edge of the concrete, delicately

batting at a fluttering bird.

"Bella!" Emma shouted, "Leave the birdie alone."

"Where'd that cat go?" Bryan asked. "She's like the Cheshire cat. Now you see her, now you don't." He shook his head. "Never mind. Back to the real quest—"

Lori cut him off. "Where'd those birds come from?"

Emma saw that her friend's hand had a slight tremor. She grasped Lori's hand and looking her in the eye said, "I'm thinking it's related to the electromagnetism."

As she talked, Emma could feel Lori's hand slowly cease its trembling and she knew her friend was okay.

"You mean like a magnet to a compass, right?" Bryan asked as he crouched down by a bird and poked it with a finger.

"Yeah," Emma said, walking over to Bryan. "Swallows are migratory so they have a compass inside their brain and, my guess is this," here she glanced up at the green-tinted sky, "interfered with it somehow."

Bryan continued to stare at the bird for a moment, then stood up and brushed his hands on his jeans.

"Well, I don't know about you two, but I'm ready to get out of this damn town!" With this, he hitched his pack onto his shoulder and strode off toward the interstate, trying his best not to step on any birds.

Emma watched him for a second then turned to Lori and said, "We'll walk for a while until we all calm down and at our first rest break I'll treat your face."

Lori nodded and, shrugging on her own bag, set off after Bryan. Emma followed them both and noticed up ahead that Bella had fallen in next to Bryan. Emma's brows drew together as she once again thought about the birds and what it meant. Things had changed and they would have to be on their guard, not only from human obstacles but from the animal kingdom as well. If the EMP bomb was affecting the brains of birds and animals, what was it doing to the world in general like the North and South Poles or the earth's core? Could the effect be powerful enough to be, at this moment, doing something to alter the earth's physical attributes? Emma sighed and, dismissing the thoughts, she decided not to think about those things until they came up. If they came up. One thing at a time, she'd take one thing at a time.

Deep in thought, Emma didn't realize her friends had stopped until she was almost on top of Lori. She pulled up short and saw her two friends peeking around the corner of a building. Beyond them, she saw three cars piled up blocking the street. The tires on the bottom car were burning and a gang of young kids were standing around arguing with each other with their backs turned to Emma and her friends.

Bryan eased back, pushing Emma and Lori with him. When they were out of ear shot, Bryan turned to Emma and Lori and said, "Okay, this is just great! What the hell are we supposed to do now! Those idiots are blocking our way and it's too far to go around!"

Lori had laid her hand on Bryan's arm to calm him down and Emma was looking around, thinking furiously. Suddenly they heard the argument escalating and two shots rang out, startling the three friends. Emma hissed "Come on!" and raced halfway back the way they had

come. Emma remembered seeing a fire escape and hoped
the gang wouldn't come down the street until they had
made it to the roof. Just as they reached it, Emma
simultaneously thought of Bella and heard more gunshots
from the front of the building. She shoved the thoughts
of Bella to the back of her mind. Damn fur ball will have
to take care of herself. More immediate she saw she was
close and leaping up, she grabbed the bottom rung of the
ladder but when she wasn't heavy enough to pull it down,
she looked down and saw Bryan realize the same thing.
Glancing quickly over his shoulder, Bryan grabbed
Emma's legs. The combined weight worked to release the
ladder and with a squeal, the ladder rumbled to the
ground. All three friends scrambled up the escape with
Bryan pulling it up after him. Making it to the roof, they
all crouched down and peered over the ledge at the street
they'd just left. No sooner had they looked over than
three of the gang came tearing around the corner and slid
to a halt looking around. The trio quickly ducked down
and tried to hush their panting breaths. Emma glanced at
Lori and saw her eyes were big as saucers. She tried to
smile reassuringly at her and Lori gave a trembling smile
back. Emma felt Bryan move beside her and glanced
around to see him easing over to a gap in the ledge to get
a peek.

Emma took stock of their supplies and saw,
surprisingly, that they still had everything.

She heard Bryan duck back down and raised her
eyebrows at him. He placed a finger to his lips in return
and shook his head, pointing to the alley. After doing this,

he glanced across at the side of the building where the car was burning. He made a motion to Emma and Lori that he was going to take a look and Emma nodded her head and took his place at the gap. She gazed down at the gang members and saw they were heading right for the fire escape. She caught her breath and looked furtively around for a way to escape. She saw Bryan messing with something at the front of the building and pushed off to go look at the back of the building. Lori caught up and whispered, "What is going on?"

Emma spoke in a low whisper too and said, "There are three guys heading for the fire escape and I'm looking for a different way off of here. I'm not sure what Bryan's doing."

They'd reached the back part of the building by now and leaning over the ledge, Emma saw there would be no escape that way. She was just pushing back from the ledge when she caught the movement of Bryan's arm back at the front of the building. Emma understood what Bryan was doing about the time the bucket he was throwing arced out over the space beyond the front ledge. She snatched Lori's arm and they darted back to the gap to watch the three gang members in the alley.

There was a loud crash and tinkle of glass as the thrown bucket connected with the windshield of one of the cars down below. Bryan joined them a moment later and they all watched as the three gang members jerked around at the noise and took off at a dead run.

As soon as the last kid rounded the corner, the three friends vaulted onto the fire escape and quietly rushed down the ladder. Reaching the bottom, they anxiously glanced at the corner where the thugs disappeared then hurriedly tried the nearest door.

Sending up a brief prayer, Emma turned the knob and shoved her shoulder into the door. It didn't budge at first, but Bryan lifted his foot and sent a powerful kick at the door and it swung open, spilling the friends into a store room. Bryan quickly closed the door and leaned against it. Lori was bent over at the waist and they were both trying to catch their breaths. Emma was also breathing hard, and she slung her pack down on a stack of pallets. After a moment, Bryan turned and blockaded the door with a two-by-four. Emma stepped to the edge of the only window and cleaning a small spot, stuck her eye to it and checked the alley. She jumped back quickly and motioned her friends over to her side. They all sneaked a peak out the window and after a second, moved away. Bryan leaned towards them and softly said, "I threw a half-bucket of tar at that pileup to distract those assholes, but they're smarter than I gave them credit for."

They had all seen, vaguely, three forms quickly coming back down the breezeway. They all held their breath as they took another look out the dirty window. The gang members, purposely, reached up and grabbed the ladder down. Emma hadn't realized that Bryan had taken the time to push the ladder back up, but was glad he had. It could make all the difference, she thought, as she watched the thugs not even hesitate as they raced up the stairs. With the ladder up, the kids hadn't even considered that their prey may have escaped. She shuddered and reached over to doublecheck the two-by-four. She looked over at Lori and saw her friend gingerly touching her cheek.

"I've got to take care of that gash," she said, crouching down with her pack and rummaging in it for the first-aid kit.

Bryan whipped his head around and forcefully whispered, "We've got to get out of here!"

Emma continued what she was doing and, calmly, without looking up, stated, "They don't know we're here and, until they leave, we're stuck here anyway." She found the kit and strode over to where Lori had sat down on a bundle of what looked like nylon climbing ropes.

Opening the kit, she heard Bryan sigh behind her.

"Yeah, you're right. I'm sorry, Lori," he said.

Lori grimaced as Emma attended to her wound and tried to make light of it, "You just keep an eye on those guys and protect us from the big, bad wolf." Then she winked.

Bryan rolled his eyes and turned back to the window.

Emma smiled at Lori's teasing and finished up with the antibiotic. After replacing the kit in her bag, Emma squeezed her friend's leg and stood. Looking around, she tried to get a better sense of what kind of store they were in. The room was obviously a supply area. Packing crates stood up against the wall and boxes were stacked around to form aisles. She had just used her knife to open one of the boxes and had glimpsed some fishing tackle when the door separating the storage room from the rest of the store burst open and a middle-aged man stood there holding a double-barrel shotgun. Emma had time to notice that he was Hispanic with short gray hair before he cocked both barrels and raised it right at them. The friends had been so shocked that no one had moved. Now Emma raised her hands in a calming gesture and softly said, "We're not here to harm you."

"Damn right you're not!" the man shouted in perfect English. "Bessie here will make sure of that."

Emma spoke quickly, knowing the man was probably just as scared as they were. "We just escaped from a gang out there and your store was the first place we tried." She turned her palms up in what she hoped was a helpless gesture. "We had nowhere else to go." She felt, rather than saw, Lori nodding next to her.

She heard a small voice behind the man speaking in Spanish to him. This seemed to perturb him and he whispered something back over his shoulder. Outside, in the alley, there was a loud noise and the Hispanic man glanced at the window. Out of the corner of her eye, Emma saw the three thugs coming back down the fire escape and yelling at each other. Obviously they weren't happy about not finding Emma and her friends. The Hispanic guy seemed to come to a conclusion and looking them over once more, he marginally dropped the barrel of the gun, and silently motioning to the friends, he stepped back through the inner doorway. The friends let out relieved breaths all around and quickly looked at one another. Emma took the lead and they followed the man through. She decided not to grab her bag, in case he took it for an aggressive move.

Once through the doorway, Emma looked around and saw she had guessed correctly. They were standing behind the counter of an outdoor store. When Lori came through, Emma heard her gasp and turned to see the reason. Squatting, huddled half behind the counter, was a little boy maybe ten years old. This must have been the owner of the voice. What caused Lori to gasp, however, were the burns all along the right side of his arm and face. Emma was better able to control her reactions, but she was still appalled. Bryan didn't hold back at all, as usual.

"Jesus!" he stated. "What the hell happened to you?"

Instead of cringing, though, the boy tilted his chin up a little and drawing down his brows said, "I was trying to get my mama out of the car!"

"Esteban!" the Hispanic man hissed, "Don't you tell these gringos nothing!"

"Oh, Papa! Just because they're white, doesn't make them bad!" he said back to the man.

Emma came to her senses and, giving in to her nurturing side, said to the boy's father, "I've got some medicine for his burns. I'm a nurse." When the man still wouldn't budge, she said, "For God's sake! You can put the gun to my head while I treat him, just let me give him medicine."

After a moment, the man wavered and with a terse nod he backed up a little to let Emma work.

"I've got to get my bag. The medicine is in it."

The man motioned with the gun to let Emma through. Bryan made the mistake of taking a step towards them and, like lightning, the man's fist shot out and punched Bryan in the gut. Bryan doubled over coughing, and Lori went down on one knee to help him. Emma took a deep breath and, putting her hands out, palms down, said in her most soothing nurse voice, "Everybody calm down." Turning first to the Hispanic, she said, "Nobody in our group wants to hurt anybody. I'm assuming you really don't want to hurt anyone either. It's obvious that you're just protecting your son and your business, so let's make a deal. I have offered to treat Esteban's burns and I will, provided you can restrain yourself from punching my friends, okay?"

The man thought about this for a minute then actually looked chastised. "Deal," he said tersely.

Emma nodded slowly and with some insight said, "It would be a lot easier for us all if we introduced ourselves so I won't have to keep thinking of you as Esteban's father." She quirked an eyebrow at him and he seemed to relax a bit more.

With a sigh he said, "Yes, okay. I am Arturo."

Emma felt relieved by this marginal victory and said, "Good. Nice to meet you, Arturo, and you, Esteban. My name is Emma, the guy on the floor sucking wind is Bryan, and the other woman is Lori. I am about to walk back to the supply room and retrieve my bag. I have this pistol on my hip which is really for self-defense and I will not give it to you."

At this the man started to raise the shotgun again, but Emma quickly went on, "HOWEVER," she emphasized, "I will not pull it on you, either, provided we can have a little truce here, all right?"

She finished and mentally held her breath. She could hear Bryan finally catching his breath and thought Arturo was going to shoot them anyway when Esteban stepped in front of his father and, using his left arm, slowly pushed down the barrel of the shotgun. Looking into his father's eyes, he said softly and earnestly, "You told me many times, 'it's not the color of their skin, Esteban, it's what's in their soul and you can see it in the eyes.' Well, Papa, I see in these people's eyes that they are good. We can trust them."

Having said this, Esteban promptly turned around and somberly motioned to Emma that he would follow her.

Emma looked back at Arturo and saw the pain of his son's injuries and the fear for his son's life, not to mention the truth of Esteban's words warring with each other behind the man's eyes. Gently, Emma laid a hand on the man's muscled forearm and said, "Your son is very wise. I say again, we're not here to hurt you."

Finally, Emma saw the man relent and lowered the gun completely. Only then did she turn to lead the boy into the back room. Arturo stayed in the other room with her friends.

She opened her bag and dug once again for her first-aid kit. Absently, she reminded herself to look for replenishments for it. She was using up a lot of antibiotic ointment and bandages.

"He's not usually like this," Esteban stated

Emma brought herself back to the job at hand and replied, "Oh?"

"Yeah, he's kind of out of sorts since this stuff all happened."

Emma inspected his wounds while trying to figure out what to say next.

"I think everyone's out of sorts since this stuff all happened," she replied absently. "I don't normally carry a gun on my hip, either." She said this last with a little smile on her face. Esteban smiled back. He was a handsome boy with the usual Hispanic coloring but with light brown eyes that Emma could only describe as golden. They were intelligent eyes and her heart ached for the loss of innocence that he, and other children like him, had suddenly suffered. She realized that no more would they be able to go to an amusement park or learn to drive a car or even, for that matter, watch a simple family movie on television while eating warm, buttered microwave popcorn with their families.

"What happened to your mother?" she asked, and instantly regretted it. His smile quickly faded and tears welled up in his eyes.

"I'm sorry," Emma said quickly, "I wasn't thinking. You don't have to say a thing."

She thought he would take her advice, but then, after Emma had cleaned the wounds and started to spray on the antibiotic, he started softly, almost too low for Emma to hear. As he spoke, Emma continued to spray on the soothing salve.

"My papa and I were here at the store. He had let me stay out from school because I had been bugging him about coming in to help. He finally let me come in since I was ahead in my studies and I think I was pestering him to death." He said this last piece with a little smile. "So I got to come in with him. We were putting away some supplies and he had just shown me the way to open up the cardboard boxes when there was a bright flash outside and a loud rumbling noise." Here, Emma nodded because she remembered all too well her experience with the bomb.

He continued, "It scared me, and I could see it scared Papa, too, which scared me even more. Papa dropped the box cutter in his hand and started toward the front of the store."

Emma could see that Esteban was lost in his memories. She had finished up with the salve and was now wrapping his burned arm, loosely, with some gauze wrap. He winced a little, but went on.

"Papa had just taken a step and all the lights went out with a sizzle like bacon when you fry it, you know?" Emma nodded and said, "Yes, I know what you mean."

This seemed to encourage him and his voice got stronger. "Well, Papa got a real worried look on his face and turned to me and said, 'Get back behind the counter, Esteban!' I'd NEVER heard him talk like that and it took me a moment to figure out he was scared. Well, I did what he said, because I was really scared, now. I didn't know what was going on! From behind the counter, I watched him reach over it and grab the shotgun. I knew about the shotgun and Papa had told me he kept it for the bad people, so I knew not to touch it. Anyway, he grabbed the gun and started to turn around when there were crashes outside. I looked over the counter and saw the cars outside were crashing into each other and people were trying to get out of them."

Emma felt the boy tremble and opened her mouth to tell him he didn't have to tell her but he went on, almost like he NEEDED to tell her.

"Mama was supposed to be on her way here, to bring lunch," he said with pleading in his eyes. His voice had gotten hoarse with the strain of telling her.

"She should have already been here. I remembered this, and running to the front of the store, I saw her car get smashed up by two other cars. I yelled to her and tried to get to her and made it to the car before Papa almost caught me, but then there was an explosion and I put my arm up to cover my eyes and, and..."

Esteban dissolved into tears and clutched Emma's neck. She hugged him back, not caring that fifteen minutes before she hadn't even known this boy existed. He mattered now. Emma fought back tears of her own as she comforted this little person who had lost his entire world. She couldn't bring it back for him but she damn sure could be there for him now.

Drying her eyes as best she could, she asked "Hey, you know what?"

He tried to sniff back his own tears as he answered, "What?"

"Your Mama knows you were there. I believe in life after death and ghosts. And I know your Mama saw everything you did. She's proud of you! She hates that you got hurt but she knows you did everything you could and I know for a fact that she loves you."

By this time she was smiling. Emma was smiling so hard she felt her cheekbones would break, just willing this strong young man to know what she felt in her heart.

She saw she had gotten through to him when he lifted his beautiful, sweet eyes to hers and said with hope, "You think so?"

She grinned back at him and said, around a lump in her throat, "Yeah, I know so. I'm a nurse aren't I? We have special powers and one of those is knowing so!" She was winging it now and just wanted to comfort him the best she could.

Esteban surprised her by throwing his arms around her neck again and whispering in her ear, "Thank you, Ms. Emma, I know so too!"

Emma held him a moment longer, then gently eased him back and changed the subject to his wounds. "I think these are going to be fine. How do they feel?"

The tactic seemed to work as he flexed his little arm and grinning said, "Much better!"

She grinned back at him and said, "Let's go see your Papa, okay?"

She saw him glance past her shoulder and followed his gaze to see everyone in the doorway and not a dry eye in the house.

Ruefully, she thought, 'So much for my bad-ass reputation.'

She stood up and, grabbing her pack, she walked back to her friends.

Bryan tried to pretend he wasn't tearing up and Lori

gave Emma a huge hug. Esteban and Arturo were hugging as well and Arturo was telling Esteban he was sorry, while Esteban was actually comforting his father.

The moment seemed to pass and Arturo was the one who spoke first, after examining his son's wounds.

"I thank you for treating Esteban, and I apologize for my earlier actions. My son was right. I usually do not act first and ask questions later," he said.

Emma tried to downplay it by shrugging lightly and saying, "We're all under a little stress. It's to be expected."

Arturo wasn't letting it go, "At least let me offer to refill some of your supplies, since you used a lot on Esteban."

She wasn't about to pass that opportunity up and said, "Do you have any first-aid kits?"

"Some of the best. Deer hunters are very accident-prone, especially when drinking alcohol." He gave Emma a grim smile and led her down the aisles to one with several backpacks of different sizes. All had the requisite Red Cross on them. He looked at a description of a couple and then stepped back and said, "Here, what do I know? You need to go through them and see which is best."

Emma smiled at him and thanked him, then bent to the task. She was amazed at how complete the kits were and, even though she wanted the largest, she knew it was too much weight to carry. She checked out the two mid-sized ones and seeing some things in the large one, she wanted to add to one of the mid-sized ones. She asked Arturo if she could do that.

"Of course, Miss, you may have saved my son's arm. Change them however you need to. It's not like I'm going to have a lot of paying customers soon."

Emma thanked him and started exchanging items in the kits. While she was doing that, Bryan, who had recovered by now, cleared his throat and awkwardly stuck his hand out for Arturo to shake. "Like Emma said, my name's Bryan."

Arturo grinned broadly and slapping Bryan hard on the shoulder he grabbed his hand and said, "No hard feelings, eh?"

Bryan winced and Emma saw him struggle not to rub his arm.

"Hey!" Arturo said, boisterously, "I know! I will give you a gift." He looked down at Bryan's belt, then, grabbing his shirt at the shoulder, he turned Bryan around and saw the .30-.30.

"Now, that's a mean rifle, you know?" he said to Bryan. "But it's really loud. Follow me," he stated with conviction, and turned to go back to the counter without waiting to see if Bryan followed.

Bryan looked at Lori, who stood next to Emma. When she noticed Bryan's look, she shrugged a shoulder and gestured him to follow Arturo. Bryan sighed loudly and followed the Hispanic.

Arturo led Bryan back behind the counter and through a separate door that Bryan hadn't noticed. The room had no windows and Arturo switched on a flashlight he had on his belt.

"This is my favorite room. The items in here are

special."

Bryan looked around and gave out an involuntary low whistle. "This is nice!"

He glanced at Arturo and saw the man was beaming with pride.

Looking back at the room, Bryan took mental inventory. The room was about the size of a large bedroom and lined up row upon row along the walls were all kinds of archery bows: Compound bows, large and small; crossbows, full-size and pistol; machetes, large medium and small; and every item was either shiny, bright metal, black, or camouflaged. There were bolts and arrows of every size and configuration as well as color and camouflage. Arturo also had an impressive array of hand knives and in the middle was displayed a survivalist table with everything from hiking boots to water purification tablets as well as, Bryan was surprised to see, fire steel. He hadn't seen that since his old friend David had showed him how to start a fire with one back in California.

He turned to Arturo, but the man had lit a lantern and was already headed to the far wall. He clamped his mouth shut and followed. They entered the L-shaped space behind the counter and stopped at a section of walls holding the crossbows. Bryan saw Arturo was deep in thought and decided to stay silent. After deliberating and handling several pistol crossbows, he chose one that was matte black and handed it to Bryan.

"I think, if this continues, you might be needing this little beauty," he stated.

Bryan gripped the pistol crossbow and hefted it. It fit perfectly in his hand and seemed balanced and easy to wield.

Arturo continued, "It has eighty-pound pull and foot stirrup for ease of draw. We'll need to get extra strings and bolts."

Bryan looked at the man like he had two heads.

Arturo saw and shaking his head, took the crossbow from Bryan. "I show you."

Quickly, the Hispanic flipped open the stirrup and used his foot while drawing the recurve bow tight. He then reached up and grabbed a bolt and slapped it in. When he was finished, he grunted and handed the weapon to Bryan. Luckily, Bryan had taken it all in and without warning turned to the far wall and shot the pistol. The bolt made a hissing noise as it whisked to its target and, after watching, Arturo made a sound of approval. The bolt had struck its intended target which was right through the trigger guard of a full-size crossbow maybe fifteen feet away.

Bryan turned back to Arturo without saying a word and repeated the process of cocking the weapon, slapping in a bolt for good measure. When he was done he lowered the pistol to his side and smiled at Arturo.

To his credit, the man just blinked twice and said, "I guess you catch on quick."

Bryan and Arturo were still chuckling when Emma, Lori, and Esteban entered. Bryan saw a gleam come into Emma's eyes as she looked around. He also saw she was carrying the mid-size first-aid kit now bulging with supplies.

"Very nice!" she said as she walked backwards around the room. Esteban and Lori followed her in but Lori walked over to Bryan with an eyebrow raised at the pistol while Esteban went to his father's side.

"Your friend here has found a new toy," the Hispanic said, grinning.

Bryan smiled a little, too, and engaging the safety, he said, "I think we should take this weapon." Glancing at Arturo he said, "That's if it's okay with Arturo."

"Sure, sure!" the Hispanic gushed, "I want you to have it. I have other gifts as well, but let's get something to eat first." He turned serious and looking at the friends, he said meaningfully, "We need to talk."

Emma involuntarily glanced at Esteban who was busy playing with the carabiners on the central table. She nodded at the man and Arturo turned to his son. "Go get the canned meat and bread." As the boy turned to go, Arturo added, "And one of those canteens of water."

Arturo started clearing the central table and motioned to some folded chairs against the wall. The friends grabbed some chairs and opened them up around the table. Arturo finished clearing a space and they all sat down. Esteban was still absent, and Arturo, in a low voice, said, "I have this feeling that you three know what's going on, so before the boy gets back, I would like for you to tell me."

Emma and her friends glanced at one another and Bryan motioned to her. "Go ahead. You're the one that told us."

Emma cleared her throat and told the man, "We believe it was an EMP bomb." She opened her mouth to explain, but Arturo was already nodding his head and Emma could see recognition in his eyes.

"Ah, that makes sense," he said

"You know what one is?" Lori asked, just as surprised as the rest of them.

Still nodding, he spoke. "Yes, I had to read up on it a few years ago when I started getting," here he paused and chuckled ruefully, "what I thought of then as crazies coming into the store asking for survivalist gear. I finally asked one of them, about a year ago, what he was preparing for. He called it a HEMP event. When he did not explain further, I went on the internet to see what it was so I could buy supplies for these people." He shrugged. "Seemed like good business."

Emma smiled at Bryan and Lori, who smiled back.

Arturo next asked a question, "Who did this?"

Emma, not smiling now, said "Well, that's the sixty-four dollar question, isn't it?"

"Sixty-four what?" Arturo asked, perplexed.

Emma shook her head dismissively and told the man, "We don't have a clue. It could have been anybody. Anyway, I figure the real question we need to ask is how long it will last?" Before he could ask, she resumed. "Unfortunately, we don't have the answer to that either."

Seeing she still had his attention, Emma continued, "I was telling Bryan and Lori that it's my belief that this green glow has something to do with the ongoing effect of the EMP on our atmosphere. As long as it's glowing, we've got problems. Will it be forever?" She felt she was asking for them all. "I hope not, but I honestly don't know. It's lasted for two days now and I'm not waiting around in this nightmare to find out."

Arturo asked, "Where are you headed? I can tell by your packs that you are going somewhere."

Emma snatched a glance at her friends and gave them a questioning look. Bryan returned it with a shrug and Lori gave a little nod. Emma didn't think it would hurt anything to tell Arturo.

She turned to him and said, "We're heading to Tennessee. Hopefully, we'll meet up with some friends of ours there." No sense going into detail.

"Are these friends going to keep you safe?" he asked, after thinking a moment.

Emma thought about Jack and said, without a moment's hesitation, "Yes, they will."

She wondered, after she had answered, why he wanted to know, but held her tongue.

Arturo stood and paced to the counter, deep in thought. She looked at her friends and, again, they shrugged.

Suddenly coming to a decision, the Hispanic man turned and said, "I want to ask you a favor." Looking pale, but determined, he continued, "I want you to take my Esteban with you."

The trio of friends were shocked. They didn't talk for a full five seconds, and then Bryan was first. "What? You can't be serious!" he squawked.

Lori was just staring, mouth opened, stunned.

Emma recovered first because she thought she was beginning to understand this man's thinking. He loved his son. He loved him enough to make a leap of faith and ask three strangers, on instinct alone, to take his son with them. Out of the dangerous chaos that was surrounding them. Arturo was choosing the lesser of two possible evils.

She stood up and went to him. Placing her hand on his shoulder, she looked into his eyes and said, "Now that your wife is gone, you don't have any family here, do you?"

With tears in his eyes, the man shook his head and said, "No. Sonia, my wife, and I were going to bring her mother and two brothers up from Guatemala at the end of this summer. We had finally saved enough money and were building on to our house so they would have a place to stay. Now?" He trailed off with a slump of his shoulders.

Emma looked back at Bryan and Lori. She knew they should talk about this, and they would, but she already knew her answer.

Esteban chose that moment to reenter the room, bringing a pillow case full of food. He stopped right after he entered, sensing the tension in the room.

"Papa?" he asked.

Arturo had already wiped his eyes and striding to his son, he took the makeshift sack from the boy and turned back to the friends.

"Come!" he said with forced jolliness. "Let's enjoy our feast! I don't think anybody is going anywhere for a while and you must be starving."

He set the sack on the table and, with a flourish, withdrew the items and placed them before the friends.

"We've got some MRE's here."

Lori said, "Hunh?"

Arturo briefly glanced up and smiled. "You are American and yet you don't know the slang terms?" he asked.

Emma rolled her eyes playfully at Bryan and told Lori, "Meals Ready to Eat is what it stands for. The military uses them in the field where free-standing mess tents aren't available. Go on, take one." She pushed one over to Lori and took one for herself. She saw Bryan reach over and grab one too.

"Thank you, Arturo," Emma said graciously.

"I appreciate the gesture," Lori said with a slight teasing tone, "but I'll reserve the thank you until after I've tried it."

Bryan had already torn into his and mumbled his own thanks through a mouthful of food. Apparently, he'd had them before. He seemed to be relishing his.

Emma bit into her own and, after swallowing, asked Arturo, "Why do you think we're not going anywhere soon?"

He looked up from his own MRE and said offhand, "I've been watching that bunch who was chasing you. They've hung around during the day and leave at night. I'm sure to get into some mischief. They did the same thing before this all happened. So I guess they will continue to do so now." He said this offhandedly.

Emma nodded, but before she could speak, Lori piped up and stated, "We'll have to wait 'til tonight then, right?"

With his mouth full, Arturo just nodded.

Lori continued, "What time do they usually leave?"

Arturo finished his meal and said, "Oh, they left early yesterday. Maybe about five or six o'clock."

"It's about noon now, right?" she inquired.

He nodded.

"So that means we have a few hours to spend. I think my friends and I should discuss everything," Emma stated with a meaningful look at Esteban. The boy wasn't paying attention and Arturo nodded to her. Emma got up and, gesturing to her friends, she said out loud, "Esteban, my friends and I are going to the other room a minute but we'll be right back."

The boy had looked up when she spoke his name and, smiling at her said, "Okay."

The three friends rose and, stuffing their trash into a nearby trash can, they left the room. Walking back to the supply room, they all waited to say anything until Bryan closed the door behind them.

"I know what you're going to say, Em, and I'm going to tell you now, I really don't think it's a good idea. I know you have a soft heart, but we can't just take this boy with us like we're adopting an animal."

As Bryan spoke he had continued over to the window. Looking outside, his face took on a look of perplexity.

Softly, he said, "Well I'll be damned!"

In apprehension, the two women rushed up beside Bryan and looked out.

There, across the street, sat Bella, calmly cleaning her front paw. She was hidden away under a box lying on its side. Bryan shook his head slowly, smiling. "Jesus! That is the most amazing cat!"

Emma smiled, affectionately, to herself.

Looking to the end of the alley, she slowly turned the door knob and eased the door open. It squealed slightly, and Emma stopped. Then, with the door barely open, Emma watched Bella stretch and then stroll leisurely to the door.

Passing between the door and the jamb, Bella sauntered over and rubbed up against Bryan's leg like nothing had happened. Looking back down the alley, and seeing that nobody had heard the door, Bryan shook his head. Grinning, he reached down and petted the cat.

Emma eased the door closed and told Bryan, "Looks like you made a friend."

Lori was grinning ear to ear and moved over to pet Bella, too.

Emma was already thinking about what they needed to discuss and walking over to the crate, she sat down. She turned her attention to her friends. Bella had finished basking in the limelight, and moving over to a clean place on the floor, promptly curled up and went to sleep.

"Em, I just don't think it's a good idea taking a kid with us on the road," Bryan blurted before Emma could talk.

Emma took a deep, mental breath while studying

Bryan's face. He was distraught, Emma could see, and this helped her ease her anger toward him. She sneaked a look at Lori and saw, to a lesser degree, agreement with Bryan.

Rolling her shoulders, Emma took a moment to answer, giving her a chance to think about what she would say.

Speaking quietly to, hopefully, calm Bryan down, she said, "You know as well as I do, you guys, that he stands better odds with us than here in downtown chaos central. Besides, we work in the medical field, it's our duty to help others."

"At what cost?" Bryan responded.

They were still staring at each other and Lori had opened her mouth to say something when there was a huge explosion outside that knocked them all to the floor. The building shook all the way to the foundation and debris rained down on them.

"HOLY SHIT!" Bryan yelled and Emma scooted over to check on Lori. She had fallen into the box of fishing tackle they'd found earlier.

She had helped Lori to her feet when Arturo stumbled in, dragging Esteban by his good arm. The boy was coughing and shaking his head. Arturo eased him down on an opposite pallet and with wide eyes said, "I think our friends have started early today. Either that or the car that was burning had a full tank."

Emma noticed that Arturo had dragged their bags with him, and she started to speak when there came a deafening pounding on the front windows. She expected the windows to break and was reaching for her bags when she saw Arturo grinning. "What?" she demanded.

He gestured with a thumb at the front of the store and said, "Plexiglas. I'm glad I invested." His smile faded, however, as he continued, "It won't hold forever. I guess my son and I are leaving also."

He finished and turned to Esteban to make sure he was okay. Emma set her hands on her hips and glanced at Bryan. Bryan threw his hands in the air and glanced at the ceiling. Emma grinned and started getting their bags ready. "Lori," she said in a low voice, "could you and Bryan finish gathering our things while I talk to Arturo?" She had to speak this last part in a louder voice since the barrage on the Plexiglas had increased.

"Sure," Lori said in a slightly trembling voice.

Emma smiled at her reassuringly, and squeezed her arm, then walked over to Arturo.

He was readying their own things as Emma approached. He glanced up at her and continued, speaking in a soothing tone to his son. Emma couldn't understand the Spanish so as he finished she broke in, "We want you two to come with us. There's more safety in numbers and once we get out of the city, you can go your own way."

Esteban was looking at her and grinning. Arturo had slowed his movements and finally stopped and listened as Emma finished.

"You don't even know us," he stated.

Gently, she smiled and said, "If I remember correctly, it was you who told your son, 'It's what's in their heart and you can see it in their eyes.' Am I right?"

He smiled ruefully back at her and said, "Yes, yes that is it exactly."

"Well," Emma breathed out and looked around at the extended group. She spotted Bella next to the back door trying to smooth the fur down that was sticking straight up all over.

Her eyes came back to the Hispanic and she asked, "Did you get everything?"

"Yes," he replied, "even as many MRE's as we can carry."

"Good," Emma said. "Thank you."

He shrugged it off and changed subjects. "If they're working on getting in the front, we should be able to slip out the back and around the side of the building. I've seen they're not too smart." He finished by tapping the side of his head and winking.

Emma was thinking out loud, "I guess we're going to have to travel in daylight," she sighed as she picked up her bag. "We can do this. We've done it before." She forced a smile at the group and seeing they were ready, reached down and whisked Bella into her bag. "Can't forget you, can we?" she murmured with a twitch of her lips. Easing the door open, she was about to poke her head out when Arturo laid a hand on her shoulder and, gently pulling her back, he gave a slight smile and nod to Esteban. Emma understood and, nodding back, let him take the lead. He wanted her to keep an eye on Esteban. With a collective breath, the rest of the group followed him out the door.

They had been traveling without a rest for four or five hours. There had been a lot of close calls. Thankfully, most of them were from drunks or otherwise inebriated people who couldn't hit the broad side of a barn. Emma's group was holed up, now, on the north side of Atlanta, in an expensive house that they discovered had been deserted in a hurry. Dishes half full of food were still sitting on the table and the house appeared ransacked. They had arrived fifteen minutes ago and, after making sure the house was empty, they all collapsed in the living room. The stench from the spoiled food in the kitchen was manageable with the door closed and the windows open. They just needed to regroup. Slumping down in an armchair, Lori wiped the sweat from her forehead and breathing hard said, "It's not supposed to be this hot yet!"

Emma slumped in another chair and dropped her bags to the floor, "I think we got spoiled to air conditioning. We weren't walking forever in a ransacked city in the broiling sun with God-only-knows-what happening to the weather, either."

The guys had all slumped on two separate couches and after mopping the sweat off his own brow, Bryan said, "We need to refill the water bottles, do you think the water here's still okay?"

Having recovered somewhat, Emma sat up a little and after glancing at Lori to see if her wound was still okay, she spoke. "I guess there's only one way to find out."

There was a rustle in her bag and Bella popped out. She turned a baleful eye on Emma then sat down and began her cleaning ritual. Emma just rolled her eyes and stood. Grabbing her own water bottles, Emma started down the hallway. She found the bathroom halfway down on the left. Stepping inside, she absentmindedly flipped the light switch. Realizing her error, she mentally chastised herself for her stupidity. Retracing her steps, she got a flashlight and returned to the bathroom. Lori had showed up at her elbow and Emma handed her the light. Bella pushed in and sniffed around.

Emma reached out, anxiously, and turned the cold water handle. For a split second nothing happened, then water gushed and sloshed out of the basin. Lori and Emma grinned at each other and Bella hissed in indignation and bolted through the door, as water sprinkled her back and tail. While Lori was filling their bottles, Emma looked for towels. As hot as it was, she was determined to take a shower.

"I'm going upstairs to take a shower." she stated to Lori.

Lori looked surprised for a minute then grinned and nodded. "Me too! God, even a G.I. Jane shower would feel good right now!"

Emma went back to the guys and handing them the water bottles, told them their plans. Bryan replied that they'd keep a lookout. Emma smiled her thanks and grabbing hers and Lori's bags, she rejoined her friend. Together they went up the long steps to the second landing. Everything on this floor appeared as if the owners might walk in at any moment. Some things were knocked askew, but for the most part things were intact. Their footsteps seemed loud in the silence. The women could hear the low murmur of the men talking below them. They looked in each room and found some guest bedrooms and a nursery. They finally came to a bathroom and Lori said, "I'll take this one."

Emma nodded and moved on, looking for the master bedroom. At the end of the hall, she turned an L and found double doors. Pushing them open, she stood for a moment taking it in. A four poster bed with opulent bedding and expensive furnishings greeted her. It was stuffy, and she went to raise the window. As Emma pushed the curtains aside, she sucked in her breath at the sight. Raising the window, she stared out at the view. The house and surrounding subdivision sat above downtown Atlanta. Maybe ten miles away, Emma saw the proud city of Atlanta burning in several places. She saw a beautiful skyline, with several buildings crumbling, and smoke, tinted green by the ever present hue, clinging with tenacious tendrils to the surrounding buildings. Sadly, Emma wondered if this was the modern version of what Atlanta natives viewed when the city burned during the Civil War. With thoughts of *Gone with the Wind* in her mind, Emma turned from the window, roughly wiped the tears from her eyes, and stepped to the master bath.

Entering the large bathroom, Emma switched on her flashlight and placed it on the counter. Double marble sinks and wall-to-wall mirrors filled her vision first. She opened a door on her left to find towels and washcloths. She grabbed one at random and, locking the door, stepped to the glass-enclosed shower and stripped down. Gritting her teeth, she jumped in and quickly started scrubbing herself from head to foot. After a couple of minutes, it wasn't so bad. The soap was deliciously scented and the shampoo was high end. Turning the water off, Emma grabbed the soft towel and briskly dried off. While in the shower, Emma had an idea. Leaving the bathroom with her flashlight, Emma stepped over to what she figured was the closet. She opened the double doors and was greeted by a closet full of clothes. She grinned and mentally crossing her fingers, she shined the flashlight around. Placing the flashlight on a chair, Emma started sorting. She found some designer sweats (Emma couldn't believe it, designer sweats!) in roughly her size and a shelf with some t-shirts. She grabbed the rest of the t-shirts and leaving the closet with her flashlight she stepped back into the bedroom. She finished dressing just as Lori stepped into the room.

"I am really having to adjust to roughing it!" Lori exclaimed.

Emma looked up at her friend and grinned at the sight she made. Her hair, still wet, was sticking out in spikes and she had goose bumps all over.

"Yeah, but doesn't it feel good to be clean?"

"I'll let you know later." Lori groused, rubbing her arms, briskly.

Emma knew Lori would be okay. One of the things

Emma loved about her was her unfailing positive attitude.

She finished, pushed the clothes in her bag, along with a bar of the sweet smelling soap, and then grabbed Lori's hand. They headed back down the hall. She felt invigorated, but at the same time, somewhat tired.

As they went back down the hall, Emma saw that the sun was almost down. Evening was coming on and she was glad. Come to think of it, she was really exhausted. Reaching the bottom floor, she turned to Lori and said "We'll let the guys shower while we fix something to eat. I saw a fireplace. Maybe we can cook some hot food."

At this, Lori smiled wistfully and said enthusiastically, "Oh my God! What I wouldn't do for something hot to eat!"

Mentally, Emma agreed. They arrived at the living room and saw that the two men were looking at something down on the road from concealed positions while Esteban slept deeply on one of the couches. As the two women approached, Bryan glanced sharply at them and, with forefinger to lips, motioned them up against the wall beside him. Emma noticed that Arturo had his double-barrel shotgun and Bryan had the rifle. Both were cocked and ready.

"What's going on?" she whispered, trying to peer out the window over his shoulder. She saw Lori go over and check on the boy.

"People down at the end of the driveway," he whispered back. "They've been milling about down there for about fifteen minutes or so. They don't look like the thugs we saw in the city, but I still don't want them coming up here. There are too many of them. Hopefully they'll go on down the road. They seem to be arguing about something."

As he said this, Emma and the two men watched as the youngest male of the group seemed to become disgusted and stating something, angrily, pointed up the drive to the house.

"Uh oh." Bryan muttered.

"Sh!" Arturo whispered.

There were three other men in the group and two women, all dressed in torn clothes, some had various bandages tied to appendages. Dirty and bedraggled, they looked like Emma and her friends. Her heart went out to them but, as Bryan stated, things were different now. There were too many of them and you couldn't afford to trust anyone. That bunch could easily cause problems for Emma's group.

Suddenly, out of nowhere, a rock flew into the group and smacked one of the women in the face.

Emma gasped in surprise. Arturo grumbled something, under his breath, in Spanish.

The friends, including Lori now, continued to watch in helpless anger as the group was surrounded by what appeared to be drunken gang members.

As they watched, the much bigger gang members surrounded the smaller group and separated the women from the men and started beating the men with clubs and bats. One of the men being beaten tried to pull out a gun and actually got a shot off but it went wide when one of the gang members deflected his arm with a lucky swing from an iron pipe.

Emma could hear Lori beside her, quietly sobbing as they watched the larger group finish off the smaller group and drag the women kicking and screaming, back down the way they had come.

Emma, sadly and with horror, vividly imagined the fate awaiting those two women. Frustration built up in her until she went over and kicked a hole in the wall next to the fireplace.

"Nice," Bryan intoned.

She rounded on him and even realizing she was venting at him, she couldn't stop. "What the hell do you want me to do? Pull out a deck of cards and sing a little ditty? Jesus Christ! We just watched several men be murdered and two women dragged off to only-God-knows-where and to only-God-knows-what to be done to them! I feel so damn helpless!"

Lori was still sobbing quietly but Emma saw she was trying to get her emotions under control. She looked over and saw she had awoken the boy and saw he was staring at her like she had three heads. Arturo still watched the driveway, but Emma could see it was clear, except for the bodies.

By this time, her rage had run its course, leaving her drained and feeling empty inside. She walked over to soothe Esteban and try to undo the damage her anger had done.

She sat down beside him and realizing he didn't know what had taken place outside, she smiled and said, "I'm just a little frustrated, honey. I let my frustration boil over and got a bit angry."

He still had big eyes, if not as scared looking when he replied, somberly, "If that's a little angry, what do you do when you're really pissed off?"

This brought a bark of laughter from Bryan, who immediately clapped his hand over his mouth and Lori snickered lightly. Emma whipped her head in their direction, which had the desired effect of silencing both of them, then turned regally back to Esteban.

"I'm sorry, Esteban, I really didn't mean to lose my temper."

He smiled shyly and said, "It's okay. I get mad sometimes too."

Emma hugged him and he hugged her back.

Having settled that, she got up and walked back to the window. Sidling up to the edge, she looked out and saw it was still deserted.

Looking at her group, she tried to distract them and said, "I wanted to cook something hot for supper. I think that fireplace is so large, we can risk a small fire, maybe cook some soup and beans or something."

As she talked, she saw the demeanor of her little group perk up. It was what she was hoping for.

Arturo looked at Bryan and said, "You go take a shower, I'll keep watch."

Bryan started to say something, but Arturo's eyes told him it was okay. Instead he shrugged and nodded, and motioning to Esteban, he said, "Come on, buddy, let's go get clean"

"Aw, man," Esteban grumbled, but followed Bryan

anyway.

As they trooped up the stairs, Lori asked Emma, "Where are we going to get wood?"

Emma smiled and replied, "I'll bet they have some charcoal somewhere. We can put a small pile of it under that fire grate. I'll go through the connecting door and look in the garage."

She grabbed a flashlight and went to the garage. Just as she'd thought, she found some charcoal and, as a bonus, some lighter fluid. She smiled a little to herself before remembering the recent events. She had to be strong. Logically, there's nothing they could have done without getting one of their group killed, or maybe all of them. She shook her head sadly and then, tucking her hair behind her ear, she returned to the living room. She saw that Lori had two cans of chicken noodle soup, beans, and a pack of crackers out. Arturo was finishing cleaning out the fireplace and Lori was looking out the window. She now turned to Emma and with her arms crossed over her chest said, "Where do you think they took those women?"

She should have guessed that goodhearted Lori would be thinking of the women too.

"Probably back to some bar. To get drunker and, and..." Lori answered her own question but then couldn't go on. She turned back to the window to compose herself and Emma patted her shoulder before taking the charcoal to the fireplace. About that time, Bryan came down the stairs with damp hair and Esteban trailed on his heels. They both looked refreshed and Emma offered up thanks for the little things.

Bryan reached the fireplace and gently took the charcoal as he addressed Arturo, "Hey, we'll get supper going, you go take a shower. You'll be amazed at how good it feels!"

Arturo smiled and thanked him, then, patting his son's head, he went up the stairs. Silently jutting his chin at Lori, Bryan looked a question at Emma. Sadly, Emma shook her head, indicating how upset Lori was. Bryan stared at Lori's back, then absently handing the charcoal back to Emma, he walked over to where Lori stood facing the window. Gently, he laid a big hand on Lori's petite shoulder and she jumped, startled, but when she turned and saw it was Bryan, she beamed up at him and Emma smiled a little, thinking of Jack and listening as Bryan tried to soothe Lori with soft platitudes. She couldn't hear, from that distance, what was said. As she turned to start the fire, she knew that just Bryan being there had made Lori feel better.

She was surprised to see little Esteban already arranging the charcoal in a pyramid under the grate his father had cleaned off.

"You've got that down pat, hunh?" she said teasingly with hands on hips.

He smiled widely at the compliment and said, proudly, "My papa took me camping last summer and he taught me how to do this." His smile faded a little and he continued, "He wouldn't let me light it though. He told me it was too dangerous with the stuff poured on it."

Emma smiled inside, and taking the lighter fluid, she

said, "It is kind of dangerous. I'll let you squirt the fluid on and then I'll light it, how about that?"

The boy beamed at her and nodded enthusiastically, so Emma showed him how and he, surprisingly, did just as she said.

"Now stand over there," she pointed behind her, "and I'll throw a match on it."

She waited while Esteban stepped over to the couch. Turning back to the fireplace, she tore a corner off the charcoal bag and lit the end. She then tossed it on the charcoal and stepped back as it flared. After a moment the fire waned and she knew it would be a few minutes while it burned down, and she had an idea.

She glanced over to her friends, then grabbed the flashlight and motioned to the boy. He tilted his head, puzzled, then followed her back to the garage. Emma was a little excited thinking about what she hoped she'd find and as they went to the front of the garage, she mentally crossed her fingers.

Arriving at the front corner, Emma reached down and laid her hand on the chest freezer she had glimpsed when she was here earlier. Hesitating slightly, she then yanked up on the lid and nearly yanked her shoulder out of its socket. Looking closer, she saw it had a lock. She looked around and saw a pry tool on a shelf. She grabbed it up and began trying to pry open the lid. She stopped to catch her breath and was about to redouble her efforts when something dangled in front of her face. Startled, she jerked back before she realized it was a key. With her eyes she followed the arm that held the key and saw Esteban standing next to her, smiling. She realized it must be the key to the freezer and she asked, grinning, "Where did you find it?"

The boy said shyly, "On that post next to the shelves." She fluffed the boy's hair and dropping the bar she took the key from him. Inserting it in the lock, she quickly turned it, not giving herself a chance to think about it.

The key turned smoothly and she lifted the lid. Both of them leaned in and looked. Emma saw she was right and there were several packs of butcher-paper-wrapped meat with writing on them. Quickly, she pushed the limp, soggy top packs away to reach the packs in the middle. They would be the ones still edible. Handing the flashlight to Esteban, she leaned back in and, perusing the writing, she grabbed five packs and lifted them out. They were sizable and, nodding to herself she closed the lid back but didn't bother locking it.

"He is interested," Esteban said.

Perplexed, Emma stopped short and looked at the boy.

Seeing her confusion, Esteban pointed down at Emma's feet. Emma looked and saw Bella, with twinkling eyes, ogling the meat packs.

Understanding now, Emma said, "It's a girl and Bella's her name."

Next, she addressed the cat, "And no, you can't have any. Not right now anyway. We'll see about later if you behave yourself."

Before striding off, Emma caught the puzzled look

that Esteban passed from her to Bella. She smirked to herself because she was used to that.

Arriving back in the living room, Emma saw that Lori was about to open the first can. Startling everyone she yelled, "STOP!"

It shocked Lori so bad, she dropped the can of soup and it rolled under the couch.

While Esteban retrieved it, Emma rushed over and embraced Lori saying, "Sorry, sorry! I didn't mean to scare you! It's just I found this meat in a freezer and wanted to save the cans."

"Jesus Christ, Emma!" Lori expelled, "You scared the living shit out of me! You could have given me a heart attack or, or," she looked around, fishing for something to say when Bryan spoke up.

"Well, I nearly pissed myself!"

This gave everyone pause and then they all burst out laughing, relieving the tension of the day.

Lori recovered first, sucking in her breath and grabbing Emma's shoulders. "Oh my God! Did you say meat?"

Emma nodded happily and showed them the five thick sirloin steaks she found in the freezer. Arturo was coming down the stairs, drying his hair. Esteban saw him first and went running to him. "Papa! Papa! Ms. Emma found some steaks!"

The man paused and fluffed his son's hair. Winking at the friends he said seriously to the boy, "What kind? Dinosaur?"

Rolling his eyes, Esteban said sternly, "No, Papa, you

know, cows...steaks!"

Arturo chuckled and continued to the fireplace, where Emma had placed the steaks on the grate. He looked over her shoulder for a moment with appreciation then, saying nothing, he went into the kitchen. The friends all looked at each other in puzzlement but soon went back to their work. Bryan went rummaging around in the garage for a lantern, while Lori was going through the bags for something to go with the steaks. Meanwhile, Emma was adjusting the grate so they wouldn't burn the steaks. Arturo came back from the kitchen with a couple of pans and a basket full of something.

"You can't have unseasoned steaks," he announced as he placed the basket full of spices down. "And you've got to have something to go with them." As he said this last, he reached in the basket past the spices and brought out two cans of diced potatoes.

Emma's mouth was watering as she stared at the potatoes and smelled the meat, just beginning to cook.

Arturo reached past the women, seeing they were frozen, and, grinning, grabbed the can opener from Lori.

Emma glanced at her friends to see their reaction and noticed Bryan had taken up his crossbow and again stood watch at the window. She hadn't even heard him return. Emma absently noted to herself that they were all changing, becoming more wary and a lot stealthier. She realized the human race had the ability buried deep inside them. It just took something like this to bring it out. Berating herself for being maudlin, she stood up and grabbed the spices from Arturo. He seemed a little surprised but let it go. Besides, he was busy making potatoes. He added a dollop of butter, which hadn't yet gone bad, to the pan and it sizzled enticingly. He then added some onion powder, dash of garlic, pepper and salt.

Emma retrieved the onion powder and pepper from him and added it to the seasoned salt she'd already sprinkled on the meat. Using a fork that Arturo had also brought from the kitchen, Emma poked at the meat absently as she gathered her thoughts. After supper, she'd get out the maps and check their route to Tennessee. They'd have to stay off the main interstate because other people would probably be using it now and she wanted to avoid any possible confrontations.

She realized the meat was done on one side and used the fork to flip them. A movement caught her eye at the window. Bryan had lit the lamp and was now pulling the heavy curtains closed around the room. Lori was helping Arturo with the potatoes and setting out bread. Esteban was petting Bella and Bella had a kitty smile on her face. The attention hog was eating that up. Smiling herself, Emma got up and went to the kitchen for some plates and utensils. She returned and removed the steaks from the fire. She took the steaks over to Lori and Arturo saying, "It's ready."

The mouthwatering aroma had filled the room and despite being very warm, she could tell the group seemed more chipper. They gathered around and doled out the food. Bryan quickly returned to the window to be lookout and Lori followed with her plate. That left Emma and the

Hispanics in a circle on the living room floor. Silence reined as they began to eat and Emma closed her eyes in appreciation as she took her first juicy bite of steak and potatoes. Warm juice trickled down her chin and she caught it with a paper towel Arturo had brought from the kitchen. The seasoned potatoes were perfect and went great with the sliced bread. The surreal setting hit her all at once and she realized that on any other day, she would have either been working at the hospital or working out in her apartment. It made her a little sad but she wasn't about to let it bring her down. The meal was absolutely delicious and she thanked Arturo and Lori for the potatoes. Esteban was sopping up the rest of the meat juice with his bread and Emma cut off a couple of small steak pieces for Bella. Bella sat down daintily and promptly finished them off, then looked a question at Emma.

"That's all the steak I'm giving you, but I'll find some cat food and a bit of water." Emma said.

She didn't notice the strange looks she got from the boy and his father, but Lori had.

"She talks to Bella all the time. Emma found her when she was a baby and they've been inseparable ever since," Lori stated.

As she talked, Esteban reached down and petted Bella's head. Bella started purring and Emma smiled as she reached into her bag for some cat food and doled it out to the feline. She then poured some water from her canteen onto her empty plate and set that before Bella.

Emma turned back to her bag and removed the map.

Seeing what she was doing, the rest of the group gathered around as she spread it out.

Arturo tapped Bryan's shoulder and held out his hand for the rifle. Bryan understood and, nodding, he slung it off his shoulder and handed it over. Arturo checked it over and walked to the corner of the window.

Emma had finished smoothing the map and said, "Okay. I'm pretty sure we're about here." She rested her finger on the map in the general vicinity of Kennesaw Mountain.

Bryan reached over and moved the lantern closer to them.

Emma continued, "I don't think we should be on a major road, so we need to figure out a route following a less used one. This road here," she said as she followed Georgia 411 with her finger northward, "is the road I want to take. It goes all the way to Pigeon Forge and I'm hoping we'll avoid most of the people."

She glanced up and caught a look of relief and agreement cross Lori's face and she knew the tiny woman was thinking about the incident earlier. Rushing on to take her friend's mind off the event, she continued, "We should sleep here tonight and rotate guards and get an early start in the morning. It should cool off a bit tonight so Lori and I are going upstairs and open some windows. Is that good with you, girl?" she asked her friend and in response Lori stood and smiled.

Bryan spoke up and said, "I'll open these down here a crack too."

Everyone was exhausted, so without a word, they all

headed off to sleep, all except Arturo, who stood guard first.

As Lori and Emma headed upstairs, Lori said to Emma, "Do you really think everything's going to be okay?"

Emma didn't want to lie to her friend, so putting on a brave face she looked at her in the glow of the flashlight and said, "We're going to do everything we can to be careful, and there is strength in numbers. We were lucky to come across Arturo. I feel we can trust him, don't you?"

Lori nodded enthusiastically and piped up, "They already feel like part of our group."

They'd reached the top of the stairs and walking into the bedroom was like walking into a wall of heat. "Wow!" Emma said, "Let's get these windows open."

As they opened the windows and made ready for sleep, they talked about how their lives had been changed forever and then, Lori asked Emma to finish telling her about Jack and as Emma filled Lori in about the rest of her one true love, little did they know, a thousand miles away, Jack Denton was in a struggle himself.

14

Ray and his little group had hiked all night and were exhausted. He shielded his flashlight and quickly flashed it on over his watch. It was 4:12 in the morning. The tree cover had been dwindling, but as long as they traveled at night it hadn't been a problem. Now, however, they had to find cover before daylight. He looked around, warily, and seeing no obvious threat, breathed a slight sigh of relief. They'd had a run-in with some wolves a few miles back and if it hadn't been for Greg's using some leftover chicken as a distraction and running for their lives, they'd probably still be stuck in trees waiting out the wolves.

He turned to his group and asked Cat if she felt like scouting for a side canyon or place to hide.

"Sure, Ray, it beats waiting here for the wolves to catch up."

He heard a snicker trying to be covered by a cough, coming from Greg's position and quickly narrowed his eyes that way.

Greg looked sheepishly at Ray who slowly slid his eyes back to Cat who was grinning playfully.

'Glad they've still got their sense of humor,' he thought to himself.

"Anyway," he said, purposefully, "we need to find a place to hole up before the sun comes up and people start moving around. I figure we're close to that little town of Gardiner and I'd like to avoid any contact."

Serious once again, Cat nodded and said, "I'll range out west of the road first, since the town's on the other side, and see what I can find."

Ray nodded and pointed to some scrawny brush up against a canyon wall. "We'll be over there."

As Cat started to leave, Ray said under his breath to her, "*Don't get caught.*"

Winking back at him, to let him know she'd heard, Cat quickly and quietly took off to the Southwest.

Watching for a second, Ray then turned and started toward the brush. As they came around the side of it, a flurry of motion startled Ray and Greg. Ray wouldn't have believed what he saw happen next if he hadn't seen it with his own eyes.

Kuan reacted to a rabbit as it was flushed from the brush. With lightning speed, he grabbed the rabbit by the neck and in one smooth motion had quickly snapped its neck.

Still in a crouch from being startled, the two other men glanced quickly at one another with amazed eyes.

Slowly the two men rose and Kuan handed the rabbit over to Greg, "It is always wise to use all the resources at your fingertips." He looked at the rabbit and quirked one smooth eyebrow. "No pun intended."

Greg just shook his head and looked at the hare.

Ray looked more appraising at Kuan and thought he needed to be more careful of this man's speed.

Looking at Greg, Ray asked, "You know how to skin that thing?"

Greg snorted and said, "Of course, went hunting with my dad."

"Well, I think we're around another bend from that

next town, so we're probably safe from prying eyes or noses. Let's cook some hot breakfast."

Greg grinned like a little kid and set to skinning the rabbit.

Kuan sat down with his back against an outcropping of rock and appeared to sleep. Ray looked over at a lone tree that looked dead from getting hit by lightning and holstering his gun, went to gather wood. He made sure to keep a sharp eye and ear out for any trouble. They should be safe from the wolves since they were out of their territory, but one never knew about wild animals.

After gathering the wood, he took it back to where Greg was just finishing up with the hare. He had the remains gathered neatly in a bundled up handkerchief. "You want to take that far away from here," he said with a serious glance and handed it to Ray.

Ray took the leavings off along the canyon wall and when he came to a large rock, he dug a hole a few inches deep and shoved the rock over it, covering all evidence of the slaughtered rabbit. When he got back to the brush, he saw Greg had the meat spitted and over a small, contained fire.

"I'm going to watch out, in case anyone smells it."

Greg nodded in agreement and turned the spit.

Ray went off into the darkness and Greg sat back to watch the fire. After a moment he glanced over at Kuan to see if he was really sleeping. When he saw Kuan was awake, he asked him, "How did you do that?"

Kuan looked over at Greg and taking a breath said softly, "I was taught by a master. He taught me how to be fast with my reflexes."

Greg waited for Kuan to say more but it seemed that's all he wanted to say.

Greg turned the spit a little farther and pondered this enigmatic man.

After a while, Ray came back with Cat in tow and rounded the brush with Cat breathing heavily.

Greg had snatched at his gun but then eased it back in the holster.

"Cat says she found a cave about a half-mile up the road and off the beaten path. As soon as we eat we'll check it out. It's going to be light soon and I want to be holed up by then. Besides, I know we need sleep."

Greg nodded and Cat slumped down against the canyon wall, down a ways from Kuan. It was obvious to everyone that she still didn't trust him. Greg surmised that Ray must have told Cat about Kuan and the hare, since she didn't look surprised about it. He got some paper towels out and took the rabbit from the spit and split it up into four portions and gave them out. Everyone was hungry, even Kuan, and they set to blowing on and eating their breakfast. Greg could tell Ray was keeping an eye out for danger, so he went ahead and pushed dirt on the fire, dousing it.

Ray nodded approval to him and Greg gave him a thumbs up.

After they'd finished and wiped their hands, they loaded up and Cat led the way with Ray coming next and Greg bringing up the rear. They all felt a little better after the meal and quietly made their way to the cave. It was on the opposite side of the canyon and was easy to see if you were looking for it.

As they reached it, Ray motioned everyone to stay as he stepped into the entrance.

Greg turned his back to the cave and kept a lookout towards the road.

He heard a click and realized Ray had switched on his flashlight.

Not hearing the roar of a bear shortly after was encouraging.

After a few minutes, Ray came back and waved them in. As they eased into the cave mouth, they could see that the roof of the cave at the mouth was about eight feet tall and slanted back fifteen feet, then abruptly ended three feet above the floor at a solid granite back. It was roughly twelve feet wide and at the back there were some animal bones of some animal who obviously hadn't been fast enough. At least they were old.

After shining the light around, Ray turned back to the group and said, "I'd like to try to find some brush to cover the mouth of the cave up somewhat before it gets any lighter outside. Cat, could you check around the inside closer to make sure I didn't miss anything? Greg and I will make quick work of the camouflage."

Cat nodded and they moved off to their separate jobs. Kuan eased himself down quietly just past the entrance and let his bags down. The team was soon finished with their chores and none too soon as the sun peeked over the eastern mountains. They were too tired to say anything more and with just a small rustling around they rolled into their beds and fell asleep. Ray remembered thinking as he was drifting off that they should post a guard, but then he thought they had covered the entrance extremely well. Besides, anyone trying to get past his barricade would make so much noise they'd be walking in to three gun barrels by the time they got in. After that, he was gone.

Ray woke with a start and realized that some noise had startled him. He lay perfectly still and waited for whatever woke him to repeat itself. After a few moments, he heard the unmistakable sound of gunfire some ways off. He quickly sat up and pulling out the map, held it up to the green glow shining through the branches and calculated quickly in his head. He hoped to God he was wrong, but it sounded like about the same distance and direction as he had thought the small town of Gardiner, Montana, would be. His moving around had awoken the others and Kuan was the only one not moving around. He was just silently looking at Ray. Ray dismissed him and glanced at his team. They were looking at him with puzzlement and he quickly pointed to his ear and out the cave mouth. Again, the gunfire came in short bursts and Cat and Greg looked up at Ray in alarm.

Ray grimaced because they all realized at the same time that they would have to investigate. This was a canyon and they would probably be seen going by the town. It was too much to hope that they would escape notice, and they couldn't waste any more time sitting until nightfall.

Ray gauged the gunfire was far enough away they could talk, so he stood up and said, "Let's get ready to roll. As much as I hate to, we've got to find out who's shooting the gun or guns and put a stop to it."

Greg sighed heavily and stated, "I knew we wouldn't be able to avoid trouble again." Pulling out his gun, he checked it over and slid it home. "Not this group! Seems every time we do something, everything turns to shit."

Ray looked over at Greg and said, "What? You want to live forever?" with a mock sneer. Cat said, "You guys! Jesus, we just need to find out what the hell is going on out there!"

She slapped her own magazine home for emphasis. And then stared sternly at Ray and Greg both.

Greg shrugged at Ray who shook his head.

Turning serious after another burst of gunfire in the distance, Ray told Greg, "You two wait here and let me scout how many are firing. Give me twenty minutes, which should do it. If I'm not back make contingency plans."

With that, Ray slipped through the brush covering the mouth of the cave and disappeared into the growing gloom.

He jogged quietly toward the scant bursts of gunfire until he came to a slight rise, indicating the road they had crossed before dawn. He had his gun out and eased up to the edge of the road, keeping his head down. He hadn't heard any shooting for a bit, so was unsure of what to expect. Just as his eyes came level with the road, a sound like an angry wasp whizzed off to his right followed by a gunshot report. He ducked back down, thinking he'd been seen. Then, with his heart pounding, he heard more bursts of gunfire and he could tell they were very close. He also realized that someone seemed to be shooting at random, not shooting at him because they saw him. This brought a brief wave of relief until someone grabbed his arm. He jerked around with a curse and landed on his back with his gun stuck into Cat's nose.

Quickly, he let up on the trigger and swept her down beside him, "Dammit! You of all people should know better than that!"

Her eyes were still wide, but then he could see her visibly getting control of herself. "I told Greg I was coming out here to help, since we didn't know how many people are shooting! I told him to just hang tight," she hissed in a whisper.

The gunfire was still sporadic and as Ray opened his mouth to say something to her, the most unbelievable, unexpected thing happened.

They heard a voice yell out somewhere beyond the gunfire, "HEY LADY, PUT THAT DAMN GUN DOWN. WE JUST WANT TO PASS BY! WE'RE NOT HERE TO HURT YOU!"

Ray and Cat turned to each other and stared dumbly: it was Jason! What the hell was he doing here? They slowly grinned at each other with the dawning realization that, potentially, this part of their mission was over. Then another thought came to Ray. Who was wielding the gun?

They would have to stop them from shooting before they could get to Jason. He saw Cat had the same thought as she nodded at him.

Ray held a fist up, motioning her to stay still. He then eased back up to the edge of the road.

As his head came level with the asphalt, his eyes took in the scene while his mind tried to process it.

There was an overturned RV as well as a stalled station wagon right next to it. Glass was scattered across the road. Ray waited out another burst of gunfire aimed back at Jason's voice. He could vaguely see a head with long gray hair bobbing around between the vehicles. He could also hear soft sobbing sounds and as he eased back down beside Cat, he knew why his boss hadn't taken the woman out. This woman must be out of her mind. With everything that's happened, most people would be hard-pressed to stay sane at all. He whispered what he figured out to Cat and saw understanding dawn in her eyes. She placed her hand on Ray's chest and said, "Let me try something, Ray."

He didn't want to let her, but seeing the pleading in her face, he relented. She saw something in his eyes and before he knew what happened, she tenderly leaned over and brushed her lips against his. This shocked him to his toes and before he could respond, she had scooted up the rise and raced to the edge of the RV.

The shooter must have caught the motion, because she let loose a barrage of gunfire right at where Cat had been just one second before. Ray thought his heart was going to pound out of his chest as he eagerly waited to see any sign from Cat. Then relief swept over him as he saw her with her back against the underside of the RV and her gun raised next to her head. She then turned to him and, smiling, winked her right eye. Ray couldn't believe it! The crazy woman.

He shook his head and watched. Cat eased up to the edge of the vehicle and quickly darted a look around the edge and then back. The woman must not have seen, she didn't shoot.

Cat looked back at Ray and raised one finger.

Okay, Ray understood, the woman shooter was alone.

Right then, Ray was startled again as a hand grabbed his shoulder. He whipped around with his gun, and saw Greg looking in amazement past him at Cat.

"Do you or Cat, either one, listen to me?" he asked, with anger and resignation.

"We do when we need to," Greg mumbled distractedly.

Ray saw Kuan about twenty feet behind Greg watching on with slight interest.

Ray dismissed him and quickly turned back to the events playing out.

Glancing quickly back at his charge to make sure he hadn't moved, Greg asked, "What's she doing?"

Ray quickly filled him in and then as they watched, Cat spoke up just loud enough for the crazy woman to hear her, "Ma'am? My name is Cat and I'm a friend. We're with the government and we don't want to hurt you. We want to help you. Why are you trying to hurt us?"

The woman had quit sobbing and gibbering while Cat talked, and she had as yet to start back up. Ray held his breath as the tension mounted.

Finally the woman spoke in a quiet quivering voice that Ray and Greg had to strain to hear. "Are you really the Feds or are you lying?"

Cat didn't bat an eye at the woman's misunderstanding. "Yes, ma'am, we're the Feds. I am agent Catherine Simmons and my fellow agents and I want to help you and understand what's happened to you. What's your name, honey?"

The woman paused long enough to make Ray antsy but then he could hear her start to cry softly in a different tone. It was relief! The woman sounded relieved. She then spoke to Cat again, "I don't want that man that's been yelling at me to come in, just you."

Cat looked over at Ray and tilted her head to where Jason's voice had come from. Ray nodded curtly at her and turned to Greg. "Look, Jason's here. I'm going over to fill him in. You and Kuan STAY here and cover Cat. This time I mean it." He mock growled at the young agent.

Greg looked up at his superior innocently, but then turned serious, "I will Ray." He said seriously.

Ray nodded back, and with another quick glance at Kuan, who hadn't seemed to move, he ducked down along the shoulder of the road and jogged toward where he'd last heard Jason's voice. The green haze of the growing light made the features of the ground deceptive and Ray had to be careful of his footing. After about twenty yards, he eased up along the edge of the road and peeked over. He saw an old black Dodge pickup about ten yards further on sitting sideways in the road with the front of the bumper pointing to his side of the road. Puzzled, he looked all around but there was nothing and no one else. In a voice low enough that he wouldn't be heard by the inhabitants of the RV, Ray said, "Jason!"

He instantly heard a rattle of pebbles behind the old Dodge as someone moved.

"Jason, is that you behind the truck?"

A thatch of dark hair poked slightly out behind the front bumper, along with the nose of a handgun.

"Shit, Ray? Is that you? Get over here before that batty old woman starts shooting again!"

Ray didn't bother to tell him what was going on; he'd tell him when he got behind cover.

Looking back at the RV and feeling confident that Cat had it under control, Ray climbed to the top of the road and skittered over behind the truck.

When he got there, he had a surprise. There was another man beside Jason. The man was at least six feet, with short blonde hair and emerald green eyes staring back at him with shocking intensity. Ray knew right away this could be a dangerous man and looked questioningly back at his commander.

Jason saw the look and said impatiently, "Ray, this is Jack Denton, the man in Cody I had to go see when the shit hit the fan. Jack, meet Ray Burch, my top agent."

The man stuck his hand out to Ray with such

swiftness, Ray almost didn't see him move. Ray shook his hand as Jack said, "Nice to meet someone who can put up with this crotchety old man longer than five minutes." He finished by adding a quirk to one side of his mouth that Ray took to be a smile.

Ray smiled back and said, "Likewise." They were going to get along fine.

Jason grumbled something to the two of them, then got back to the subject.

"We've got a crazy old lady holed up in that RV and we just got here about twenty minutes ago. When we got here, she just started shooting away, for no reason. I've tried to reason with her, but every time I say something, she just starts firing that automatic rifle!" He looked over at Ray. "Any suggestions?"

Ray answered, "Cat's up there now trying to talk her down. The lady let Cat go in behind the RV about ten minutes ago. From our side, she sounded scared. You know Cat, behind all that tough exterior, she's a softie. We should hear something shortly. I say we just hang tight."

Both men were just looking over at him.

Denton said, "Cat?"

Both the other men realized at the same time that Jack didn't know Agent Simmons, but Jason spoke first. "It's the female member of the team. She's clever, fast, and sharp as a tack." He looked at Ray then. "And, as Agent Burch put it, she has one flaw, in my opinion, she does have a soft heart. It's one of the reasons I almost didn't pick her for this mission. Of course, now it might turn out that's just what we needed."

Ray saw Denton nod out of the corner of his eye then turn back with his rifle and watch the RV.

Something dawned on Ray and he looked at the two men.

"Wait a minute! How did you two get this far so fast?"

Jason looked at the agent strangely, for a minute, then understanding settled on his face along with a slow smile.

"We drove here," he said, deadpan.

Behind Jason, Jack continued to watch the RV but shook his head, silently.

Ray dismissed the man and looked back at Jason, "You what? I know for a fact, you could not have driven here!"

Jason took mercy on his agent and said, "Well, you're right. If you try to start a newer car it wouldn't work. But, Jack and I realized that cars made in our day didn't have computer chips and so we took a gamble and tried to start one of Jack's neighbor's trucks, and voila!" here, he gestured at the Dodge, "It worked!"

Ray stepped back, looked at the pickup, and without thinking said, "This old thing?"

"That's no way to talk about the transportation that's going to get us where we need to be!" he said, mock sternly. "Besides," he said, on a more serious note, "it's all we've got."

Ray took another look at the truck and on second thought, guessed it to be the most beautiful thing he'd ever seen. If it ran.

"Hey!" Jack hissed, "Here they come."

The men looked over the hood to see Cat and the woman, who was still sobbing, walking slowly towards them. It bode well that Cat's arm was around the older lady's shoulder and she was talking softly to her. Behind Cat, Ray caught a glance of motion and realized that Greg had moved up to where Cat had been behind the RV. Realizing that Greg could see him, Ray held up a fist telling Greg to hold there. Greg gave a slight nod and Ray turned his attention back to the women. Studying the older woman, Ray saw she was dirty and had cuts and bruises over the parts of her body he could see. He surmised she must have been in the RV when it crashed. That means she must have been out here for a few days. Jack must have realized the same thing. Ray noticed the man moving towards the truck cab and saw him reach in to get a backpack. Smoothly, he removed a canteen and some rolled towels. He finished this just as the women arrived. The men all kept their distance as Cat eased the woman down on a camp chair Jason had retrieved.

"These are my friends, Sheila. They're Feds too."

The woman named Sheila glanced up quickly at the faces surrounding her and stated in a tiny voice, "I'm sorry I shot at you. I was just so scared and lost without Gerald." She looked back down at her hands in her lap and Cat filled in the rest.

Apparently, Gerald was her husband and had been driving the RV when the E-day event occurred. Cat said the man must have had a heart attack and swerved across the road and eventually turned the monstrous vehicle over. At the time, Sheila was all the way in the back of the vehicle and when it turned over, she had been tossed around pretty good.

Jack softly interrupted, once, to ask, "Sheila, did your husband have a pacemaker?"

She looked up quickly at Jack, then back down at her lap, then slowly nodded her head.

Ray looked quizzically at Jason who gave him a brief shake of the head.

Jack handed the canteen and towels to Cat and said quietly so as not to disturb the older woman, "There's food wrapped in the towels. Why don't you get her settled down with some food and water and hopefully she'll calm down a little more."

Cat looked at Denton suspiciously.

Jason saw Cat's reaction and said, "It's okay, Cat, he's one of us. His name's Jack Denton."

A strange look came in her eye. She quickly covered it but not before Ray had seen. The other two men didn't notice.

"Thanks," she said as she took the proffered items.

Ray made a mental note to ask her about it later. Jason motioned Ray and Jack to the other end of the truck and when they had assembled there he spoke. "Same thing as before, Jack?"

Jack nodded and said, "Yeah, pacemaker quit, then, well, then the heart quits."

Ray caught Jason's attention and told him he was going to get Greg and Kuan.

"Sounds good, Ray. You all come around the back side of the truck here so we don't frighten the woman."

Nodding, Ray turned and quickly strode to where he last saw Greg. Greg saw him and waited.

"What's going on?" he asked.

Ray motioned toward the truck. As they walked, Ray replied, "Some older lady whose husband had a heart attack and flipped the RV. She went a little crazy. That's all. Understandable under the circumstances. Cat talked her down and now they're getting her some food and water." Ray looked over to check on Kuan. He had followed them and now stood serenely, leaning on his staff.

About that time, Jason walked up and said, "It's good to see you in one piece. How much trouble did you have?" He addressed all this to Ray and Ray saw Greg start to open his mouth and say something smart until Ray frowned at him. Greg promptly closed his mouth and turned away, but not before Ray caught him grinning. Jason caught some of the exchange and lifted an eyebrow at Ray.

"I'll be here with Kuan. Why don't you go through the station wagon and see what you can find, Greg," Ray told the young agent. He knew it would keep the young man busy and possibly out of trouble. Greg nodded to him and went to the vehicle.

Turning to Jason, Ray saw he was still looking at him. "Young guys," Ray said with a shrug. This seemed to pacify Jason because he went on. "I'm glad you got the target," he said, stepping up to Kuan.

"I'm standing right in front of you, sir, and I can speak and understand perfect English." This came softly from Dai Ji Kuan.

Turning to Ray, Jason had a sheepish smile before he turned back and addressed the slender Chinese, "I'm sorry, Mr. Kuan, it's been quite an adventure these last few days but that is no excuse to forget my manners. Welcome to the United States and thank you for agreeing to help us with this problem. Now I think it's a bit more problematic." Jason started to turn away but Kuan snagged his sleeve, "I don't believe those were the correct words used. I said I would come over and see what could be done to alleviate ALL the problems." Jason looked at the man quizzically for a moment then smiled and nodded. He remembered, now, that the Chinese were sticklers on perfection and this man was just correcting Jason in his wording.

"Yes, of course." he replied and turned back to Ray. Ray was splitting his attention between Greg going through the station wagon and Cat over by the truck.

Jason said, "I'm going to see how the old woman is doing and try to get her to let us go through her RV for supplies."

Ray watched as Jason walked toward the truck and it took him a moment to register the fact that all of a sudden Jason was on the ground, writhing. Then he heard the report and realized Jason had been shot! He grabbed for Kuan then realized the man was already diving for cover, next to him, by the truck. Ray looked over at the station wagon and saw Greg's face twisted in concentration and his pistol aimed out toward the sound of the gunshots. Glancing back toward the back of the Dodge, he saw Cat had also moved quickly and had shielded the older woman at the back of the truck, also away from the shooter. Ray couldn't see Jack. Then he saw movement under the truck as Jack reached out and grabbed Jason's arm and quickly dragged him under the pickup and against the inside part of the left rear tire. The older woman had started crying again.

Another shot rang out and the front windshield of the station wagon shattered, blowing glass all over Greg's back as he ducked just before it happened. Ray heard muffled oaths coming from Greg's position and he smiled grimly at himself at Greg's spunk. Sobering at the current situation, Ray looked back over the scene and mentally planned what to do next.

Before he could act, however, another shot rang out and Ray flinched but then relaxed when nothing happened. He heard a scream out away from their ring of cars and glanced over at Cat, who had a surprised look on her face. She then shrugged.

Ray glanced at where he could see Jack working on Jason. He was just about to call out to him when a young girl's voice yelled from out beyond Ray's vision, "I GOT HIM! YOU CAN COME OUT NOW!"

Greg raised an eyebrow to Ray and Ray shook his head back at him curtly. He didn't believe right off the bat that they were saved that easy.

"COME OUT AND SHOW YOURSELF!" he yelled into the green gloom.

Ray could see Cat peeking out toward where the voice had come from and saw her tense, indicating she was watching something. She raised her gun and tracked whoever it was that was approaching. He glanced back at Greg and held up a fist telling him to stay put. Keeping the Dodge between himself and the incoming figure, he ran in a squat to the bed of the truck and carefully peeked over.

Walking in from a line of scrub brush was a young teenage girl. She was wearing jeans, boots and a button up shirt and ball cap. She appeared, to Ray, to be about fourteen or fifteen years old. She walked confidently to the front of the truck and, reversing the handgun, simply handed it to Cat as she looked steadily into the woman's eyes. "Good riddance," the girl stated. She then collapsed at Cat's feet.

Ray almost reached her to catch her before she hit the dirt, but didn't quite make it. The first thing he noticed was that she weighed next to nothing. The second thing was that she seemed to be covered in bruises. He gently laid her on the ground then took his jacket off and placed it under her head. Sheila had quit crying and seemed to take an intense interest in the young girl and took over from Ray. She lifted the canteen and gently started to tend to the teenager.

Ray turned away and quickly headed toward where Jack had dragged Jason out from under the truck. Jason was pale but seemed in pretty good condition. Jack had torn open the shirt over Jason's left bicep and was digging in his backpack for a first-aid kit. Ray leaned over and said, "How's he doing?"

Jason opened his eyes and said, between gritted teeth, "I'm shot in the arm, I'm not on my deathbed."

"That answers my question well enough," Ray spoke up. He noticed a clean, bloody hole through the muscle in Jason's upper arm. He then turned back to see if the girl had come back around. He saw she had and Cat and Sheila were trying to talk to her.

Greg had come over to Ray from the station wagon and now asked, "You want me to go out and check the shooter?"

"Yeah, just be careful, in case she didn't finish the job." Ray said.

Greg nodded and silently disappeared. Ray glanced back at Jack tending Jason before going over to the women. When he got there, Ray saw that Cat was trying to slow the girl down from guzzling the water.

Cat finally got the canteen of water from her and asked gently, "What's your name?"

"Ashley," the girl answered, shakily. Ray stayed quiet so as not to spook the girl and let Cat take the lead.

As he knew she would, Cat started with the easy questions. "What's your last name, Ashley?"

"Cook, my name's Ashley Cook." Her voice was getting stronger and Ray could tell this little waif had a lot of spunk.

She returned Cat's look and asked, "Do you have anything to eat? I haven't eaten in a couple of days."

This startled Cat and she said, "Sure, honey, let me go get you something. You just sit right here. Nobody's going to bother you, okay?"

Ashley nodded and eased her back up against the side of the old Dodge, wincing as the bruises brushed against the metal.

Cat got up and tilted her head at Ray as she started walking around to the bed of the truck.

When they reached the back, Ray saw that Jack had just finished up a nice looking field dressing on Jason's arm and Jason had ripped the sleeves off his shirt and was gingerly slipping on his jacket.

"What's the story with her?" Jason asked Cat.

"Not sure yet. Her name is Ashley Cook and she hasn't eaten for a couple days. I was going to see if you had some food to give her before I talked to her some more."

As Cat said this, Ray looked around for Kuan and spotted him standing between the truck and the station wagon, leaning on his staff.

Ray brought his attention back to the conversation and heard Jack telling Cat, "Sure, we have some ham biscuits in that light brown satchel in the truck bed."

Cat thanked him and stepped over to the truck whipping out her flashlight and shielding the face. She rummaged in the truck bed, grabbed the satchel, and Ray followed her back to the girl.

As they reached her, they saw Sheila was sitting next to her and they were quietly talking. Ray thought Sheila seemed a lot better, but, then, it could just be wishful thinking.

Ray pushed these thoughts aside as he returned his

attention to the girl. 'Ashley,' he thought to himself, 'I have to remember her name is Ashley.'

Cat eased herself down next to Ashley and the girl tiredly smiled at her. Cat reached into the satchel and brought out two biscuits and handed one to Sheila and one to Ashley. Sheila looked confused for a minute then beamed at Cat and thanked her. Cat smiled and said, "You're welcome."

As Cat and Ray turned their attention back to Ashley, they saw she had already taken a huge bite but was chewing slowly with her eyes closed, and Ray could see she was savoring every morsel.

As they were waiting for her to finish eating, Ray caught movement out of the corner of his eye and saw Greg walking up to him.

Greg was looking over at Cat and Ashley and carrying a rifle. When he got to him, Ray asked, "What'd you find?"

"Middle aged man, scruffy looking, had this .22 rifle and a handful of ammo in his pocket."

Ray waited for him to say more and when he didn't he turned his gaze back to Ashley.

"I guess we'll have to wait and see what the girl has to say."

Jack and Jason joined Greg and Ray, and quietly Ray filled them in.

"Sure glad it was a .22 or I'd have had a hard time tying my shoes," Jason said with a frown.

"You're lucky it went clean through," Jack stated.

Jason ignored him and asked Ray, "What's the girl

say?"

Ray shrugged and said, "Not much. She has bruises all over and is thin as a rail. When she gets done Cat will find out what's going on."

Jason nodded and motioned the other men to the other side of the Dodge. Once they got there, he made sure they were out of earshot of Kuan and the women, and asked Ray to fill him in on their trip. Ray obliged and by the time he finished, Cat was walking over to them and Ray could see over her shoulder that the other two women were resting and seemed satisfied.

Ray raised his eyebrows in question to Cat and she sighed, "Looks like the man you probably found out there was Ashley's stepfather. Apparently he had been beating her and her mother for the last two years. I get the impression he's sexually abused her too, but she didn't say as much."

She put her hands on her hips and continued, "When the EMP bomb went off, it seems he went crazy and choked her mom to death during one of their arguments. Ashley didn't know this until she came out of hiding after he left. She found her mother on the floor in the kitchen. She said she didn't even notice what had happened to the power, the green sky, none of it. All she could think about was following her stepfather and killing him. She said she had just caught up to him and saw him shoot at Jason and that's when she shot him in the back of the head with one of his own guns."

Cat was sadly shaking her head as she said the last part. "She seems pretty calm now, but God only knows what's really going on under the surface."

Everybody was staring at the two women and Jason spoke up. "Well, shit. We can't leave them here."

Jack sighed, then said, "I have plenty of room at the ranch and people who can look after them until we can get this all figured out. Might as well bring them with us."

At this point Ray said matter-of-factly, "Anybody want to fill us in on where you all came from and where we're going next?"

The sun had been up for a bit by this time and even though the sky was still green, it didn't seem to bother the birds and they were singing all around the little group.

Jason looked at Ray and said, "We need to get going so let's load everybody up and I'll fill you in on the way. We're going to Jack's ranch in Cody." He winced as he moved his injured arm. "We'll have a few hours' drive to tell you all about it."

Ray nodded and the group broke up, preparing for the next leg of their trip.

Before getting into the driver's seat, Jack gazed longingly to the east towards Tennessee and mumbled under his breath, *"Come on, Emma, I feel you're still alive. Make it to Pigeon Forge and I'll come get you."*

With that said, he turned on his heel and climbed in the truck.

15

Emma rolled over in her sleep and her right hand flopped onto Lori's left injured cheek, eliciting a yelp from her friend. This brought Emma straight up in bed and she looked over at Lori and realized what had happened.

"Oh, Lori! I am so sorry! I am so used to sleeping by myself, I guess I spread out too much."

Lori was still gingerly holding her left cheek and sitting up in bed. "That's okay, it feels better today, but still kind of sore."

"Let's change the bandages and I'll put some more Neosporin on it."

Emma quickly got off the bed and looked around for her backpack before remembering that she had left it downstairs.

She smiled at Lori and said, "I gotta go down and get my bag, I'll be right back."

Lori smiled and nodded at her and began to change her clothes. Emma turned to the stairs and headed down. Before she left, she found herself glancing out the window to see if the sky was still green and saw it was. She sighed to herself as she descended the stairs but quickly smiled as she reached the bottom and saw Esteban petting Bella.

"I think she likes me, Emma!" he stated with excitement in his voice.

Emma smiled bigger and agreed, "She does indeed."

Happy to see the feline and young boy making friends, Emma went over to get her pack and saw Arturo repacking both his bags.

Emma saw some of the items he had out on the table and she walked over to get a closer look at them. Arturo didn't seem to mind her staring at the things and Emma whistled low at some of the items she saw.

"Nice!" she stated, as she took in the water filtering systems, para cord, flint sticks, and other survival gear.

She had seen these items before, and had planned on buying some online when she had enough money, but time had run out before she got a chance. She could see the items were very particular to doomsday preppers and she said as much to Arturo.

He agreed, saying, "Yes, I have been 'prepping' for a while now."

With an easy smile he continued, "You see, I have become one of those 'crazies' just like my customers. Looks like it was a good thing I did!"

Emma caught the humor in the Hispanic's voice and smiled good-naturedly with him. "I think me and my little group are VERY glad you are a prepper and that you have decided to come with us." Turning serious now, she stated, "Thank you, Arturo for being here."

The man made a mock bow and returned to packing his gear. Emma continued to her backpack and as she reached it, she saw Bryan coming out of the downstairs bathroom and stretching.

"One thing I already miss is a real bed," he stated.

Slinging her pack over her shoulder, Emma replied with a wan smile, "I feel guilty about you guys watching out for us all night, but I sure appreciate it. I'll take first watch tonight to make up for it, okay?"

Bryan did a mock eye roll and said with a sigh, "If you must!" and Emma playfully punched him in the arm on the way by.

She stopped next to Esteban and pulled out the antibiotic spray and tapped him on the shoulder.

He turned and saw the can and his shoulders sagged.

"Aw, come on buddy, you know we have to get that burn healed up. Just because it's doing better doesn't mean we give up and let it get infected, right?"

He smiled and rolled up his sleeve for Emma to spray his arm, and she could see it was a lot better.

"Wow! That's looking real good!" She praised him to help make him think of something else while she doused the wound with the spray can.

He hissed a bit in expectation of pain, then smiled up at her when he felt just the soothing liquid.

"It doesn't hurt like what my dad put on it!" He then glanced over at Arturo at about the same time the man looked up at them both and innocently said, "What? I only had Campho-Phenique!"

Emma looked at him funny for a moment, then remembered a paper she had to do on early antiseptic remedies in America and realized that, actually, the remedy was a great choice for antiseptic properties and that the phenol was used for the slight numbing of nerve endings and she slowly nodded her head.

"Not bad, Arturo, not bad."

He seemed to relax and smiled back at her. "My momma swore by the stuff, and Esteban seems to be better."

"That he is," Emma conceded.

She made a mental note to realize that they were going to have to use unconventional methods for everything from now on, not just treating wounds, and she would have to start thinking out of the box. If they came across a book store, maybe she would look for a book on home remedies or homesteading.

She realized Esteban had walked away during her musing, and she continued up the stairs to Lori.

As she reached the bedroom door, Emma saw that Lori had spiked her brunette hair up and was just finishing dressing, so she went on in and set her bag on the bed.

Pulling out the Neosporin, she told the little woman to sit down and removed the small bandage from her cheek.

"Ouch!" Lori hissed, then reached up and took the bandage from Emma.

"The tape hurts worse than the cut," she intoned.

Easing the bandage off the rest of the way, she looked at Emma apologetically.

"I'm sorry, it's feeling much better!" she said brightly.

Emma smiled gently at her friend and said, "That's good! Let me get a good look at it."

With that, Emma led Lori over to the window where she could have a little more light, albeit green light.

After leaning in with a serious look on her face and gently prodding to make sure there wasn't any pus,

Emma smiled at her friend and said, "You are looking good, sister! Let's just put some more on today and leave the bandage off so it dries out a bit and see how it is by tonight."

Her friend smiled gratefully at Emma and nodded.

As she finished tending to her friend, Emma glanced across the room and noticed a woman's watch shoved back behind a book. She stepped over and picked it up, noticing that it was a Swiss watch and it was still working. This made her raise her eyebrows and weighing her thoughts, she reached in her bag and brought out a small silver coin. Flipping it in the air, she caught it then gently placed it where the watch was.

Lori noticed and asked, "What was that for?"

Emma shrugged her shoulders and said, "I have no idea if the owners of the house will come back, but if they do, and notice the watch and food are gone, I want them to know that a moral group of people stayed here and my conscience will be clear knowing we paid for what we took."

Lori's eyebrows were furrowed and then they smoothed out as she seemed to understand.

Quietly she said, "You want to try to keep a semblance of civility," as she slowly nodded her head.

Emma slowly nodded back and smiled. "Yes, that's it exactly. We can't lose our souls in the process of changing."

Looking down at Lori, Emma saw she had on a baggy pair of sweats from the closet, a t-shirt, and a pair of her own tennis shoes that she must have gotten at the apartment before they left.

She saw Lori had her own bag on her shoulder and saw she was ready, so Emma swung her bag up and, grinning, said, "Let's go!"

Downstairs, they saw the guys were ready also so, without a word, Emma nodded and scooped Bella into her bag. They all headed out the door, warily, and ducked behind some low bushes.

After witnessing what had happened the previous evening, they wanted to make sure they were not observed. Emma glanced over at Arturo and saw he had some small binoculars out and was scanning the area. When he lowered them, he looked over at her and nodded. With a deep breath Emma stood up and started walking across the lawn away from the drive. The rest of the group followed with Bryan and his crossbow next to her and Arturo bringing up the rear. As someone who was familiar with the great outdoors, Emma trusted her ability to read how animals acted when humans were near. Judging from the birds in the nearby trees squawking and the chattering of faraway squirrels and other animal sounds, it was a good bet that there were no other humans close by. But it was always good to be doubly sure.

They came to a low fence that bordered the property and climbed over it, handing bags to each other until they were all over the top.

Emma found it interesting how a small group of people could come together cohesively in a crisis and was glad for everyone who was here.

They had decided to cut across to Highway 41 and to follow that north awhile until it came close to I-75 and then shadow I-75 North until they hit Highway 411. All of which had to be done with minimal human contact.

She looked up and noticed they were coming up to a road, so she gestured to her little group and hunkered down behind a large pine tree.

As everyone but Arturo gathered around, Emma dug out her trusty atlas and laid it on the ground.

Looking at it, and then looking around at the landscape, she pointed to a place on the map. "I think this is where we are, and that," she said, pointing to the far off road, "is 41."

Lori squinted into the gloom at where Emma was pointing, and Bryan just briefly nodded as Emma stuck the atlas back in her bag.

As they rose and got ready to step out from behind the trees, Emma noticed something and said, "Sh!" before dropping back down and waving her friends down. To their credit, everyone dropped down almost as quickly as Emma did and Bryan had his crossbow up to his eye, checking the perimeter. Nothing moved, but Emma kept her hands flattened to keep everyone down as she scanned the road.

"What'd you see?" Bryan breathed, right next to her shoulder.

Emma continued to watch the road as she lightly whispered back to him, "Nothing, there are no animal noises."

Emma could sense, rather than see, Bryan listening

to his surroundings and about two seconds later they saw movement on the road they had been headed for.

Their little group dropped completely flat on the ground as they all saw the movement at roughly the same time.

Quietly, Emma's group watched the group of people walking north and Emma noted that they were different from the group last night. The group last night were loud, unruly, and probably drunk, and they were dressed like thugs.

This group was smaller, had both men and women in the group, and were dressed similar to Emma's group. They were very quiet, seemed timid, and she could see that each member had some type of weapon, from handguns to baseball bats. She figured that they were a group just like her group trying to get somewhere safe. Mentally, she wished them well and waited as they disappeared below her field of view.

As they waited a few more seconds, Emma could hear the birds start to sing again and the insects start their chirruping. She sent up a mental thank you to God for her ability to notice the quieting of the animals.

They all sat back against the large tree and breathed a little easier.

Emma spoke up then and stated, "We're not going to be able to follow any road. We'll meet up with all kinds of people and we don't want that. We won't know if they are good guys or bad guys and I don't want to try to figure it out at arm's length."

She looked around and saw Arturo smile and nod at

her; everybody else just looked scared or nervous, but she could tell they were all with her.

Again, she pulled out the atlas and looked at their choices. She could only see one thing to do and that was to head due north to Tennessee.

She traced a line to a place she had been before, Red Top Mountain State Park and lodge on Lake Altoona, and a plan began to form in her head.

"Here," she said, "I've been here before. If we can make it to this point, today, we can camp out around this area and there will even be water!"

She got more excited as the plan became clearer in her head.

"Most people will want to stay around civilization, at first, in case the electricity comes back on." She glanced around and saw they were listening closely and went on, "However, we are pretty sure that's not going to happen, so we are going to go straight here!" As she finished up, she tapped the map at Red Top Mountain.

She continued, "We can probably make it today, if we keep our heads down, and then camp there for tonight. If all goes according to plan, we can head out tomorrow by crossing the lake at a bridge or something and head straight to Tennessee!"

She said this last with such conviction that everyone just looked at each other and nodded.

Bryan said, "All righty then, let's do it!"

Emma smiled and rummaged in her bag for a compass and finding it, replaced it with the atlas. All this activity in the bag must have ticked Bella off, because she promptly jumped down to the ground, vigorously shook herself, and glared briefly at Emma before bounding into the woods.

As Emma tried to get her bearings with the compass, Esteban said worriedly, "Hey! Where's she going?"

Emma ignored him, but Lori said, "It's okay, sweetie, she always comes back," and gave him a smile which seemed to comfort him.

Emma figured out that the compass wouldn't work and threw it back in the bag. She looked around to make sure there was only their little group and asked her friends, "Is everyone ready?"

When everyone nodded back at her, she hitched her bag up and strode off toward what she thought was north. Coming to Highway 41, they crossed quickly and without incident, and pulled up into the trees. It was getting warm and Bryan passed around the canteen.

Continuing on, Emma paid attention to her surroundings and was surprised that they hadn't seen more people, not that she wasn't glad. As she thought about this, she turned to Bryan who was behind her walking next to Lori, and asked her two friends what they thought.

"I don't know, Em," Lori stated and Emma could tell the two were seriously thinking about the question. Emma kept walking through the underbrush and finally came to a plausible answer.

Most people were a lot like turtles. When something happens, they stay where they think they are safe and familiar with their surroundings until something forces them out. This was only the second day after the bomb exploded, so most people would still have food, water, and shelter. They would most likely stay in their homes until the water or food ran out or someone forced them out of their homes. In some ways, Emma thought their group was smart to leave when they did. If this was a long-term event, as her gut told her it was, then now was the best time to move away from the population. When there weren't too many people yet. The second thing she realized if her thoughts were correct, was that most of the people they met now were probably up to no good.

With these thoughts running through her head she saw that they were coming to another road. She stopped and knelt to let the group catch up.

Seeing her stop, the group quietly knelt next to her and looked down at the map she had retrieved.

They had crossed several small streets with no problems and had been walking a couple of hours. Her best guess said that this was Duncan Road and they would have to walk beside it for another couple of hours before they got to the country club. She told her friends this. Then, putting the things away, they checked that the road was empty and scuttled across while Arturo backed them up. As Arturo finished crossing, Bryan passed the canteen again and everybody headed out.

This time they were able to walk more in a group. To pass the time, Emma told them her theory on why they hadn't met many people. As she finished, Arturo piped up and said, "It makes sense. That is how I have seen people too. The bad ones are the ones we need to keep an eye out for now. They will be searching for people such as us."

Emma nodded as she agreed. "Yes, that's what I was thinking. That's why I want to go to this country club to hole up. Maybe no one will be there, and it will be surrounded by a golf course instead of houses close by."

Everyone nodded agreement and they pushed on.

Sometime later, they came to the edge of a golf green and knew they had made it. They had only had two other run-ins with other groups. Each time, Emma's group had seen them first and had let them go on by. Both groups had been rowdy, drunk and up to no good and Emma had thanked their lucky stars that neither group had seen hers. All this stress was wearing the group out, she could tell, and glancing at her new-found watch she saw it had taken them almost five hours to get to the club. She knew they needed to regroup and she was thinking about getting some rest and starting out tonight when they were less visible. She would see what the group said.

There looked like there was a golf cart path across the road and checking both ways, they quickly crossed over. Following the path, it took about fifteen minutes to reach the clubhouse and not seeing any movement they eased up with their backs against a wall.

There was a window next to Arturo and Emma raised her brows at him to ask if he would check it out. He nodded and winked and eased up to the window.

Quickly he darted his head around then back and shook his head at Emma to tell her he hadn't seen anything. She nodded and the group followed her in a crouch around to the back of the building. There was a dumpster and a back door. Just past the door was another window. Emma had her gun out and eased up to the back door and tried the knob, already knowing it was locked, and she wasn't disappointed. She shook her head back at her friends and moved to the window. She stuck her gun into her jeans and tried the lock, again finding it held tight. She looked in the window with her hands cupped around her eyes and could see it was some kind of office in disarray. She didn't see anybody in the office. Moving back to the group, she huddled there and told them what she had seen.

"I'm going to break the window. We need to refill our water bottles and regroup."

They nervously agreed and as they kept a look out, she took the butt of her gun and smashed the glass right above the lock. Everybody jumped at the preternaturally loud sound. They froze like rabbits, waiting to see if a hawk would swoop down on them. When nothing happened after a couple of minutes, everybody began to breathe again and Emma pushed out the remaining glass. She reached in to unlock the window and raised it up. It slid easily and Emma was just squeezing through when she heard the distinctive click of the hammer on a six shooter. It was right next to her ear and she froze, while her heart skipped a beat.

A deep, gravelly voice said, "I been watchin' y'all for

a few minutes and I'm going to give you the benefit of the doubt but this is what's going to happen. You are going to come on in and so are your friends. Then, we're going to go into the common room. Y'all are going to tell me just what the hell you think you're doing trespassin' on club property!"

All this time, Emma had not said a word, just listened, and had been frozen half in and half out of the window. Now she nodded her agreement and said as much, "Yes, sir, we don't mean any harm. Can I tell my friends what is going on so they don't get trigger happy?"

The voice chuckled and said, "Why don't you do that." And Emma heard the man back up a pace.

Emma still hadn't moved but in a slightly louder voice so her friends could hear, she told them, "There is a man in here with a gun on me. I don't think he means us harm but he wants us to slowly come in and tell him what we're doing here. Please keep your weapons pointed down since he is pointing his gun right at my head."

There was an intake of breath which Emma knew was Lori, but otherwise no sounds. Slowly, she continued into the room and kept her hands raised as the rest of the group followed suit.

When everyone had made it, the rough voice spoke, "I want you all to lay your weapons on that desk."

No one moved for a second and then Emma slowly reached to her gun and laid it on the desk, paving the way for her friends to do likewise. After hesitating, the men followed her lead.

"Just so you know, I'm not going to hurt you, I just

want to find out what's goin' on. Go through that door with your hands up, single file, and have a seat."

Emma started and her friends followed. As she went into the next room, she saw it was the main room of the club with couches and chairs. Everyone found a place and she was glad to see Esteban sat with his father, close to him on a loveseat.

It was gloomy in the room, even though it was daylight outside, and Emma watched as the man reached over and switched on a flashlight.

It brightened the room and everybody was able to get a good look at the man behind the voice.

As the man eased into a chair, he kept the gun on the group. Emma could see he was an older man, possibly around mid-sixty years old. He had a thatch of gray-streaked wiry black hair that was mid-length and had a short beard to match. He had piercing light brown eyes and Emma could tell that this man didn't miss much. He was wearing faded jeans and a t-shirt with Pine Tree Country Club logo over the left breast.

"Since you seem to be the bold one," here he motioned at Emma, "why don't you tell me who you all are and what you're doing breaking and entering." He smiled and Emma opened her mouth to protest, but then thought better of it.

She snapped her mouth closed for a second and calmed herself.

She started again, "My name is Emma Hudson and these are my friends." Here she gestured to the group.

Pointing around to each person, she gave their

names, finally ending with Arturo and Esteban.

When she finished the introductions, she looked back at the man and started at the beginning and it took all of thirty minutes to relay their brief journey from the cafe up to where they were now. She told the barest of details, leaving out the part about Pigeon Forge and why they were going there. She wanted to only give this man exactly what he asked for.

When she finished, they all sat quietly while the man seemed to digest this. Some of them shifted in their seats

After a while, when the silence was getting uncomfortable, Bryan softly cleared his throat and said, "Sir, can we ask who you are?"

The man seemed to come back to himself and realize he still had the gun trained on the group.

He lowered the barrel and laid the gun on the arm of the chair as he spoke. "I'm sorry, desperate times call for desperate measures. My name is Carl Henderson and I'm the caretaker here at the club. Well, at least I was, up until two days ago."

They all seemed to relax after Carl laid the gun aside, and Emma even let out the breath she didn't realize she'd been holding.

"Seems like the world has gone to hell in a hand basket. I've watched the sky turn green and all sorts of people cut across the greens. Nobody has tried to get in here until today." He continued, looking back at the group, "No electricity, and I had to drag two dead old men off the puttin' greens and down to the golf cart shed. Wasn't sure what to do with 'em, since I gathered the world had turned upside down. I just wrapped 'em up in some tarp I had down there until the lights would come back on and I could call the police. Doesn't seem like that's goin' to happen anytime soon though, does it?"

This last question he directed at Emma. He sensed that she was the leader of the group.

She looked back at her friends and they all seemed okay with her trying to explain her theory on what had happened.

"Mr. Henderson, if you want, I can tell you what I think is going on, but first we'd like to get comfortable. We tried to break in here because we need to refill our canteens and have something to eat. Would you mind very much if we did that?"

The man seemed startled that she would ask and then said, "Well, sure, I didn't mean to scare y'all. I was just coverin' my ass."

He smiled at them all then and everyone seemed to loosen up completely at the words.

"Let me show you where you can get water. It's about the only thing that seems to still work."

At this, he rose and grabbed the gun and flashlight. Looking to make sure they followed him, he led Emma and Bryan back to the food service area behind the bar and pointed at the faucet.

Bryan refilled his own canteen and grabbed Emma's and did the same.

"I'm going to grab the other bottles," Bryan said while looking a question at Carl.

The man nodded and Bryan eased back over to the

group and gathered the empty bottles.

While he did that, Emma looked back at Carl and asked, "Why'd you stay here after the sky turned green? If you don't mind my asking," she put in hastily.

Carl didn't seem to mind and he gazed back steadily at Emma and replied simply, "I have nowhere else to go, this is my home." He could see Emma was confused, so he continued, "You see, I'm a vet, army actually, and I was also homeless. Long story short, Miss Margaret, she's the head honcho around here, she used to volunteer at the mission in downtown Atlanta and she got to know me. Well, about five years ago, she just up and offered me this job, and I've been here ever since. It's a good job and the benefits include a small apartment down in the cart shed. I've been real grateful, but I should've known it wouldn't last." He looked sad and Emma felt sorry for the old man, then he went on, "I've had the pistol all this time. She wouldn't have liked it none, had she known." He grinned at this part and Emma could tell the old man genuinely liked his boss.

"I'm sure she would have understood," she told Carl. "What happened to her?"

At this, Carl shrugged and said, "When she and the others found out their cars and phones didn't work, they all left, on foot. Most of 'em live around here, so I guess they just walked home. After that, nobody came back."

Emma nodded her understanding.

"We do appreciate you letting us rest and get some water."

This change of subject seemed to work and the man

said, "I saw y'all comin' from a ways off and you didn't look like much trouble, but you never know. Can't be too careful."

Emma smiled at the man. "No sir, you can't."

After that, they all gathered back in the common room and were just settling in when there was a commotion in the office they had just broken into. Carl was up on his feet in a flash with the gun pointed at the room and everyone else had tensed, when out strolled a calico fur ball with golden eyes. Everyone relaxed except Carl. "What the hell is that?"

At this, everyone seemed puzzled at first and then it dawned on them that Carl didn't know Bella.

First Lori began to snicker, then Bryan, and in a few moments the whole group was laughing except Carl, and he was looking at everyone as if they had all lost their minds.

Between bouts of laughter, Emma told Carl who Bella was and he slowly lowered the gun. "Damn cat scared the bejesus outta' me!"

This release of tension brought on more laughter as everyone realized that Bella had scared all of them at least once.

Carl seemed to think about something and then said, "Go get your weapons. We may need them, now that the window is broke."

This seemed to sober everyone up and Bryan said he would retrieve them.

Arturo spoke up and said he would keep watch and asked Emma to keep an eye on Esteban. She nodded and the Hispanic disappeared into the next room.

When Bryan returned, Emma started going through the bags and bringing out food. She went ahead and fed Bella to keep her out of their hair. Everyone grabbed an MRE and Emma took one to Arturo.

Back in the common room it was quiet as everybody ate, and Emma remembered her manners and offered Carl one.

"No thank you. I still have food here and as a matter of fact I just ate."

Emma nodded and finished her own meal.

As she finished putting her trash in the kitchen trash can and sat back down, she spoke up. "I feel better. Now I can tell you what we all think has happened."

She repeated her theory and spoke about what she had watched on television and what they had all witnessed in getting to this point.

After a little bit, she wound up by saying, "So I hate to say it but, I think this is the way things are going to be for a while."

Carl had not said a word during the story and continued to sit for a minute and process everything Emma had said.

Emma looked over at her friends while she waited, and saw that Esteban was playing with Bella with a piece of string. She smiled to herself then looked back at Carl as he spoke.

"You know, that is the craziest thing I have ever heard, and if you would have told me that three days ago, I would have thought you were plumb off your rocker.

Now, though, it all makes perfect sense, as scary as it sounds."

With that he was quiet once again, and Emma could see he was thinking again so she waited patiently.

Bryan got up and, stretching, said, "I think I'll check on Arturo." He took his crossbow with him and disappeared into the office. Emma saw Lori look after him as he left and then turned to Carl as he spoke.

"If what you think is true, and I think it is, then where are you all going in such a hurry?"

Emma cleared her throat, to buy her a moment to think, and then said honestly, "I really don't want to tell anyone where we are going." She glanced up to gauge his reaction and saw that he was still calm and she went on, "Let me just say, we have a place in mind and I am meeting up with people I know."

This seemed to make sense to the old man and he nodded slightly as if to confirm something in his mind.

"Well, far be it from me to keep someone from just passin' through. You're welcome to stay here tonight and I'll even give you some things from the pantry. Tomorrow you can be on your way."

Emma thanked the man but said, "We'll get some rest, since you'll let us stay here, but I think we're going to leave in the middle of the night tonight. It's dawned on us that moving at night may be safer than the daytime. We've seen a lot of drunk troublemakers out during the day and it seems they're passed out by nighttime and we can sneak past them easier."

This seemed to make sense to the man and he

agreed.

Getting out of his chair he headed to the kitchen but said over his shoulder, "Make yourselves at home, I'll gather you some supplies you might could use."

As he was about to disappear into the kitchen, Emma asked if there was a place they could shower. He gestured across the room to an alcove and Emma thanked the man.

When he was gone, Lori piped up and said, "I swear you make some strange friends!"

Emma rolled her eyes at Lori and after telling Bryan and Arturo that they were going to shower, she grabbed her bag and she and Lori went to the women's dressing room. Again, it was dark and Emma switched on her flashlight and laid it on the table.

"I hate to complain, but I sure do miss hot water," Lori groaned.

Emma smiled at her friend and said, "Better cold water than no water at all!"

"True that," her friend sighed, and turned on the shower head.

The two women emerged, clean and exhilarated, and Emma was finishing combing through her damp hair. She saw that Bryan had returned and was talking to the old man. Esteban had stretched out on the couch and fallen asleep. Bella was perched up on the mantle above the large fireplace and Emma just shook her head at the cat.

Bryan noticed they had come out and said, "The evil witches return!"

Lori threw a punch at his arm while Carl guffawed.

Emma slumped down in the overstuffed chair and told Bryan, "You warlocks can go get clean if you want. I'll go relieve Arturo."

Bryan laughed and grabbing his bag headed to the alcove. Emma took a breath and hoisted herself out of the comfy chair and went to the office to relieve Arturo.

They had all showered except Esteban, who was still out on the couch, and had gathered back in the main room. After checking supplies, Emma glanced at her watch and saw it was six. She looked up at her friends. "I think we should all try to sleep until midnight and then leave at night."

They all looked at each other and agreed it would probably be best.

She laid out the atlas and pointed to a small lake a little ways away.

"This is Aubrey Lake. I think we should shoot for here, following along the edge of I-75 until we come here to the junction of Highway 411. If we push hard, we can make it by morning. The thing about lakes is that there is water and usually cover, as in trees and brush. We can hide out there and sleep, taking turns, until nightfall. Then we can head out to our next destination."

Everyone seemed to see the wisdom in this and it was agreed.

"I'll take watch until 9:00. Who wants last watch?" Emma asked.

Arturo was already lying on a makeshift bed on the floor next to Esteban and gestured that he would. Emma nodded to him and taking the rifle, went into the office.

After a few minutes, she heard footsteps and looked up to see Bryan coming through the door. He settled next to her and they watched the greens before he said, "I was talking to Carl while you two showered. He told me about a guy that comes to golf who has a horse farm. Lots of horses. He says the guy's farm is north of the I-75, 411 junction. That's right by where we are going!"

Emma slowly nodded her head, thinking.

"We would have to pay him for them, if he would even sell some." She was thinking about the silver she had brought along and hadn't told anyone. If they could get a good address and find the man's farm, it would definitely be worth a try. She made a mental note to ask Carl for good directions before they left.

"You're right," Bryan said with a sigh. "We don't have anything to trade."

Emma could see that Bryan was thinking about walking all the way to Tennessee and she patted his arm. "Don't give up so easily. We'll see."

The time passed uneventfully after Bryan went to lie down and Emma spent most of that time thinking and planning. When she finally looked at her watch in the covered glow of the flashlight, she saw it was 11:30 and she stood up to stretch. Quietly, she went back into the common room and grabbed the atlas and, taking it back into the office, she checked out something she had thought of. After seeing her hunch was right, she nodded to herself and put the atlas away. She gave it a few more minutes, then went to wake the others up. It was going to be a long day.

After waking the others, Emma went to see if she could find Carl and nearly ran headlong into him coming out of the kitchen.

"Whoa there, Missy!" he said after steadying her arm.

"You scared me!" Emma snorted, then noticed he had some mugs and a kettle of deliciously scented coffee.

"Good Lord above, is that coffee!?!" she stammered.

Carl grinned ear to ear and nodded, "There's a small wood-burning stove in the kitchen and I thought I would surprise y'all."

Emma didn't know what to say, but she didn't have to. The others were gathering around the bar like it was Christmas day. Carl set the kettle and mugs on the bar and went back to the kitchen. As they all poured some coffee, he returned with a small bottle of creamer and some local honey.

"I don't have any sugar, but this here is local honey for sweetening your coffee."

The group looked at each other. Clearly none of them had ever used honey in their coffee but then shrugged and tried it out.

Almost as one, they all rejoiced at how good it tasted and thanks was given to Carl from the bunch of them.

He seemed pleased and before anyone could say something else, he reached around and brought out two medium-sized jugs of the amber honey and proudly gave them to the group.

"Wherever you are going, if this doesn't get set right for a while, you're going to have to do some bartering and this may help out some."

The group sat stunned for a moment, then Lori reached up and gave the old man a huge hug, which Emma could see caught the old man off guard.

"You are the sweetest man I know!" Lori gushed, which further confounded the man, and to Emma's delight she saw him blush.

Carl disentangled himself from Lori and gruffly stated under his breath, "It's the least I could do." And mumbling something else, disappeared back in the kitchen.

They all savored the rest of the brew and when they were almost done, Carl came back in the room more composed than when he left.

Emma took the time to change subjects and retrieving the atlas, she laid it in front of Carl and said, "Bryan was telling me about the man you know who has a horse farm. I was wondering if you could show us, on here, where his farm is."

The old man hesitated, apparently having second thoughts.

Emma decided she needed to set the man at ease and she felt he could be trusted, so she spoke up. "Listen, I know we all just met, but we are trying to get to a place in Tennessee. If we can find some horses and TRADE for them," she emphasized, "then it will make this little journey go a lot easier."

Carl looked at each one of them intently.

With a sigh he spoke. "I may be an old fool, but I think y'all are good folks."

He reached across the light of the flashlight and

looking more closely at the map, stabbed a finger at a point north of Aubrey Lake near a road call Cass White.

"It's right off here somewhere. He took me up there a couple of times to do some work for him. Nice fella' by the name of George Brewer. It's been a while, he doesn't get to golf as much as he would like. If you get there, you tell him Carl Henderson says hi."

Arturo had woken Esteban and had given him something to eat out of his bag. Emma told Carl thank you and called the group to gather around. Seeing that Carl had disappeared again, she set about telling the group what she had thought of. "I noticed something here."

They all leaned in and squinted at the map in the low light.

Emma was running her finger along a light gray line that left a spot close to Aubrey Lake and ran all the way up next to Pigeon Forge.

Before she could say it, Arturo said it for her. "Railroad tracks!"

Emma nodded and said, "It makes perfect sense. With the EMP blast, the microchips on the trains are fried. They won't be running but it's a perfect track through the woods and hopefully no one else will be using them yet." She shrugged, "If they are, at least it might not be as bad as roads."

She looked up at everybody to gauge their reaction and saw they thought it was a good idea.

Putting the atlas away she kept speaking, "If we can get some horses, it'll be that much faster."

They were all looking a little relieved. Apparently, walking the main roadways was bothering them as much as it was bothering her.

Emma was anxious to get started so she grabbed her bag and made sure she hadn't left anything. Slinging it over her shoulder, she grabbed her Glock, stuffed it in her waist band, and looked around for Carl. The rest of the group were finishing rounding things up and Emma spotted Carl standing quietly by the office doorway. She walked over to the old man and looked up at him as her friends fell in behind her.

"We sure do appreciate everything you've done for us. Are you going to be okay here?"

The man grinned behind his beard and said, "I'll be fine, it's folks like you that are in danger. You never know what strangers are gonna do, so keep your guard up."

With that, he tilted his head at the broken window, and stepped back.

Emma took a deep breath and looked around for Bella. Noticing the cat was almost standing on her foot, she scooped her up, gently placing her in the pack on her back, and off they all went into the gloomy, quiet night.

16

Emma rubbed her eyes as she squinted through the shrubs. They had been walking all night and had finally made it to the lake they had seen on the map.

They had stayed on the railroad tracks and had pushed hard to get here, to the south side of the lake. The journey had been more unnerving than they had expected. Before they had gotten out into the country, they had heard more gunshots, screams, and explosions than they had anticipated. Walking along the tracks, however, had seemed to keep them hidden, as Emma had hoped, and they'd only had to hide a couple of times when groups of people had come crashing across the tracks.

It was almost daylight and they needed to go to ground. Her group was on the edge of the lake in a grove of trees and shrubs big enough to give them cover and they had gotten off the tracks and crossed a cultivated field to get here.

She looked around at her friends and could see they were as tired as she was.

"I'm tired, you guys," she stated without preamble, and slumped down in the grass.

Arturo eased Esteban down to the ground. He had been carrying the exhausted boy for the past half mile, and Emma could only guess how he had done it.

Lori and Bryan just plopped down where they were, and Emma could hear how hard everyone was breathing. Everybody just rested for a while as the green sky got lighter.

After swigging some water, Lori piped up, "I'll say it again. You would have made a great drill sergeant, Em."

Bryan barked a laugh and Arturo quietly chuckled. Emma just smiled and nodded her head; she was too tired to do anything else.

"Yeah, well, this drill sergeant is exhausted," Emma said, and before she could ask, Arturo said he would take watch. Emma thanked him with her eyes and, bundling her pack under her head, she more passed out than went to sleep.

Sometime later, Emma was ripped from her deep sleep by sharp stabs of pain in her head. She sat straight up and gave a yelp, clapping her hands to her head. All the activity and noise woke everyone around her and before she knew it, Bryan was pointing his crossbow all around with a bleary expression on his face. Even Lori had whipped out her knife and was staring at Emma. After a moment, Arturo, too, appeared with the rifle to his shoulder and everyone was staring questioningly at Emma.

She looked around and saw Bella shaking her head and trying to spit out some of Emma's hair.

"Dammit, cat! One of these days, someone's going to kill you for that!" Still puzzled, everybody seemed to relax a bit. Bryan asked, "What the hell?" Emma had collapsed back down and pushed the cat away, but she was wide awake now.

"Oh, Bella does that sometimes when she's hungry," Emma replied.

"Well, I damn near skewered her!" Bryan retorted.

Emma smiled, tiredly, and said, "I know, Bry, I'm sorry. Thanks for letting her live."

Only moving her arms, Emma reached in her bag and got a handful of cat food out and, finding a clear spot, spread it out for Bella. Then, with a sigh, she sat back up and got her some water, too.

Everybody had relaxed and sat back down, so Emma rubbed her eyes and pulled out the atlas.

As she looked at the map, she took out a bag of beef jerky and had some for breakfast, sharing it around to her friends.

"We're real close," she said absently, and traced her finger north of their current position to where Carl had said the horse farm was.

Suddenly, there was a gunshot close by in the direction they had come from. They all jumped and laid flat. Arturo had the rifle out and was looking through the bushes toward the sound. More gunshots sounded and, as the group watched, they could see a firefight had ensued at the motel they had sneaked past in the night.

Everybody looked at each other with differing expressions of sadness or fright and they knew they had to get going.

Emma silently pointed to their bags and everybody loaded up.

With one last glance over their shoulder, they eased away from their hiding spot, keeping it between themselves and the battle. They were still on the south side of the lake and needed to skirt around it to the East, away from the motel. Hunched over, they silently made their way East. Just as they rounded the far edge of the lake, there was a large explosion behind them and they turned just in time to see a fireball rising into the sky, and several people with guns raised were storming the front of the motel. The group was far enough away not to be spotted, but close enough to see what was happening.

"Jesus..." Bryan muttered.

Lori had a look of horror on her face and Emma could see that Esteban had tears running down his cheeks. Emma sighed and turning back to the east, they all continued on their course. As they walked, Lori moved up beside Emma and asked, "Do you think it will be better in Pigeon Forge?"

"I don't know, I hope so," she answered honestly. "All I know is that there are vacation cabins and some are isolated. We can settle in and defend ourselves for a while until Jack arrives."

Bryan had moved up beside them and had heard that last part. "Who is this guy, Em?" he asked now, "Why don't you tell me a little more about him."

They had rounded the east end of the small lake and were now headed into some more trees and Emma paused as she thought about where to begin.

"STOP RIGHT THERE!" a man's voice shouted from the trees ahead of them.

Emma caught her breath and berated herself for not paying attention. Arturo had swung the rifle up and was swinging it back and forth as they all searched the gloom for the owner of the voice. Whoever it was, he was well hidden. It just looked like, well, trees.

"Lower your rifle and put your weapons on the ground," the voice said.

Nobody moved.

"Come on, I'm not going to ask again!" the voice stated angrily.

Emma knew what they had to do so she moved, slowly. Reaching down to her waist, she removed the Glock and, bending down, placed it at her feet. Bryan and Lori followed suit, but, out of the corner of her eye, Emma saw that Arturo wasn't budging and, in fact, held the rifle steady on the speaker.

"Put the rifle down, mister," said the voice menacingly.

Emma slowly raised her hands and spoke. "Just a minute! Everybody just calm down!" She said this to Arturo, as much as to the man in the trees.

To the unseen man she spoke now, "We aren't here to cause trouble. We're just passing through. My name is Emma Hudson, I'm a nurse and these are my friends." Emma hoped that by telling a little about themselves that she would make the man see them as more human.

"We're coming from Atlanta and heading to Tennessee." She hesitated, then added, "We have family there."

By adding that last part, she hoped she wouldn't have to explain why they were heading to Tennessee. She shouldn't have worried as was evidenced a moment later.

"You're a nurse?!?" the voice demanded.

"Y-yes," Emma stuttered, puzzled.

Silence reigned for a few seconds and then the man spoke again, "I'm going to step out and I'll lower my rifle if he will agree to lower his."

Emma knew the man meant Arturo and she looked over at the Hispanic and nodded.

Arturo wasn't pleased, but he briefly nodded back.

There was a rustling noise by a tree about thirty yards ahead of the group and then a camouflaged man stepped away from a huge oak tree.

Right away, Emma could see that the voice belonged to a very young man, probably late teens or early twenties. There was some more rustling to their group's right and left sides and three more camouflaged men stepped out of hiding. Emma realized they had really been surrounded.

She felt, rather than heard, Arturo stiffen and she lifted her left hand at him and shook her head a little and he relaxed.

As the four men slowly came closer, she could see they were all very young but well-armed with high-powered rifles. They also seemed to be alert to all their surroundings. This told Emma that they were knowledgeable in woodcraft.

Emma and her group waited patiently and when they arrived in front of her and her friends, she could tell that something was haunting the young speaker. She waited for the young man to speak.

"How good of a nurse are you?" he asked of Emma.

Her slim eyebrows pulled together in confusion as Emma answered, "Good enough, I suppose, why?"

The young speaker seemed to come to some decision and he rushed his words, "My father has been shot in his side and the bullet is still in him. Can you come take a look at him?"

It all made sense now. She looked at her friends in question and got shrugs from all around. She realized this would slow them down, but because of who she was, she couldn't just walk away.

Sighing deeply, she turned back to the young man and said, "We'll come with you and I'll look at him if you will all quit pointing your weapons at us and treat us as equals. We're not here to rob or hurt anybody."

The boy nodded thankfully and Emma continued, "And tell us your names."

The boy had the decency to blush and said, "I'm sorry, my name's Josh and the two guys over there are my younger twin brothers, Tony and Zack. This," he said, pointing to the last young man, "is our friend and neighbor, Ryan."

"Nice to meet you. Now, we're wasting valuable time," Emma stated. "We're going to pick up our weapons and you lead the way to your dad."

The young man nodded and stepped back. Emma and her friends retrieved their weapons and she motioned Josh on.

Emma walked for a while beside Josh and then asked, "So what happened? How did your dad get shot?"

Josh glanced at her then, looking around, said, "Those gunshots you heard over at the Best Western? Those people came to our ranch first." He shrugged, "I

guess they were just going down driveways. We were all
out in the barn doing our chores when we heard our dog,
Bear, start barking. Dad started to go out the barn door,
then stopped and jumped back, motioning us to get our
rifles." Here the young man looked angry and explained
to Emma, "We've had to keep our guns loaded since the
day this happened," he said, motioning to the green sky.
"We've had nothing but trouble since then." He didn't
have to elaborate further; Emma could only imagine and
she nodded for him to go on.

"Anyway, we grabbed our rifles and each of us found
an opening and looked out to the front driveway where
there is a clearing. We saw a group of ragged looking
people easing across the clearing toward the house. They
all seemed to have a weapon and dad yelled at them and
told them to leave. As soon as they heard his voice they
just started shooting at us in the barn." Here, Josh looked
perplexed and shook his head, "I don't know why they
didn't just leave." He mumbled, almost to himself, then
resumed telling Emma what happened, "We ducked
behind cover as the bullets just kept hitting the barn. As
soon as there was a lull, I could see dad's face and he was
furious, so he swung up to a window and started firing his
rifle at them. I don't think he was trying to actually shoot
them, or he would have. I think he was trying to scare
them off, but they just started shooting back and it was
like an Old West gunfight. Bullets were flying everywhere
and after a few minutes it was quiet." Emma could see
the haunted look on the young man's face as he
continued.

"I looked out to see where they were and could just see them leaving back up the driveway. I guess they didn't expect us to give them that much trouble, but we did and they left. I was relieved and turned around to look for everybody and saw dad, lying on his back next to a hay bale. He was holding his side and I could see blood was seeping through his fingers and soaking his shirt. When I ran to him, he said he'd been shot. I told Zack to get some rags and lifted dad's shirt to look." Josh pointed at his left side, just above his waist. "The bullet hit him here and I looked at his back to see an exit wound but there wasn't one. I could tell dad was in a lot of pain and as I pressed the rags to the bullet hole to stop the bleeding, he told me to go get Doc Watson, our vet that comes to the house when the horses are sick. He lives about two miles away, and I was on my way to get him when we came across you all."

Here the young man stopped talking and looked at Emma. "I hope you can help him and I'm not wasting my time."

For a brief moment, Emma was offended, then put herself in Josh's shoes and realized she would have said the exact same thing.

"I'm not a doctor, but I have a master's in nursing and I've worked at Piedmont in Atlanta for the past seven years. I've seen gunshots a lot and have helped doctors in the emergency room, I'll do what I can for your dad."

Emma didn't know that Lori had been listening until her little friend spoke up and said, "She's the best there is. I've heard doctors say that she should have gone to medical school." With this defiant statement, her friend just glared at Josh and this seemed to placate the young man.

By this time, they had all reached a clearing, and Emma could see a good-sized ranch style house in the distance with some barn buildings sitting a little away from it. All of a sudden a dog started barking loudly and Josh yelled, "Bear! Hush up! It's just us!" and the dog came running up, wagging his tail. Josh reached down and patted the big brown mutt's head and motioned Emma and her group to follow him to the cluster of out buildings.

When they reached what Emma could see was the main barn, Josh called out to his dad that they were coming in and Emma heard a male voice grunt loudly in return.

Looking over her shoulder, Emma could see that Arturo and the other three young men had taken up positions in the yard with Esteban staying at his father's side. Bryan and Lori were right behind Emma as she and Josh entered the dusky light of the barn.

As her eyes adjusted to the light difference, Emma looked around and saw all the things you would expect to see in a barn—tools, hay bales, and horses!

She wrestled her mind back to what she was here for and searched intently for Josh's father. Josh was moving over to a window and Emma followed. There, on the other side of a hay bale with splatters of blood on it, she saw him. He was sitting up with his back against the barn wall, holding a wad of rags against his left side, low, by his hip. She could see that his face was pale and he was breathing heavy.

The man was smiling slightly at Josh, and the young man said, "I found these folks out by the lake and she's a nurse so I brought her instead. How are you doing, dad?"

The man nodded at his son and Emma could tell from her experience in the ER that the man was in pain but didn't seem to be mortally wounded.

Emma stepped closer and told the man, "My name is Emma and yes, I'm a nurse. Can I see your wound?"

The man seemed to relax a little and nodded. Emma knelt next to the man and rummaged in her bag for a flashlight and her first-aid kit.

She lifted the ball of rags the man had been holding against his side, and switched the flashlight on to examine the wound.

She saw that it, luckily, must have been a small caliber, possibly a .22. Blood was just oozing from the hole and it wasn't a large hole. Sending up a prayer of thanks, she said, "We need to lay you flat and put your feet up on that bale, but first I need to look at your back." He nodded curtly, from the pain, and, replacing the rags against his side, Emma helped turn him on his uninjured side and lifted his shirt to thoroughly examine his back for an exit wound. The man grunted in pain and Emma mumbled apologies as she searched but found no exit wound. As she looked at the man's back, however, she noticed a slight bulge about an inch from the man's spine on the same side as he had been shot and she felt of it. This got another hiss of pain from the man and confirmed Emma's suspicions.

She helped lower the man to his back and told him, "I think the bullet is under the skin right where you felt me poking." She felt the man's wrist and counted heartbeats as she looked at her watch and after a minute she nodded to herself and said another silent prayer of thanks as she found his pulse fast but steady and strong.

She grabbed the man's feet and raised them up onto the hay bale, then turned back to talk to the man.

"It looks like you've been shot with a .22 caliber. I don't think it hit any vital organs or you would probably be dead right now. Your pulse is strong and steady, so I think you were very lucky. Now, that being said, of course, without a hospital to do medical tests, I can't be sure, but I think the main thing is to stop the bleeding and try to clean the entrance wound and make sure it doesn't get infected." Here, Emma paused to see if the man would ask any questions. When he didn't she continued, "I could dig the bullet out of your back but I don't think that would be smart, since it seems to be in muscle and not hurting anything, and that would just be another entrance for infection."

As she quit talking and there was silence, the man seemed to breathe a little easier. Emma could see he was thinking and she waited.

Finally the man spoke. "I think you're right," he said in a deep voice, and Emma could tell the man was exhausted.

"I don't want you to dig that thing out, just leave it in," he resumed. "Josh, get your brother Zack and help me to the house. Make sure Tony and Ryan keep an eye out for strangers, tell them to shoot first and ask questions later!" he said, angrily.

Emma shook her head and said, "I don't think you should move yet."

The man stared a hole through her as his sons reached down and helped him stand, "You just pretty much told me I had a flesh wound. I've been lying here for an hour and haven't died yet. I think I'll be okay getting to the house, don't you?"

In reality, she did, and she didn't think she could change his mind so she did the only thing she could, she nodded.

As the boys helped their dad to the house, the rest of her group gathered their things and followed the trio.

Emma checked to make sure Ryan and Tony were standing guard, then went into the house to try to help.

As the two boys reached the living room, their dad pointed gruffly at the couch and the boys lowered him gently to his back. As the older man caught his breath, Emma asked them where they kept their medicine.

"Down the hall, first door on the left is a bathroom with a medicine cabinet," Zack said quietly. Emma could tell he was pretty shook up over all this. Squeezing his arm and smiling at him encouragingly, she moved off down the hall to look for some antiseptic. She could have used hers, and she still would if the men didn't have any, but she was thinking of her own little group and didn't want to deplete their supplies if she could help it.

Reaching the bathroom, she flipped the light switch

before she remembered and when she realized it wouldn't work, berated herself mentally before getting out her flashlight.

Swinging it around, she found the medicine under the sink, as well as the medicine cabinet on the wall, and she searched the supplies to see what they had.

She found a bottle of hydrogen peroxide, almost full, and a half tube of antibiotic ointment. Looking at some of the other things, she also found a bottle of half-full Darvocet, not quite expired, and some gauze. Leaving the bathroom, she headed back to the living room where Josh and Zack had settled their dad onto the couch and Bryan and Lori were talking quietly by the front door.

Emma stepped over to the couch and raised her eyebrows at the man.

He nodded and she proceeded to patch the man up. After she finished about fifteen minutes later, the bleeding had slowed way down and she felt pretty confident that he would be sore but would live. The man was very lucky and she told him so.

He seemed to be in a little less pain and said, "I want to thank you for coming to help me. You didn't have to, and I appreciate it."

Before she answered, Emma doled out two of the Darvocet and, fishing out a bottle of water, handed them to the man. "These are painkillers that I found in your cabinet. They're not very strong, but will take the edge off the pain while you heal. As for coming to help you, it's what I do and I was glad to find you in as good a shape as I did. You're welcome."

The man swallowed the pain pills and then said, "By the way, my name is Mitchell, Mitchell Roberts." He tried to reach out a hand to shake but winced and Emma patted him on the shoulder instead. "It's very nice to meet you, Mitchell, although I wish it could have been under different circumstances." She smiled as she said this last part.

The man smiled back at her in some pain, but she could tell he seemed better.

As the pills seemed to already be working, Mitchell mumbled, "Get the boys to make you something to eat, you're all welcome here." With that, he seemed to pass out and Emma spread an afghan, which was on the back of the couch, over him and turned to Josh. The boy was looking at his father with tears in his eyes and Emma could tell he was worried.

"He'll be okay," she reassured him and his brother, "I've seen a lot worse at the hospital and they survived."

This seemed to mollify them and Josh turned to Emma, Lori, and Bryan. "Well, are you all hungry? I could fix you something to eat. It's the least we could do for helping our dad."

Emma's stomach rumbled at the thought of food and she smiled and nodded gratefully.

As Josh went into the kitchen and Zack sat down next to his dad on the couch, Emma went over to speak to her friends.

Bryan spoke first. "He was lucky that was just a flesh wound!" he said under his breath.

Lori spoke over his last words, also in a whisper, "He

should be glad we were there at the right time and place!"

Emma nodded and hushed them. "The point is we're here now. I need to find out where George Brewer's house is and find out if they know him. We've got to keep moving and I want to get some horses."

She was whispering too, and realized it looked suspicious so she just turned on her heel and went into the kitchen, where Josh was.

As she entered, she saw the young man had placed his rifle by the door and had started a fire in the wood-burning stove. "Eggs sound good to everyone?"

She could tell he was still somewhat worried about his father, but he was putting on a brave face.

She spoke up and said eggs were great and could she help.

He nodded and pointed to a basket of eggs and got a cast-iron skillet out.

As they worked together, Emma thought about what she was going to say and then just asked, "Josh, do you know a man named George Brewer? He's supposed to live up this way, somewhere on Cass White Road."

Josh had paused and looked over at Emma as she finished.

"How do you know old George?" he asked.

Emma shrugged and said honestly, "I met a man last night that knows him and he said he thought he lived up this way."

Josh was silent as he got some chunks of cheese and some bread out and Emma thought he wouldn't answer, but then he did. "Mr. Brewer is our neighbor to the north

and we went to check on him after the explosion and
found him dead out behind his barn. We guessed he had
a heart attack. He lived by himself and only had three
horses, so we buried old George on his place, properly,
and dad said to bring the horses back here where we
could care for them until things went back to normal. I'm
thinking that's not going to happen anytime soon."

This last seemed to depress him and Emma quickly
tried to think of something to take the young man's mind
off the current situation. Before she could think of
something, Lori had walked up and heard the last part.
She started to open her mouth, then looked puzzled and
Emma realized the little woman was staring out the
kitchen window that faced north. Emma saw the blood
drain from her friend's face just before she turned to see
what had startled her so bad. As she turned to look out
the window, she realized there had been a pressure
building in her ears and she was just starting to hear a
howling noise as she stared straight north out across the
backyard. Bryan had noticed all this as well and as he
looked out the same window, he reached over absently
and grabbed Lori's upper arm. As the trio looked on, it
was as if Emma could see Josh was turning in slow
motion to see what they were looking at. They all stared
in horror as a rolling wall of white blew through the trees
and barreled across the two acres of backyard toward the
house. For a split second, Emma's mind could not
process what her eyes were seeing. When it did, the hair
on the back of her neck stood up as the howling
increased to a crescendo. She didn't know how it could be

happening, but knew, at a gut level, she was right.

She opened her mouth and screamed, "GET DOWN!"

At the same time, she grabbed Josh and threw herself behind the kitchen island they had all been standing at. Out of the corner of her eye, she saw Bryan had continued on from grabbing Lori's arm to dragging her with him.

All four of them collapsed in a heap just as the wall of white smashed into the house and rocked it to its foundation. Emma could hear windows all over the house imploding under the pressure and she felt sure the entire house would be destroyed.

The billowing, blistering white wind was white due to stinging snowflakes! It was bone-chilling cold. Emma huddled with the other three and concentrated on trying to take a breath. It was like being immersed into a frozen river after coming out of a sauna. After what felt like an eternity, but was probably more like three to four minutes, the wind subsided somewhat. It was enough for her to suck in a freezing breath and open her eyes a crack. As she shivered in the cold weather, she took stock of her surroundings. She saw that the wind was still swirling through the house. Everything was covered in snow and frost and Emma could see her breath in the room. She had never experienced this before in her life! Not even in Wyoming.

She could feel that her friends and Josh were also starting to stir and as they moved away from her she shivered. It had to have dropped fifty degrees in just minutes, but that was impossible! She shook her head at the thought; nothing was impossible anymore.

Getting to her feet, Emma suddenly thought about Mitchell, the wounded man. She started to move toward the couch but her foot slipped on the cold, icy floor and she nearly fell. Steadying herself against the bar, Emma continued more cautiously around the corner. She looked up to see Mitchell and his son Zack, huddled against the floor. Mr. Roberts was wincing as his son was just pushing to his feet.

"Mr. Roberts! Are you okay?!?" she asked.

Wincing as he sat up and leaned his back against the couch he asked, "What the hell was that?"

Emma swept her hair behind her right ear as she knelt next to the man. She raised his shirt to examine his wound and mumbled, "I think it's a blizzard."

The man just stared at her. She saw that his wound had started oozing blood again. She applied some clean gauze and pressed his hand back against it.

"A blizzard?" Mitch asked, incredulous. "It's April in Georgia, for God's sake!"

Emma finished up with his bandage and rose to her feet. "Well, I'm from Wyoming and I'm telling you, it's a blizzard."

Emma ignored the man's stunned expression and was now shivering. Blowing into her hands, she looked around to see where everyone else was.

Lori and Bryan were huddling together near the kitchen island. Josh was helping Zack up and murmuring to his dad and brother. Swinging around, she looked for

Esteban and had just spotted him when the front door flew open and Arturo and Tony stumbled in, supporting Ryan between them. Emma grabbed the door and slammed it closed behind them and they eased the young man down on a recliner.

Before Emma could ask what happened, Arturo told them the story.

"We were watching the front driveway when this hit and it slammed Ryan into a tree. I think he's broken his leg. Tony and I were walking ahead of him and we got blown into some bushes."

She moved to Ryan to check his leg.

Vaguely, she heard Bryan and Lori talking to Arturo as he checked on his son. As she was using her knife to cut open the right jeans leg of Ryan's pants, she felt someone drape a jacket over her shoulders and she said a silent prayer for the warmth. Examining the wound, she could see the skin starting to swell over an area about four inches around on the outer part of the young man's leg. It was covered with scrapes, but other than that, the skin was unbroken.

Emma glanced up into Ryan's eyes and said, "I'm going to poke on your leg a bit. It may hurt some."

She could tell that Ryan was in pain but he nodded briefly to let her know to go ahead.

She nodded back at him and gently started to examine the young man's injury. She twisted the leg out and got an immediate hiss of pain, then pressed on the outside of the wound to see if she could feel broken pieces of bone that shifted separately instead of together.

The young man hissed again, but not as much and this relieved Emma.

She pulled over an ottoman and pillow to prop the young man's leg up, then quickly slipped her arms into the too-large jacket on her shoulders. Blowing again on her hands to warm them, she spoke to Ryan and whoever else wanted to listen, "I don't think you broke it, but if you did it's just a hairline fracture. We need to clean those scrapes so they don't get infected. I saw some anti-inflammatory pills in the bathroom that you'll need to take for a few days and I would keep weight off that leg until it can heal, say, maybe a week."

She glanced around before heading to the bathroom and grabbed her flashlight. It had been gloomy before the blizzard hit, now it had grown even darker.

She also saw that everyone had some kind of blanket or coat on and she figured Mitchell had told his boys to do this. She was glad, since she could only do one thing at a time. As she walked down the hall, she heard the older man direct his sons to start barricading the broken windows against the wind and to start a fire in the fireplace. Searching the entire bathroom, she came up with anti-inflammatory pills and remembered she had left the hydrogen peroxide and antibiotic next to the couch.

Returning to the living room, she grabbed the other items she needed and finished fixing up Ryan's leg.

As she finished, the young man thanked her profusely and she waved him off and told him he was welcome. She elevated his leg back up on the ottoman and turned to see what else she could do.

Bryan and Lori were helping to hammer wood over the blown-out windows as were Josh and Tony. Zack was almost done lighting a fire in the fireplace and Emma could hear the wind still howling outside as she searched out Arturo. She found the man huddled with Esteban in his arms and Emma's breath caught as she feared the worse.

She stepped quickly over to where the Hispanic man and his son were huddled and she laid a hand on his shoulder. The man jumped at her touch and she smiled an apology down at him and could see worry in the man's eyes.

"What's wrong, Arturo?" she asked.

"I didn't want to say anything last night, but he's had a fever since we left the golf club. I thought he would get better, but it feels like the fever is worse, and he's not acting right, he keeps saying he's tired."

Emma bent down to feel his forehead and cheek and sure enough, he was hot. She had been afraid he had been injured in the onslaught of the storm, which would have been bad, but this wasn't good either. She told Arturo she needed to look at his burn and they pulled his sleeve up to check the burn, but it looked like it was healing well. Pulling the boy's sleeve back down, Emma frowned as she thought about what could be causing the fever. She told Arturo to hold on and she went over to Ryan and got the anti-inflammatory. She'd made up her mind as she bent over and gave two of the pills to Arturo and reaching over to her bag, also gave him a bottle of water.

"I don't think the fever is related to his burn. If it

was, his burn would be inflamed as well. He hasn't complained about it hurting, and I think it may be just a cold or a virus. Children get fevers all the time. We just need to watch him over the next couple of days until we get to Tennessee."

The man nodded but still looked worried, but Emma couldn't help that right now. She stood to see what was being done.

Mitchell was resting on the couch. Zack had finished and there was a roaring fire in the fireplace. The windows were shuttered and Bryan was now helping Lori tidy up.

Emma's mind returned to her original problem and as she stood watching, her mind quickly pored over her quandary. As much as she wanted to stay and help out the Roberts family, she was being pulled north to Pigeon Forge. Glancing out the windows, she could see it was blowing and snowing strongly. They would have to wait and hope that the storm let up quickly. She had no idea what to expect in this bizarre situation. She sighed. Emma wasn't good at being patient. Next, she had to see if she could talk Mitchell into selling her Mr. Brewer's horses. That would be her next step.

Having made this decision, she went over to help Bryan and Lori as they finished cleaning up.

"How are you guys?" she asked as she reached them. Bryan chuckled as he dumped his dustpan full of glass in the trash can. Lori looked up at her with wide eyes, though, and asked, "What else is going to happen that we aren't expecting?" Emma thought she was being funny, but then saw she was serious.

"Honestly, I have no idea. All bets are off and we just have to learn to roll with the punches. I'm going to go talk to Mr. Roberts about some horses. We can't leave until this storm blows out." She didn't add *if* it blew out. "When we do, we'll have to have some supplies, winter AND summer."

Emma saw Lori sadly shaking her head as she walked over to where the older Roberts lay on the couch covered with blankets.

"How are you doing, Mitchell?" she asked as she checked his dressing.

"Not too bad," the rancher answered. "That pain medicine is dulling the pain some and making me sleepy. How's the boy?" He nodded at Ryan.

"He's going to be fine," Emma replied. "I don't think he broke his leg, I think it's just severely bruised. He'll need to stay off of it for a while. I would make him some crutches."

Mitchell nodded and stayed quiet for a bit.

Emma took this opportunity to speak up about what was on her mind. "Mitchell," she said to make sure he was paying attention, "I know you don't know a man named Carl Henderson." She waited and when he confirmed he didn't, she went on, "We met him at the Pine Tree Country Club yesterday. He took us in and helped us. He then told us about a man who used to golf there every once in a while, by the name of George Brewer." She saw recognition dawn at the mention of Brewer's name and she went on. "Mr. Henderson knew we were wanting some horses to get where we were needing to go, so he told us how to try to find Mr. Brewer." Here she paused, warring with herself over how much to tell him, then went on. "I have a little bit of silver and I was going to offer to negotiate with Mr. Brewer over some horses." She saw that the man was watching her intently, so she continued, "Just before this storm hit, I was helping Josh with the eggs and he told me what happened to Mr. Brewer. I am very sorry to hear about him, by the way, I am thinking he probably had a pacemaker, am I right?" When the man nodded in amazement, Emma resumed, "I saw another case right after the explosion happened where a man with a pacemaker just died. Instantly, so I don't think Mr. Brewer even knew what hit him."

She paused to let all this sink in and to gather her thoughts. Before she could speak again, however, Mitchell asked her, "How do you know all this? What's going on? Are we under attack?" He was struggling to sit up and Emma laid her hand on his shoulder and shook her head trying to get him to relax back down. When he didn't, she told him, "I'll tell you all I know in just a minute. I need to ask you though, will you sell me Mr. Brewer's horses?"

After she said all this, she could see the man was mulling this over and she held her breath.

She realized that she hadn't heard anything in the room around her for a few minutes and she looked around. Everyone had heard the exchange between Mitchell and herself. They had all gathered near, with the exception of the Hispanics and Ryan, but you could tell they were all listening closely.

Emma returned her attention to Mitchell just as he began to speak. "I don't know how you know all this, but I am grateful for what you've all done, so I tell you what I'll do. I will give you George's three horses if you will do something for us."

As he spoke, Emma let out her breath and listened closely.

He continued, "Tell us what you think is going on and why. Also, tell us where you are going or, at the very least, promise when this is all over, you'll come back and visit and return the horses. I'm going to have to hand them over to George's family or the authorities when the electricity comes back on."

Emma could tell that the man was saying this last part for the benefit of the young men in the room and that he wasn't at all sure this last part would happen.

She nodded and glancing up at Lori's smiling face she turned to Mitchell and stated, "You have yourself a deal! We'll also need tack and some supplies, and I'll be glad to pay for that."

He hesitated, thinking, but then nodded sharply. "Agreed."

Emma heard her friends breathe a sigh of relief behind her and was glad the deal was done. She noticed that the room had warmed up nicely but realized everybody still hadn't eaten.

"I tell you what," she said again, "why don't we make something to eat and we'll all sit down and discuss everything. It doesn't look like we'll be going anywhere for a while." She glanced out a window for emphasis.

Mitchell nodded again, wincing in pain, and Emma patted his knee as she stood up.

"I'm going to make something to eat. Do you want to help me?" she asked Lori and her friend nodded.

The two women moved into the kitchen and Emma saw that the eggs hadn't broken. She sent up a mental thank you to God and started looking around for utensils and cooking pans. She could hear conversational voices in the living room and realized that everyone was starting to talk and get along. As she found the skillet and where the utensils were, she readied everything and her friend was getting the fire going in the wood stove.

As Emma was beating the eggs, she suddenly thought of Bella and hesitated for a brief second. After breathing deeply, she continued. There was nothing she could do about the cat right now, she'd just have to take care of herself.

Lori finished with the wood stove, stepped up close to Emma and whispered, "How long do you think this blizzard will last?"

Emma frowned and answered, "I don't know, Lori. I'm hoping it'll blow itself out by tonight. If we can find some warm clothes, I'd like to rest up today and leave tonight."

Before Lori could answer, there was a voice at her shoulder and Arturo said, "Emma, I can't take Esteban into this with a fever. I'm going to ask Mr. Roberts if we can stay here a while until my son is better."

Emma could see the man was torn about it, but

could understand his decision.

"We will miss you, Arturo, but of course you're right. I don't think the fever is serious, but taking him out into this would just be inviting more complications."

The Hispanic man smiled with relief and hugged Emma before going back over to Esteban.

This unexpected development weighed on Emma. It meant that she, Lori, and Bryan would have to make it alone. On the other hand, they would have fewer people to worry about watching, so in the end, it evened out.

They had finished fixing the meal and were serving it on plates. Lori let the others know it was ready, and Emma took a plate for Ryan and Mitchell over to them. Ryan thanked her with a big smile, but Mitchell said he wasn't hungry. Emma nodded in understanding at the rancher and kept the plate for herself.

She sat with everyone else in the spacious living room and they all dug in to their food. In the quiet, they could all hear the house creak in the wind that was still blowing outside and Emma couldn't help an involuntary shiver. She was thankful for the shelter and dreaded the thought of having to get out in this but it was something she had to do. That brought her around to thinking about Jack and her family and she could only pray that they were okay.

She noticed that everybody was almost finished eating so she decided to speak up.

She started her story at the point when she and her friends had been eating lunch just before the burst and by the time she finished, an hour later, the whole room sat enraptured by what she had revealed. They asked questions when she told them about her theory on an EMP blast, and she was surprised to find out that nobody had heard of it.

She answered their questions as best she could with her limited knowledge from a TV show and finally everyone sat silent, and completely stunned.

As she waited for the knowledge to sink in, she got up to look out the window. Emma was surprised to see that the wind had died down and that it had quit snowing altogether. Very strange weather, but, then again, they were in very strange times.

In a soft voice Mitchell asked, "So, where are you all going now?"

Emma hesitated as Bryan and Lori looked at her to see how much she would divulge.

"Tennessee," she replied, "I have family there." This wasn't so much a lie as she hoped it was a half-truth. She hoped her family would be there eventually, and so she felt good about the admission.

The man nodded and said, "Well, you are all more than welcome to stay here if you like, but I understand if you have to leave."

This gave her an opening to ask about Arturo and Esteban staying until the boy got better.

Before she could speak, however, Arturo took over and asked Mitchell himself. After thinking for a second, the rancher agreed.

"We'll need an extra set of hands while I heal, so I think it'll work out for all of us. Now, if you all don't mind, I'm really tired, so I'd like to get some sleep."

They all agreed and the three friends moved into the kitchen to make their plans while Josh and Zack cleaned the dishes.

Emma had brought her bag to the kitchen island and as they sat at the bar, she opened the dog-eared atlas once again and plotted a course.

"Now that we have horses," Bryan said, "we'll be able to push a little harder and get there in, what, Emma? A day?"

Looking at the map, Emma shook her head. "I think it'll take about a day and a half. We're going to have to go through this wilderness area to, hopefully, avoid other people."

Bryan nodded, but Emma could tell something was bothering Lori, so she asked her what was wrong.

Lori looked embarrassed as she told her friends, "I've never ridden a horse."

To Emma, who had ridden horses since she could walk, this was, at first, unbelievable. But then, as she thought about it, she quickly hid her surprise.

"It's okay, we'll take two horses and you can take turns riding double with me and Bryan."

The little woman looked immensely relieved and Emma hugged her friend to let her know it was fine.

"Let's get some rest and then we'll get going."

Her friends nodded and finding places near the fireplace, they settled in.

A few hours later, the friends were up and packing their things. This woke the others up and Mitchell told

Josh to take them out to the barn and help with the horses.

Emma walked over to the rancher as Lori and Bryan finished their packing and reached down to hug the man.

"I want to thank you for all you've done for us." Reaching out her hand, she gave the man a small roll of silver dollars. "This is for the food and supplies. It may come in handy if the power stays off."

The man pushed her hand back and told her to keep it. "You've done more than enough to repay me. I wish you luck and safety. I think you all will need it."

This seemed to tire the man out and Emma smiled her thanks and gave the man another hug. "Keep that wound clean and keep taking the antibiotics for another week. You should be okay."

The man winked at her in answer and she turned away.

Searching out Arturo, Emma told the man, "When Esteban gets well, come find us."

She said this as hugs were exchanged between the friends and the Hispanic said that he would try.

She nodded smartly, then bent down to check Esteban's forehead, which seemed better, but the boy slept on. She tousled the youngster's hair with a little smile, then grabbed her bag and stood up. She saw Josh was waiting on them and pulling her flashlight out, they stepped out into the cold night air. Looking at her watch, Emma saw that it was just before midnight. The wind had died down completely but the air was cold enough to see her breath. Emma was thankful for the winter clothes and supplies the Roberts family had given them and told Josh this. The young man nodded his welcome as they stepped into the barn. Emma switched on her flashlight and shined it around the inside of the warmer stable. There were several curious horses staring back at them. Josh was already moving over to the horses they were going to use and Emma let him know that they would only need two of the horses; Josh pointed out the two that they could have.

"The saddles and other tack are over there," Josh said, pointing to a room opposite the horses.

As Emma took a step toward the room, there was a rustling of loose hay above her head, in the loft, and a shadowy form jumped down almost on top of Emma's head.

Attesting to everyone's hair trigger nerves, in a split second there were four weapons pointed at the form before everyone realized it was a cat. Bella, to be exact.

"Shit!" Bryan gasped, before pointing his crossbow away from the feline. Everyone relaxed at the same time and Lori even giggled, shakily. Bryan was still speaking. "I swear she does that shit on purpose!"

Josh was looking puzzled and Emma realized he didn't know who Bella was. Glancing at Bella, who was cleaning a paw unperturbed, Emma told Josh who the cat was. Josh still looked puzzled but slowly nodded.

Emma just sighed loudly, then continued to the tack room for the saddles and equipment.

While she and Bryan started grabbing the saddles, she pointed out things for Lori to grab and they headed back to where Josh had retrieved the two horses.

Emma saw two geldings, one a bay and the other a sorrel. She gauged them to be somewhere between 10 and 15 years old and seemed to be about 14 hands high. They both stood still and calm, which was a good thing. They had their ears pricked toward Emma and her friends. Lori stopped a few feet away but Bryan and Emma continued slowly up to the horses. They stayed fairly calm and Josh told her that George used to use the two as trail horses because of their good disposition.

Emma set her saddle down and softly spoke to the bay, rubbing his jaw and ears. The horse shifted his stance but seemed unfazed by her ministrations.

She saw that Bryan was talking soothingly to the sorrel and that Lori was still hanging back and nervous. Well, she would deal with her friend's fear after she gained the horses' trust.

"What are their names?" Emma asked Josh.

The young man shrugged and mumbled, "I don't know. We didn't know George that well. He'd just bought his place a few years ago."

Turning back to the bay she spoke to him softly, "Well, I guess we'll just have to find a good name for you two." And then the horse nudged her with his nose, and she knew then that they would get along.

Patting his shoulder, Emma proceeded to saddle him and put his bridle on.

Only when she finished did she look over to see Bryan was almost done with the sorrel.

Glancing over her shoulder, she saw Lori was

watching all this intently, and Emma knew her friend was trying to memorize the process. Giving one last pat to the bay, she stepped over to her little friend. "What do you think?"

Lori glanced nervously at Emma but said bravely, "Tell me what to do, Em."

So Emma took a few moments to tell Lori the important things about horses and her friend listened intently.

Meanwhile, Bryan had gotten their packs onto the horses along with a bag of grain. She was surprised that he was checking all the hooves. Most people wouldn't have known to do that.

Returning her attention to Lori, she asked, "You ready to try?"

Her friend looked at her, drew her shoulders up, and nodded briskly, "Yep, let's do it!"

Emma squeezed her friend's arm and led the way to the bay. She was going to have to figure out a name for him, she thought distractedly.

Arriving at his side, she checked the cinch and made sure the stirrups were the right length. Leading him over to a stool, she stopped him with his left side next to it. She noticed the bay with his head swung back looking at Lori and admonished him, "Just give her a break, Leroy," and a name was born.

Lori had hesitated while stepping up on the stool and asked incredulously, "Leroy?!? You're going to name him Leroy?" Rolling her eyes, Emma's friend stepped up smoothly on the stool and settled in the saddle, looking for all the world like she had done it a million times.

Emma's jaw dropped open and she and Leroy stood frozen for a good five seconds before they heard a bark of laughter from Bryan. Emma could see Josh was smiling openly as well.

Emma shrugged after getting over her amazement and then, after scooping Bella up in her backpack, she swung up in front of Lori.

Walking the bay over to Josh, Emma reached down her hand and shook the young man's. "Thank you, Josh. Take care of our friends and your family and watch your backside."

The young man grinned up at her and said, "We'll be fine. You all watch your own."

With that, they all made sure they were bundled up and away they rode.

17

On a lonely dirt road in the dead of night, frogs were croaking and there were night sounds all about. Around a bend in the road, two large shadowy figures appeared, making their way slowly but methodically towards the end of the long driveway. As they reached the end, the smaller of the two pushed their hood back and told the other, "We're here."

The larger figure revealed itself to be two people on horseback and they came to a stop next to the lone figure on the first horse.

It had taken three long, uneventful days of riding through the backwoods, but Emma and her two friends had finally made it to the cabin that she and Jack had shared so long ago. Jack had said the owner was a family friend when he had grown up in Tennessee. Emma vaguely remembered that the man was wealthy and had vacation homes all over the world. The chances of the man being at this one was very slim. Emma sent up a prayer just in case.

She swung her leg over Leroy's rump and slid to the ground. Her legs were shaky and sore and she almost collapsed before clutching the saddle. She hadn't ridden a horse in many years and her body now shouted in protest.

She saw that Lori and Bryan were suffering the same fate as they scrambled off the sorrel. Emma smiled softly as she returned her attention to the cabin and noticed, thankfully, that all was quiet and dark.

She stepped up to her friends and said in a low voice, "You two hang out here, with the horses. I know the layout and can get in and check it out."

They both nodded, too tired to put up an argument.

Emma pulled her Glock and handing Leroy's reins to Bryan, she began to ease her way around to the side of the cabin. She remembered a large propane tank on the west side of the cabin and underneath the cap on top of it was where the owner hid the key. At least, that's where it was last time. She continued to ease around the cabin and was thankful that the snow had melted the day after they left the Robertses' place.

Emma and her friends had had plenty of time to discuss where the abnormal weather had come from. She had told them about an article she had read online. It had talked about the classified government program called HAARP or High Frequency Active Auroral Research Program. Some people thought it was really a program researching the use of electromagnetism to change or control the weather. She had told them what she had read, but nobody really knew what was happening. Since none of this had ever happened before, the whole world was essentially in uncharted territory.

Realizing that she had reached the side of the cabin, she hesitated for a couple of seconds to listen and see if she saw or heard any movement. Not sensing anything, she hooded her flashlight and flipped it on. She let out just enough light to see she was about ten feet from the big propane tank and she moved close to it. She reached with one hand to lift the cap and her heart dropped when she didn't see the key. She would just have to break in like she had at the country club. Moving past the propane tank, she located a basement window, reached down with the base of her flashlight, and broke open the window. The noise seemed loud in the night, and she waited to see if anyone would respond. After about a minute and all was still quiet, she pushed out the rest of the glass and slid into the cabin. Her sore legs threatened to give out and she steadied herself against the wall. She stood still for another minute to check again if anyone was moving in the house. When there still was nothing, she felt that the house was indeed vacant and completely unshielded her flashlight. Aiming it at the stairs, she quickly went up them and through the basement door into the kitchen. Shining the light around, Emma could see that it had been a long time since anyone had been here. The kitchen was bare and she walked into the living room. She saw all the furniture was covered with drop cloths and there was a thin layer of dust over everything. She let out a sigh of relief and walked out the front door onto the porch.

She signaled her friends. As she watched them start the long walk to the porch, she moved back into the living room and let the memories wash over her.

She remembered it exactly as it appeared now, but with love and warmth. She remembered a fire in the fireplace and hers and Jack's whole beautiful future ahead of them. After a moment the emotions threatened to overwhelm her and she ruthlessly reined them in, wiping a lone tear from her cheek. She forced herself to think about the here and now. They had made it here. All they had to do now was to stay safe and wait. She knew Jack would come. He was still alive, she felt it, and as long as Jack was alive he would come for her.

ABOUT THE AUTHOR

Stacey Livingston lives just outside of Atlanta, Georgia. At 45 years old, she has traveled all over the United States as a diagnostic medical sonographer. She has also met a lot of different people. Over the past 23 years, she has always wanted to write stories, but never found the time to. Now that Stacey has settled in one place and is in semi-retirement, she has decided to start with a thrilling tale that captured her imagination. Along with her three cats and best friend, she enjoys day-to-day life and the opportunity to spin tales for everyone's enjoyment.